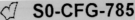

"How long have you been a whore?"

"I beg your pardon?"

"I was told you were a dock-whore," he explained.

"Oh," she said, clucking her tongue at what she must consider his deliberate misunderstanding of her words. "It's dock-tore, as you well know."

"Oh," it was his turn to say. Dock-whore meant healer in some countries, he recalled now. He supposed, with chagrin, that lewd-tenant didn't mean anything lascivious, either.

"Sit up," she demanded then, turning away from him to write something on a parchment pad.

"Sit up? Does that mean we are not going to couple?"

"Unbelievable!" she muttered under her breath. Then louder, "You could say that. Not now. In fact, never."

"Ah, milady, you should never say never. Not to a Viking."

SANDRA HILL

Wet & Wild

AVON
An Imprint of HarperCollinsPublishers

This is a work of fiction. Names, characters, places, and incidents are products of the author's imagination or are used fictitiously and are not to be construed as real. Any resemblance to actual events, locales, organizations, or persons, living or dead, is entirely coincidental.

AVON BOOKS
An Imprint of HarperCollins*Publishers*
10 East 53rd Street
New York, New York 10022-5299

Copyright © 2004, 2011 by Sandra Hill
ISBN 978-0-06-201923-3
www.avonromance.com

First Avon Books mass market printing: December 2011

Avon Trademark Reg. U.S. Pat. Off. and in Other Countries, Marca Registrada, Hecho en U.S.A.
HarperCollins® is a registered trademark of HarperCollins Publishers.

Printed in the U.S.A.

10 9 8 7 6 5 4 3 2 1

*This book is dedicated with much love and respect
to my good friend, Sherry Hogan Dudik.
Sherry is a writer of fine inspirational pieces,
but what she doesn't realize is that she is the
inspiration . . . to everyone she touches.
Having survived more tragedy in her life than
any normal person could bear, Sherry just
continues on with a smile on her face.
No wonder everyone loves her.
No wonder I am blessed to call her my good
and constant soul-friend.*

Wet & Wild

CHAPTER ONE

☙

T *upping his life away, looking for a better day . . .*
Ragnor Magnusson was in the midst of swiving the
most beautiful woman in all the Norselands, and he was bored.

In, out, in, out, in, out, ho, hum. He barely stifled a yawn.

On the other hand, Inga Sigundottir, young widow of a
Norman jarl and daughter of the Danish King Svein Forkbeard,
said, "Oooh, oooh! You are soooo good, Ragnor, but must you
go so fast? I want this to last forever."

*Of course I am good. But fast, you greedy wench? For-
ever? Hah! I have been plowing the field betwixt your thighs
for an hour at least. Bloody well reach your peak already,
m'lady.* That was what he thought, but what he did was slow
his strokes to a snail's pace.

Inga's eyes rolled back in her head.

No surprise to Ragnor. He was an expert at the bedsport
when he chose to be. After all, he was a Viking.

Then, whilst Inga moaned and writhed beneath him, even
as he did his in-and-out exercise, he scratched his buttock,
wondering idly if there were fleas in the royal linens. Then
he squeezed one of her nipples, knowing it was expected of
him, thus producing more moans and writhing. He pondered

whether there might be any roast boar left from the evening meal down in the castle kitchen. Yea, a slice of boar on a piece of manchet bread, washed down with a horn of ale, would go over nicely about now, even though it was well past midnight. But, alas and alack, he had work yet to complete . . . bed work.

For a brief moment, Ragnor entertained the notion that he might be getting old. He was only seven and twenty. That was too young to lose the enthusiasm for coupling. Wasn't it? But then, he'd lost enthusiasm for just about everything these days . . . a-Viking, trading, running the royal estates at Norstead, even fighting. That last was particularly alarming. He was born and raised to be a warrior. If not soldiering, what?

It had all started when his comrade-in-arms, Skorri Leifsson, died last year in battle. Ragnor had held his best friend in his arms while sword dew flowed steadily from the neck wound delivered by a Saxon blade. Nay, truth be told, Ragnor's low spirits had begun long before Skorri's death. There had been a hole in his heart and in his life since the death of his father, Magnus Ericsson, and nine siblings in a presumed shipwreck more than ten years past. Before that, he'd lost his beloved uncles Geirolf and Jorund Ericsson, Geirolf's wife and twin daughters, and his grandparents Lord Eric Trygvasson and Lady Asgar. So many deaths!

"Why did you stop?" Inga asked peevishly.

With a jolt, Ragnor pulled himself back to the present. He smiled down at Inga, her blond hair spread prettily about the pillow, her blue eyes staring up at him with a mixture of concern and arousal and impatience. She wrapped her long legs around his hips, not about to let him escape. Her lips were red and swollen from his earlier kisses.

His manpart was buried in her sheath. He might have lost the "enthusiasm," but his cock had not. In fact, it twitched.

She smiled up at him, as if he'd just paid her a compliment.

He waggled his eyebrows at her. It was not her fault he'd lost the "enthusiasm." She deserved better.

Lifting her legs over his shoulders, he began to pound at her then. Short, hammering strokes that brought her to her peak, and then beyond.

Inga nigh screamed with pleasure.

Seconds before he reached his own peak, he withdrew and spilled his seed upon her stomach with a long sigh of satisfaction.

"Noooooo!" Inga shrieked and grabbed his wilting staff in both hands, trying to jam him back into her body.

"Huh?" His eyes bulged at the agony as she squeezed him hard and pulled. Every man knew . . . and every woman of experience should know . . . that a sensitive organ such as a cock deserved better treatment after being the instrument of milady's pleasure. Quickly he pried himself out of her viselike grip. If he hadn't been wilting afore, he would be now. The pain was excruciating.

On her knees, she now whacked him about the head with her pillow. "By your leave, milady, have you gone demented?" he asked between whacks. Sex affected people in odd ways betimes; once, Ubbi the Ugly claimed he broke out in boils afterward, but perchance that stemmed from another cause. Ragnor had ne'er heard of sex turning a woman demented, though. Some men, yea, but that was usually from lack thereof.

She still reached for him, trying to pull him back inside her . . . which was ridiculous, really. Trying to put a wilted lily back in a slick pod was like . . . well, putting an egg back in the chicken. Impossible.

He laughed, which made her even more angry. Baring her perfectly white teeth at him, she snarled, "You bastard!

You cur! You lying, cod-sucking, too-charming son of a whore!"

Have a caution, Inga. Your true character is showing. "I never lied to you," he proclaimed indignantly as he grabbed her in his arms and lifted her so that her feet dangled off the rush floor. "Stop squirming, Inga, and tell me what this is all about."

Tears welled in her eyes. "Why? Why would you not give me your seed? Am I not beautiful enough? Was I not pleasing in the bed furs? By the gods, my father will thrash me for failing. And he will thrash you, too, for compromising me."

"I don't think so." Ragnor was referring to the thrashing, as well as the compromising. But then he went stiff with alertness. Setting Inga down, he backed up a bit. "Your father . . . he sent you to my bed furs?"

"Of course," she wailed, swiping at the tears which now overflowed and ran in rivulets down her cheeks. "Dost think I would dare such scandalous behavior without his blessing?"

Hah! 'Twas not I who made your virtue forfeit. Ragnor had heard of Inga's "scandalous behavior" with several other men; she was no untried virgin. Understanding dawned slowly. It had been a trap, set by the wily Danish king, ruler of all Jutland. Ragnor was not a king in his own land, but he was of noble birth . . . a chieftain of wealthy estates left by his grandsire in Vestfold, the rich southern region of Hordaland. Forkbeard schemed to join their families in wedlock . . . *lock* being the key word. He wanted to ensnare yet another Norse family into his spiderweb of intrigues.

But Ragnor was no fool. Ever since he'd lain with his first maid at age thirteen, he had tried to be careful not to breed babes hither and yon, and as far as he knew, he'd been successful. He had been taught a harsh lesson about the perils of virility by his father, who begat thirteen children. Children who gave him no end of trouble.

Ragnor grinned and gave himself an inward pat on the back at his escape.

"You dare to find mirth in me?" Inga narrowed her eyes at him and looked as if she might punch him in the mouth.

"Not in you, sweetling. Do not take it personally."

"And why not? Would it be such a horrendous thing if your seed took root in my womb?"

Yea, it would. "I do not wish to wed . . . yet."

"Yet?"

Not ever. "For years and years."

"If your father were here, he would force you to marry . . . to carry on his line."

If my father were here, he would not need me to carry on his line. He would have any one of my six half-brothers do the deed. "My father would understand my reluctance," he insisted.

But would he? Ragnor mused. *Or would he tell me that family is everything, and it is time for me to start my own?*

"Well, if you will not wed with me, you had best do me a favor," Inga declared. "You owe me that at least."

Ragnor had to laugh at her turnabout. They were both standing there, stark naked. She no doubt wanted to couple with him again.

Torolf, where are you when I need you? Where that thought came from, Ragnor did not know. His brother had been dead these many years . . . the last time he'd seen him, they'd both been rogues to the bone and both sixteen years old—born a mere sen-night apart to the same father but different mothers in different locales. Often folks mistook them for twins, so identical was their appearance, except his hair was black and his eyes blue, while Torolf's hair was blond and his eyes brown.

Their mischievous personalities had been the same, too. Ragnor recalled more than one occasion when the two of them had taken one lusty lass betwixt them in the bed furs. That was what Inga needed now. Two men to satisfy her needs. Torolf would have been "up" for the game . . . Ragnor just knew he would, his brother's preference ofttimes being for blond-haired women, while he preferred the rarer red. He liked his women to have a brain, as well, whilst Torolf had claimed it took no brain to spread one's thighs. *By the gods, you can still make me smile, Torolf, even when you are in far-off Valhalla.*

He glanced at Inga, standing afore him in all her blond, naked glory, a pensive expression on her face. His brother would not have said her nay.

Inga stamped her small foot in the rushes to mark her impatience.

For the love of Frey! She does *want me to swive her again. Can I?* He glanced down betwixt his legs. Turned out the lily was not dead after all. Turned out he did not need his brother after all.

Still, he thought, *I miss you, Torolf. Even after all these years.*

"About that favor, Ragnor," she said sweetly.

Yea, she wants me again. Oh, well! A Viking's work is never done.

But then, Inga surprised the spit out of him.

"Dost think there is any leftover boar down in the kitchen? Could you bring a little late-night repast for me to sup on?"

He laughed. What else could he do when his lady friend was more interested in meat than . . . well, meat?

Six months later, and deeper in the doldrums . . .

"Stop wallowing, Ragnor."

Madrene! By the gods, I am trapped now.

"Wake up, you lazy lout. 'Tis well past dawn, and much work to be done."

Work? What work? He tried to look at his sister, but his eyes seemed to be glued shut.

"Have you smelled the garderobes lately? They need to be limed. The outside privies, too. The mound of manure by the stables resembles a mountain."

I thought I was in the fires of Muspell afore, but, nay, hell is yet to come.

"And have I mentioned the moats? Holy Valhalla! We must needs start digging a trench to drain the stagnant water lest it breed pestilence. Not to worry, brother dear, I will show you how."

Dig a moat? Me? Now? I cannot open my eyes, let alone pick up a shovel.

"Shame on you for neglecting your duties so, brother. Tsk-tsk-tsk. All for the sake of wallowing. And one more thing . . ."

Ragnor groaned inwardly. Anytime a woman said "And one more thing," any sane man knew to run for cover. 'Twas trouble coming, pure and simple. *Is there aught more irksome than a nagging Norsewoman? Why does she not find herself a lustsome Viking man to keep her busy in the bed furs?*

Madrene was still rambling on in her irritating, I-am-better-than-thou voice. He inhaled and exhaled deeply for strength, knowing that ignoring his shrew of a sister was not going to make her disappear. Ragnor lifted his head from the tabletop where he had been pressing his forehead and sat up as straight as he could under the influence of the alehead madness. Very carefully he turned his heavy head to glare at Madrene. She sat beside him on the dais of his great hall at Norstead, her efficient fingers working thread through a handheld distaff and spindle. Brooches adorned each of the straps on her long, open-sided apron. A ring of keys hung from one of the pins, marking her authority. A troll-warrior in an apron! Well, not really a troll. Madrene was pleasing to the eye in some ways, he supposed, with her blond hair and shapely figure . . . till she opened her mouth.

The only things more active than her tongue were her hands. Never let it be said that Madrene succumbed to an idle moment in her over-efficient life. She'd probably already counted his bed linens, inspected his kitchens and store-rooms, not to mention the cess pits. Each sweep of the rough yarn through her fingers was like the sound of fingernails scratching across a rusty shield.

The fat cat draped across her shoulders like a fur mantle irritated him, as well. Black it was, though ill-named Rose. The furry monster had shifty gray eyes that regarded him with distaste as it hissed. Ragnor was the lackwit who had given Madrene the mangy gift when he'd returned from the eastern lands two years ago. The animal used every opportunity to annoy him—scratching his arms, pissing on his boots, once even landing on his male parts as he slept.

From the light seeping through the bladder windows, he realized it was morn and he still sat at the high table of the dais of his great hall. House servants and thralls bustled about on their daily chores. He must have sat here through the night . . . or was it two nights? With a grimace of distaste over the fuzziness of his tongue, he declared, "Vikings . . . do . . . not . . . wallow."

"Hah! Vikings wallow better than any halfbrained men I've ever met."

"Are you saying that I am a halfbrain?"

The cat made a sound he could swear was "Yes!"

He decided in that instant to buy Madrene a dog. A big dog. One that disliked cats.

Madrene knew as well as he that intelligence ran especially high in his brain. He spoke numerous languages. Numbers and words stuck in his mind on first hearing them. Sagas, once heard, imbedded themselves in his memory. He could survey the goods in a laden ship and within seconds precisely calculate their market value.

But he supposed that having intelligence didn't translate into acting intelligently, leastways in Madrene's assessment of him.

Holy Thor! My head is pounding. I need a horn of mead . . . or a death-blow to the half of my brain still alive and throbbing . . . or a good knock that would teach me the sense never to drink again or engage my sister in conversation. Further elaborating on her charge of his being halfbrained, he said, "I am smarter than the average Norseman." *But not smart enough to shut my teeth.*

"Not when it comes to drinking." She stopped her infernal spinning and stared at him for a long moment. The cat jumped off her shoulders, which was a feat in itself, considering how fat it was, and went off to annoy someone else, or catch some of the mice that abounded in the dirty rushes. "When did you get back?"

"A sennight ago."

"A sennight?" she exclaimed. "And you have not come to see me?"

Madrene ran the family farmstead. It bordered the royal fortress—his home—though it was many hides distant, two hours by horse. The farmstead was a prosperous estate, but nothing compared to his home—the vast lands and buildings that once belonged to his grandsire, Eric Trygvasson. He loved this place, Norstead, especially the timber castle built in the motte-and-bailey pattern with its highly carved eaves and beams, its great hall which could easily seat two hundred of his hird of soldiers, six huge center hearths, and hundreds of hectares of mountainous land dotted with fjords leading down to the sea. Outside the fortress castle were the smithy, armorer's shed, stables, barns, kitchens, a brewery, a bakehouse, storerooms, and massive exercise fields for his soldiers . . . all enclosed within a wooden palisade. Yea, he loved Norstead, but apparently not enough. Why else would he stay away so much?

As for Madrene, he should have visited her. She was all the family he had left. But whenever he saw her, when he went to the farmstead, he remembered too much. That was why he kept his distance . . . that, and her nagging. Still, he saw the hurt in her blue eyes . . . the same pale blue as his own, he'd been told . . . though her hair was blond and his was black.

He shrugged. "I was busy."

"Busy!" she snorted. "Doing what?" She glanced pointedly at the empty goblet sitting on the table before him. "And, by the by, I hear that King Svein has a bone to pick with you."

"Pffff! Six months ago he tried to trap me into marrying his daughter. He did not succeed."

Madrene raised her eyebrows at him. "The way I hear it, he almost succeeded." As always, the Norse gossip vine had stretched its tendrils all the way from Denmark to Norway.

Not surprising. "That third leg of yours will get you into trouble yet."

Third leg? "Madrene! You may have seen twenty-eight winters, but that gives you no excuse for unseemliness. Tsk-tsk." He grinned as he spoke.

It was Madrene's turn to say, "Pffff!" She shook her head at him. "Men always let their dangly parts lead them down the wrong path. Methinks it started with the Christians' Adam, whose lustsome nature caused him to eat the forbidden apple."

He and Madrene had been raised in both the Norse and Christian religions, but still he found amusement in her quoting of the Scriptures. Neither of them was very religious.

"Do not smirk at me, brother. You know I am right. And whilst we are on the subject . . ."

He groaned and put his face in his hands.

". . . would it be such a bad thing for you to marry Inga? She is pretty enough. And biddable. And apparently wanton to some extent."

"All good qualities in a wife, I presume?" he asked with a laugh, raising his head once again. "Biddable! Hah! What would I do with a biddable wife? There is one thing I would discuss with you, though . . . something, uh, personal?"

She arched her eyebrows in question.

"When I was with Inga, and we were engaged in . . . you know . . ."

She arched her eyebrows higher.

". . . I did what I was supposed to do, but I had no . . . um, 'enthusiasm' to speak of."

Madrene's lips trembled with a half smile. "That was six months ago. Libertine that you are, how has your 'enthusiasm' held up with other women?" She choked on her own stifled laughter.

I knew I should not have discussed this with Madrene. She does not take me seriously, not by half. Still, he blundered on, "There have been no others. Dost think something is wrong with me?"

"I don't know. Have you truly not lain with any other woman in all that time? I mean, 'tis unremarkable for me—I have not known a man in five years. But you? By thunder, 'tis a miracle."

He could not tell for certain whether she made jest with him. He felt himself blush, and he never blushed.

"None? Well, well, well." The expression on her face was marked by equal parts disbelief and amusement.

Rose, who sat a short distance away licking her fur, hissed out what could only be a snicker.

"'Tis not that I can't. I just don't want to. I seem to be yearning for something more. And you misspeak in calling me a libertine, truly you do. I do not fornicate any more than the average Norseman."

"Which is an excessive amount."

I cannot believe I am having this conversation with my sister.

She squeezed his arm and said, "Ragnor, methinks you are finally growing up. At the ripe old age of twenty and seven! Praise the gods! You need a soul-mate, not just a bedmate."

"I take exception to that conclusion. Why is it that women always think the answer to every man's problem is marriage? Soulmate? There is no such thing."

He had no chance to discuss the matter further because Madrene motioned over a housemaid, who carried a tray with a large metal cup on it. When Ragnor recognized the contents, he protested, "Oh, nay. I could not . . . please . . . stop shoving it in my face, Madrene." His sister forced to his lips her usual concoction for curing the aftereffects of the mead madness. It was warm and green and slimy. The fact that it usually worked was beside the point.

"Stop being such a whineling."

"Yech!" he said as he swallowed the horrid mess all in one gulp. It landed in his stomach with a thud, and soon thereafter he began to feel better . . . once he stopped gagging.

"About your marriage," Madrene persisted.

"You overstep yourself, sister," he cautioned. "I am the jarl here."

"Am I supposed to be impressed?"

"Well, nay, but you should treat me with more respect . . . and stop bringing up marriage."

"You are the last male in the line. You must have sons . . . legitimate sons . . . if our father's bloodline is to continue."

Ragnor would have asked why Madrene did not do the job herself, but he knew better. Her husband, Karl, had put her aside five years ago for failure to breed. Pronounced barren, she had vowed never to wed again. Personally, Ragnor suspected Karl was not that great a husband or lover, and that the fault might have lain in him . . . at least partially. But he decided not to broach that subject with Madrene. She would no doubt bring up her "dangly male parts" theory again.

"I will consider marriage someday," he promised. "But it will be on my own terms. With a bride of my choosing."

Madrene nodded.

"In the meantime, I will be departing in a sennight or two."

"A-Viking?"

"Mayhap." Most men of his acquaintance went raiding in the spring, after planting, or in the fall, after harvest. It was midsummer now, but the land did not bind him as it did others. "Or I will join forces with other Norsemen to assault the Saxons."

"Come, brother, let me help you to your bed furs. You need to sleep for a good long time. Then we will discuss your future plans."

Leave it to Madrene. She did not berate him for his plans to go a-Viking or soldiering. She was a good Norsewoman. A strong female. And handsome, too, when she was not nagging. He only wished she'd been able to find a husband who pleased her, in hearth and heart, but most especially in the bed furs. Forget that nonsense about soulmates, a good bedmate would do.

He looped his arm around her shoulders, though he did not need her to lean upon, and she wrapped her arm around his waist. As they walked through the great hall, heading toward the staircase leading to the upper chambers, she said, "I know what this is all about, Ragnor."

"What *this*?"

"Your mood. 'Tis that time of year. Midsummer. That was when our father left with nine of our brothers and sisters on his sea voyage."

"And never returned," he finished for her.

"Yea, never returned. Dost think there is any chance they are still alive?"

He shook his head at her, sad that she would even ask the question. "Nay. You know *Faöir* would have sent us word. He would not disappear for eleven years without telling us, if he were still alive."

"I know," she said on a sigh. "Still, we have no proof. Just news of their longship having been in Greenland and beyond. Then nothing."

"They are dead, Madrene," he said gently. "Betimes, though, I wish that we had gone with him on that fateful trip."

"Then we would be dead, too."

He shrugged as if that might not matter so much. Odin's breath! This kind of talk would put him in an even darker mood. He tried to brighten up Madrene, at least, if not himself. "Well, we still have each other. And I will not be leaving for a good many days yet. Shall I challenge you to a game of *hnefatafl* this evening?" He leered at her like some crafty gambler.

She smiled back and nudged him in the ribs with her elbow for his teasing. "I always win, you rogue, unless you cheat. Methinks 'tis time you brought me a few more baubles back from your adventuring. Yea, that is what I will take for my prize this time. A woman can never have too much amber . . . or gold."

Ragnor laughed and hugged her to his side as they walked up the stairs. Inside, though, he thought, *What a sad and lonely pair we are!*

CHAPTER TWO

❧

A thousand or so years later. . . . Are we having fun yet? . . .

"Magnusson! Get your hairy ass up here and give me fifty. You are one sorry sonofabitch! You run like a girl. You breathe like a girl. Pff-pff-pff! Are you a girl? Are you, Viking?"

Ensign Torolf Magnusson, the object of that tirade, looked up at his instructor, Master Chief Petty Officer Ian MacLean, and wondered idly if that bulging vein in his tormentor's forehead might just blow. One could only hope.

"Haul ass, boy," the Master Chief continued to yell. "Remember, winners never quit. Are you ready to quit? We haven't had a quitter today. Yet. You ready to give it up, loser? Huh? I'd love to have *you* ring the bell."

Oh, shit! Here we go again. Like I would ever quit over a dickhead like you. Like I can't handle a measly spill into a mud pit. You're not going to break me. I survived Hell Week. I can survive you. Torolf, one of the eight members of Team Five in SEAL Class 500, crawled out of the ditch where he had fallen during the obstacle course known in BUD/S training as the Devil's Spawn. BUD/S was the acronym for the SEAL training program Basic Underwater Demolition/Seals. Training was done here in Coronado at the Naval Special

Warfare Center. Sometimes, like today, Torolf wondered why it had always been his dream to be here.

He spat a wad of crud out of his mouth, wiped the mud out of his eyes with the back of his dirty hand, then levered himself up and out by muscle-strained arms. Standing to attention, he said, "Yes, Master Chief, sir."

Master Chief MacLean stood glaring at him through dark Matrix sunglasses, hands on hips. On his shirt shone the coveted trident pin that all SEAL wannabees aimed for. Better known as the Budweiser, the trident pin, featuring an eagle grasping Neptune's pitchfork in one claw and a weapon in the other, was granted only to men who had gained SEAL status.

Without having the order repeated, Torolf dropped to the ground to do fifty push-ups, on top of the five hundred he'd already done that day. And it was barely oh-nine-hundred on a bright California summer morning.

His seven teammates, equally wet, dirty, and bone-tired, stared with seeming solemnity at him as he completed his "punishment." None of them cracked as much as a grin, knowing full well that they could be next.

Seaman Justin LeBlanc, that crazy Cajun from Loo-zee-anna, did wink at him, though . . . a brief flutter that could be interpreted as a blink if noticed by the chief or any of the three other instructors in attendance. Cage was his swim buddy. In SEALs, swim buddies could never be more than six feet apart.

Petty Officer Second Class Sylvester "Sly" Simms, a big black dude from Harlem who used to model men's tighty whities for *Esquire*, gave the chief a surreptitious finger behind his back.

Petty Officer First Class Travis "Flash" Gordon crossed his eyes, as if a bug had suddenly crash-dived on his nose.

Seaman Frank Uxley, nicknamed F.U. for obvious reasons, didn't blink or gesture; he'd been doing duck squats all morning for failure to help lift his IBL (Inflatable Boat, Large) fast enough in a predawn surf op. No way was he chancing a repeat of those hamstring-punishing exercises.

Lieutenant (jg) Jacob Alvarez Mendozo—JAM—moved his lips slightly; he was probably praying, being an ex-Jesuit priest. JAM always claimed he had God on his shoulder, while all Torolf had was that puny-assed Thor.

"You boys need a little loosening up before breakfast," the Master Chief said. "What say we go for a short run . . . say ten miles?"

What a comedian!

Torolf knew that ten miles meant it would probably be fifteen . . . maybe more. It would be an uncomfortable run in heavy boondockers, with sand between their toes and in every bodily orifice from their early-morning beach roll-arounds. They were in full ruck today, which meant BDUs and carrying about seventy-five pounds of military field gear. At least they weren't carrying their IBLs on their heads while they ran, which was the norm.

Torolf refused to show the Marquis de Master Chief his displeasure. There had been a contest of wills going on between him and the "Lean-Mean" from the get-go. Hell, they all knew what a "Mac Attack" meant, and it had nothing to do with hamburgers. The chief prided himself on being the "professor of pain."

The chief yelled out one of his usual nauseating inspirational quotes: "The journey of a thousand miles begins with one step."

"Or with a lot of bitching," Torolf muttered to himself.

"My sister's going to run with you boys today," the chief announced. "Hope you can keep up with her."

There was a communal groan as Lieutenant Alison Mac-Lean arrived. Though she had spent less time in the service than her older brother, she out-ranked him. Ian Maclean had attained the highest rank an enlisted man could reach, master chief petty officer. But with the injustice typical of the military, any person who graduated from officers' candidate school outranked the highest enlisted officer.

Lieutenant MacLean was clad in running shorts and a U.S. Navy T-shirt. She didn't have any breasts to speak of, like many extreme female athletes, though her long legs bordered on spectacular. Her red hair was short and tousled. Torolf was tall—six foot four—but Lieutenant MacLean had to be close to six foot herself. And big-boned. He liked his women blond and petite. Nope, she was not his type at all.

On the other hand, Ragnor would like her, he thought of a sudden. His brother, whom he hadn't seen in more than ten years, had always had a preference for redheads and women with brains. Why he would be thinking of Ragnor now, he had no idea. *I'm probably hallucinating from exhaustion.*

Lieutenant MacLean was a physician here at the naval base with a specialty in sports medicine. She and two other physicians worked exclusively with the trainees and SEALs themselves, checking them out after every evolution. The teams had their own medical facility at Coronado with excellent, much-used rehab capabilities, all of which were headed by the good lieutenant. Often called upon to work with the muscle-related injuries the SEALs sustained in their grueling workouts, she even went out on field ops on some occasions. The SEALs program barred females, but Lieutenant MacLean was as close to a female SEAL as they came.

"Do you think she's a dyke?" Flash asked as they fell in behind the chief, his sister, and three other instructors,

jogging slowly off the "grinder"—the asphalt P.T. arena—
and heading toward the beach.

"Hell, no," F.U. answered with a laugh. "Where'd you get
that dumb-ass idea?"

"She's so big," Flash answered. Flash was only about five
foot ten; so any woman taller than he would seem big.

"And big means lesbo? You are such a frickin' asshole."
That was Cody O'Brien speaking. He and Flash hated each
other with a passion because 1) Flash loved country music;
and 2) Cody hated country music. Simple as that.

"Takes one to know one," Flash answered.

"Asshole or lesbo?" Cody countered.

"You are achin' for a breakin', man," Flash snarled.

"Hoo-yah! Kiss my achy breaky ass, sweetie pie," Cody
said, laughing.

"Sticks and stones may break my bones, butthead."

"Well, that retort came right out of kindergarten," Cody
said. "Oops, that's how far you went in school, isn't it?"

"I think she's a hottie." JAM spoke right over Flash and
Cody in his educated Mexican-American accent.

None of them had even broken a sweat yet, but they
would in another mile or five. For now, they were able to
talk and run at the same time. They all looked at JAM. For
an ex-priest, he wasn't all that priestly.

"JAM, JAM, JAM, you poor boy! I think you need to get
laid," yet another of the SEAL trainees chimed in. This time
it was Frank "Pretty Boy" Floyd, the team's hands-down
quintessential ladies man from Bangor, Maine. He had been
a race-car driver before entering the SEALs. Race-car drivers
were known chick magnets, apparently, or so he told them
on numerous occasions. Humility was not one of his strong
suits.

"Eff you," JAM said. Definitely not priestly.

"You called?" F.U. replied. It was a standing joke among them, and they all laughed.

"Actually, JAM's right. She's not bad. I like Lieutenant MacLean," Torolf said. "And as for big, lots of Viking women are tall. Nothing wrong with that."

They all groaned.

"Oh, no! Not the Viking crap again, Max," Sly said, bringing up the rear. All the SEALs and SEAL trainees were given nicknames, his being short for Magnusson. "I swear, I am going to puke if I hear one more story about how great it was to ride the open waves in a longboat, or wield a sword that has a name, or eat dried fish back in the freakin' Norse-lands."

Everyone laughed again, including Torolf, who had told them a story or two about eating the dreaded lutefisk in the dead of winter or on a long-ship when out on a prolonged voyage. Not that they'd believed any of it.

"You all think this is funny?" the Master Chief called back to them. Thank God he hadn't been able to hear their words, especially about his sister. "Well, then, let's pick up the pace. And how about a little jody call, boys? It's your turn, Petty Officer Gordon. Remember, if something's hard, it must be worth doing. Let's hear it, loud and clear. Tell us why hard is good."

"I don't know but I've been told," Flash yelled out.

"I don't know but I've been told," they all repeated, keeping beat with their running as they chanted.

"Navy SEALs are mighty bold."

"Navy SEALs are mighty bold," they sang back.

"Ladies watch how a SEAL runs."

"Ladies watch how a SEAL runs."

"SEALs have real hot buns."

"SEALs have real hot buns."

"But we all know why the women flock . . ."

"But we all know why the women flock . . ."

" 'Cause SEALs have got a great—"

"Gentlemen!" the Master Chief interrupted, turning and jogging backwards as he addressed them. "Do not go there! There's a lady on board."

Flash grinned and finished, ". . . sweet talk."

And the rest of them chanted back, " 'Cause SEALs have got a great sweet talk."

"Sound off, one, two . . ."

"Sound off, one, two . . ."

"Three, four."

"Three, four."

When their running exercise—which did end up being fifteen miles—was over, the Master Chief yelled over to Flash, "Petty Officer Gordon. In my office at nineteen hundred hours. We need to discuss your choice of *grody* jody lyrics. Perhaps a bit of Gig Squad will teach you to be a better composer." Gig Squad, held for one hour after dinner, consisted of the usual physical-torture punishments, like sit-ups and duck squats, but they were inflicted outside the instructors' offices, where everyone passing by could witness the humiliation. Poor Flash! They'd all been there at one point or another in the past three months.

Torolf walked up to the chief's sister, who was bent over at the waist, breathing heavily. It had been a grueling run, and her hair was wet and plastered to her head, no longer fluffy. He had to give her credit. She had kept up nicely.

"Sorry if we offended you," he apologized, even as he breathed deeply in and out, like she did, to get his heart rate down.

"No problem," she said without looking up.

He felt rather guilty over his teammates' remarks about her physical appearance and decided to be a nice guy. "Excellent run, Alison," he said. Using her given name probably crossed the line, but what the hell. Maybe she would like to get to know him better. He was a good-looking guy. He could be charming. He decided to give her a shot.

She straightened and gave him a level look, taking in his sudden interest in her sweat-soaked T-shirt, which revealed that her seemingly nonexistent breasts did, in fact, exist. *Hoo-yah!* They more than made up for her height. With a laugh of understanding, she said, "Drop dead, swabbie," and walked off.

So much for giving her a shot. Shot misfired. I wonder if Ragnor would have done any better.

Soon after, Torolf walked with his SEAL trainee buddies toward the dining hall, sweat still rolling off his body in rivers. He and the other guys walked a little funny from being rubbed raw between their legs by the wet sand. Despite his being in prime physical condition, his knees felt like rubber after all that exercise, and the day had barely begun. Alison MacLean walked straight as a poker in front of them, as if the run had been a snap for her.

"I think she likes me," Torolf pronounced with a grin.

His teammates turned as one to look at him.

Cage spoke for them all. "As my granny always says to my sister, 'Darlin', a man and his ego doan make the gumbo boil.'"

"What the hell does that mean?"

"It means Alison MacLean doesn't give a rat's ass about you," Cody interpreted. "Or any of the rest of us."

Dreams of being Demi Moore . . . uh, G.I. Jane . . .

"Did my guys offend you today, Allie?" her brother asked as they sat down to eat in the officers' dining room.

"No. I've heard more suggestive grody jodies, believe me . . . some of them from women," she answered. "If I get offended over a little bad language, I'll never make it on a SEAL team."

Ian shook his head sadly at her. "Sis, it ain't ever gonna happen. Bullshit movies like *G.I. Jane* aside, the Navy will never open the SEALs program to women. And it's not a sexist thing, either. There are good reasons why—"

She put up a halting hand to stop the explanation he was about to give. She'd heard it too many times before. From him; from her father, Rear Admiral Thomas MacLean, a member of the U.S. Government's Task Force on Terrorism; from her brother Ross, a Navy pilot; from her brother Clay, a midshipman at Annapolis; and from dozens of Navy personnel through the years. That didn't mean she would give up, but in the meantime she'd gone to medical school and was putting her talents to good use in other ways, indirectly fighting the terrorism she and her family abhorred . . . with good reason. "We'll have to agree to disagree," she insisted.

He started to say something more, then stopped with a shrug of surrender. They both dug into their lunches, eating silently.

"I saw Magnusson talking to you. What was that about?"

"Nothing."

"Was he hitting on you?"

Alison had to laugh. Always the brother, looking out for his little sister. Not that she was little. "Not really."

"I'll kill him. Did he ask you for a date, or say something vulgar? These guys don't have the sense God gave a goose when it comes to their trash mouths."

Ian should talk! She'd heard more than a few blue words

pass through his lips. "No, Ian, he didn't ask me for a date. And give me credit for being able to handle myself if he did. Jeez! It's not like he pinched my butt or anything."

"You don't take matters seriously enough. Maybe I should stop you from running with my teams."

"If you issue such an order, I'll kill *you*. Really. It helps me stay in top shape. I need to push myself."

"You look fine. Beautiful, in fact."

She patted his arm. "You're my brother. Of course you would think that, but I've got news for you . . . I am not beautiful. Beauty isn't what I'm aiming for anyhow when I talk about being in top shape. It's important that I be as physically fit as any SEAL if I'm called out on a field op to provide medical aid to a team . . . *or* if the Navy ever gets its act together about female frogmen . . . frogwomen, that is."

"You never give up, do you?"

"It runs in the genes, honey," she said, pushing her plate back. "I'm going to dash home for a quick shower before I do my afternoon rounds."

"I know your apartment is convenient for you, but I still wish you'd move in with me." Ian had been bugging her to move into his house in San Diego since his fiancée dumped him six months ago, but Alison had refused. "Especially with those phone calls you've been getting lately."

Alison had made the mistake of telling her brother about the "breather" phone calls she'd been getting the last few months. Sometimes there were as many as six on her answering machine when she got home from work, and the calls came during the night, too. "They stopped weeks ago," she lied. Really, all she needed to do was change her phone number. And she would, when she got the time. No big deal!

Ian worried about her in other regards, too. Her entire

family did. Ever since her fiancé, a Navy SEAL, had been killed in a Lebanese bombing five years ago. But she was fine now. Except for an extreme hatred of terrorists.

When Alison was assigned to Coronado last year, she had rented an apartment—the whole second floor of an old Victorian house. "The Island," as many locals called Coronado, even though it was really a peninsula, included a small town of tree-lined streets with Victorian homes juxtaposed with bungalows. White sand beaches lined the Pacific side and the scenic San Diego skyline graced the bay side. It was also home to the North Island Naval Air Station on the north side, and on the south end, the Naval Amphibious Base, where the SEALs trained. Downtown San Diego was an eight-mile ride over the Silver Strand, the neck of land that connected the "island" to the mainland.

Her independence was important to her, but, more than anything, she loved her apartment, antique plumbing and all. Rather than tell her brother that, she said, "Sam would never let me move into your house, anyhow." Sam was the huge white cat he'd inherited from his ex-fiancée—the only thing Sheila had left behind.

"You have a point there," he replied with a grin. The man did love his cat, though he pretended that he just put up with him.

Just then, a young aide to the base commander walked up to their table. "Excuse me, Master Chief, sir, you need to come outside right away. There's been an accident."

"*What*?" they both said at the same time.

"Is it Doofus again?"

Harry "Doofus" Harrison was a trainee on Team Two . . . the clumsiest oaf God ever created. Last week he fell off the climbing wall and almost knocked an eye out. The week before, he'd almost drowned himself in two feet of water. But, to give him credit, he had heart out the wazoo.

"Nope, not Doofus this time. Team Five was crossing the road over from the grinder when a private food-service truck came barreling through. Drunk driver. Wasn't watching where he was going."

"Anyone hurt?" Alison asked, morphing into her physician mode. She and her brother had already risen and were heading out, following the petty officer.

"Couple of guys got minor scrapes, but nothing serious, thanks to Ensign Magnusson. He jumped in front and pushed his teammates back."

"And Magnusson?" she asked, alert to the concern in the sailor's eyes.

"Magnusson is in pretty bad shape."

CHAPTER THREE

※

A-Viking he did go, a-Viking he did go, hi-ho the . . . uh-oh! . . .

Ragnor had left his homeland a sennight ago, but already he was having regrets. He'd expected to do a little pillaging of Saxon churches and rich farm estates, drink some stolen ale, perhaps sample the wares of some Saxon maids, overall have a good time and return home a little richer come autumn.

What he had not expected when he'd joined his four longships with six of Forkbeard's was the twenty Saxon ships manned with hundreds of armed soldiers that he saw on the horizon, royal banners waving in the breeze.

"Uh-oh!" the king said to Ragnor even as he motioned for one of his larger longships to pull up alongside so he could jump over.

Ragnor gave the old slyboots a killing glance. "*Uh-oh? That is all you can say? I smell something stink-some, you wily whoreson. What is this about?*"

Svein ducked his head guiltily. "I might have kidnapped King Ethelred's sister and her babe, along with some holy relics and a chest or two of gold coins."

"*Might have*? When might you have done this?" *I must be*

demented to have joined forces with this lunatic. I knew he was not to be trusted. Aaarrgh!

"When you were off emptying out that monastery near Winchester."

Good honest work! Relieving fat priests of their jewel-encrusted chalices. Unlike . . .

So you planned this all along, you slimy bastard!

"Why?" Ragnor asked through gritted teeth.

"Revenge for the St. Brice's Day Massacre, if you must know. My sister Gunnhild was among those murdered . . . and she a voluntary hostage." Svein batted his lashes in an exaggerated fashion and even feigned wiping away a tear. *The old bag of wind!*

"That was several years ago, and Ethelred has paid you much danegeld in recompense since then. Not to mention your massive retaliation three years later." Ethelred was a strange and disturbed monarch, everyone knew that, but that did not excuse this unprovoked affront by Svein.

"My wrath is mighty and still unappeased," Svein said with a shrug.

Frankly, Ragnor believed that Svein was using the St. Brice's Day Massacre as an excuse to pillage and plunder endlessly.

As the king's longship side-butted against his, Svein nimbly leapt onto it, and called out to Ragnor, "Good battle, my friend!"

Hah! Some friend. But Ragnor had no time to dwell on that now. "To arms!" he yelled to his men, who jumped off their sea chests and took out weapons and armor, both leather and chain mail. The shields, stored along the rim of the outside of the longship, were quickly lifted and readied for use. Within minutes they were ready to engage the fast-approaching enemy. Sails were lowered and anchors thrown to steady the "fighting field." The men-at-arms in his other three longboats followed suit. "It appears we are going to battle this day," he shouted. "May Thor's great hammer Mjollnir be with us all."

His men raised their swords high as they cheered and banged their shields. He pulled out his own favorite broadsword, "Foe Fighter," laying his battle-axe "Head Crusher" at the ready. After that, he donned a sleeveless, knee-length tunic of chain mail. Unlike some of his men, he disdained to put on a leather or metal helmet with nose guard. It was all in Odin's hands now, after all . . . or the Christian One-God. He said a silent prayer to both.

Svein's largest longship, the one onto which he'd jumped, managed to escape, but the rest of his vessels remained for the fierce battle which soon ensued.

At first there were war whoops aplenty on both sides, along with shouts of "To the death!" or "Mark them with your spears!" or "See you in Valhalla!" But after an hour of fighting, the only sounds resounding on all the ships were the din of battle—swords ringing against each other and the screams of the dying. The deck of Ragnor's ship was slippery with blood. Bodies lay about, both Saxon and Viking, staring sightlessly upward. Some were minus limbs or even heads. It was a scene out of hell itself.

At the sight of all this carnage, Ragnor remained calm and dispassionate on the outside, but inside he felt like vomiting with horror. His sword nigh smoked with skillful deathdoling; his soul nigh smoked with despair. So many good men would break the raven's fast this day. So many!

Ragnor's men were well-seasoned soldiers; he was lord of the swordplay himself. But the foemen's force triply outmanned them. Taking a slight respite to catch his breath, Ragnor was surprised from behind by a huge Saxon who latched one arm around his neck and used his other burly arm to lock Ragnor's sword at his side. The brute must have weighed twice as much as he, and Ragnor was a big man.

A spurt of rage burst through Ragnor then, both for himself and all his dead comrades. With the energy of a berserker, he broke free and raised his broadsword high, about to split the skull of his attacker down the center. But the redhaired monster, whose yellow teeth were bared, with spittle running down the sides of his mouth, lunged for him and slid on the bloody deck, hitting him square in the chest. Ragnor's buttocks struck the ship's rail, and both men went overboard.

He struggled in the briny depths, pulled down by the weight of his armor and boots and by the Saxon warrior, who would not let go of him. First things first. Ragnor squeezed the throat of his enemy till his eyes bulged and his body went lifeless. Then he attempted to rise to the surface, his lungs burning. But he was down too low, and he kept sinking lower.

As water filled his mouth and nose and then his lungs, he felt lightheaded. There was no pain as peacefulness overcame him.

So this is how it feels to die. Not so bad. Mayhap my father and my brothers and sisters experienced the same thing. Ah, well. I would not have wanted a straw death. A Viking should not die in his sleep.

He floated then, still underwater.

I wonder if I will meet up with my family again today.

I wonder if Valhalla will be as grand as the elders have proclaimed, with walls made of golden spears and a roof of golden shields.

He laughed with morbid mirth as another thought came to him. *I wonder if the Valkyries, those famous female warriors, will manage to bring back my "enthusiasm."*

A strange white light appeared before him at the end of a long tunnel. Was this the channel to the afterworld? He wanted to go toward the light, desperately. But off to the left side he saw a fleeting, older image of his brother beckoning him away from the light. He alternately laughed, then winced with pain. Had he been wounded in battle, too? And to the right he saw a red-haired goddess, also beckoning him away from the light. Her green eyes were huge with fear. She was in some danger, and she appeared to need his help.

How strange! Ragnor thought.

But then he thought no more.

The deed was done.

Shattered dreams . . .

"No way! I am not dropping out of SEALs," Torolf raged at Master Chief MacLean from his hospital bed.

"You have no choice," the Master Chief said.

"I *will* graduate into the teams. This has been my dream for too long to give it up now. No friggin' way!"

"You can 'roll back' after you've fully recovered. You won't even have to start over with a new class; you can pick up in training where you left off." The chief smiled kindly down at him, which was really scary . . . seeing the Professor of Pain smile at him. Sort of like Hannibal Lecter patting you on the head before he dined on your eyeball. "You don't even have to repeat Hell Week."

"No way!" Torolf repeated.

"You've suffered a major concussion, your body is bruised; your face is black and blue. You need to recuperate," Lieutenant MacLean, the physician, said.

"Commander Britton has signed you off for one month's leave," the chief said in one of his "don't argue, I am God" voices. He laid a set of orders on the bed, down near Torolf's feet, which were covered with a light blanket. "I'm assuming you'll want to go home to Sonoma to rest. There's a plane leaving at oh-nine-hundred tomorrow. Make sure your doctor there gives the hospital here regular updates. Good luck!" He saluted then and spun on his heel. At the door he turned and said, "If it's any consolation, I think you would have made a good SEAL. And I would welcome the chance to kick your butt if you return." With those words, the chief left.

Torolf glared at the chief's retreating back and at his sister, the physician, who remained. It was probably silly, but he felt like crying, and he didn't want to do it in front of a female.

"It really is for the best," she said.

"Drop dead," he said, repeating her words back to her.

She just smiled, not at all offended. Therefore he decided not to apologize.

After that, everyone left him alone, fearing his dark mood. In the middle of the night, Torolf rose from his bed, very carefully since he was still in pain. He dressed himself and made his way out of the quiet medical facility, unnoticed. He had a motorcycle no one knew about parked in a private garage in Coronado, against regulations. He would drive home to the family vineyard in Sonoma . . . or maybe he'd go somewhere else to get himself back in shape. He wasn't really worried about being stopped, because, after all, he had orders giving him a one-month medical leave.

As he left Coronado a half hour later, traveling across the Silver Strand, he wondered if he would ever return.

Damn straight I will, he answered himself almost immediately. *I am a Viking. Vikings never quit.*

Die Hard, Die Soft . . . Whatever! . . . Dead is Dead . . .

Ragnor shot straight up in the air from the water, like a dol-
phin, took a huge gulp of air, then felt himself being shoved
back under by a heavy hand. He'd always prided himself on
being leather-lunged, but this was ridiculous.

Apparently, he hadn't died after all . . . not yet. And neither had his Saxon enemy, whose hand was pressed down on
top of his head.

Enough is enough! Drawing on some inner energy and
the will to live . . . now that he knew life was within his
grasp . . . he shoved the hand aside, kicked the man in the
groin, then swam swiftly to the surface. To his surprise,
other heads bobbed to the surface around him, but they
swam to a nearby yellow boat, and a measly boat it was, bigger than a small fishing boat but smaller than even the small-
est long-ship. It wasn't even made of wood.

"What the hell was *that* about down there?" a man yelled
in his face as he, too, came to the surface. It was not the
Saxon warrior he'd been struggling with when he'd almost
drowned, although this man's short brown hair had a reddish tint, too. It must be another Saxon warrior. With a thun-
derous expression on his face, the man yelled out to what must
be his comrades, "This jerk-off just kicked me in the nuts,
deliberately." Then he blinked as if in sudden recognition.
"Magnusson, you dumb sonofabitch, what are you doing
here? I thought you were gone." A vein in his forehead looked
as if it might burst.

Well, of course he had kicked him *deliberately.* The man

had been trying to drown him. As for being *gone*, he'd thought so, too. But how did the man know his name? He shrugged, guessing that his wordfame must have spread even to the Saxon lands.

Immediately he was surrounded by a half-dozen men. The leader—the one who'd been down there with him— pointed sharply to the left and bellowed right in his face, "Get your ass out of the water. Pronto! I have a few things to say to you, Ensign Magnusson."

End-sign? Is that a vile name in the Saxon language? Hmmm, I thought I was proficient in the English tongue, but mayhap not. This fellow speaks with an odd accent. He focused his brain, trying to understand the words in context.

Ragnor had a few things to say to *him*, too, but then he noticed the direction of the Saxon's pointing. It was a shoreline. How could that be? When he'd gone down, his ship had been on the high seas. Could it have drifted during the battle?

Frowning with confusion, he swam toward shore. Meanwhile, other men crawled into the yellow boat, which they rowed along beside him. Some of them stared at him in compassion. It was a considerable distance, but he swam well, and besides, being alive gave a man the stamina to go on even under the worst of situations. He suspected this was going to be a worst-type situation.

"A-ten-hut!" his attacker screamed as he and some of the men in the boat waded onto the sandy beach. At the shouted order, seven of the men stood stock-still with their hands at their sides, staring straight ahead. He figured he should do the same. When in enemy territory, it was best to blend in and not call attention to oneself . . . though kicking that man in his male parts certainly must have made Ragnor stand out.

"Why are you still here?" the leader asked, coming up to stand in front of him, practically nose to nose.

Well, I know I should be dead, but what kind of a question is that? "Because the gods wanted me to stay," he offered tentatively.

"Don't give me any of your wise-ass answers. And you know the proper way to address me, Ensign. *Yes, Master Chief, sir.*"

Ah, as I suspected, he is the chieftain. "It was not—" He stopped when he saw the glower on the leader's face. Apparently, he hadn't really expected a response.

Now the chieftain was gaping at his arm rings. "I thought I told you on the first day of BUD/S to ditch those friggin' bracelets. Have you got a death wish?"

"Nay, I can honestly say I do not have a death wish," he said, then added, "Chieftain, sir. And as for these"—he tapped the etched gold arm rings on his upper arms—"I never take them off. Good luck, they are."

The chieftain said a well-known Saxon word that sounded like luck but was not. "I swear, Magnusson, in a hostage situation you would be the first one released, because your constant talking would drive them nuts."

"I take offense at—" The chieftain's unbridled growl cut Ragnor short.

"Well, boys, since Magnusson here is such a glutton for punishment, and since he thinks it's A-okay to defy doctor's orders, to join an op uninvited, to wear jewelry, for chrissake, to strike an instructor, and to mock the Master Chief by calling him Chieftain, why don't you *all* give me one hundred push-ups, followed by a five-mile run. One for all and all for one, right?"

That was a lot of data, even for an excessively bright man to comprehend. Once he'd processed as much as he could, Ragnor thought, *I understand now. This chieftain wants to*

establish his authority by having us refer to him as master,
as well as chieftain. I can do that, if it will save my life. But,
really, I call no man my master.

"Yes, Master Chief, sir!" the seven men surrounding him
said as one, then shot Ragnor dirty looks before dropping to
the ground, legs straight, arms braced. They began lowering
and raising their stiffened frames, never quite touching their
chests to the ground. He dropped down, too. After a few clumsy
attempts, he got the rhythm and kept up with his fellow prisoners . . . if that was what they were.

What a silly way to punish prisoners! I saw Ivan Split-
Nose sever body parts of prisoners one time, piece by piece,
just to amuse himself. And torture! Whoo-ee, the Saxons
have nothing on the Arabs in that regard.

Soon they were done with the absurd "push-ups," but did
they stand still and relax? Nay. The chieftain and some of
what must be his assistant leaders yelled, "Fall in," and the
lackwitted prisoners began to run in the sand. Apparently
running was a punishment, too. Pfff! Wait till he told Svein
Forkbeard about this. The Saxons would be an easier target
in the future once he gave their enemy that information.
"Not to worry, Svein, if they capture you, they will punish
you with running. Ha, ha, ha!"

"Get your ass in gear, Magnusson," the leader shouted, "or
do you want to do a few extra miles?"

How would I know? I do not even know what miles are.
But he was a quick learner and assumed it had something to
do with distance. He said, "Yea, Master Chieftain, sir," which
did nothing to soften the chieftain's glower. Soon Ragnor
caught up with his fellow prisoners. They all, himself included,
wore boots and garments similar to loincloths except bigger, with short legs. That was all. They were bare-chested and

bare-legged. As he ran alongside the men, he noticed something else about his new comrades. They were all bald . . . or nigh bald, except for stubble.

He thought he heard the leader mutter to one of his aides something that sounded like, "What's with that 'yea' business?" and the response he got was, "You know Magnusson and that spacey Viking talk of his." But then they ran up ahead, leaving a distance between them and the prisoners.

"What caused all of you to go bald?" he asked one man running in tandem next to him on the right . . . a tall man with muscles aplenty. In truth, they all had muscles aplenty, just like him. "Do they feed you so poorly here? I have heard that scurvy will do that to men betimes."

"Cut the Viking crap, Magnusson," the man said, staring straight ahead. "You'll get us all in trouble . . . more trouble than you already caused. Kicking our team leader in the balls . . . have you lost your bleepin' mind?"

"Mayhap," Ragnor said. "By the by, you talk funny."

"*By the by*, asshole, you're the one who talks funny," he said with a snort of disgust. "*Mayhap!* Jeez!"

Ragnor decided not to take offense at the asshole remark . . . for now. "But back to your baldness . . . I hate to tell you, but you all look ridiculous with those shiny pates. Like bloody monks. Holy Thor, I will eat grass afore I let my appearance go like that."

"He must have hit his head harder than anyone thought," another prisoner commented, loud enough for Ragnor to hear but low enough that their captors up front could not.

"I've got news for you, Viking," still another prisoner said. "Your head's been shaved the same as the rest of us."

That news drew Ragnor up short. Impossible! Still, he raised a hand to his head . . . his bristly head. He roared with outrage. "I will kill the man who did this to me." *How dare*

*they cut my hair? I am not an overly vain man, but I had
very nice hair. Somebody is going to pay for this.*

*Aaah, what difference does it make? I am alive, thank
the gods! And hair grows back . . . I hope. There are worse
things in life than a bald head . . . like no head.*

Another question nagged at him. *When did they cut my
hair?*

*And remove my armor and replace it with these small
clothes and leather boots?*

*And where are all my seamen and soldiers? Dead? All of
them? Am I the only prisoner taken in that battle?*

He continued to run, pondering these sorry events. Every
once in a while the chieftain or one of his cohorts ordered
the men to run into the surf and get wet, then roll around in
the sand, before resuming their running. *Strange people!*

Looking sideways to the left, he noticed a tall, slim man
with brown skin. "Are you a Moor?" he asked, trying to be
friendly.

The brown man gave him a disbelieving look before staring ahead again. "Did you just call me a moron? You really
are a dickhead. The only reason I'm not gonna beat the crap
out of you is that you probably have a concussion."

Ragnor frowned. "You say me wrong. I did not say more-
on, I said Moor . . . ah, I see. More-on must be a derogatory
word in your language. My apologies if I gave offense. I
meant Nubian."

"Nu . . . nu . . . nubian," the brown man sputtered.

"And as to that other. Nay, I am not a dickhead, I am a
Viking."

There were snickers all around then, followed by a remark from the brown man, "Dumb shit!"

"So, are you a Moor, Sly?" another prisoner asked the
brown man.

"More or less," the brown man, whose name must be Sly, answered with a chuckle.

"I knew a man named Sly at one time. Sigurd the Sly."

Sly just ignored him.

"You know, there are eight of us prisoners. We could easily overtake those four enemy up front," Ragnor advised. In truth, he could take all four of them himself, but he did not want to appear boastful.

This time all his fellow prisoners turned to look at him and as one they repeated Sly's assessment of him, "Dumb shit!"

"But—" Ragnor started.

"Just shut up," the brown man said.

"Petty Officer Simms," the enemy leader called back, turning and continuing to run backwards, "do I hear you engaging in conversation with Ensign 'I've Lost My Mind' Magnusson? Perhaps you would like to help us pick up the pace with a jody call?"

The brown man, presumably named Simms as well as Sly, surprised Ragnor by beginning to chant out a sort of song, which the other prisoners repeated back to him:

"I don't know but I been told."

"I don't know but I been told."

"Navy SEALs are good as gold."

"Navy SEALs are good as gold."

"But we ain't SEALs yet, nosirree."

"But we aint't SEALs yet, nosirree."

"Three more months and we are free."

"Three more months and we are free."

"Till that time we toe the line."

"Till that time we toe the line."

"We got pain, but we don't whine."

"We got pain, but we don't whine."

"Sound off, one two . . ."

"Sound off, one two . . ."

". . . three, four."

". . . three, four."

Silence reigned then except for the rhythmic pounding of boots on sand . . . until Ragnor asked Sly, "You all want to be turned into animals?" He did not really believe in all that fantasy nonsense, but many Vikings did. Dragons, trolls, magic, and such. Still, he was beginning to wonder if he really was dead and had landed in one of the other worlds many Norsemen believed in . . . not Asgard, like the Christian heaven, or Muspell, like the Christian hell, but someplace in between where humans might be turned into animals.

"Huh?" Sly said.

"Seals? Your song . . . and a very fine song it was, too . . . spoke of wanting to become seals. Which is a mistake. I have met more than a few of those slimy animals in my time, and they do not lead a pleasant life. Their breath is most stink-some. It behooves you to reconsider, believe you me."

Sly gave him another of his disbelieving looks and said, "Suck my dick."

Ragnor was smarter than the average Norseman, especially when it came to languages, and he did not need an interpreter to tell him what *dick* meant. Sly's slur was comparable to Dar the Dangerous's favorite saying, "Lick my manroot." But he decided not to take offense and answered with dry humor, "Thank you, but, nay, I do not think I will partake of that pleasure."

Laughter surrounded him then, even from Sly. And one man behind him remarked, "You are in rare form today, Max."

At first he thought the man was addressing someone else, then realized that Max must be a shortened name for Magnusson. He liked it. And, yea, he was in good form, as the man said . . . but not as good as he'd originally thought. *That* he realized when their running punishment went on and on and on. For at least an hour they ran, up and down the beach. All of them were aromatic, to say the least. He had sand in his boots, sand in his small clothes, sand in his mouth and ears. He'd thought his leg muscles strong, but apparently he was not as strong as these fellow prisoners. His thighs and calves screamed with pain, whilst the other men, including the enemy leaders, just loped along.

When they finally stopped, with the leader yelling, "Fall out," then "At ease," the other men were bending over at the waist, walking in slow circles, and breathing easily. He, on the other hand, sank to the ground with a thud. He panted as loudly and heavily as a warhorse after a siege.

The chieftain hovered over him within seconds. "Are you all right, Ensign? Should I call the medic?"

Well, that is interesting. Concern from a captor? And medic—what is that? Ah! "Nay, I have no need of a healer. I was winded, that is all."

"You've been injured. You had no business coming out here today, sailor."

Of course I was injured. You would be, too, if you'd engaged in a sea battle, fought off a horde of bloody Saxons, then almost drowned. He shrugged, and stood. He and the chieftain were about the same height and build. "You are wrong. I had no choice."

"It's your funeral, buddy." The instructor walked off, shaking his head as if Ragnor were a hopeless case.

Ragnor began to walk with the other prisoners, heading toward the enemy's great hall—oddly called a chow hall—where presumably they would be fed. They were crossing a wide exercise field now . . . not pounded dirt like his exercise fields at Norstead, but rather a hardened mixture, like

pitch that had been baked with crushed stone. Many people
bustled about on the roads and walkways, some of them
dressed in white apparel—white *braies,* white *sherts,* even
white head coverings. Others were dressed in matching light
brown garb, and still others in a fabric mixing brown, black,
and green, which would be almost invisible in a forest, he
would think.

Just then the sight of a familiar figure stopped him in his
tracks.

"Who is that?" he asked. His heart began beating wildly
with excitement. It was the woman from his vision . . . the
one who had beckoned him away from the white light.

"You know who that is," Sly told him. "That's the Master
Chief's sister, Lieutenant Alison MacLean. The doctor."

*She is a lewd-tenant? I like the sound of that. Lewdness
in a woman is always desirable. And a dock-whore? Is this
my lucky day? She does not appear to be in trouble at the
moment. Where is the fear . . . and danger . . . I sensed surrounding her?*

The woman was dressed all in white, like many of the
men, right down to wearing men's *braies.* She was tall, much
taller than the average woman, and slim. Her hair was short
and red. Her legs were exceedingly long. Her skin was a flaw-
less peach color with a slight tint of gold and dotted with freckles. Her eyes were green. All this he saw in one sweeping
glance from her head to her toes.

"She's the most beautiful woman I've ever seen. Nay, that's
not true. She's the most desirable woman. Magnificent."

"Huh?" his comrades said.

The woman had just noticed them. When her eyes connected with his in passing, they returned immediately, then
widened with surprise. Yea, he was a good-looking man. An
Arab princess had once told him that he exuded virility.

Even bald, he would imagine he could turn a female head. He puffed his chest out and waited for her to approach.

Several of his fellow prisoners laughed. One of them asked, "What's with the interest in the good doctor?"

All the others had opinions, too.

"That must have been some knock on the head."

"The chief is going to make seal soup out of this bozo."

"I'm taking bets she flattens him for looking at her like that."

"I think he's got a hard-on over frickin' G.I. Jane."

"No one has a hard-on after a fifteen-mile run. His jock strap must be full of sand, just like the rest of us."

"This is more fun than Bourbon Street during Mardi Gras."

"Man oh man, I can't decide whether I should go eat or stay to watch this fiasco unfold."

They all stayed.

But Ragnor did not care about their teasing. He looked at the woman who strode toward them with fire in her eyes.

"It would seem I have regained my 'enthusiasm,'" he murmured to himself. And for the first time in what seemed like forever, he smiled.

CHAPTER FOUR

❧

Can hormones cause brain meltdown? . . .

"A-TEN-HUT!" she yelled out when she came face to face with the idiot SEAL trainee.

At first he just gawked, but then he stood at attention, staring rigidly back at her, nothing improper in his posture, everything improper in his eyes. Her Grandma MacLean always said that some people had talking eyes; his were speaking a mile a minute and all of it sextalk.

When did that SEAL trainee get so handsome? Even wearing those god-awful SEAL issue swim trunks, dripping with sweat, dusted with sand, covered with bruises, reeking of body odor, he exuded a compelling masculinity.

Since when did she start to notice one man in this ocean of testosterone here at Coronado?

Since when did the heat in a man's eyes make her melt a little bit inside? Not for five long years.

Since when did her eyes lower to a man's middle and wonder . . . ?

I must be losing my mind.

"At ease." With a whooshy exhale of disgust, she asked, "What are you doing here, Ensign Magnusson? I thought you were gone."

He gave a whooshy exhale of disgust, too, resting his hands on his hips.

I am not looking at his hips. I am notnotnot. How could a man have such a narrow waist? Aaarrgh!

"That is the selfsame thing the chieftain said . . . your brutish brother, I think he is. I will give you the same reply I gave him. I, too, thought I was *gone*, but here I am." He smiled widely at her, like she should be glad he was still here. His smile was pure rogue. And, Lordy, Lordy, he pushed the boundaries by referring to his team chief as brutish . . . even if Ian was just that, on occasion. "Is it not fortunate . . . for both of us . . . that I survived?"

"If that is a pickup line, it's pathetic." The goofball! Really, some of these SEALs were off-the-wall crazy with the stunts they pulled on a daily basis, but to walk out of a hospital bed back into the rigors of the elite SEALs training program . . . well, it defied belief. Not to mention flirting with his superior officer. If he was flirting.

He frowned in confusion. "I have always been good with languages. I am fluent in eight and can read and write two of them. But then, most countries in proximity to the Norselands speak mutually comprehensible languages, even the bloody damn English. I do not understand some of your words, though, even in the context of surrounding words. Like 'pickup line.'" As he rambled on, he continued to frown. Then his face brightened with understanding. "Oh, do you infer that I am being smooth of tongue? Deliberately insincere? If so, you say me wrong, milady. I can assure you that my attraction to you is honest and fierce. By your leave, milady, willst join me in my bed furs tonight?"

"Bed furs? Bed furs?" she sputtered out. *Don't beat around the bush, buddy.* Alison had once gone on a blind date with a guy who announced before they'd even gotten into his car, "I

have three condoms in my pocket, baby. What say we forgo
the dinner-and-movie crap and burn some rubber?" Needless
to say, they hadn't burned any rubber . . . in his car or otherwise.

But this jerk here in front of her was waiting with actual
expectancy. Hah! If he hadn't already sustained a blow to
the head, she might just give him one. She gritted her teeth
and counted to five—ten being beyond her limits at the moment. And, no, she was not going to think about the totally
unacceptable ripple of pleasure that had gone through her at
his outrageous bed invitation. "You were ordered to go home,"
she said in as level a voice as she could manage.

"I was?"

"Don't play innocent with me. I was there."

"You were?"

"And stop looking at me like that."

"Like what?"

"Like you are seeing me without my clothes."

"That I am." He waggled his eyebrows at her.

"Ensign!"

"Call me Max, like my fellow captives do. Or Ragnor."

"Ragnor? Why would I call you Ragnor?"

"Max, then." He shrugged as if it didn't matter either way
to him. "Could we go somewhere private where we could . . .
talk?" The mischievous gleam in his blue eyes could not be interpreted in any other way than man-to-woman sexual interest.

Blue eyes? That observation stopped her short. *I thought
his eyes were brown.*

And that stubble of hair on his head . . . it appears black.
She frowned with confusion. *I could swear the Viking's hair
was blond.*

*Hah! I know only too well how vain some of these self-
proclaimed studs are. He probably dyed his hair and wore*

*contact lenses, just for vanity's sake. Which is an infrac-
tion, of course . . . wearing contacts.*

*Like he would care. Case in point. Look at those arm
rings back on his biceps again. Ian will kill him for that in-
subordination.*

"We have nothing to talk about. And certainly nothing involving bed furs. Go home," she said finally. Let the Navy
handle all his other offenses; she didn't need to add sexual
harassment to the load. All she cared about was his health . . .
although he did not look unhealthy at this moment. In fact,
he looked very . . . healthy. *How come I never noticed those
twelve-pack abs before? Or his sinfully flat stomach? Or the
fullness of his lips? Or . . .*

*Holy smoke! Since when do I notice physical appear-
ance? This place is overflowing with prime male flesh, most
of it wrapped around egos the size of a Goodyear blimp. No
big deal!*

"I do not think I can," he said.

*Huh? Oh, he must be referring to my order that he go
home.* "Why not?"

"Methinks the gods want me to be here."

"The gods?" She barely suppressed a groan of frustration. SEALs and pilots were the most superstitious military
men she'd ever met. She recalled how her fiancé used to
insist on wearing his undershirts inside out whenever he left
for a new mission. Ian wore a crucifix that had been a
Christmas gift from Grandma MacLean. Her father had
worn mismatched socks. She guessed "the gods" fit right in
with that superstitious nonsense. So it was with forced patience that she inquired, "Why? Why would 'the gods' want
you here?"

He shrugged. "I know not, but I have a suspicion that you
may be involved. The moment I saw you, I felt some . . .

connection." He gave her a slow head-to-toe survey that left no doubt what connection she might have, if only she would give the nod.

"I beg your pardon," she sputtered some more. Good Lord, he must have suffered a harder blow to the head than the X-rays had shown. Alison knew her physical limitations. She was no beauty and never had been. Besides, she'd met up with this guy numerous times over the past three months, and he'd never mentioned this "connection" before. "Does your head hurt?"

"My head? Hah! My whole body hurts. Didst know our captors made us run endlessly in the sand, after first trying to drown us?"

"Drown-proofing," she said.

"Huh?"

"It was the routine drown-proofing exercise designed to show trainees how to survive in a field op involving a water insertion or extraction."

"Huh?" he said again, then paused a moment before inquiring slowly, "Are you on the enemy side or the prisoners' side?"

She was about to answer his ridiculous question when she noticed his face go white and his eyes widen with shock.

"Oh!" he gasped. "For the love of Odin, where am I?"

"I knew it, I knew it. You are still in shock, sailor, and you have no business engaging in extreme physical activity. You probably shouldn't even be out of sick bay."

He didn't hear her, she could tell. Instead, his head pivoted here and there as he seemed to notice the surroundings for the first time.

"What . . . what are they? Those metal boxes on wheels?" he asked, pointing to various jeeps, trucks, and cars moving around the periphery of the base.

"Transport vehicles. For carrying people and goods," she answered hesitantly, as if speaking to a child. Actually, his question had been childlike. What kind of game was he playing now?

"But there are no horses pulling them." Before she had a chance to comment on that ludicrous statement, he had another question. "And *that*?" he asked, pointing upward.

"A plane. And over there, a helicopter."

"Do people go up in them?" His face was bloodless with seeming shock.

"Of course."

He shuddered. "What a strange land this is!"

"Are you all right?"

He nodded.

"We'd better go back to the hospital so I can check you over."

"And all these buildings. With glass, no less! Is glass not a precious commodity in your land? Where is the royal castle, by the by? Or the fortresses? All I see are square buildings, and so many people in the same attire walking about. White, brown, and that odd mixture of brown, black, and green. All identical. And not a one of them carrying a sword or battleaxe. Are they captors or captives?"

"Really, you're pushing this game too far."

"I wish I had Foe Fighter with me."

"A musical group? You wish you had a musical group with you?" Alarm rippled through Alison as she wondered if she might need help to restrain this man. He was clearly delusional.

"What musical group?"

"Foo Fighters. The musical group that sang 'My Hero.' "

"That is absurd. I was referring to my favorite sword, Foe Fighter. Although it did prove to be my hero on more than one occasion."

He doesn't look deranged. Maybe he's just pulling my leg. "I am not amused."

"Hah! Neither am I amused. I thought at one point that I had died and gone to the other world—Niflheim or Muspell—especially when your brutish brother tried to drown me."

Aaarrgh! "He didn't try to drown you. As I said before, that was a drown-proofing exercise, so that you could learn to stay underwater for a really long time."

As if she'd never spoken, he went on, "I rejoiced when I walked onto land again."

"That's not unusual. Lots of trainees feel an immense relief after sustained punishment, which is what near-drowning must feel like."

He cast her a look of incredulity, as if she were the one spouting nonsense. "Now I am beginning to believe once again that I did indeed die, and this is some strange region of after-death that the elders have never heard of." He swept a hand in a half circle to indicate their surroundings. "Well, leastways there are no giants or trolls here. I feel weak as dragon piss at the moment and not at all up to fighting off monsters."

"Are you hallucinating? Do you have a fever?"

"No fever, but I am hot." He winked at her suggestively on that last word and took her by the upper arm. "Did you say something about a hospitium and checking me over? Dare I hope there are private rooms in your hospitium? There are? Good. I find that I am not too weak for that. Methinks I will like this 'checking over.'"

Surely he can't be implying . . . "It's just an examination, for heaven's sake."

"In the nude?"

He is! "Maybe. Probably."

He nodded his satisfaction at her answer. "Will there be bed furs involved? I assume those red blotches on your cheeks indicate 'Nay.' No matter. I must say, I have ever been partial to a midday swiving, especially when the enthusiasm is on a man . . . better than a midday repast, for a certainty, though I could use a horn of mead."

I am not going to ask him what swiving is, or enthusiasm. I'm afraid I already know. "Mead? Are you referring to beer? You know alcoholic beverages are not permitted on base." *Nor is midday swiving.*

As if she had not spoken, he said, "Is it not wonderful that I have regained my enthusiasm for the bedsport . . . and all because of you?" He smiled widely at her.

Alison was speechless.

Let's play doctor . . .

Ragnor followed the woman—Lieutenant Alison MacLean— into a building, presumably the hospitium, then down a narrow corridor, smiling the entire time.

He knew her name because of the small badge she wore on her *shert* front. As to his smile, well, there was something about the male body that defied nature. The man could be battered and bloody, he could be exhausted, he could be on his deathbed, for the love of Frey, but the sight of a female arse swaying from side to side in front of him could raise the sap of even the deadest tree. Especially when that arse filled form-fitting *braies.*

And there were three things to keep in mind here:

—Alison had a very fine arse, as outlined by said white *braies.*

—He was far from dead.

—His enthusiasm was back with a vengeance, and this female would do well to avoid Vikings in the heat of enthusiasm, unless she shared the enthusiasm . . . may the gods be so inclined.

About to open a door at the end of the corridor, Alison glanced back over her shoulder, noticed the direction of his stare, and blushed bright red, once again. He rather liked the idea that he could make her blush. Then she backed into the chamber.

But that was all right. He'd seen enough to know she more than merited his renewed enthusiasm.

He followed her into the room, which was much like the other rooms he'd seen along the way. So much white! White walls and ceilings. White patterned floor. White parchment-like paper on a high bed-table. With all the glass windows letting in the sunlight, it was almost blindingly bright. This was unlike any hospitium he'd ever seen afore, certainly unlike the one attached to the minster in Jorvik, where he'd once been treated by the good monk-healers after a gruesome battle. But then, everything he'd seen here thus far was unlike anything in his experience.

She waved to the right and said, "Go into the bathroom and give me a urine specimen."

"What?" He looked into the chamber, which had a white porcelain bowl attached to the wall and a larger porcelain chairlike thing sitting on the floor, which had water floating inside.

"Here." She handed him a clear cup, which looked like glass but was not. "Relieve yourself into the toilet"—she pointed to the porcelain chair—"but give me some in the cup."

Toy-let. The porcelain chair is a toy-let, he told himself so that he would remember the word. Then, "Give you what in the cup?"

"Urine."

You're in . . . you're in, he repeated in his head, but it made no sense. He could tell Alison was getting exasperated at having to explain everything to him. "I'm in *what*?" *Oh, this is too much!* he thought as understanding dawned on him like a cloudburst. He did know what urine was. "You want me to piss in a cup?"

"Of course."

"Are you going to drink it?"

"Don't be an ass. Just do it." She shoved him into the bathing room and slammed the door after him.

He did, in fact, piss in the cup and cover it with a lid. Some healers used animal urine in their healing arts. He supposed that was what Alison wanted with his piss, though he was not certain of that fact. Did she gather piss from everyone? If so, she must have a goodly amount. *Yech!*

He finished pissing in the toy-let, which was quite an experience . . . especially when he found that if he pushed a certain lever, the water and urine washed away, down a hole in the bottom. Just to be sure, he pushed the lever five more times, till he was unable to coax any more piss from his organ.

Then he examined the porcelain bowl attached to the wall. He discovered that hot and cold water came from the silver pipes and rushed down a drain in the bowl. The Romans had such marvels, he had heard, but never had he witnessed them himself.

Glancing upward, he saw a mirror on the wall . . . one that was much clearer than any polished brass he'd seen in the past. To his horror, he got a really good look at himself. His hair was so short, he was nigh bald. He had oozing cuts and bruises on his face and on his shoulders and chest . . . mostly from the battle that morn with the Saxons.

Had it really only been less than a day since he had fallen overboard with that Saxon warrior? Had Forkbeard truly escaped? Were all his men dead?

He shook his head from side to side, not understanding any of what was happening to him.

Next he touched a silver box on the wall that held soft, parchmentlike towels. Another container held liquid soap which squirted out when touched in a certain place. He knew it was liquid soap because he'd been fiddling around with some of the levers and ended up with splashes of water and splotches of the slick stuff all over the place. When he'd tried to wipe it up, it bubbled slightly, like soap. He decided to wash some of the stink off himself.

After he'd washed and soaped and rinsed and washed and soaped and rinsed and dried himself off with the parchment towels, which he carefully folded and laid on top of the toy-let, since he was unable to shove them back up into the silver box, he pissed and flushed two more times.

"Ensign Magnusson, *what* are you doing in there?" Alison opened the door a crack to peer inside.

"Bathing and pissing," he answered, walking past her. Some women did not know enough to give a man privacy. She was just like Madrene in that regard. "What did you think I was doing? Pleasuring myself? I do not do that." *Much.*

"Do you have any idea how close you are to landing in the brig?"

"Mayhap I would know *if* I knew what a brig was." In truth, Ragnor was getting as exasperated as the good dock-whore over his inability to understand all the new words in this land.

"Lie down on the table," she ordered, pointing to the high bed-table with the parchment cover.

"Why? It hardly seems big enough for coupling. We could just as easily do it against the wall, or on the floor." Now that he had his enthusiasm back, he was not too particular.

She made a whooshy sound of disgust and pointed again.

"I'm going to ignore that remark . . . *this time.* Keep it up, though, and you will most definitely find yourself in hot water."

He started to ask what she meant by hot water—*was it a method of torture?*—but decided he didn't really care. "Shall I take off my garment first?" he asked. "I washed my man-parts and buttocks in the bathing room to remove all the sand, but I had to put the dirty small clothes back on."

Her jaw dropped open before she shut her mouth abruptly. "No, you don't have to remove your shorts. I can pull them down myself."

I like the sound of that.

She put a necklace of black cords with a silver pendant around her neck, then inserted two of the ends into her ears and pressed the pendant against his chest. It was cold, but he soon got accustomed to it. If this was foresport in this land, he found it mighty strange. "What are you doing?"

"Listening to your heart."

"What is it telling you?"

"That you have a strong heartbeat. A little rapid, but that's to be expected, I suppose."

"Well, yea, I would say so . . . with you leaning over me, nigh touching me with your breasts."

She jerked back.

"Nay, sweetling, do not draw away. I like your touching me with your breasts." He reached up to draw her back down, closer, but she swatted his hands away. Touchy she was, like a nervous virgin, which he did not imagine she was at her advanced age.

She pretended indifference to him, but he was not fooled. Her breasts grew full and peaked at his words. Even though she now wore a white coat over her *shert*, he could tell that about her. There were many things he did not understand about this land, but the interplay betwixt a man and a woman . . . ah, that he clearly understood. He was not a Viking for nothing.

Grabbing another device, she wrapped a black band around his upper arm, below his own gold arm band, and inflated it somehow so that the binding became extremely tight. Then she watched an arrow on a circular piece of metal as it moved amongst some numbers.

"Now what are you checking?"

"Your blood pressure."

"My blood is hot for you, I can tell you that without some special device."

"Tsk-tsk-tsk! I'm not measuring the heat of your blood, just how fast your heart is pumping it."

"Hah! I would warrant it is racing like a hunted reindeer." He looked pointedly at her breast region again.

"You would be right. It *is* high . . . but not alarmingly so."

She unwrapped the band from his arm and began examining his head. "Where is your head wound? And the swelling . . . there is no swelling." She gazed at him with confusion and a bit of alarm.

He shrugged.

"You had a concussion," she said, still frowning. "There is no evidence of that on your head now."

"I am quick to heal," he offered as an explanation.

"Plus, you've got lots more wounds and bruises on you today. Did you get all these during training exercises this morning?"

"Undoubtedly. Your brother is merciless in the torture. But, nay, truthfully, most of them came from the battle. Those Saxons can be brutal. Not that I did not inflict as many wounds myself, many of them mortal ones."

She did not appear impressed.

Quietly and with obvious puzzlement, she cleansed some of the cuts with a stinging ointment and closed several others with small metal clamps she called butterflies. By then, she'd arrived at his waist, and his enthusiasm reared its head, making a tent of his small clothes. He wondered if she would have the nerve to actually examine him there. He would bet she would be impressed.

She did. Uncover him. With a sigh of surrender, she pulled the stretchy waistband down to his thighs, exposing his nether region.

But she was not impressed. Or not so he could tell.

The skin surrounding his standing cock and ballocks had been rubbed raw from the sand during his incessant run this morn, but it was naught to be concerned about. When she touched one particularly abraded area, his cock jerked, then lengthened.

He smiled.

"Stop it. Stop it right now."

"Stop what?"

"You know what."

"How can I stop *that*? You have brought back my enthusiasm, praise the gods! 'Tis your fault, not mine."

"Yeah, well, how would your *enthusiasm* feel about a bucket of ice-cold water?"

He pretended to ponder her question as if she were serious . . . which she could not be. *Could she?* Then he answered, "In all honesty, I think it would douse my enthusiasm, good and true. But why do such a thing?"

She handed him the same jar of ointment she'd applied to his cuts and told him to smear them on his raw skin.

"I would not know how," he lied. "You do it for me."

"Figure it out," she asserted firmly.

"Do you fear your own arousal if you touch me?" he asked.

"Get a life," she said.

He wasn't sure what that meant, but he was fairly certain it was not a compliment.

After he'd ministered to his own abrasions, she flicked the waistband of his small clothes up with a sharp snap and ordered, "Roll over so I can check your back."

He did as she asked, being careful to adjust his thickened manpart so he would not hurt himself. While she ran her cool fingertips over his back and buttocks and legs, treating the cuts there, he asked, "How long have you been a whore?"

"I beg your pardon." She said that in such a shrewish manner, he was reminded once again of Madrene. Shrewishness must be an inherent trait of most women, which some managed to bank down, while others let it run rampant.

"I was told that you are a dock-whore," he explained.

"Oh," she said, clucking her tongue at what she must consider his deliberate misunderstanding of her words. "It's 'dock-tore,' as you well know."

"Oh," it was his turn to say. Dock-whore meant healer in some countries, he recalled now. He supposed, with chagrin, that lewd-tenant didn't mean anything lascivious, either.

"Sit up," she demanded then, turning away from him to write something on a parchment pad.

"Sit up? Does that mean we are not going to couple?"

"Unbelievable!" she muttered under her breath. Then louder, "You could say that. Not now. In fact, never."

"Ah, milady, you should never say never. Not to a Viking."

"Listen," she said, turning and leaning back against the wall, arms folded over her chest. "You are in perfect health. I don't understand how, but you are."

"I could have told you that. So why don't you just hop up here and—"

She put up a halting hand. "However, I am very concerned

about your mental health. Maybe you are putting on an act. If you are, it is sick. If not, you are in deep need of some counseling."

"From whom?"

"A psychiatrist."

"What is a sigh-kite-tryst?"

"Brain doctor."

"Why in bloody hell would I need a brain doctor?"

"To see if you are suffering some aftereffects from your brain concussion."

"I have no idea what you just said."

"Here's the bottom line, Ensign Magnusson. I am inclined to ring you out of SEALs training and send you home."

"You could do that? Take me home to the Norselands?"

"That's not what I meant. I wouldn't personally escort you anywhere. But I do have the authority to ship you out."

"Dost that mean you would force me to leave here?"

"For your own good."

"Would I still be a captive?"

"You are not a captive. You are here voluntarily."

"I am?"

"This is a ridiculous conversation."

Ragnor thought about the ramifications of what she'd just said. *I am not a captive? Then what am I? Does that mean all those men I thought were fellow captives are here voluntarily? Do I want to stay here with them . . . or wander elsewhere in this land? Or out to sea? Alone. Nay, best to stay with the enemy I know. Not that I know much about this enemy.* He glanced up at Alison, beginning to conclude that this woman was of the enemy camp. Yea, he would like to know his enemy better.

"Nay!" he said firmly. "I will not leave."

"It is not your decision to make."

"Yea, 'tis. I will not leave. You cannot make me."

"Be reasonable."

"*You* be reasonable."

She sighed. "Okay, here's the deal. The only way I am going to sign you off medically is if you agree to start seeing Dr. Feingold on a regular basis."

He sighed, too. "Another dock-whore . . . I mean healer. The brain dock-whore, I presume?"

She nodded.

He snorted with disgust but said, "I will try one meeting, but that is all I will promise for now."

"Fine. I'll set up an appointment."

"What do I get for being so accommodating?"

"What'd you have in mind?" He could tell that she immediately regretted her question.

He grinned. "Many things are on my mind. But a kiss would suffice for now."

"I better not have heard what I think I heard," a booming male voice said behind him. Ragnor turned to see the evil captor, Chieftain MacLean, glaring at him.

"Ian," Alison said to her brother, "lighten up."

"You are out of line, sis. You may outrank me, but this man is under my command." His eyes flashed angrily at her, which Ragnor did not like . . . not one bit.

"Do not take out your fury with me on a woman," he cautioned the chieftain. Standing to his full height, he glared at the man, who was clearly taken by surprise by his defense of Alison. "I have decided to take Milady Alison under my shield. That means any insult to her is an insult to me."

Alison and her brother gaped at him as if he'd grown another head. "How dare you?" both of them yelled at the same time.

"I dare much because I am a man of honor. A Viking."

The chieftain made a low growling sound deep in his throat, and Ragnor took the battle stance—legs widespread, hands on hips—prepared to fight. By the gods, he missed his sword.

Alison stepped between the two of them and put a hand on each of their chests. "Enough! No one is going to fight here." Addressing her brother, she said, "Ian, this man is in perfect physical condition. I don't understand how, but he is. On the other hand, it's obvious that he's suffering some delusions. So he has agreed to meet with Dr. Feingold."

"Can he return to training?" the chieftain asked with a snarl.

She nodded. "For now. His continuance will be conditional on Dr. Feingold's report."

The chieftain smiled, and it was not a pleasant smile. "Come with me, then, Ensign Magnusson. You want to play games, do you? Well, I'm going to show you some Navy SEAL games, guaranteed."

"Well, thank you very much," he told the chieftain as they walked off. "Mayhap I will show you a few Viking games, as well." Over his shoulder, he winked at Alison.

She almost smiled.

CHAPTER FIVE

*O*nly the lonely . . .

Alison arrived home at seven that evening.

She pulled into the driveway, but then just sat there for a few minutes, motor running, while an old Hank Williams ballad played out, "I'm So Lonesome I Could Cry." Yep, that about said it all. Tears misted her eyes as a crushing sense of loneliness overwhelmed her with surprisingly sudden force. She had a job she loved, a good family, the dream of one day becoming a SEAL, and an apartment she took great pleasure in decorating bit by bit.

It was that damn Viking, she concluded, swiping at her eyes. Ever since she'd met Ensign Magnusson this afternoon, she'd felt alternately exhilarated, then depressed. And so lonely she could die. Why? What was it about the SEAL trainee with the overblown ego and warped sense of humor and, okay, a body to die for that pulled at her heartstrings . . . and other strings, as well. Like maybe lust strings.

She smiled at her musings, turned off the motor as ol' Hank crooned off into the sunset airwaves, and got out of the car, briefcase in hand. She had a ton of paperwork to do tonight.

"Hi, Lillian," she called out to her landlady, who stood amidst her rose bushes in the front yard, watering them with the soft spray nozzle of a hose. Lillian Kelly had to be over fifty years old, but she wore tight blue jeans, a halter top, and sneakers. She'd recently dyed her waist-long gray hair a soft blond; it was pulled back now into a high ponytail. Lillian was the hottest middle-aged woman Alison had ever met.

The dozens of magnificent species that adorned the flower beds were a testament to Lillian's thirty-some years of precious care. Well, care by her *and* her longtime husband, Al. Al had taken off last year with his thirty-year-old dental assistant. To everyone's surprise, Mrs. K. hadn't been all that broken up over the philanderer's departure. "The old fart has been boring me silly for twenty years now, and he wasn't all that hot the first ten, either," she'd told Alison when she'd attempted to sympathize with her. "Good riddance to bad rubbish."

"Hi, sweetie," Lillian replied now. "Beautiful evening, isn't it? Not too hot. Your mail is on the hall table. Come down for some lemonade and chocolate cake later, okay?"

Alison smiled widely. She had a sweet tooth that could not be denied. "You bet."

After stepping up to the wraparound porch of the old Victorian house—painted yellow with blue shutters—and going through the ornate double doors with their side panels of stained glass, she gathered her mail, then went up the wide staircase. She unlocked the door to the second-floor apartment and went in, checking over the mail, mostly bills, as she entered.

Almost immediately, her body went on high alert.

Someone had been in her apartment. She could tell by the altered position of the cushions on the sofa—she was anal about positioning Grandma MacLean's needlepoint pillows on her antique camelback sofa. The wrapped birthday gift for Ian on the kitchen counter seemed a bit wrinkled, as if it had been opened and rewrapped—though she couldn't be sure that she hadn't done that herself when she'd put some personal photos inside the wallet she planned to give him. There was definitely the faint scent of cologne . . . male cologne . . . that very intense Drakkar, she was pretty sure.

Quickly she opened the top drawer of her desk, situated by the door, and took out her pistol. She already knew it was loaded, but she checked anyway. Only then did she move slowly about the two-bedroom apartment, checking every space, every window. There was a half-open window in the kitchen, overlooking the backyard. Had she left it open this morning? Probably. Who would ever expect someone to enter a second-floor apartment by way of a wobbly rose trellis? Mrs. K. was here most of the time, but not always.

Once she returned to the living room, she noticed the blinking light on her answering machine. Five messages. She knew before she even turned them on who it would be. The Breather. No words, just the loud sound of heavy breathing. The creep was probably jerking off while she listened. But wait, he had said something on the last message: "Bitch!" There was an odd accent to the voice, noticeable even with only one word . . . possibly Middle Eastern.

Alison felt like freaking out, but she couldn't afford that luxury.

What should she do?

Call her brother? *No!*

Talk to Mrs. K. to alert her to the possible danger and urge her to keep her own doors and windows locked? *Yes*.

Call the police and have them dust for fingerprints? Alison was reluctant to call the cops. She was a strong woman who could take care of herself. But that was being foolish.

Phone calls were one thing; breaking and entering was quite another. With a long sigh, she decided that she had to make the call. It was the right thing to do.

She would not tell her brother, though. Not yet, anyhow. Ian would have her moved out and into his house before she could say, "Oh, brother!" How could she ever expect to be considered suitable SEAL material if she was unable to protect herself?

Thus it was that two hours later, she, Lillian and Detective "Call me John" Phillips from the local police sat at her kitchen table drinking lemonade and eating chocolate cake. The other cops had already left after dusting for fingerprints, to no avail, and taking the tape from her answering machine back for the file they were starting on her case.

"Be careful, both of you," John said. "Two women living alone today. Pfff! You've got to be more careful about keeping doors and windows locked, even when you're only outside in the yard, or making a quick run to the grocery store."

"I don't like having to change my life for some pervert," Lillian said. For they were assuming that the person who'd invaded Alison's apartment was the same person who made the Breather phone calls. "Besides, no one entered *my* apartment."

You tell 'im, Lillian, baby!

"Hey, the first access to the second floor is through your front door. If you don't care about yourself, you have to be protective of your tenant," he pointed out.

Lillian ducked her head sheepishly at the reprimand.

You tell 'er, Mr. Law & Order!

John winked at Alison, to show he was being tough to be kind. And for personal reasons, as well, she suspected. She could tell he was attracted to her, though he was being subtle about his interest and entirely professional in his words. He wore no wedding band. A definite plus. In fact, single status was an essential in her dating requirements.

Alison leaned back, studying the detective. He was about thirty-five, over six feet tall, had a slight receding hairline but was not unattractive. Unfortunately, Alison felt zilch when she looked at him. And wasn't it a sad reflection on her life of late that she'd been turned on today by a crude goof-ball who talked like an eleventh-century Viking, but turned off by a perfectly nice, college-educated officer of the law?

"I would suggest some other things . . . like maybe a dog." John was talking to both of them.

"Not for me. I love animals," Alison said, "but I'm gone too much. It wouldn't be fair to the dog." And if she ever did make the SEALs, an animal would be totally out of the question. She would be gone for days, even weeks at a time.

"Hmmm," Lillian said. "I always wanted a pet, but Al was allergic to pet dander. Yes, a dog would be a good idea."

"Let's go to the animal shelter tomorrow," Alison suggested, giving Lillian's hand a quick squeeze.

"Do they have pit bulls there?" Lillian asked. And she was serious.

"Uh, I don't think a pit bull is necessary," John quickly inserted, barely stifling a grin. "What you want is a dog that will bark when a stranger enters your property, not an attack dog. Small breeds can be just as effective."

"Okay," Lillian agreed. "But not too small. I don't want a tiny wussy dog that resembles a skinned rat."

Alison exchanged a smile with the detective, who was rather good-looking when he smiled. Maybe she shouldn't be striking him out before she gave him a chance. Not that he'd really asked.

But then he did, just before he left. "Can I call you?" he asked.

She hesitated only a blink of a second before nodding.

"What we really need is a man," Lillian said when Alison returned to the table.

"Was that a *we* in there?"

Lillian shrugged. "Maybe. Though in my case I'm not interested in marriage again. A little sex wouldn't be unwelcome, though." She tossed her head as if daring Alison to make fun of her for such an idea, which Alison would never do.

"And what makes you think I need a man?" Alison inquired.

"Oh, honey, you need a man more than anyone I know," Lillian said with a laugh.

"Should I be insulted by that observation?" Alison asked, laughing as well.

"Not at all. You've just been too long without, honey, and I don't just mean sex."

You got that right. How about five freakin' years? For some reason, the image of a six-foot-four Viking in shorts flashed through her mind. He was sex, and then some.

"Why are you smiling?" Lillian asked.

Because my brain has become lodged in my crotch. "Nothing," she said, trying to make her face expressionless. But it was too late.

"You met a man!" Lillian accused with a whoop of delight.

You could say that. At first Alison was going to deny it, but then she conceded, "I met a man."

But that was all she would say.

Whoever said "No Pain, No Gain" wasn't a Viking . . .

Ragnor had been in this strange new land, which he'd discovered was called Ah-mar-ee-ca, less than a full day, and every bone and muscle in his body hurt, while his brain roiled with confusion. He had been in deep trouble before—*I am a Norseman, after all . . . trouble finds us even when we are not looking*—but never anything like this.

He reclined on a pallet in the sleeping quarters where the SEAL trainees were housed—*That's what I am, apparently . . . a SEAL trainee . . . may the gods be laughing behind their hands!*—having just completed what should have been a sybaritic hot showering. But he was not happy. In fact, he was sorely tired of people either gaping at him or laughing at him or saying things he could not understand. Like that little stick with a brush on the end. How was he to know it was a tooth-cleaning brush, and the sweet mint paste in the tube was not for eating, but polishing? Even worse, when he'd pulled those silver packets from his metal lock-her, everyone—*everyone*—had burst out laughing just because he did not know what a cone-dome was. And wasn't it a marvel—a liberation for men and women alike—that conception could be controlled in this land?

For some reason, when he'd learned the purpose of the cone-domes, immediately an image of Alison had come to his mind . . . and what he would like to do to her with those protective coverings. He also thought momentarily of his father, Magnus Ericsson, and how he could have used about a hundred of those cone-domes over the years. The last he'd seen his father, Magnus had taken a vow of celibacy for this very reason . . . not wanting any more than thirteen children.

Ragnor planned on taking about a thousand of those little marvels with him when he returned to the Norselands . . . *if* he ever returned to the Norselands.

And that was another thing that troubled him. He had always been considered an exceedingly intelligent man. He could recite sagas after hearing them only once. He learned

languages of other countries so amazingly fast that some
called it magical. He had a brain for strategy in battles, for
puzzling out mysteries, for tabulating the direction of the
sun in figuring time, for adding figures. He had even studied
the stars and sun and moon under Arab astronomers. He
could read and write. But in this country, he felt nigh dumb
under the weight of all the complex marvels that the people
of this place accepted as everyday happenstances.

But that was neither here nor there. He saw from the corner of his eye that his fellow SEAL team trainees were approaching his bed . . . with some ill intent, he would warrant
by their expressions. All of them, himself included, wore
nothing more than drab *sherts* and short underpants.

He had been lying on the pallet with his arms folded behind his head. Sitting up cautiously, he prepared himself to
bolt if they attacked . . . though why they would do that, he
had no idea. They had all suffered equally that day under
the punishing hands of Chieftain MacLean. Climbing a
rope wall as high as a mountain, up and down and up and
down like a bunch of bloody squirrels. Running incessantly,
often with the yellow boat on their heads. Ducking bullets in
"evade and escape" escapades; bullets were this land's version of arrows shot out of special weapons called guns.
What fun that had been, just barely escaping death! And all
the while the chieftain had been yelling out his usual pithy
sayings, like, "Most wars are lost, not won!" Ha, ha, ha! Always he and his comrades had been wet and sandy. And sore.

Give him a good sword and he would show the chieftain
a thing or two about "evade and escape."

His seven boat teammates sat down on either side of him
on his pallet and on an adjoining one. SEAL trainees from
the other boat teams walked about or lay on pallets around
the barracks . . . a hundred of them in all.

"Dude, we've decided to give you an intervention," the one called Sly told him, placing a comforting black hand on his knee.

Ragnor was not comforted at all, probably because he did not know what an intervention was. "Will it hurt?" he asked.

They all laughed.

"It will hurt us more than it hurts you," said Flash.

Uh-oh!

Flash came from a country called Alley-bam-ha. He loved listening to music on a magical black box about such subjects as cheating hearts and beer-drinking buddies, much like the sagas of the Norseland. Cody, who sat on Ragnor's other side, hated Flash's music and much preferred songs by the arrow maker, like "Walk This Way."

Strange, strange people in this strange, strange country! he thought, not for the first, or fiftieth time.

"Max, you weirded us out with your behavior today," Flash said. "We're going to help you out, though, buddy. We are going to cover your ass."

They all nodded.

"How?" he asked cautiously. He wasn't sure he wanted any of their hands on his arse . . . or covering other intimate body parts either.

"You took a hit for us when you shoved us back and got slammed by that truck," JAM explained . . . though it wasn't much of an explanation, since Ragnor didn't know what a truck was. Earlier today, Ragnor had been surprised to learn that JAM, the quiet one in this group, had been in training to become a Christian churchman—a priest—before deciding to become a SEAL. "Your concussion is our concussion."

For the love of Frigg!

"It's obvious that you're still suffering from the effects of that blow to the head. Hopefully, it's just temporary, and your memory will come back. In the meantime, we're going to help cover for you." It was F.U. speaking now. Even Ragnor knew what F.U. meant, but why anyone would want a vulgarity for a name puzzled him immensely.

"Pretty Boy"—who had been dubbed thus because he was, well, pretty, if such an appellation could be given to a man— added, "It's a good thing we're well into Phase Two of training and that a lot of our class-work is over with . . . especially Hell Week. You're in acceptable physical condition, so, with a little coaching from us, you should be able to get by."

"Acceptable? Acceptable?" Ragnor sputtered. "I am in prime physical condition."

They all rolled their eyes at his assertion.

"Did I not swim fastest in the timings today?" he reminded them.

"Yes, you did, bless your heart . . . and raised the bar for all of us. You've heard the expression 'It pays to be a winner.' Well, in SEALs you change that to '*You* pay to be a winner,'" complained Cage, the man with the lilting accent who happened to be his swim buddy, as if a man his age needed a swim buddy. Cage was from the Southern country known as Lose-anna. They had dragonlike animals there the size of longboats; these ally-gate-oars swam in the swamps and gobbled up people. Or so Cage claimed. "Holy crawfish, when I saw you hit the water slicker'n snake snot I knew we were in trouble. Well, not to worry, pal, we're gonna help you."

"One for all and all for one," Sly declared.

Ragnor's seven comrades reached their right hands into the center and clasped, so he did the same. "Hoo-yah!" they all yelled. Ragnor figured that must be a war cry.

Yea, this was war. For him, anyway.

"So from now on, you follow our lead," JAM said. "If

you don't understand something, watch and listen. We'll help you."

Ragnor nodded hesitantly.

"It's settled, then," Flash announced, looking at each of them individually.

Well, not quite everything. "Where does Alison reside?" Ragnor asked.

At first, silence reigned as they gave him a communal gape.

Then Cody inquired, "Do you mean Lieutenant Alison MacLean? Your superior officer? The Master Chief's sister?"

He nodded.

Everyone groaned.

Except him. He stood, explaining, "I would like to take a handful of those cone-domes with me over to her keep."

"Why?" Flash asked.

"To practice." Really, he wasn't the only one who suffered from dimwittedness in this group.

Sly pulled him back down to a sitting position on the pallet, and everyone crowded closer.

"We need to explain a few things to you," Flash said.

They were all grinning.

"About what?"

"The birds and the bees," F.U. said.

Dimwitted, for sure.

"And the rules and regulations of the Ewe-Ess military," Sly added. "It's called fraternization, Max, my boy. Maybe even sexual harassment."

Birds, bees, sheep, soldiers, sex, and hairy asses? I think I have landed in a dimwit hole.

CHAPTER SIX

❦

Me-shock, you-shock, roar-shock . . .

"And what do we see in this picture?" Doctor Fine-gold asked as he held up yet another indecipherable black blotch on a white background.

Ragnor grunted his disgust at this silly game he was being forced to play with the brain doctor . . . a man in at least his mid-forties with curly brown hair and window-glass jewelry that fitted over his eyes with thin gold bands over his ears.

"A man and woman coupling upside down."

"Really?" The doctor seemed fascinated by his answer as he cocked his head from side to side, trying to see the same image. "And this one?"

"Female nether lips."

The doctor's widened eyes were the only indication of his surprise. "And this?"

"Breasts. Big ones."

"And this?"

"Three tongues."

"And this?"

"Three tongues and the Viking S-Spot."

The doctor put the placard down and gazed at him with interest. "What is the Viking S-Spot?"

"'Tis a secret. You have to be a Viking to understand."

*Believe that, and I have a fjord in the northernmost Norse-
lands to sell you.* "All I will say is there are tongues involved.
And exploring."

"We seem to be somewhat preoccupied with sex today."

*What is it with this "we" business? I am the only one be-
ing grilled with questions. And, yea, I am preoccupied with
sex. Ever since I got my enthusiasm back and nowhere to
direct it. And not sex in general. Sex with one particular
lady doctor.* That was what he thought, but what he replied
was, "*We* are men. Are *we* not supposed to be preoccupied
with sex?"

"So, you are saying that it is natural for men to be preoccupied with sex?"

Aaarrgh! The man never answered his questions, and
this was Ragnor's third session with him. As far as he could
tell, they were going nowhere and the doctor had yet to examine his brain, though if he even dared to wield a sharp
object or hammer near his head in an attempt to break open
his skull and peer inside, Ragnor would be forced to defend
himself.

"Actually," Ragnor began tentatively, "I have had a problem of late." *Here I go again. Just like with Madrene. Some
men have running bowels; I seem to have developed a running tongue.*

"A sexual problem?" the doctor asked, practically rubbing his hands together with glee that Ragnor would reveal
some secret. "I used to be a sex therapist."

*Wonderful! A healer who treats two essential organs . . .
top and bottom.* "I lost my enthusiasm for coupling for a long
time, but now it is back with a vengeance."

"Enthusiasm? Lack of enthusiasm? Do you mean impo-
tence?"

"Nay!" a horrified Ragnor replied quickly. "I was able to

rise to every occasion and perform, but my heart was not in it for a while, and I fear the, uh, malady may return."

"Hmmmm."

Ragnor hated it when the doctor said "hmmmm." It meant that the brain healer did not quite believe him. It also meant he was about to ask him one of those "we" questions.

"How long has it been since we have engaged in the sex act? And how do we feel about that?"

"I do not know about you, but it has been more than six months for me. And, believe you me, that is a long time for a Viking."

"Hmmmm," the doctor said again. "But you mentioned this lack of—what did you call it?—*enthusiasm*, as if it were in the past. Have we passed the threshold, so to speak?"

"The first time I saw Alison, enthusiasm hit my cock like a tidal wave of lust. And it has been at high tide ever since."

"Uh-oh! Do you mean Lieutenant Alison MacLean?"

"The very same. And do not tell me about fraternization rules. My manpart does not recognize that word." He gazed at the doctor, waiting for some actual advice, which would be a welcome change.

"Lust is wholesome . . ."

I already know that. Tell me something I do not know.

". . . as long as we men control our impulses."

Why should we?

"I would suggest you direct your lust elsewhere . . . perhaps toward some woman not in the military. And, of course, it goes without saying that the female must be willing."

Ragnor drew himself up straight. "I have ne'er taken an unwilling partner in the bedsport."

"Well, yes, but the Navy frowns on *bedsport* between its officers of different rank."

Ragnor waved a hand airily.

"Does Lieutenant MacLean share this, uh, attraction?"

"She has not said so in words, but, yea, she does." *She must.* "I have a sense about such things." *Usually.*

"Be very careful," the doctor cautioned, studying him for several long moments. That was another of his tactics . . . long silences in which the other person became uncomfortable and then broke the silence by talking too much. Not that Ragnor would do that. "I must admit, you puzzle me, Max . . . you don't mind if I call you Max, do you? Good."

"Why do I puzzle you?" he asked. Ragnor had tried his best to be careful, having been warned by his teammates not to disclose too much about his problems to the shrink— that was the name for a mind healer in this land—for fear it would give the leaders cause to expel him from SEALs. Although he hadn't recalled that warning when babbling about his enthusiasm woes.

"I've talked with all the SEAL trainees, and each has a different reason for being here. Why are you here?"

Because the gods decided to punish me for some reason? Because the Norns of Destiny caused me to make a wrong turn on the white pathway to Asgard? Because Alison needs me? He liked that last reason best.

"Why do you want to be a SEAL?" the doctor persisted.

"I do not precisely want to become a SEAL," Ragnor revealed carefully. He knew now that becoming a SEAL did not mean turning oneself into an animal; rather, SEAL stood for SEa, Air, and Land—an elite military group. But he already belonged to an elite military group—Vikings. And if he wanted to punish himself, with much less pain, he could go off and become a Jomsviking with their rules of celibacy or join the Varangian Guard with not-so-celibate rules.

"Then why are you here?"

"That is a good question," he said, leaning forward with his elbows on his knees. "Mayhap you could give me some hints."

"Many men want to become SEALs to prove something to themselves, or others. They want to show that they have the physical and mental stamina to survive."

"Is that not a bit like putting yourself in the dragon's mouth to prove you have no fear of death?"

The doctor just smiled at him. "Other men like the fact that women are attracted to SEALs."

"They are?" Ragnor asked with interest.

"Oh, yeah."

He shrugged. Attracting women had never been a problem for him. "Hmmm. 'Tis much the same in my land. Ladies, no matter the country, flock to warriors . . . especially Viking warriors. Whoo! We have to knock them away with a stick betimes. Ha, ha, ha! But seriously, 'tis a known fact that we Norsemen enrich the blood of the countries we conquer by mating with their women. We are taller and more handsome than the average man, which means our children will be, too. Not me; I make my best effort not to spread my seed hither and yon. Of course, we Vikings bathe more often, which no doubt has something to do with our attraction. There is naught more distasteful to a woman than to swive with a stinksome man, or so I have been told."

He grinned to show he was half teasing, but Doctor Finegold stared at him, open-mouthed. Ragnor had perchance let his tongue wag a bit too much. Again.

The doctor shook his head as if to clear it and said, "Still other men want to become SEALs to serve their country. It is a noble profession."

"That is a strange notion to me, allegiance to a country. We Vikings pledge our fealty to a particular leader, ofttimes out of friendship or to defend our homes, but rarely is it for loyalty to country. But then, we do not have such noble principles in our land. Liberty and freedom for all. That would engage any man's allegiance."

"You are an amazing man."

"Yea, I am," he said with no modesty. "But to answer your initial question, I will be honest with you. I am here because I have nowhere else to go . . . at the present."

The doctor frowned. "Why would you say that? You have a large family and a nice home and—"

How would you know that? I have discussed my family with no one. Hmmm. Ragnor put up a halting hand. "Nay, I *had* a large family, but they are gone."

The doctor gasped. "How could that be? I saw in your files that you have a father and ten brothers and sisters."

"All dead, except for one," he replied flatly. Again he wondered how the doctor knew of his family. And what were files anyhow?

"What? How?"

"Drowned."

"Why, that's horrible." The doctor put a hand on Ragnor's forearm and squeezed. "I can see how you would be disoriented a bit and how you would see the SEAL program as a substitute family. Yes, it all makes sense now."

"It does?"

"MAGNUSSON!" someone bellowed out in the hall, beyond the closed door of Doctor Fine-gold's hospitium chamber. "Has anyone seen that frickin' Viking?"

Doctor Fine-gold rolled his eyes, then got up and went to open the door. Leaning out, he chastised Chieftain MacLean. "Tsk-tsk-tsk! This is a medical facility, Master Chief. You can't come barging in here disturbing the patients."

"And my patience is sorely strained." Ragnor grinned

with satisfaction when the chieftain's face turned nigh purple with rage or embarrassment or both. Still his leader blundered on, "It's oh-nine-hundred, Magnusson, and you should be down on that beach ready to run. Why don't you just ring out and save us all the trouble?"

After being here at Coronado for four days, Ragnor had learned that any SEAL trainee could ring out at any time, and six of them had done just that since his arrival. "Ringing out" meant quitting the program and returning to regular military duty. Ragnor had never been a quitter and he was not about to start now. And who knew what "regular military duty" entailed? Probably something equally distasteful.

Besides, it irritated the chieftain that he wouldn't ring out. And Ragnor did so enjoy irritating the chief.

"We're done for the day," Doctor Fine-gold told the chieftain, "but I would appreciate you not barging into my office in the future, Master Chief MacLean."

"Yeah, well, I never did have much use for shrinks," the chieftain said. "What are you two doing in here anyhow?"

Ragnor brightened and picked up one of the blotch pictures and showed it to the chieftain, "We were just looking at a picture of you."

"Huh?" the chieftain said, gawking at the two black globes with a tiny stem in the middle.

"I call it 'Chieftain's Manpart,'" Ragnor said, waving good-bye to the doctor, who was having trouble hiding a grin. Ragnor stepped around the gurgling chieftain, whose fists were clenched and whose forehead showed a throbbing vein.

"Ensign, you are going to run your butt off today, after which we are off to San Clemente Island for some land warfare lessons. I personally aim to shoot your balls off."

Nag, nag, nag. Really, this chieftain is worse than my sister Madrene. A thought occurred to Ragnor then. "Are you married?"

"No, I'm not married . . . not that it's any of your business."

"Would you like to meet my sister Madrene?"

The chieftain closed his eyes and seemed to be counting. "Ensign, report for Gig Squad tonight."

"Does that mean you have no interest in Madrene? You might like her. She is blond and buxom and . . ." *the worst shrew in the world.*

"Did you hear me, Magnusson? Gig Squad. Tonight."

Ragnor ignored the mention of Gig Squad. He'd been assigned that after-dinner punishment every single night he'd been here. All it involved was one hour of pushing-ups, jumping jacks, duck walks, squat leaps, and other silly games meant to wear down the muscles.

"You know, Ensign, I don't think you *really* want to be a SEAL. It's not enough to want it; you have to hunger for it."

Oh, bloody hell. Another of his inspire-you sayings. He's worse than Snorri the Sleep-Inducing Skald. "That's all right. I ate an apple a short time ago, so my hunger is appeased."

The chieftain clenched his fists and growled something that sounded like "Friggin' come-he-diane!" Ragnor understood the "friggin'" part since it was a common word here amongst sailors, but not the other term. No matter!

Smiling with seeming innocence at the chieftain, he asked, "Will Alison be running with us today?"

"That's 'Lieutenant MacLean' to you, mister, and you better not be harassing my sister," the chieftain said through gritted teeth as they walked together toward the exercise arena.

"I can honestly tell you that I have never hair-assed anyone in my entire life. And I would definitely have no inclination to put hair on your sister's bottom." *I have other ideas for her bottom, but you don't need to know that.*

The chieftain continued to gurgle.

Which Ragnor took for a good sign.

Beware of ladies on the prowl . . .

"That dog is hopeless," Alison said with a laugh.

"Sam is not hopeless. He just has 'sit' and 'lie down' mixed up," Lillian said, also laughing.

She and Lillian had been trying to train the German shepherd puppy for the past two hours, to no avail. Sam, who was only six months old, just stared at them with his big ears pointing upward and his tongue lolling happily.

He did bark a lot, though, and that should be a plus. In fact, Alison had barely been able to sleep since his arrival because of all the barking down below. He barked at passing cars, even when they were one block over. He barked at his dreams when he was snoring away. He barked at moths. He barked at the beep of the microwave. He barked at everything. They hoped he could be trained eventually to bark only at strangers on the property.

She and Lillian had been diligent about locking doors and windows, spotlighting the front and back yards at night and generally watching their backs. Those precautions along with the barking dog made them feel a little safer. Besides, Alison had had no Breather phone calls for the past three days, which they took as a good sign.

"I think I'll go upstairs and take a bubble bath with a nice glass of cool wine and a good book," Alison said.

"Sweetie, what is wrong with you?" Lillian shook her head. "It's Saturday night. You're young. You should be out, dating, meeting new people. Didn't that detective call you?"

"He did, but I just didn't feel up to all the small talk that goes into a new relationship. Not tonight."

Lillian arched her eyebrows in question.

"If you must know, today is the anniversary of the day David was killed." David had been her fiancé. He and other SEAL team members had been caught in a brutal bombing by terrorists they had been hunting down in Lebanon. Ian had been one of those team members . . . the only one to survive. It seemed like yesterday, but it had been five years ago. She swiped angrily at the tears that filled her eyes.

"Oh, my goodness!" Lillian stood and gave Alison a sympathetic hug. "Well, you are definitely not staying home tonight. We've got to do something to wipe out those memories."

"Like?"

"Girls' night out, honey."

Oh, boy! Me and Lillian out on the town. I don't like the sound of that. "What did you have in mind?"

Lillian tapped her chin thoughtfully, then smiled mischievously. "The Wet and Wild."

"Lillian! That dive hardly seems like your kind of place."

"And what is my kind of place?" she asked with mock indignation.

"Well, for one thing, they play country music there."

"I like country music. Well, some of it. It makes me smile."

"Me, too," Alison admitted. "But this bar has an archway you have to go through to enter. It sprays a fine mist of water on you so that—"

"—you have a wet T-shirt," Lillian finished for her, smiling ear to ear.

"I've only been there once, and Ian about had a fit when he found out. It's a civilian hangout, but some military guys go there, too."

"Your brother is too uptight by half."

"Tell me about it."

"You know, I've been thinking that what I need in my life is one more big fling."

Alison, who was down on her haunches petting the dog and only half listening, almost fell over. "What?"

"Really. Before menopause kicks in and my brain is muddied up by hot flashes, I want a meaningless, hot-as-sin affair. No strings. A mature stud. Yep, that's what I want."

"And you expect to find that at the Wet and Wild. Mrs. K., that bar is down and dirty. Not the Mature Ladies Singles Club."

"Pfff! If I wanted that, I'd go to church."

"Don't be surprised if someone pinches your butt."

"Do you think?" Lillian asked with exaggerated interest. "I haven't had a good butt pinch in decades. Sweetie, don't look shocked. At my age, any attention is a compliment."

"I'm not sure about this."

"Come on. It's just the kind of place we need tonight. A beer. Some greasy food. A little lust and laughter."

"Okaaay, but I'm not wearing a T-shirt."

"Well, I am," Lillian said.

When they prepared to leave the house a few hours later, Lillian was indeed wearing a T-shirt emblazoned with the glittery logo "Still a Fox" tucked into a pair of tight blue jeans.

And Alison, who'd decided to throw caution—or perhaps her brain—to the wind, had opted to wear not a T-shirt but an even more outrageous white tank top tucked into her own tight black jeans. She even had cowboy boots on; they'd been an engagement gift from David, who'd had a wry sense of humor. Somehow, she knew David would approve of her wearing them tonight. Once he'd even made love to her wearing nothing but those expensive boots. "Wanna get down and dirty, baby?" he'd asked her more than once.

Oh, yeah! "Are you ready?" she asked Lillian as she got into the passenger seat of her Mazda.

Lillian nodded with a mischievous grin. "And rarin' to go."

"The question is whether the world is ready for the two of us."

Down and dirty, here we come!

CHAPTER SEVEN

&

*F*riends in low places . . .
  "Hey, Mad Max, time to get down and dirty."

Ragnor ignored the intrusive voice of one of his comrades—probably his swim partner Cage—as he lay splatted face down on his pallet, where he'd fallen fast asleep after a quick showering several hours ago. "Go away," he mumbled.

They'd returned to the base from San Clemente Island, where they'd been engaged all day in "sneak and peek" or "escape and evade," covert operations designed to teach them how to move about unseen in enemy territory. When they weren't crawling about in the mud and brambles, they were doing "surf penetrations" for the same purpose. Their faces and arms had been "cammied up," meaning camouflaged with greasepaint so they blended in with their surroundings. Down and dirty, for a certainty!

Before going out for that "field op," they'd been taught hand-to-hand combat in a hall with padded walls and floor. Ragnor had taught the burly instructor a thing or two, including how to employ a proper garrote when a silent kill was required, or the proper way to engage an enemy head-on when a sword was not at hand. Really, these soldiers with all their fancy weapons did not know everything about war. To his surprise, they did not appreciate his input.

He'd missed dinner but did not care, with every muscle in his body screaming from the past three days' exercises at San Clemente. War games, they called them. More like torture games, if you asked him.

And he was sick to death of the chieftain's sayings, which were designed to be inspirational but were mostly just downright half-brained. Like his latest, "Pillage before you burn, boys . . . ha, ha, ha," as if every good soldier didn't already know that. He suspected it had been a bit of sarcasm on the chieftain's part directed at him. He had not laughed.

Aside from the physical torture, he was in mental anguish as well. He just did not understand how another country could have so many advanced weapons, horseless vehicles that could travel across land or air, flameless lighting, running water, glasslike apparatuses that fit over the eyes enabling a soldier to see at night, and so many other marvels. Why had he never heard of this country before? He still was not sure that he hadn't fallen into some after-death realm. He didn't feel dead, but then, how would he know how dead felt?

He had survived more than one sennight in this new land, thanks to his comrades in SEALs who'd explained many things in hushed tones so the chieftain would not overhear. And they covered for him when he blundered.

"C'mon, Max, the chicks are waiting for us." It was Pretty Boy speaking. "Well, they're waiting for *me*. Don't know about you ugly ducklings."

"You're a swan, all right, Pretty Boy," Flash remarked. "All feathers and no meat."

Ragnor cracked his eyes open to slits to gaze at his wonderful, albeit lackwit, comrades.

"Hah! You're just jealous of my pretty feathers. Besides, I got meat. And chicks know I got meat," Pretty Boy countered, patting his groin for emphasis.

"We Cajuns are better than anyone at drawing chicks. We don't need no pretty faces, either. All we gotta do is wink and drawl out, 'Come here, darlin'.' They melt every time," Cage proclaimed. "*Laissez les bon temps rouler*. Let the good times roll, baby . . . Loo-zee-anna style."

"I am not hungry." Ragnor finally inserted himself into the bizarre conversation. "Besides, I am not overly fond of chicken. I much prefer boar . . . or shank of reindeer."

Pretty Boy laughed. "You'll like this kind of chick, my man."

"We need a little B & B for our R & R," Flash put in.

"They mean bootie call," Sly explained, as if his words were any clearer. "Booze and Broads for our Rest and Respite."

"A honky-tonk. A little music, a little dancing, a little beer," Flash further explained. "And easy women."

That got his attention. "Beer? Dost mean there will be mead available?" He rolled over and sat up on his pallet. He would give just about anything for a horn of mead.

"You betcha," Flash said.

Even at night, sleeping time was not their own. Sometimes they were awakened by loud shouting, or banging of clubs on trash can lids, or whistles or bullhorns or weapons going off, just so they could be marched down to the ocean where they would sit in the surf for hours on end. Tonight they'd been given a rare night off, but Ragnor could not imagine that a drinking hall was what their leaders had in mind. "I cannot believe our chieftain and his cohorts in punishment would allow us to go to such a place. Do we have leave to depart the base?"

"No, we have a limited liberty, but what they don't know can't hurt us," Flash answered, waggling his eyebrows with mischief.

"Well, mayhap I will go with you, then," Ragnor agreed. "Where exactly are we going?"

"The Wet and Wild," Flash announced with a big grin.

"Well, count me out," Cody yelled from several pallets away. "I don't need any she-done-me-wrong songs. I want good ol' rock 'n roll." Cody did a little dance that involved swiveling his hips and thrusting his pelvis in a suggestive manner. "I'm off to Rock 'n Suds. Besides, it's deep in San Diego, where we're sure to evade a Mac Attack."

"Me, too," F.U. and Sly said as one, walking toward the door with Cody, both of them wearing the blue *braies* he'd noticed many men wearing in this country, along with U.S. Navy tea-ing *sherts*.

"Count me out both ways," JAM said.

Everyone turned to look at him.

His face bloomed red as he disclosed, "I have a date." JAM was dressed in the white uniform some of the military men wore. The contrast with his dark complexion was startling, and probably attractive to women. JAM came from Mexico, where skin color was somewhat dark, but not as dark as Nubians, like Sly . . . although Sly was not from the land of Nubians. He came from a country called Man-hat-ten. Very confusing!

"Whooee, ya gotta watch them quiet ones," Flash said. The others added randy remarks on the former priest-to-be's prowess in the bed furs. Like youth-lings they were. In truth, like Vikings they were. He guessed that men in all lands of whatever age liked to tease each other about their virility.

"Do you like country music?" Flash asked him.

"What country?"

"Never mind," they all said with communal disgust. "Never mind" was a common saying here.

Two hours later, they were sitting at a back table in a

drinking hall named the Wet and Wild, wearing uniforms of tight faded-blue *braies*, short-sleeved tea-ing *sherts*, and light-weight running shoes. *What a country! Special shoes just for running!* And of course they all had handfuls of cone-domes in their pockets, just in case they got lucky. Ragnor didn't need to have "getting lucky" explained to him.

Little had he known that the place's name, Wet and Wild, came from the wetting down of females, and males, who entered the premises, thus turning their upper garments nigh transparent. Not a bad idea! Mayhap he would suggest it to his castellan when he returned to the Norselands. Women who entered his great hall for a feast would have to endure a bucket of water over the chest area first. On the other hand, women like Madrene might just bop any man who dared such with the flat side of their own broadswords. Besides, a wet *gunna* didn't give quite the same effect as a wet tea-ing *shert*. Oh, well!

He, Flash, Cage, and Pretty Boy had just finished off platters of chicken wings doused in a red sauce that about blistered the tongue, followed by hard pretzels that about broke the teeth. This was considered fine dining in Ah-mare-ee-ca. Now they just sat, drinking long-necked bottles of mead—rather, beer—discussing subjects that are important to mankind. Like fake orgy-ass-ems.

They'd had to explain the word orgasm to Ragnor first, as they had so many words in the past few days. He'd told them that Vikings used the word "peaking" instead of orgasm. Same idea.

"Man, I hate it when women fake it." Flash shook his head with disgust. "When I broke it off with Janine last year, she told me she'd been fakin' all along. That she hadn't come one single freakin' time."

"She was probably lyin' just to get back at you," Pretty Boy said.

Flash shrugged. "Maybe, but how's a guy to know?"

"*Mon Dieu*! You just ain't doin' it right, if you have to ask that," Cage opined. Cage always had an opinion, especially about women. To his mind, Cage-huns—that was the culture he came from—did everything better.

"Bullshit!" Flash said. "I been doin' the deed since I was fourteen. I guess I've learned everything there is to know about screwin' by now."

"I just let the woman do all the work," Pretty Boy said. "Then, if she has any complaints, it's her fault. Come or don't come, it's up to her." It wasn't surprising that Pretty Boy would think something like that, being so full of himself.

"Betimes I fake my own orgy-ass-ems," Ragnor revealed, before he had a chance to bite his tongue.

Everyone turned to gawk at him. Then they hit him with a barrage of comments.

"Liar!"

"Impossible!"

"Well, you topped us with that one, Max. Hoo-yah!"

Finally, after they all stopped laughing, Flash swiped at the tears of mirth rimming his eyes and asked, "Not that I believe you, but how would a guy be able to fake an orgasm?"

"*Mais, oui*," Cage added. "Women have the 'ooh-ooh-ooh-you-are-killing-me-baby' routine down pat, but a guy can't hide the visible facts. Either he wilts or he doesn't."

"Hah! You would be surprised how many women don't bother to look. They are selfish creatures at heart. Furthermore, 'tis just as easy for a man to say, 'Ooh-ooh-ooh-you-are-killing-me-sweetling.' "

"But why?" Pretty Boy wanted to know. "Why would a man want to fake it? What's the fun in that?"

Ragnor shrugged. "Boredom. Once you've tupped two hundred women and more, the novelty wears off."

"Two hundred?" all three of his comrades sputtered.

"Get out of here!" Pretty Boy snorted with disbelief.

"Are you pullin' our legs?" Flash asked.

"Two hundred sounds about right for me, too," Cage said, then burst out laughing. "Hot damn! Ain't male exaggeration the greatest!"

"You do not believe me," Ragnor concluded. "Well, 'tis naught to be proud of anyhow. I never actually counted, but, really, I have seen seven and twenty winters. I have been tupping since I was thirteen, and those first few years, my brother and I could not get enough. I have . . . had . . . a brother who was the same age as I, and we had this unspoken competition to see if all the maids in the Norselands could warm our bed furs."

"A twin? You're a twin?" Cage asked.

Ragnor shook his head. "Not twins. We were born of the same father, but different mothers from different countries only days apart. We were similar in appearance—almost twinlike, I suppose—except I am dark and he was light."

"You said *was*," Pretty Boy said with touching gentleness.

"Yea, my brother died, along with my entire family. All ten of them. Except for my sister Madrene."

"Good God, man! All of them died? How?"

"Drowned, probably." He shrugged. "I still miss them, especially my brother."

Cage put a hand on Ragnor's shoulder and squeezed. "I'll be your brother."

"All of us will," Flash said, squeezing his other shoulder.

"You betcha," Pretty Boy put in, too.

Ragnor couldn't help himself. Tears misted his eyes. He could not speak over the lump in his throat, but he did nod his thanks to each of them.

He hadn't realized till that moment just how lonely he had been feeling of late, and not just since coming to this new land. He missed his brother and the camaraderie they'd always shared. And he missed his best friend who'd died last year. No wonder he'd felt as if his life were unraveling, as he'd told Madrene.

But he had no more time to dwell on that misery because a group of musicians stepped up to a platform and broke into a rowdy song about boot-scooting boogers, of all things. The drinking hall erupted with cheers and laughter as patrons hooted out their appreciation for the song, some of them singing along, and some of them stepping onto the sawdust floor to dance. And what a dance they were doing! The women shook their arses in their tight *braies* and jiggled their breasts; that he liked. But some of the men looked downright silly, in his opinion, with their off-rhythm, flailing, unmasculine moves.

"Okay, losers, time to show you how the winners operate." Pretty Boy stood, cracked his knuckles and flexed his fingers in an exaggerated manner, then sauntered over to the bar, where he leaned back on his elbows and waited. Within seconds, he was approached by a woman wearing extremely tight white *braies* and a wet tea-ing shirt which showed off her prominent breasts. She kept flipping her long blond hair over one shoulder with a saucy toss of her head.

Soon the band changed rhythm to a slower-paced song, something about friends in low places. Pretty Boy stepped out onto the dancing floor with his newfound woman friend, along with a dozen or so other couples. What they did then pretty much amounted to foresport.

"*What* is that?" Ragnor exclaimed

"Dancing," Flash answered.

The couples stood face to face, arms wrapped around

each other, moving foot to foot with an occasional swirl tossed in. In essence, body rubbing. And the women allowed it? In public? What a land!

"Are they going to fornicate in public, too?" he asked.

"Hell, no! It's just dancing," Flash said. "And actually, I've seen you out there a time or two before, buddy. So don't knock it."

"You have seen me dance? Knock what?" *Why do people keep reminding me of events I cannot recall? I know I would remember doing something so wicked in public.*

"Watch this," Cage said. Making eye contact with a young lady with flowing black hair who was standing across the room with a long-necked bottle of mead in her hand, he crooked his forefinger, beckoning her to come over to him. To give the wench credit, she didn't jump at his command, but she did throw her head back and laugh. Then she crooked her finger at him. "Whatever you want, *chère*," he murmured, chuckling. With a grin, Cage stood, downed the rest of his beer, then danced his way over to her. In truth, Cage's dancing was quite good, unlike the uncoordinated movements of the other flailing males out there. Within seconds, Cage and his female were dancing together, creating quite a spectacle of themselves.

"And what do you call *that*?" Ragnor asked Flash, the only one of his friends left behind.

"Dirty dancing."

"For a certainty," Ragnor agreed. Cage had been right about one thing he'd boasted of so often. Those Cage-huns did know how to dance.

Flash left him then, too, to find his own partner . . . a blond woman of medium height who reminded him a bit of Svein Forkbeard's daughter Inga. He hoped Flash was being careful; if this wench was as designing as Inga had been, he'd find himself wed-locked afore he knew it, cone-domes or not.

After that, he just leaned back with his long legs crossed at the ankles and propped on the next chair, watching and listening. No need to make conversation. No need to get up and meet some woman. No need to make a fool of himself dancing. He was on his third bottle of mead, so it was not surprising that everything spun around him and the talking, laughter, and music came together into a pleasant buzz.

Suddenly, though, he saw something that caused his wandering gaze to halt, then look again. Walking through the water archway was a tall red-haired woman in leather boots, tight, tight black *braies*, and a sleeveless, neckless white *shert* which was now damp. It was Alison MacLean. Even from across the room, he could see the outline of her breasts. *Now, that is a gift from the gods.*

Ragnor gulped and set his bottle of beer on the table. He wanted nothing to cloud his vision now. Should he get up and go to her? Or should he wait for her to notice him?

As if reading his thoughts, Cage danced close to his table and warned him, "Don't you dare, cowboy. That woman is off limits."

Pretty Boy soon followed, noticing the direction of Ragnor's stare. Alison was laughing at something her companion said . . . an older woman similarly attired, except that she wore a short-sleeved tea-ing *shert* with some words on it. "No freakin' way, Max. Don't even think it," Pretty Boy said, his arms wrapped around the pretty blonde as they danced in place. "Remember what we told you about fraternization."

It was no surprise that Flash showed up next. "Man, you

are going to scorch the good doctor by looking at her like that. Cool down, Max. Go find yourself another woman. Or stand under the water archway to cool off." Flash danced off then, his good deed done for the night.

They were right. Alison MacLean spelled trouble for him. He would be in this country for only a short time . . . he hoped. No sense landing himself in the military prison called a brig because he lusted after the wrong woman. Still, his heart raced and his blood warmed just watching her walk across the dancing hall.

She headed toward a table where, to his surprise, Doctor Fine-gold was seated, and rose to greet Alison. No wonder Ragnor hadn't recognized the brain healer before. He wore dark blue *braies*, like just about everyone in the hall, a multicolored, long-sleeved *shert*, and high-heeled boots which gave him some additional height. Alison appeared to be introducing the older woman to Doctor Fine-gold before they all sat down at the table. Alison's back was to Ragnor, which gave him plenty of opportunity to observe, undetected.

He relaxed somewhat, with his legs still propped on the other chair, and indulged in another long swig of beer. He should take the recipe for this beer back home to Madrene, who prided herself on her skill in brewing mead. She always looked for new recipes. He made a mental note to himself of things to carry back with him: cone-domes, beer, running shoes, weapons known as guns, and toothpaste. Idly he wondered if his trip back to the Norselands would involve near-drowning again, and whether all those items could survive a water dousing. He smiled to himself at his mind meanderings.

The serving wench brought him another cold beer, which he sipped now, not wanting to become *drukkinn*. Pretty Boy, Cage, and Flash stopped by periodically, checking on him, no doubt to make sure he didn't "make a move" toward Alison. They even offered to introduce him to some wenches, an offer he declined.

He watched through slitted eyes as Alison talked animatedly to her woman companion and Doctor Fine-gold. Mostly, though, the conversation took place between the older woman and Doctor Fine-gold; the woman had to have a number of years on Fine-gold, but Ragnor could see the sexual interest between the two.

That was neither here nor there. His interest—sexual and otherwise—lay with Alison. He saw her only from the back and the side when she turned periodically. It was enough. From the back, he could see clearly the muscle definition of her shoulders and upper arms. This was not the kind of soft woman he was accustomed to, but a female as hard-bodied as some of his SEAL comrades. Oh, not in an unfeminine way. She had all the curves that marked her as a woman, but they were sharply defined. He found that he liked that about her. Hard and soft all in one package. In other words, irresistible.

She'd combed her wavy red hair off her face and behind her ears, from which dangled gold hoop ear ornaments. Her lips had been painted ruby red and her cheeks rouged slightly. Her lashes were long and golden red.

Just looking at her made him feel good.

What kind of children would they produce? Red-haired girlings with green eyes like her? Black-haired boylings with blue eyes like him? Or different combinations, like red-haired boylings with green eyes, or black-haired girlings with blue eyes, or red-haired boylings with blue eyes, or black-haired girlings with green eyes, or . . .

Aaarrgh! I must be losing my mind. Thinking about children! Holy Thor, I'm turning into my father.

While his mind had been wandering, something had

been happening at Alison's table. Doctor Fine-gold and the other lady got up to dance, and some fellow in light brown pants and a short-sleeved *shert* came over to talk to Alison. She seemed to know him. They talked for several moments, with the fellow leaning over the table, one hand propped on the back of her chair, way too intimately for Ragnor's tastes. Then Alison stood and walked out onto the dance floor with him.

Ragnor's feet hit the floor with a clomp. But he didn't rise immediately. Instead, he watched as the imprudent fellow swirled her about to a fast song . . . "Honky-Tonk Something or other." The man with the death wish who dared to touch Alison looked like an idiot. Alison, on the other hand, took Ragnor's breath away, and he had already been breathless. She raised her arms, which lifted her small breasts. Swayed her hips. Showed off her nicely rounded arse. Swung legs that were sinfully long. Through two songs he watched, knowing that his three SEAL comrades watched him just as closely, worried that he was going to do something that would land them all in the brig.

He did not mind quietly observing the exhibition that Alison and her male friend put on to the rowdy songs, but once the musicians moved into a slow rendition of "Crazy"—*and wasn't that appropriate for his mood of late?*—Ragnor could not sit still and allow another man to embrace his woman in such a familiar way, all in the name of that fornicating exercise they called dancing.

And, yea, he thought of her as *his woman*. No question about that.

He cared naught if Alison smiled invitingly at the rogue. No one should be allowed to hold her except him.

Standing abruptly, Ragnor stomped out into the middle of

the dance floor and tapped her shoulder. She turned to look over her shoulder, then jerked with surprise. "Max! What are you doing here?"

"Dance with me," he said without any preamble. It was not a question.

"Get lost, bozo," the guy said. He lowered his hands from the back of Alison's waist and turned to confront him.

Ragnor ignored the man, not even caring if *bow-sew* was an insult. Instead, he repeated to Alison, "Dance with me."

She stepped in between him and the other fellow. "John, this is Ensign Magnusson. Max, this is Detective John Phillips, a local police officer."

"What need have you of a police officer?" Ragnor asked, having learned from his SEAL comrades that police, including detectives, enforced the law in this land. Was Alison in some danger, as he'd originally thought?

"Ensign? You're an ensign? What the hell are you doing approaching a superior officer, boy?" the policing man asked, and not in a pleasant manner.

The *bow-sew* he had been willing to accept, but *boy* from a man only a few years older than himself? *Hah! I do not think so!* Ragnor drew himself to his full height, which was a half head taller than the policing man, who, incidentally, had a retreating hairline Ragnor was pleased to notice. "Go away afore I have to rearrange your nose. Or pull out what little remains of your hair."

"Are you threatening me?"

"A Viking never threatens. We just do."

The fellow had the nerve to roll his eyes. "A Viking, for chrissake. You Navy SEALs are something else!" He probably knew Ragnor was a SEAL or a SEAL trainee because his *shert* proclaimed him so. "Not only do you SEALs think you're God's gift to women, but now you claim to be a friggin' Viking besides. Give me a break!"

"I would be more than pleased to oblige you," Ragnor said. "Which body part would you like me to break first?"

Out of his side vision, he saw that Pretty Boy, Cage, and Flash had lined up behind him, probably outraged over the SEAL slur. Turned out there were a few other actual SEALs in the bar, aside from the trainees, and they had heard the remark, too, and were not happy, if their clenched fists were any indication. Still others of the nonmilitary ranks moved toward the policing man.

"Whoa, whoa, whoa!" Alison said, putting a hand against both of their chests. "John, back off a bit. Ensign Magnusson is a . . . friend of mine." Her face turned bright red at the word *friend.* "Go back and sit at the table. I'm going to dance with him. I'll rejoin you shortly. Okay?"

John appeared reluctant to agree, but finally he nodded and averted a fight by walking back to the table and picking up a bottle of beer, which he emptied in one long, angry draft.

Alison turned her attention to Ragnor then. And she was nostrils-flaring, eyes-blazing angry. "You jerk!" she said, and took him by the hand, pulling him toward the far back region of the drinking hall.

"You are looking very comely tonight, Alison," he said.

"Screw you!"

I'd rather screw you, he thought but even he knew better than to say that aloud. He was watching her arse as she marched in front of him. One cheek up, then down, the other cheek up, then down. Very nice rhythm she had going there. He smiled.

Just then she glanced over her shoulder and noticed the direction of his gaze. *Uh-oh!* It had been his experience that women had a particular sensitivity about their arses, unlike men, who rarely thought of their backsides, being much more interested in their front sides.

She glared at him as if he were lower than a pile of dragon shit.

Reluctantly he lifted his gaze from her buttocks and inquired as sweetly as he could, "Where are we going?"

Not so sweetly, she replied, "Somewhere private . . . where we can't be seen."

Thank the gods, even if her voice is not dulcet-toned with welcome for me, she has something private in mind for us.

"Stop grinning."

He pressed his lips together. "Whatever you say." They'd arrived at their destination, which appeared to be a storage room. Boxes of beer, rows of toy-let parchment and nappykins filled both sides of the wide aisle.

She stopped, turned, and continued to glare at him.

"What now?" he asked when the silence went on and on.

"I'll tell you what. You and I have got to come to an understanding. There is nothing between us, and never will be."

He raised a hand to interrupt. "I must disagree. I am here in this land because of you. I sensed your danger . . . and your allure, truth be told."

"Bull crap! I have no allure."

"Oh, yea, you do. Just looking at you makes me breathless. Not just here tonight in your tempting attire. If I see you from across the grinder at the base, all straitlaced in your white uniform, my heart skips a beat; it truly does. When you run with the teams, I can barely stand for anyone to glance your way. I recognized you the minute I first saw you . . . not just from the near-death vision I had, either. I hate to say it—you are obviously not in a receptive mood—but I suspect you are my destiny."

Her mouth dropped open. Speechless, she was.

But not he. He just blundered on. "My grandmother, Lady Asgar, may she rest in peace in her Christian heaven, always said that there is but one woman for each man in our family. She said we would recognize our destiny when we met her. I ne'er believed it before, but I do now. You should know, milady, that I lost my enthusiasm for the bedsport a good long time ago, but it is back with a vengeance now that I have met you. You are my destiny, to be sure." *I cannot believe I just said that. Where did it come from? I never thought that stuff about destiny before this moment. Is it true? Or is someone else speaking with my tongue, like mayhap the jester god Loki? I wonder if near-drowning affects the tongue? Or a man's good sense?*

She shook her head and laughed. "That is the biggest crock I have ever heard. Does that line usually work for you, Ensign?"

He shrugged. "I do not know. I ne'er tried it afore." He could feel his face heat with embarrassment. Flowery words were not his normal style. Usually, he just looked at women, and they came to him.

"What do you want from me?" she asked, not mincing words.

Your mouth . . . your breasts . . . your womanparts . . . your body. "A dance." *Oh, good Lord, even I recognize how pathetic that sounds.*

"You want to dance?"

For a start. "Yea."

"Why in God's name would I do you a favor when you've behaved so badly?"

"I behaved badly? When?"

"Aaarrgh!"

"There are many words and sounds I do not recognize in

this land, but *aaarrgh!* is not one of them. What have I done to make you *aaarrgh!* except ask you to dance?"

She rolled her eyes. "Fine. Let's freakin' dance."

Fine. I won that argument. But not really. "Uh, I should tell you something."

"What now?"

"I cannot dance."

She rolled her eyes again and added a laugh. "Then why did you ask?"

"I asked before because I did not want another man holding you. I ask now because I need an excuse to get you in my arms and melt that cold shield you have wrapped about yourself. You are mine, and the sooner you recognize that fact, the better."

"What?" she shrieked. Some women liked a man to be possessive about them; others did not. Apparently, she was one of the latter. And she was as good at shrieking as Madrene. Mayhap it was a talent inherent in all women.

"I am a quick learner, though," he said, holding his arms open for her to step into his embrace.

"One dance," she said icily, "and that's it. If we're lucky, no one will see us. If not, we are both in big trouble." She stepped into his arms and put her hands on his shoulders. Through the half-opened doorway, they could clearly hear the music—a song about love and misery, a universal partnership, he supposed.

"I meant no trouble for you," he started to say.

"Shut up," she said.

Well, that was certainly blunt. "I love it when you talk rough to me."

She growled.

Not a good beginning to our love affair, Ragnor thought, but then he got lost in the pleasure of holding Alison and did not think anymore. He looped his arms around her waist as he'd seen other men do on the dancing floor with their partners. But that was not enough. Not nearly enough. He yanked her closer so that her breasts pressed against his chest, her face nestled against his neck, and her groin fitted itself against his groin. The scent of some floral fragrance enveloped him like an aphrodisiac. Not that he needed any passion prodders.

Saints and Valkyries! He almost swooned at the sheer wave of pleasure that rippled through him at that bodily contact.

He groaned.

She groaned.

He smiled against the top of her hair, especially when she shifted from foot to foot to the beat of the music, thus rubbing her breasts across his *shert* and her womanhood against his most appreciative manhood.

"Dance, dammit," she ordered. Her voice was shaky, which could be either a good thing or a bad thing. Good, he decided.

He did dance, as best he could, trying to follow her rhythm, which pretty much amounted to swaying from side to side.

"This is such a mistake," she whispered against his ear.

He wished she would say more because her breath in the whorls of his ear was akin to the most erotic touch, as if she had tongued him there, or somewhere even more provocative. "What?" he asked, even though he'd heard her plainly.

"This is such a mistake," she repeated.

And he smiled as delicious spirals of pleasure rippled out from her breathy words. "Put your tongue in my ear, sweetling," he urged.

"What?" she squawked, and tried to pull away.

He held on tight. *Bloody hell, I didn't mean to say that aloud.* "Just teasing. Just teasing." *Mayhap later.*

They were both silent then as they swayed to the music. He liked this dancing, he discovered. He'd thought that at twenty and seven he'd learned everything there was to know about lovemaking, but he'd been wrong. This was a new, more subtle form of loveplay, and he was enjoying mightily her unwitting tutoring.

She brushed her breasts across his chest.

He followed through on the return brushing.

She undulated her hips against him.

He saw stars, then returned the favor.

She gasped.

He took a deep breath in an attempt to slow down his burgeoning excitement.

She ran her fingertips over the back of his neck and up over his close-clipped skull.

He swept his open palms over her back from her waist to her shoulders, then back to her waist. Over and over, each time creeping lower till—*thank you, gods and goddesses*—she allowed him to cup her buttocks, to pull her even tighter against him.

The band moved on to a new love-and-misery song, but he barely noticed, so engrossed was he in the marvel of dancing with this woman . . . *his woman.*

Finally, when he could bear no more of this exquisite torture, he drew his head back and looked down at her. Her eyes were closed and her lips dreamily parted; he realized that she was only half aware of the emotions overtaking them both.

"Alison," he whispered. "Open your eyes, dearling." He wanted her fully aware when he took them to the next step.

Lazily she opened her eyes. Their green color was misty with arousal. "What are you doing to me, sailor?"

"What are you doing to me, siren?" he whispered back.

Then he lowered his lips to hers. And sweet, sweet, sweet was the taste of her mouth. He swept his lips across hers, to and fro, learning how they fit together. When he got it just right, he slanted himself over her parted lips and plunged his tongue inside. A bold thrust to show his hunger for her.

But instead of drawing back from his assault, she opened her mouth wider for him, and she sucked softly on him.

He whimpered his pleasure.

She whimpered, too, when he began the slow in-out tongue-dance of lovemaking. His hips were following suit below. And then they moved to the wall, where he positioned her with her arms over her head, hands clasped, bodies as close as any two bodies, fully clothed, could be.

He wanted to cup her breasts and suckle her.

He wanted to open her black *braies* and slide his fingers into her woman-fleece.

He wanted to be inside her, sheathed to the hilt.

All these things he yearned for, in good time. For now, he relished the sheer joy of kissing her, and being kissed back in return.

"I did not realize how hungry I was," he gasped out once when he came up for air.

"Nor I," she said, arching up to resume the torturous kiss. This time, her tongue was in his mouth, and she was showing him with expertise that she knew the rhythm of lovemaking, too.

"You are so screwed."

"Not yet, I'm not," she murmured with a smile against his panting mouth.

"I didn't say that," he told Alison, though he wasn't sure she heard him.

Chuckling erupted behind them. Male chuckling.

"I told you he'd go half-cocked," someone said. "Well, maybe not half."

Then more chuckling.

Awareness seeped into his lust-ridden brain, and he pulled back slightly, bracing his forehead against hers as they both tried to slow their panting breaths.

"Yep, screwed tight and about to be delivered, straight to the brig," another male voice said behind them.

"I told you he wouldn't listen to us. Look at that boy carry on," still another voice said. "Whoo-ee, the chief is gonna have his head on a platter."

"Go away," Ragnor growled to his three comrades, who were standing in the now fully open doorway, grinning like lackwits.

"Not on your life!" they said as one.

"Oh, God!" Alison exclaimed, her face flaming. In truth, she looked mighty good to Ragnor with her kiss-swollen lips and her eyes still glazed with passion. Her nipples stood out in her disheveled tea-ing *shert* as testament to the arousal she could not deny, and her *shert* wasn't even wet anymore. "What did you do to me?"

"Me?" he said defensively. "What did you do to me?"

"Jerk!" she said, shoving her palms against his chest and stomping toward the doorway, where the three lackwits parted for her. "If any of you say anything about this," she warned just before she passed through, "I will have all your heads on a platter. You won't need to rely on my brother for that."

With those words, she practically ran down the hallway

toward the musicians, who were once again wailing out something about love and misery. *Isn't that the truth?*

Ragnor's three comrades gave him their full attention then, shaking their heads at what they must have considered idiocy.

Cage spoke for all of them when he asked, "Was it worth it?"

He grinned, and without hesitation replied, "Oh, yea!"

CHAPTER EIGHT

What was she thinking? . . .

By the time Alison made her way back to the table where Lillian and Abe were still talking up a storm, her heart rate had slowed to about two hundred beats a minute and her blood was only scalding hot. She didn't know if she was more angry or more aroused.

What was I thinking?

I wasn't thinking. That's the problem.

Did I have too much to drink?

Nope. I can't blame it on beer brain.

Is it the anniversary of David's death that has put me in this vulnerable state?

A little bit, maybe.

Is it hormone overload?

For sure.

Maybe it's as simple as loneliness.

Yep, that, too.

Would any man have done for me in my current state?

Hmmm. John was dancing with me moments before, and I wasn't affected at all.

Merciful heavens! I've got the hots for a Viking.

With a sigh of hopelessness, Alison looked from Lillian to Abe and back again. They were talking about the psychiatrist's favorite hobby, raising prize orchids in a small greenhouse attached to his house. Obviously, they shared a common interest in horticulture. But it was more than that, Alison realized with a smile. These two sizzled, despite their age difference. She saw that in the way they looked at each other, even when discussing floral fertilizers. Not to mention the way they touched each other occasionally . . . fingertips on a forearm, a pat on the thigh, a not-so-casual arm around a shoulder.

Alison wished them well. Both of them were good people.

"John left," Lillian informed Alison suddenly, as if just noticing that she had returned. "It was obvious when you were gone so long that . . . well, you know?"

She nodded, not really concerned. She would call the detective tomorrow and apologize for her rudeness.

"I don't like to interfere in a colleague's personal life," Abe said hesitantly, "but do you think it's wise to get involved with an ensign . . . and a SEAL trainee, to boot?"

"I'm not involved with him," she stated as firmly as she could, as much to convince herself as them, she supposed. "It was just a momentary blip of the brain."

You are my destiny, he had said. Why his words flickered through her mind just then, she did not know. But what an odd thing for him to say. Not at all like the usual pickup line.

Lillian made a snorting sound of disbelief, her gaze sweeping over her in a way that told Alison she should have stopped off at the ladies room on her way back. Putting the fingertips of one hand to her mouth, she realized that her lips must be bruised and swollen from all their kissing. A hand to her head also disclosed that her side barrettes were dangling and her hair was in disarray. She wasn't about to look down at her chest area, afraid of what she would see. "Okay, so it was a big blip," she admitted with a self-deprecating laugh.

Lillian and Abe joined in the laughter, and she took a

long swig of her lukewarm beer. If she didn't laugh at herself, she might just start crying.

She had told Lillian earlier tonight that the Wet and Wild was down and dirty. That was just what she'd gotten. Down and dirty, Viking style.

Just climb behind my shield, baby . . .

"Listen, buddy, you can't go over there," Cage told Ragnor for about the hundredth time.

In fact, Cage and his other two friends held him back forcibly from crossing through the drinking hall to the table where Alison sat with her female companion and Doctor Fine-gold. Fortunately, John the Hair-Losing Policing-Man had departed.

"I just need to talk with her," he insisted. "No kissing, just talking."

"Uh-uh-uh," Flash said. "I think it's time for us to go back to the base." The other two nodded.

"Without using any of your cone-domes?" It surprised him that his friends would give up their own bodily pleasures to remove him from the temptation of Alison MacLean. But then, he'd once done the same for his friend Skorri when he'd been *drukkinn* and about to make a fool of himself over a married lady whose husband wielded a broadsword with great expertise.

"Just give me one second to apologize; then I will leave with you," he promised.

The three of them looked at each other, about to relent.

"You promise to leave then?" Cage asked.

"Unless she invites me to her bed furs. Then I cannot promise that I will leave her side."

"Man oh man, you are delusional," Pretty Boy commented, shaking his head.

"I don't know about that," Cage said thoughtfully. He and Pretty Boy still had a firm hold on Ragnor's arms, while Flash was standing in front of him, as if he could block his escape. "Last I saw, he was tickling the good doctor's tonsils with his tongue. I never thought she would allow that. So I wouldn't bet against our Viking stud here."

"Forget the tonsils. He was dry humping a friggin' lieutenant against the wall," Flash pointed out with his usual crudity.

"A wall-banging knee-trembler, for sure," Pretty Boy agreed with an admiring grin.

"That's it!" Ragnor said, breaking their hold on him with sharp elbow jabs to either side, then stepping around Flash with a quick feint right, then left. He swaggered toward Alison's table—*if naught else, Vikings had swaggering down to an art form*—with the three lackwits following behind him like bloody shadows.

"Uh-oh!" Doctor Fine-gold said when he saw Ragnor approach.

The older woman looked his way and said the same, "Uh-oh!"

Alison turned in her seat to see what they were uh-ohing about and snapped, "Go away!"

He had never been good at taking orders from women . . . from men either, for that matter. So, he sat down next to her at the table. His pestsome shadows stood behind him, not wanting to miss a bit of the spectacle they assumed he was about to make.

"Milady, I offer you my apologies," he said, donning the most sorrowful face he could manage. *In truth, I am not all that sorry. Not for kissing you. Not for your kissing me back.*

Not for pressing you against the wall. Not for the near-coupling. But I am sorry that you are sorry. Even he recognized what a sorry apology that would make, so he shut his teeth. For once.

"For what? Annoying me? Embarrassing me? Kissing me?"

"He kissed you?" the older woman said, delight ringing in her voice. "Is he the one you mentioned, honey?"

"You mentioned me?" he asked brightly.

"No, he's not the one," Alison said, but he could tell she was lying.

"What did she say about me?" he asked the other woman.

She just smiled and reached out a hand in greeting. "Hi, my name is Lillian Kelly, Alison's landlady. This is Abe Feingold. And you are?"

He shook her hand and nodded to Doctor Fine-gold. Before he could speak, Alison spoke up.

"He already knows Dr. Feingold. Lillian, this is Ensign Magnusson. Max. A SEAL trainee. He was just leaving."

"I was?"

His shadows chortled behind them.

"And these are his fellow trainees, Ensign Frank Floyd, Seaman Justin LeBlanc, and Seaman Travis Gordon. Goodbye, everyone."

After shaking hands all around, they all just grinned, except Ragnor. When she was about to turn her back to him, he quickly said, "I would like to discuss why I acted the way I did. I probably came on too forcefully, but a man cannot take lightly the destiny thrown his way by the Norns of Fate."

"Oh, God! Not that destiny crap again." She put her face in her hands and groaned.

"Destiny?" Doctor Fine-gold said, propping his chin on his elbows on the table. "We never discussed destiny in our sessions together. Were we perchance repressing our innermost dreams?"

We, we, we. This is not about "we," I assure you. Fortunately, Ragnor didn't have to respond, because the lady named Lillian responded for him. "Are you saying that Alison is your destiny, sweetheart?" Lillian asked him. When he nodded, she remarked, "How sweet!"

He glanced toward Alison and grinned. No one had ever called him sweet before.

Alison stuck her tongue out at him.

Which was oddly arousing.

His three laughing comrades excused themselves to go off and find their night-mates, probably figuring that he couldn't do anything too bad with Doctor Fine-gold in attendance. Little did they know!

"Alison, Abe wants me to go over to his house to see this special night-blooming orchid he has cultivated, but I don't want you going back to the house alone," Lillian said. "Will you come with us?"

"No, you go ahead without me. I can drive home alone. Don't you worry about me."

"Sorry, Abe. I'll have to pass for tonight. We had an intruder break into our house this week. Plus, Alison has been getting alarming Breather phone calls for some time," Lillian explained.

"Ah, so that's why you got the guard dog," Abe remarked, nodding his head in approval.

Alison and Lillian both smiled.

"Sam is hardly a guard dog. Not yet," Lillian said.

"But he does bark a lot," Alison added.

Ragnor sat up straight at all the talk of intruders and breathers, wondering if the latter referred to fire-breathing dragons. He wouldn't be surprised in this land where people flew in the air and cooked food without fires. "Are you saying that someone, or something, is endangering you?" he asked Alison.

She shrugged. "Let's just say I have reason to be cautious. That's how I met Detective Phillips. He was sent to the house to investigate after the break-in."

"I knew it! I knew it! I told you that I was called here because you are in danger," Ragnor told Alison. "Well, you are not to fret. I hereby take you under my shield. I will protect you."

Alison rolled her eyes. "You took me under your shield before," she pointed out.

Insufferable wench! She does not halfway appreciate the protection a man's shield provides!

Abe and Lillian stared at him with a mixture of confusion and admiration.

"I had an odd experience when the chieftain attempted to drown me, and while I was walking toward the light, Alison beckoned to me because of some danger she faced," Ragnor explained to Abe and Lillian. "Even then, afore I actually met her in person, I sensed she was my destiny. Plus, I do so like a woman with red hair, a nice arse, and a little intelligence. Not too much intelligence, mind you. Just a mite."

Alison was no longer rolling her eyes, she was gaping at him with disbelief.

What? Did she think I was making up all that destiny stuff? She must think I'm demented. And, really, has she no sense of humor? I was teasing about the arse business. Not that I don't like her arse. But . . .

"You are demented," she said.

"The chief . . . I'm assuming that you are referring to Master Chief MacLean . . . he tried to drown you?" Doctor Fine-gold asked Ragnor with consternation.

Finally, someone is outraged on my behalf.

"It was just drown-proofing exercises," Alison explained.

"Hah! Since when do you drown-proof someone by drowning him?" Ragnor demanded.

Abe and Alison exchanged looks that pretty much translated to *He's mixed up in the head*, but Lillian smiled at Ragnor as if he'd just created the sun. So he addressed his next remark to her. "You are not to worry about Alison tonight. I will accompany her home and ensure her safety."

Lillian nodded hesitantly.

Abe looked skeptical.

Alison stated vehemently, "No, you will not." Then, "Besides, you're not permitted to drive."

I probably am not permitted to be here in this drinking hall either. And that hasn't stopped me. Or my comrades. "Drive what?"

"A car, you imbecile."

He didn't know what "imbecile" meant, but a car he did understand. It was one of those horseless wagons used to transport goods and people in this country. If you asked him, a good horse would suffice, but then, no one had asked his opinion on the matter. "Nay, I do not drive a car, but I can accompany you, then walk back to my sleeping quarters. Or run. I am getting very good at running. Ha, ha, ha!"

She did not even smile at his jest.

Lillian answered for her. "Yes, you could walk, or run, back from our place."

"Traitor," Alison muttered under her breath to Lillian.

"You are under my shield now, milady," Ragnor repeated once again, as his final word on the matter. "Do not push the bounds of what is seemly for a woman by arguing with me."

Alison made a gurgling sound as if she were speechless but had lots to say.

Good.

Lillian stood and took Abe's hand. "We will be on our way then, and leave you two to resolve the matter."

Abe looked at Lillian and asked, "Are you sure?"

"I'm sure," Lillian said.

Bless you, Lillian.

"I'm going home now," Alison said soon after the couple left. "And don't you dare follow me out of this bar. If I'm seen leaving with you, my career is dead in the water."

Never dare a Viking, milady. 'Tis the first lesson most young ladies are taught at their mothers' knees. He let her leave on her own, but he was not about to give up. Soon he followed her, with as much subtlety as a very tall, bald Viking in tight *braies* could manage.

She had just unlocked her car and opened the door when she noticed him. "You again. What a pest!"

"You did not think me pestsome when you were kissing me till my eyes rolled back in my head."

"I was not . . . oh, look there." She stared at a car that had just driven up. It was loaded with laughing men in military uniforms. "Get in this car right away before someone sees you."

He fumbled with the latch on the door and finally got it open. With great difficulty he managed to squeeze himself inside, though it was a tight fit. His knees pressed up against his chest, and his head touched the ceiling. His tight *braies* became even tighter. In truth, he feared the blood supply might be cut off to his most precious body part.

"Oh, good heavens! Put the seat back," she ordered when she noticed how scrunched up he was.

"How would I do that?" he grumbled.

"The lever is on the floor by the door." After a moment, he got the seat moved all the way back. It was still a tight fit for his tall frame, but better than before. "Put on your seat belt," she advised. He watched how she did hers and did the same for himself. Now he truly did feel like a sausage, confined by the tight pants and the belt.

She drove across the parking area and onto the roadway at a high rate of speed. He braced his feet on the floor and held tightly onto the edge of his seat. "Must you travel so fast?" he asked.

"Fast? I'm only going twenty miles per hour," she said, as if that explained away her foolhardiness. Then, probably just to annoy him, she sped up the horseless wagon and they nigh flew down the roadway.

"I am not afraid," he said—though no one had asked—whilst closing his eyes for the collision that was sure to come.

She just laughed. "You act as if you've never been in a car before."

"I haven't."

"Puh-leeze. At least while we are alone, drop the Viking nonsense."

"You consider my being a Viking nonsense?"

"I don't doubt that you are of Norse descent. Maybe you are even from Norway originally, but this constant use of Old-Norse-style words and this constant misunderstanding of modern words . . . well, it's getting old."

He had no time to defend himself because she slowed down the car, presumably approaching her home, and he saw a shadowy figure in the side yard. "Stop the car!" he yelled.

"What?" she yelled back at him as she pressed her foot down hard on a floor lever, and they came skidding to a stop.

"How do I get out of this bloody belt?" He tried but could not release himself. By the time she'd showed him how and he'd managed to find the door handle, the man was no longer to be seen. Still, Ragnor vaulted from the car and ran to the side yard, then all around the house, searching. The only thing he found was a still-smoking tow-back-hoe stick, which had been discarded in the grass. He pinched out the hot end and put the butt in the pocket of his *braies*.

"Max? What's going on?" She came up beside him as he stood surveying the street. From inside, a dog could be heard barking wildly.

"There was a man skulking around your house when you drove up," he told her.

He saw the alarm that widened her eyes.

"No dragons, though," he assured her.

"Stop kidding."

"Hah! Dragons are not a kidding matter, believe you me."

"Have you seen many dragons, Max?" she asked mockingly.

"Nay. They are elusive creatures." Actually, he felt silly saying so because he was not sure they existed.

Meanwhile, she went back to her car and got a weapon from one of the compartments . . . a small gun.

He arched an eyebrow at her.

"I want to be armed before entering the house . . . just in case."

He was about to tell her that he would enter first and protect her, but a weapon might be useful as well. "Do you have any idea who the man might be?"

"I have no idea. All I know is that someone entered my place several days ago. Didn't take anything. In fact, he took great care not to be detected. The only clue we have is that I've been getting Breather telephone messages on my answering machine."

Ragnor knew what a tell-a-fone was, though he could hardly credit that it worked the way Cage had explained it to him. Later he would puzzle over that marvel. For now, he was more concerned about the danger that obviously threatened Alison. "What is a Breather?"

She quickly explained, and he understood that it was a man threatening a woman in a cowardly fashion. Either to scare her or to get his man-pleasure in a perverted fashion. A danger to Alison, either way. "You need a guard."

"That's why Lillian got herself a guard dog this week." She motioned toward the house where the dog was yipping and yapping.

She went up the front steps, gun in hand. He needed a weapon of his own. To the right, he saw a long-handled rake propped against the porch. Quickly he stomped on the rake end to break it off, thus giving him a makeshift spear, which he raised over his head, battle-ready. Holy Thor, he wished he had his sword, but this would have to do. Tomorrow, come hell or Valhalla, he was going to find a smithy where he could purchase a new sword.

At the cracking noise, Alison glanced back over her shoulder and gasped. "Good Lord, you look like an ancient Viking warrior."

"That I am," he said. "Though not so ancient."

In the still of the night . . .

The minute she unlocked and opened the front door, Sam made a barking, flying leap for Max, who caught the animal in one arm, his other arm being occupied with his wooden "spear." Ragnor staggered backward, just catching himself from toppling over at the unexpected furry catapult. Then Sam, the not-so-great guard dog, proceeded to lick the Viking's face with wild abandon.

Alison laughed. How could she blame the puppy? She'd been pretty much licking the guy's face tonight, too.

"This is your guard dog?" Ragnor asked as he put the animal back on the floor. Sam's tail was wagging a mile a minute as he rubbed himself against Ragnor's pant leg. Ragnor grinned at her.

Geesh! Don't grin at me like that. I hate grinning men. I hate your grin in particular. Any minute now I'll be wagging my tail and rubbing myself against your pant leg.

"Why are you looking at me like that?" he asked in a silky voice that implied he knew just what she'd been thinking.

"Some warrior you are! In fact, some SEAL trainee you are, standing here chit-chatting when there might be someone lurking inside this house."

His face flushed.

That was an unfair criticism, Alison realized immediately. And unkind. But really, she had to keep her distance from this guy; he had the strangest effect on her.

"You are correct in your criticism, milady. I am distracted when I am around you. A good warrior must be focused." He pushed her behind him then, even though she had a gun and he had only a rake handle. For some reason, his presence made her feel safe.

Carefully they examined all the rooms on the first floor, along with the doors and windows. Everything was secure. Next, they moved up the stairs to her apartment, which was locked and secure, as well. She told Max, "Whoever was outside never entered. Maybe you were mistaken. It could have been just the shadow of a tree."

He turned from where he had been examining some framed photos on the mantel. "There *was* a man." He showed her a cigarette he'd picked up in her side yard.

It was a slim European brand. She put it on her desk. "Okay, then, maybe I'd better call John."

He bristled. "The policing man? Why? Am I not protector enough for you?" He'd moved to her sofa, where he ran his palms over the silk fabric, then fingered the lace curtains behind it.

"No, it's not that. I just think I should put in a report."

He waved a hand of dismissal, sat down in a recliner that had belonged to David, then gasped when it flew back, bringing his feet upward. Once he realized that he hadn't done anything wrong, and that the chair was actually quite comfortable, he sighed his satisfaction. Good thing the vibrator didn't kick on. "Do your reporting in the morn. After daybreak, John of the Declining Hair will be able to examine the damp grass outside as well. For clues."

John of the Declining Hair? Is he making a joke? Or could he be jealous? Oh, my goodness, Alison, don't you dare be pleased over making a man jealous. How freakin' pathetic! That's even more pathetic than sucking the saliva off a perfect stranger's tongue in a honky tonk storeroom. Or almost a stranger. Wet, for sure . . . and wild, for sure, too. Aaarrgh!

"All right. I'll call the police in the morning," she agreed. "You can leave now. If you don't get back to the base soon, you'll probably be in trouble. Muster is usually at oh-five-hundred and it's about midnight now."

"I'm probably already in trouble. In truth, I am always in trouble with the various chieftains anyway, especially your brother. One more spate of 'trouble' won't bother me." He got up out of the chair in one lithe movement. She usually crawled off clumsily.

She had to smile, not about his too-smooth body moves,

but his using that odd word. "Why do you call him a chieftain? That must irritate the hell out of Ian."

"Well, yea, it does irritate him for some reason. And, yea, I continue to do so for that very reason." He grinned mischievously at her, and she had the oddest inclination to wag her tail . . . or jump his handsome bones. "But, bloody hell, that is his title, is knot?"

"He is a Master Chief."

He shrugged. "Same thing."

She followed him out of the living room into her kitchen, which was large and roomy with a round oak trestle table sitting in an alcove featuring a large floor-to-ceiling bay window that overlooked the back garden. In the distance could be seen the bay and the San Diego skyline.

"Any culprit wanting to enter your keep could easily break these windows and gain access. You should wall it up, or move elsewhere."

"I love those windows, and this kitchen, and this house. I'm not moving anywhere."

"Then you need a protector, and not just a silly pup," he asserted. The dog was already sleeping near her front door, waiting for Lillian's return, no doubt.

"The puppy will grow up, and he can be trained to be a better guard dog. What are you looking for in there?"

He was opening and closing the refrigerator, seemingly fascinated by the light that went on and off, and by the cold air coming out. "What do you call this?" he asked.

"A refrigerator. It keeps food cold so that it doesn't spoil, as if you didn't know."

"I do not suppose you have any leftover boar and manchet bread?" he inquired, peering inside again.

"Are you hungry?"

"Hah! Does a Saxon lie? Do snakes slither? Do priests pray? Do men tup women? Do dogs in heat—"

She held up a hand, laughing. "I get the message." She pushed him aside and began to take items from the fridge—boiled ham, sliced cheese, potato salad, pickles, mustard, and three-quarters of a chocolate layer cake left by Lillian several days ago.

"Why don't you take Sam outside to do his business while I set the table?" she suggested.

He nodded and went off.

This is absolute insanity . . . bringing a guy who is practically a stranger into my house . . . when I'm his superior officer . . . when he's a SEAL trainee . . . when I am so attracted to him my toes curl. She could not seem to help herself. By the time he returned, she had set all the items out on the table.

As if he hadn't been gone for fifteen minutes, he resumed their previous conversation. "As to that other suggestion of yours, I will remain here with you till Lillian returns and the house is fully secured. Or till daylight. Whichever comes sooner."

At first she was going to argue, but she was too disconcerted by his implication that Lillian might stay out all night. "What would make you think that Lillian would stay out all night with Abe Feingold?"

"Alison," he said, his tone chiding her for even asking the question.

She felt herself blushing. "She's older than he is."

"That would signify how?" he asked with amusement, already picking at a piece of ham. "Some of my best coupling has been with older women. And you? Have you never lain with a younger man?"

He was stone-cold serious. "Actually, there haven't been that many men in my life. None since my fiancé died."

He cocked his head with interest. "You are . . . were . . . betrothed?"

She nodded, wishing she hadn't brought up the subject.

"What happened?"

"He was killed by a bunch of scumbag terrorists."

"I have been hearing much about terrorists in the SEALs training. And, yea, they are scum, no matter what country they come from." He continued to eat, then asked, "How long ago was that?"

"Five years."

"Five years since you have made love with a man!" he exclaimed. Then he smiled . . . one of those horrible gloating male smiles.

She smacked him on the upper arm.

"Why did you do that? I was just smiling."

"Yeah, but I could tell what you were thinking."

"You could?" He smiled some more. "That with your prolonged celibacy and my renewed enthusiasm, we should be incredible together?" He waggled his eyebrows with exaggerated lasciviousness.

"We are not getting involved," she asserted, although it already felt as if they were involved.

"What? You do not find me attractive?"

Hab! More like I find you too attractive!

"Wait till my hair grows out. Then you will see how handsome I can be. Before they cut my hair, it hung down to my shoulders. Black as ebony, it was. When I took extra care to make war braids on either side of my face, intertwined with amber beads, women fell at my feet." He waggled his eyebrows some more.

She didn't know whether the waggling eyebrows or his odd mention of war braids disconcerted her more. Deciding that a change of subject might be appropriate, she said, "I notice that you watch everything I do, then you do the same."

"Like?"

"Like when we are eating. You watched me make a sandwich before making one of your own, then cut it in half exactly the same way. You waited to see which utensil I picked up to eat potato salad before you did the same, and you're using your fork with some awkwardness."

He nodded. "I never heard of a sand-witch afore. Nor did I ever use a fork. There are so many new things in this land that sometimes I feel dumb, but I assure you I am not. In fact, my brain is almost too sharp. I remember everything . . . which my father considered both a bane and a blessing. A bane because I was always reminding him of things he said years past, exactly how he said them. A blessing to him in that I could recall word for word any saga ever told round the hearths . . . any message ever given, even years later. And languages—I pick them up like that," he said, snapping the fingers of one hand.

"A photographic memory?" she asked.

"I do not know about that. I just know that I learn quickly."

"Hmmm, maybe not photographic, since that involves the written word. More like genius or Mensa level, which I highly doubt." She rose from the table and went into the second bedroom, which she had converted into an office. She came back with a small book. "Have you ever read Dickens?" she asked. "Of course you have. Every schoolkid has at one time or another."

"Actually, I have only read three books. Two of those were in Latin and the other in Arabic. None of them was Dick-

hands. It sounds rather perverted." He grinned at the idea of her mentioning something perverted.

She blinked at him with confusion. Why did he continue to pretend ignorance of so many words? "Okay, this is *A Tale of Two Cities*. One of my favorites of Dickens. 'It was the best of times. It was the worst of times,'" she began, and continued to read through two full pages.

When she stopped, he stared at her, fascinated. "That was very interesting," he said. "Read more."

"Maybe later. For now, let's see whether you can recite back anything I said."

He did. Perfectly.

"That was incredible. I don't believe it." She went into her office and came back with a small Bible, a Koran, and a collection of Emily Dickinson poetry. He passed every one of her tests. "What's your I.Q.?"

"I don't know," he said hesitantly. "What's yours?"

"One hundred and forty-five, and that is very high. I graduated from high school at sixteen and med school at twenty-two."

She could tell he weighed each of her words and, when he answered, "The same as yours," she knew he lied. But why? Did he fear she would be intimidated by a smarter individual? Or had he never been tested? "Do you mind if I ask Dr. Feingold to give you an I.Q. test?"

He hesitated. "Will it hurt?"

She laughed. "No, it won't hurt." She looked around the table then and realized that all the food had disappeared. He must have been ravenous. "Are you still hungry?" she asked.

"No, my hunger is well satisfied," he said. "The hunger for food, that is."

She ignored his suggestive remark and said, "I have chocolate cake if you'd like dessert."

He just stared at the cake she put on the table, then dipped a forefinger in the sinfully rich chocolate frosting. He closed his eyes and sighed.

"Yep, Lillian's cake always has that effect on me, too. I confess to having a sweet tooth." She cut him a huge slice and put it on a plate, handing him a fork. "Would you like milk with that?"

"I much prefer mead . . . or beer." He was testing the consistency of the cake with the tines of his fork.

"With chocolate cake? I don't think so. I have a few cans in the back of the fridge, but believe me, milk goes better with cake."

He settled for milk, and ate not one but three slices of the cake. She ate two small slivers herself.

They smiled at each other when they finished as only two chocoholics, or dessert lovers, could.

"The running will be extra hard for me tomorrow after all this food," he proclaimed, rubbing his very flat, very hard stomach.

"But was it worth it?" she said.

"Ah, well worth it."

In the silence that followed, Alison began to feel uncomfortable. It was past midnight and still Lillian hadn't returned. They would surely hear the dog barking when the front door opened. And as the silence continued, he stared at her in an intense manner that caused her to avert her head. To avoid looking at him, she made quick work of putting the dirty dishes in the sink. When she came back to wipe off the table, he was still staring at her.

"Is there something else you want?"

He nodded.

"What?"

"You."

CHAPTER NINE

*S*he who hesitates is laid . . . uh, lost . . . uh, same thing . . .
    Me? He wants me?

Oh, my goodness! Oh, my goodness!

Are those butterflies in my stomach? Or bats in my belfry?

What do I care that he has the hots for me? Lots of men have the hots for me.

Hah!

Well, occasionally a man has the hots for me.

I shouldn't even care. What would I want with a crude, ignorant guy like him? He's not my type at all. Not that I have a type.

He sure knows how to kiss, though. Don't I know that from personal, up-close experience!

Betcha the sex would be spectacular.

What is sex? It's been so long since I've had it, I'm not sure I'd recognize it if it hit me in the face . . . or down lower.

What is wrong with me?

I should tell him to just get lost.

That was what Alison thought, but what did Alison do? She hesitated.

That was all she needed to do.

She hadn't said yes, but she hadn't said no, either. To Max's mind, it probably meant the same thing.

"You are considering it," Max said, watching her closely. To his credit, he didn't gloat as he confronted her with the fact. She probably would have had to kill him if he did.

"No, not really considering it." Which was a lie. "That would be ludicrous." Which wasn't a lie. "I just hesitated, that's all. A momentary blip in sanity."

"Hah! Every Norseman worth his salt, whether he be soldiering or seducing, knows to take advantage of the tiniest chink in the enemy's armor . . . not that a lady-love is the enemy. To the Viking man's mind, hesitation on a lady's part screams, 'Take me!' "

"Lady-love? I am *not* your lady-love. Definitely not. Not even close." *But, man oh man, that "take me" bit strikes an erotic nerve.*

"Not yet, mayhap. But soon." With a wild Viking whoop of joy, he lifted her in his arms, swung her around in a circle, then carried her down the hallway to her bedroom.

She was so surprised by his action that all she managed were a few gurgling sounds . . . which he probably took as sounds of appreciation for his ability to lift her so easily. Meanwhile, her feet dangled off the floor and she clutched his shoulders to keep from falling. He probably considered it an embrace. She should lift one hand and smack him a good one.

"Have you lost your mind?" she asked. They were eye level with each other.

"Lost my mind over wanting you," he said, giving her a quick kiss on her open mouth. It was just a kiss. A little kiss. But she felt it all the way to her toes. How pathetic was that?

Her eyes went wide. Her jaw hung open. She hoped she wasn't drooling.

"Shhh," he said, sensing that she was about to protest, finally. "Do not attempt to talk down my ardor, as women are wont to do, always talking everything to death. My enthusiasm is back, and that is cause for celebration." He tossed her onto the bed, so expertly that her head landed on the pillows. It was a low bed, with no footboard. So, he immediately catwalked on all fours up over her, spreading her thighs in the process. Then he settled himself on her.

She saw stars. Literally.

He groaned with pure male satisfaction.

Darn it!

She groaned, too.

Darn it!

Really, she couldn't help herself. He felt so good pressed against her. If she let herself, she might very well have an orgasm just by lying under the handsome hunk. It gave a whole new meaning to "getting laid."

But it was more than that. There was something elemental about the weight of a man's body on a woman's. She'd forgotten how that felt. *Oh, David! I miss you so much!* Tears misted her eyes in remembrance. For one brief moment, she considered arching her back and offering herself to this man, just to forget what she had lost.

Enough! Get a grip, Alison. You cannot do this. "Get off me, you big lug," she gasped out, once a tiny smidgeon of sense entered her fuzzy brain. "And stop smirking."

He laced his fingers with hers and braced himself on straightened arms. He kept her pinned to the bed with his lower body. "I was not smirking. I am just happy."

"Stop being happy."

He laughed. "You do not want me to be happy?"

"Not at my expense." She would have wiped her wet eyelashes if her hands were free.

"You missay me, milady. We are *both* about to be happy."
He bucked his hips several times to show her how happy.

She pulled one of her hands free and swatted him on the
shoulder. "Aaarrgh!"

"I love it when you growl, sweetling. It ripples through
your body from your mouth to your toes and some important places in between, if you get my meaning."

I get your meaning all right. I'm rippling there, too.

"Can you do it again?"

What? Ripple? Oh, God! Does he know I'm rippling? "The
Navy has rules against this," she pointed out, which sounded
lame, even to her.

He made a great show of looking from right to left. "I see
no Navy here. Just a man. And a woman. The only rules are
those we ourselves make . . . or break."

"I can't do this, Max."

"Why? Do you abhor lovemaking, as some women do?
Or is it just me?"

She shook her head. "To tell you the truth, you tempt me.
For the first time in five years, I am tempted. So, no, it's me,
not you, that's the problem."

He cocked his head to the side.

"You scare me," she said.

"Me? I have done naught to frighten you." He stiffened with
affront. "Do you regard me the same as your stocking man?"

Stocking man? Stocking man? Oh, he means stalker. "No,
not like my stalker. The very fact that I would be attracted to
a man who is almost a perfect stranger is what's scary. It is
so out of character for me. I don't do one-night stands. Usually there is love, or some type of commitment involved."
Not that there's been either of those for five years. She
shrugged. "I don't understand. I guess I'm just particularly
vulnerable tonight."

"Destiny," he said. "That is what this is all about. The first time I saw you I knew . . . I just knew. It sounds like something romantic the skalds would speak about in their sagas. But there is a bond betwixt us. Not love. Leastways not yet. Truth to tell, probably not ever."

She had to smile at the horror that swept over his face at the L-word.

"And as for commitment . . . hah! I barely know what I am going to do a minute from now, let alone next sennight, or next year. I must needs take one day at a time."

She didn't understand half of what he said, but the gist of it was . . . a fling, that's all he wanted. Was that so bad? Before she had a chance to voice that ill-advised notion, he said, "But there is no need to weep over it." He released her other hand, then rolled over onto his side.

She had to restrain herself from pulling him back, so empty did she feel without his weight.

Bracing an elbow on the bed, he rested his head on his hand, then used the thumb of his free hand to wipe the skin under one of her eyes, then the other. "Why do you weep, sweetling? And why are you vulnerable tonight?"

"My fiancé died five years ago today," she blurted out before she had a chance to bite her tongue.

He nodded, as if he understood . . . which he couldn't possibly. "You told me earlier about the death of your betrothed . . . at the hands of terrorists, I believe. But I did not know that today marked the anniversary. In truth, my sister Madrene and I were discussing this very subject a short time ago."

She frowned in confusion.

"The death of a loved one marks a person for life. The hurt and emptiness never really go away, despite the years. 'Tis an irony that I have been thinking so much about my brother this week. Betimes my heart aches with yearning for him." He shrugged. "We shared the same father but differ-ent mothers. Born in far distant lands on almost the same day. Methinks we were heart-twins, if there is such a thing."

Smiling, she remarked, "Your father was a busy man. Making babies in different countries at the same time."

He smiled, too. "That he was. Thirteen children in all were born of his seed."

"Thirteen!"

"What can I say? He was a very virile man."

When he smiled at her the way he was right now, so ten-der and genuine, she simply melted. There was no other way to describe his effect on her. "And you? Would you like to have a big family someday, like your father?"

"Hah! I would prefer no children . . . or mayhap one, if the right woman came along. I know too well the chaos of a household full of squalling, squabbling brats. And I have changed my share of stinksome nappies to last a lifetime. Phew!"

"I can't picture you cleaning a baby's bottom."

"Someone had to do it. Nursemaids kept quitting on my father all the time, and none of his wives or mistresses stuck around for long."

A soldier with a gentle side. That is some tantalizing com-bination. "You are really something," she said.

"Yea, I am," he agreed. "Now can we make love?"

She laughed and swatted him playfully.

"Tell me about your betrothed who died. What was he like?" Even as he asked the question, he twirled the curls surrounding her face around a forefinger. He seemed fasci-nated by her hair, which had always been the bane of her life. Red and frizzy. He seemed enthralled by it.

It took her a moment to recall his question. "David was good-looking, I suppose, though not outstandingly so."

"Not as comely as me, eh?" He arched his eyebrows at her. Now his wicked fingers traced the line of bare skin from her neck over her shoulder and down to her wrist. That, too, seemed to fascinate him.

She swatted him again. "No, he wasn't as good-looking as you, but he had a wonderful personality. Everyone liked him."

"I am personable . . . when I choose to exert myself," he said in a little-boy voice. As he spoke, his fingers tracked the neckline of her shirt . . . definitely not in a little-boy manner.

"And David had a wonderful sense of humor. We were always laughing when we were together."

"That is one of the best things about us Norsemen. We know how to share a good jest, mostly at ourselves."

I can see that by the mischievous gleam in your eyes. Laughing eyes, that's what you have. But they were talking about David, not Max, or at least they should be. "He was brave and loyal, especially to his country and his fellow SEALs. He probably would have been a lifer if he hadn't been killed. A military career was all he ever wanted."

"I am a warrior for life, too. Oh, I must needs run the family estate when I am home, but fighting is what I do. It is who I am."

"Tsk-tsk-tsk! You asked me about David but keep talking about yourself."

"And your lovemaking?" he inquired, ignoring her criticism.

She probably shouldn't answer such an intimate question, but she did. "Excellent. We were very compatible, in and out of bed."

His brow furrowed.

"Now what?"

"Methinks I am jealous of your lover, if that is what

squeezes my heart so. I have never been jealous before, so I cannot be sure."

"Jealous? Of a dead person?"

"I think of you as mine."

Oh, good Lord, this guy is smooth.

"And when you speak of your continuing affection for this man, dead or alive, I feel threatened . . . nay, cheated . . . in some way," he explained. "My grandmother, Lady Asgar, would have said I've finally met my destiny."

There he goes with that destiny business again! "You are so odd," she said with a laugh.

"Good odd or bad odd?"

"Definitely good," she admitted. "Look how you changed my tears to laughter."

"Well, then, I must certainly deserve a reward." He was stone-cold serious.

"And that would be?" She stiffened with suspicion.

"A kiss. That is all. A mere kiss." And he was still serious.

Beware of men who take their kissing seriously. "Hah! There is nothing mere about your kisses."

"A compliment, sweetling? I do not know if my already bruised heart can take the shock." He chuckled, even as his face lowered to hers.

She could have stopped him, but she didn't want to. For the first time in a very long while, she wanted to forget rules and regulations, forget what was appropriate for the widow of a brave soldier, forget her reputation as a Navy doctor and daughter of a high military official. She wanted to be just Alison MacLean, woman. She wanted to live in the moment.

And she did.

He didn't come on too strong. If he had, she probably would have panicked and shoved him away. Instead, he wet her lips with his tongue, then moved his mouth seductively over hers in a slick dance of persuasion. No words were spoken, but his kiss spoke for him. He teased and his kiss said, *So you think you can resist me?* He nipped and it said, *So you think you can resist me?* He licked and it said, *So you think you can resist me?* He pressed and shaped and pressed and shaped and it said, *So you think you can resist me?*

When she opened her mouth to him, he moaned, and, oh God, when did a man's moan touch her so? Ever? Then he plunged inside her mouth, taking her to a whole other realm, and it said, *I cannot resist you.*

Alison suckled his tongue reflexively.

He plundered her mouth with a sexual rhythm as old as time.

They both went wild then. His hands were everywhere. Her hands were everywhere. He was on top of her again. But, no, that wasn't good enough. She shoved at him, rolling him over on his back. Then she was on top of him. And it felt so damndamndamn good.

She lifted her head and smiled down at him. "You taste like chocolate."

His blue eyes glazed over with passion. His mouth was puffy and wet with passion. He looked as if he couldn't speak. She probably looked the same.

"You taste like woman," he said finally in a hoarse whisper.

"Is that good?"

"Oh, sweetling, that is exceedingly good."

He combed his fingers through her hair and pulled her down for another kiss. While her mind focused on his kiss, his hands made quick work of pulling her tank top out of her jeans. She sat up again, astraddle him, to help him get the garment up and over her head.

Then he just stared at her, wide-eyed with dismay, not

appreciation. He must be disappointed in her small breasts. She tried to climb off him and slink away in embarrassment, but he held her firmly by the waist.

"What is that?" he asked, nodding his head toward her breast region. "A chastity belt for the bosom?"

"Huh?" Only then did she realize that it was her nude lace bra, not her breasts, that were causing his dismay. "Don't be silly. It's just a bra . . . an undergarment."

"Does it come off?"

"Oh, please! A man of your experience should be able to take this off one-handed."

He just continued to stare at her with dismay.

While he watched, she undid the front catch and shrugged out of the garment. The confusion left his face, replaced by pure male appreciation.

"You're beautiful," he said.

"No, I'm not. I'm too small. Big breasts are—"

He put a forefinger to her lips to hush her protests. "I always thought I favored big-bosomed women, but it was a cruel jest the god Loki was playing on me all those years. Little did I know I was just waiting for you. You are perfect. You are the fulfillment of all my fantasies. How could I have been so blind?"

He shaped her breasts from underneath. They barely filled half of his big hands. Then he flicked the nipples with his thumbs till they budded with sheer joy.

Alison almost swooned at the pleasure that shot out in erotic ripples from his fingertips to every part of her body, especially between her legs, where hot liquid pooled. The ache he created there and throughout her body was so pleasurable it was almost painful in its intensity. Never, never, never had she been aroused so quickly.

"Help me," he said as he attempted to undo the snap on her jeans.

She laughed and rolled over onto her back beside him. There was no way anyone would get these tight jeans off unless she was in a prone position. While she undid the pants and pulled down the zipper, he moved to her feet and yanked off her boots. All she wore now was a pair of nude lace bikini underpants, which he eyed with parted lips.

Just before he reached for them, she said, "No. It's your turn now. I want to see you, too."

He smiled with supreme male confidence in his body, which he knew she would like. At any other time, she would have liked to hit him upside the head for his arrogance. Now, she just wanted him to hurry up. Sitting on the edge of the bed, he removed his shoes and socks, then stood and shucked his shirt, jeans, and Navy issue briefs. All in record time.

He stood before her for several long moments, allowing her to look her fill. He was very tall . . . about six-foot-four, she would guess. His head was almost bald thanks to the SEALs training haircut, but not unattractive since he had a nicely shaped head and a devastatingly handsome face. Black lashes framed compelling blue eyes. A straight nose. Full, well-defined lips. Straight white teeth.

But it was his body that caused her heart to race. He had broad shoulders and muscles everywhere, though not in a bulked-up weight-lifter way. And the erection that stood out from his center was either a compliment to him or to her; either way, it was impressive. And he knew it.

When she arched an eyebrow at him, he shrugged. "I told you that I have my enthusiasm back, sweetling. Aren't you glad?"

"Oh, yeah!"

"Now you," he demanded. "Stand so I can see all of you. And take off that scrap of nothing. Though it is very enticing, I suspect I am enticed enough and soon may embarrass myself like an untried youthling if I get enticed any more than I already am."

With that rambling discourse which amounted to "Hurry up, babe, I'm horny as hell," which should have repulsed her but didn't, she slid off the bed and stood for him, stepping out of her panties. She stood at the bottom of the bed while he stood at the side. She couldn't remember a time in her life when she'd been so unafraid of showing off her body with all its imperfections.

"You know, Max, I'm just as likely to embarrass myself if you don't get on with this," she said with uncharacteristic brashness.

At first he frowned, but once her words sank in, he smiled.

CHAPTER TEN

❧

New World swiving, compared to Old World swiving . . . no comparison!

Ragnor looked and looked and looked at Alison's nude body. Then he looked again. He even walked over to her and circled her body, viewing it from all angles. He didn't touch her. Just looked.

She wore only the gold hoop ear ornaments, which was curiously erotic. Her legs and underarms were hairless.

She was taller than most women and big-boned, her shoulders broader than usual for a female because of all her exercise. Muscles sculpted her upper arms, her back, her thighs and calves, even her buttocks. But she was not all hardness everywhere. He knew from his recent touch that her small breasts were soft, and her belly would be, too. Not to mention her woman folds. For a certainty, there would be softness there . . . plus muscles, he hoped, imagining how they could grasp his manpart. In essence, she was built like no other woman in his experience, and he had seen plenty.

As an added benefit, not that he needed extras, her nether hair was red, too. He smiled. Ever did he favor red-haired women, especially when they were red all over.

For a brief second, he thought of his brother Torolf. How Ragnor would love to regale him with tales of this human

goddess he had found! How he would boast that his woman—
and, yea, he thought of her as his woman—was the best in all
the lands. Torolf no doubt frolicked with his blond Valkyries
in the other world, but Ragnor could not be envious when he
had such a flaming beauty of his own.

"You remind me of those warrior goddesses that legends
speak of in my land."

Her body stiffened with affront.

*Why is it that women are so sensitive about their bodies?
It is true in every land where I have traveled. Do we men
ask if our teeth are yellow, or our buttocks too fat, or our
armpits too stinksome? Nay, we are confident in ourselves.*
"That is a compliment, dearling."

Her body relaxed, but only slightly.

*Perchance she needs another compliment or two. I can
do that.* "Methinks you would give as well as you got in the
bedsport," he observed, continuing to scrutinize her myriad
muscles.

"You better believe it, buster, but I'm beginning to think
you're all flash and no substance, with all this dawdling."

*So much for compliments! Hmmm. She thinks to direct
this loveplay, does she? I think not!* "Not dawdling," he cor-
rected her. "Savoring." *Bloody hell, I am good.*

"Savoring?"

"Anticipating the reward to come." *Very good! How do I
come up with this stuff?* "Do you not engage in foresport in
your land."

"Foreplay? This is your idea of foreplay?" She laughed.

*Is she laughing at me? She'd better not be. She is proba-
bly just happy that she is about to be the recipient of my
lovemaking. I hope.* "Yea, 'tis foresport, as I said. Do you not
tingle, even a tiny bit?"

He stood in front of her, forcing her to look him in the

eye where he could gauge her honesty. "You are tingling, all right," he pronounced.

Her face bloomed with color. "And you? Are you tingling, too?" she asked.

By the gods, I relish a woman with a mind of her own. No molding her to my pattern. She will be what she wants, and that is fine. More than fine. "Like a bell."

He picked her up by the waist and elevated her so they were of even height. "Anxious to move on, are you, wench?" He swept his hands down and behind her, cupping her buttocks from underneath, and touching the wetness between her legs with his fingertips.

She let loose a howl of surprise . . . or outrage . . . or just plain tingling, and tried to squirm out of his embrace. He laughed and launched them both onto the bed, which creaked noisily but held up under their combined weight. She tried to move so that she would be on top, but he pressed her back to the mattress.

Then he did what he had been yearning to do since she'd walked through that water spray at the drinking hall. He put his mouth to first one breast, then the other, bringing the nipples to hardness. As he suckled hard and rhythmically on their pebbled tips, she arched high off the bed and keened out her pleasure. *If she was not tingling before, she is now, I warrant.*

He was about to move lower, to skim his lips over the smooth skin of her abdomen and belly, but she grabbed hold of both his ears and held him fast. "Don't . . . you . . . dare . . . stop," she gasped out.

He tried to raise his head and tell her that her wish was his command, but not only did she press his face to her bosom, tightly, but she wrapped her legs around his waist to hold him fast, also tightly. *Not a bad position to be in!*

So, like any good soldier, he did as commanded. He wet her nipples. He blew them dry. He nipped them with his teeth. And flicked them with his fingertips. He massaged both breasts at the same time. He took practically a whole breast in his mouth and sucked her hard against the roof of his mouth.

The whole time she undulated her hips against him and whispered encouraging words, like, "Yes. There. Harder, dammit. Oh, my God! I think . . . I think . . . ooohhh!"

With a long wail of bliss, she reached her peak, just from his ministering to her breasts. *What a woman!*

But now, after putting on such a wanton show, she buried her face in the crook of his neck like a shy maiden. He felt a wetness on his skin. "What? You cry for what purpose?"

She refused to let him draw back to look at her.

"I'm embarrassed. How pathetic you must think me. To come just by being touched a little bit."

That was not a little bit of touching. That was a lot, milady. And if "come" means what I think it means, here I come . . . any second now. So enough talking! "Hey, I almost peaked, too, and you haven't even touched me . . . yet. Do you want to? Touch me, that is?" He jiggled his eyebrows at her.

And she did. The witch! She took hold of his member and tried to guide him between her spread legs. He closed his eyes for a second as stars exploded in his head. *What is it about women grabbing hold of my manpart? First Inga. Now her. Ouch!* "Whoa, whoa, whoa!" he said, carefully extracting himself from her grip, which had actually been rather gentle. "Can you help me put on a cone-dome?"

"Huh?" she said.

And people in this land think I am dumb! Without moving himself off her body, he leaned over the side of the bed and reached for his den-ham *braies.* From one of the side pockets he extracted the silvery packets and dumped them on the mattress.

Her eyes went wide before she hooted with laughter. "You brought ten condoms with you tonight? Are you sure that's enough?"

How would I know if it's enough? I do not even know how they work. Or if one or several are worn at a time.

"You expected to get lucky tonight? Talk about overconfidence!" A glimmer of teasing danced in her green eyes.

"I brought them 'just in case,' not because I expected anything." His words sounded defensive, even to him.

She tore one of the packets open with her teeth. Then she did the most amazing thing. She rolled a thin sheath over his cock, like a second skin.

"Holy bloody damn hell and Valhalla!" he exclaimed at the intense pleasure that shot through him. He blew out a few short breaths to regain his self-control.

Then he did what he was meant to do . . . his destiny. He plunged inside her hot, clasping folds, to the hilt, and let loose with a wild Viking yell of victory, or defeat, or just plain wonder at the magic of the gods-given gift of sex. One thing was certain. He was tingling.

Meanwhile, she stared at him with horror that her insides were clasping and unclasping and clasping and unclasping him in welcome. The talented wench reached another peak, praise be to Frey.

He must be doing a wonderful job of pleasuring her. Or was the talent all with her? Either way, he couldn't wait to see what he . . . or she . . . would do next.

Leaning down, he brushed her lips with his, then braced himself on taut arms over her. Still imbedded in her, he feared that any move on either of their parts would end the game too soon. "Do . . . not . . . move," he warned.

"As if I could!" she replied on a soft moan.

He closed his eyes and tried to think of nonsexual things. Like smelly lutefisk. Like cleaning out his moats. Like Madrene's nagging. Like an ugly boil he'd once seen on a bull's arse. Like grains of sand blowing in a desert storm.

"What are you doing?"

"Counting," he rasped out.

"My blasted orgasms?" she inquired with self-deprecation. "That's just great!"

He opened his eyes. She stared up at him through eyes as green as a rare Norse pasture. Her red curls were tousled in wanton fashion. Her swollen lips bespoke his passionate kisses. Her inner folds no longer moved around his manpart, but they encased him like a tight glove.

"Your peaks are my pleasure," he informed her. And that was the truth. If women only knew what a tribute their arousal was to a man's ego!

"What a nice thing to say. But I think you've peaked me out."

"You have not yet begun to peak," he assured her.

"Please! That is such a macho thing to—"

He spread her thighs wider with his own thighs, then forced her knees up almost to her chest, thus allowing him to slide even deeper inside her.

She gasped and stared at him in disbelief. Reaching up with both hands, she brushed her fingertips across his nipples. He arched his neck backward at the extreme pleasure-pain that mere caress caused. Then he forced her hands away, holding them above her head on the mattress.

"You didn't like that?" She cocked her head to the side in question.

"I loved that, but I am hanging by my fingernails from a

cliff, sweetling, and I must needs control this bedsport. This time, leastways."

"Oh, you *must needs*, huh?" With a choked laugh, she put her feet on the bed and arched up her hips, pushing him upward as well, which required great strength. Then she did the most incredible thing. Deliberately, she made her woman channel milk him. Three times in a row she did this. His eyes nigh crossed in his head. No longer could he control the sap that ran hot and heavy through his body.

As slowly as he could, he withdrew from her, then thrust inside again, slowly.

She whimpered.

He did it again.

She whimpered again.

Over and over he rocked in and out of her tight channel till beads of sweat covered his brow and the wet sound of their slick coupling was like music of the most erotic sort.

"Faster," she urged.

He went slower. "Do you like that?"

"Oh, yes! Just like that."

He tried a different way.

"Again."

He went back to the first way. 'Twas always best to remind a woman who was in charge in the bedplay.

"Please."

"Ah, I thought you'd never ask. Like this?"

"Ohmigod, yes! Do it again."

He did, and then some. He continued to thrust in and out of her, long strokes that were becoming shorter and harder. She locked her heels around his buttocks, trying to get more of him. He had no more to give.

This time on his withdrawal, he paused, reached between

their bodies, and lightly strummed that engorged bud buried in her woman-fleece. She screamed and began to buck wildly till he took her hard, hard, hard.

With a sort of hysterical irrelevance, he recalled being bored in the midst of swiving Inga and any number of women the past few years. He recalled wishing it just to be over. Not so with Alison. Now he wanted it to last forever.

But alas and alack, he was only a man, and all good things must come to an end. He might have screamed then, too, but he could not be sure, so overpowering was his release. Over and over he spurted his hot seed till he became light-headed with ecstatic torture. Even then, his body continued to thrust into her with reflexive after-spasms.

For a long time, he lay atop the panting wench, trying to regain his breath. When he finally raised his head and gave her a quick kiss of thanks, he told her, "You were wonderful." As an afterthought, he added, "I was wonderful."

"*We* were wonderful," she said.

And that was the truth.

She tied him up in knots . . . literally . . .

Max had fallen asleep almost immediately.

SEALs trainees learned special fast eye-movement exercises which allowed them to practically fall asleep at will, taking advantage of five-minute catnaps when necessary, even standing up. Still, the guy had to be physically exhausted from the sleep deprivation that was typical of SEALs training. Plus, she credited herself with some of the depletion that had knocked him out cold.

Snoring lightly, he lay on her bed, totally relaxed, as only a man who'd just been truly laid could do. His arms were tossed over his head in complete abandon. His legs were spread a bit. Even at rest, his penis was half erect.

He filled her bed—took it over, actually. Alison should have felt as if he'd invaded her space, now that the explosive passion had waned. But oddly, she liked the way he looked there. Truthfully, a foolish part of her felt as if he belonged there.

Would any man have done tonight? She doubted it.

She was happy, that was all she knew, and she had Max to thank for that unexpected bonus to her night out on the town. Not just for the sex, which had been spectacular; good heavens, the guy took staying power to a whole new level. Sixty-minute man, for sure! But that was not why she was so thankful . . . or not totally. Somehow, Max had helped her close a chapter on her old life by reminding her that she was a young, healthy woman. Five years of mourning were ended. Just like that. She would always miss David, but life moved on. Max had helped her see that.

She put her panties and bra back on and went into the bathroom. When she returned, he opened his eyes and said, "Come back to bed, sweetling."

She smiled at the clear invitation in his eyes. He was still lying on his back, totally relaxed, with his arms upraised. Even the hairs on his underarms were attractive to her. Talk about total sex appeal!

She had something she wanted to say to him. So she sat down on the edge of the bed near the bottom, wanting to put some distance between them.

He grinned at her obvious distancing maneuver.

"Thank you, Max," she said, wanting to get that out of the way right off.

He arched his eyebrows at her. "Thank *you*."

"Not for that. I mean, yes, for *that*, but not exactly."

He chuckled at her floundering. He probably affected lots of women that way.

"What I'm trying to say is that you helped me forget for a little while tonight. More than that, I'm finally going to be able to stop dwelling on the past and what might have been."

He nodded his understanding.

"And while I'm thanking you, I also have to apologize," she added, feeling her face heat up at what she needed to say. "I'm really embarrassed over my behavior with you. Jeesh! You must think I'm really pitiful. I mean, I never lose control. But I did tonight . . . more than once."

"Three times," he told her bluntly. *The cad!* "But you are not to feel bad about that. It is a woman's role to lose control in the bedsport and the man's role to maintain control."

"That is the most macho drivel I have ever heard!"

"You do not believe that?"

"I do not believe that."

"Well, I admit that some men . . . weaker men than we Vikings . . . have less control over their bodies. Not me, though."

"You are so full of it!"

"I can prove it."

"How?"

"There is naught you can do that would force me to lose control . . . unless I chose to do so."

Is he teasing me? Setting me up? Hmmm. He appears to honestly believe his own hype.

"But do not feel bad about that, dearling. It is the way of the world. Men lead, women follow."

She growled her displeasure at his words.

The clueless twit just rolled over onto his side and beckoned her to come to him with a wagging forefinger.

She considered giving him a different finger. "Listen, buddy, I grew up in an all-male house. My mother died when I was eight. There was only my dad and my three brothers. If there is one thing a tomboy like me understands, it's the lure of a dare. Are you daring me to prove that you can maintain control . . . no matter what?"

"Of course not. I would not be so unfair." He still beckoned her with his finger. His erect penis was doing some beckoning of its own. "I know that you could not win such a dare. The advantage is all mine."

Ooooh, you are gonna get it. "You are going to be so embarrassed," she warned, moving over to her dresser, where she rooted through a drawer.

"What are you searching for, sweetling?"

"These," she said, turning and holding up a handful of silk scarves.

"What? You are going to dance for me? As appealing as that may be, it will not cause me to lose control."

"Dance? What are you talking about?"

"I saw some Eastern women in a harem who used scarves to dance about on soft carpets. Except they were in a tent, not a wooden keep like this."

"A harem, huh?" she said skeptically. "No, I'm not going to dance."

"Too bad for me." He put on an exaggeratedly sad face.

"I'm going to tie you up."

"Really?" He brightened at that news. "Why?"

"Because this time when we make love, it will be *my* way. I'm making sure of that."

"And you thought I would object to your way. Why?"

"Oh, not object, per se . . . just take over. As you said, you're accustomed to being a leader instead of a follower.

It's about time you had the tables turned on you. Are you game?"

He nodded hesitantly.

And so Alison, who hadn't had sex for five years and was making up for it bigtime, tied the big guy's arms to the headboard posts and his spread legs to the side boards.

His half erection was no longer half.

CHAPTER ELEVEN

*C*ome here, my dear," said the fox to the pigeon . . .
    Women were so simple. For the love of Frigg! They believed everything a man told them, no matter how outlandish.

I mean, really! Even a halfwit knows that a man's body is designed to lose control at the slightest provocation. A maiden's smile. The twitch of a curvy arse. Breasts, legs, woman-fleece, the small of a slender back, softness, hardness, toes, eyelashes, just about anything turns a man's brain to porridge. I remember the time Torolf's sap started running just from watching Dagne Hildedottir eat a carrot.

Ragnor smiled to himself as he observed Alison preparing to make him lose control. He'd baited the trap and lured her in slowly with his subtle dare. Not every man would have been able to succeed at such. But then, he was a Viking.

In truth, he could break these bonds in an instant, if he wanted . . . which he did not want. It wasn't that her knots were tied inexpertly. But he was strong. He could pull the bed posts out if necessary.

"So, do you engage in bondage often?" he inquired lazily.

She smiled as she tied the last of her knots on his left ankle. "Hardly. Like, not ever." Then she asked him, "And you?"

"I can honestly say that no one has ever tied me up afore. Not an enemy in battle. Not a woman in bed-play." *But I am willing to try anything.*

"A first for both of us, then," she said, clapping her hands together with mock exuberance.

"And I have never tied up a woman either, in case you are interested in that information," he added.

She blushed prettily, though she pretended his comment did not disconcert her. "Maybe later."

Lucky, lucky, lucky, that is what I am tonight. Thor must be paying me back for that lost battle. "Have I told you how much I like your body?" he asked. She was wearing scant undergarments, including the chastity belt on top. They were erotic in the way they called attention to her womanparts.

"About five or ten times," she said, clearly pleased by his compliment. "I like your body, too." She blushed some more at that admission.

Well, who would not? "Really?" He knew he had a good body, but it was always nice to hear it. And it was especially gratifying to hear it from Alison. He wanted to please her, in all ways.

"How do you feel about peanut butter and honey?" she asked suddenly.

"Huh?" How did they get from good bodies to food? "I mean, I like honey well enough. As to that other, I do not know. Why?"

"You've never had a peanut butter and honey sandwich? Aaaaah, you are in for a real treat. I suspect you're a sugar-holic, like me, if your appreciation for Lillian's cake was any indication."

She left the bedchamber and soon returned with a tray, which she placed on the bedside table. First, she broke off a piece of the sand-witch. It contained two slices of soft white bread with a brown paste and honey inside. He wasn't so sure about that brown paste, which resembled something a babe might emit into a nappy. But before he could voice that concern, she shoved it in his mouth.

He sighed. "You are right. It is surely an ambrosia of the gods."

"Hmmm. Maybe I need a taste."

He thought she would take a bite of the sand-witch, but no, she reached for a glass container and dipped her finger inside, coating it heavily in the brown paste. Then she proceeded to drizzle honey on top from a miniature bear with a nozzle in its head. Next, she proceeded to spread the combination all over his lips. And these substances, unlike what had been on the sand-witch, were warm and liquidy. They must have been heated in her kitchen.

This is not much of a sex game so far. "I thought you said you wanted a taste. Oh." *On the other hand . . .*

She leaned forward and began to lick at his mouth. Wide swipes of her tongue at first. Then nibbles. Then, without warning, she plunged her tongue inside to taste him. If he could have, he would have shot up into a sitting position, so intense was the pleasure-shock of her invasion.

For the first time, Ragnor began to wonder if he was the fox or the pigeon in this game.

"How does it . . . rather I . . . taste?" he asked as calmly as he could. He hoped she didn't glance downward because then she would see just how un-calm he was.

She did.

He moaned inwardly.

She winked at him. The saucy wench. Then said, "I'm not sure how it . . . rather you . . . tastes. Perhaps I need more of a taste."

And the wily wench knelt on the mattress between his

spread thighs and slathered both of his nipples with the gooey mess. The bed linens and their bodies would be sticky with the concoction by the time this exercise was finished, but not to worry! She made quick work of licking him, and biting him, and then—Help-me-gods!—sucking him over and over and over till he nigh bolted against his restraints. *Yea, Thor is really, really sorry for not coming to my aid in that battle.* Meanwhile, maintaining self-control was proving harder than he'd expected.

"How's your self-control?" she asked, peering up at him from his wet nipples with the seeming innocence of a born siren.

What self-control? "Just fine," he lied. "How's yours?"

"Fair to middlin', honey. By the way, how many times did I 'embarrass' myself before?"

"Three," he answered hesitantly. "Why?"

"Tit for tat, skippy," she hooted gleefully.

"What does that mean?"

"It means, sweetheart, that you are going to come three times before I'm done with you."

"Three times!" He tried to laugh, but it came out as choking. Finally he managed to say, "Sweetling, I am good but not that good. Oh, wait. I already peaked once, so two more times. Easy." *Holy Valhalla, when did I become such a braggart?*

"Easy, huh? Sounds like another dare to me. Baby, you have never lost control the way you will tonight."

A little tremor of something approaching fear went through Ragnor then, especially when she made a line with the warm peanut butter and honey from his chest down to his navel and farther still. In fact, she chuckled wantonly before combining a huge gob of both substances on her fingertip and spreading it up one side and down the other and all around the knob of his most appreciative cock.

He tried desperately to say something intelligent, but all he managed was, "Glubfh, glubfh, glubfh . . ."

"Lost any control yet, cupcake?" she asked as she sucked the remaining substance off her finger with a finesse that would do a harem houri proud. Then she began to lick her way to paradise. Paradise to him, leastways.

In the end, she took him in her mouth. And wasn't that just about enough to make his manpart explode and his brain melt? Just before he spurted his seed, she drew back and watched him surrender his self-control.

"Two down, one more to go," she announced triumphantly.

He would have said something brilliant if he could have spoken above a whimper.

While he wheezed like an aged warhorse, she stood and waved jauntily at him. "I'll be right back, sweetie. Don't you go anywhere."

As if he could! He was no doubt stuck to the mattress by the honey-nut paste. He should get up and strip the bed of its linens. He should go into the showering room and wash off the mess. Later, he decided.

She is going to pay for this indignity . . . a mind-boggling, wonderful indignity but indignity nonetheless. Yea, she had "embarrassed" herself three times, but she was a woman. That was different. He must show her that he held the upper hand. But how?

Hmmm.

He smiled when an idea came to him.

Tit for tat, Viking style . . .

Alison was in the bathroom. After cleansing herself of the peanut butter and honey paste residue, she prepared a soapy washcloth, a wet rinsing cloth, and towels to take back to the bedroom. Time to clean up the boy before moving on to Round Three. She would get fresh bed sheets from the linen closet on the way.

She looked in the medicine-cabinet mirror, well pleased with herself. Her red hair was a mess of curls. Her cheeks were flushed. Her erect nipples pressed against the thin lace of her bra. She was excited beyond belief at how she'd been able to make Max lose control and what was yet to come . . . pun intended.

She hadn't had so much fun in years.

"Your friend Lillian came home."

She jumped at the voice behind her, and saw Max leaning against the jamb of the open doorway . . . a door she had specifically shut before coming in here moments ago. "What . . . what did you say?"

"I said that Lillian came home. You probably didn't hear her or the barking dog because the water was running in here. She popped in to get Sam and tell you she would lock up."

"Did she see you?" she asked, glancing pointedly at his bare body, particularly one part.

He just grinned.

Strolling past her, he whacked her on the bottom with an open palm, then proceeded to spread his legs and pee into the toilet. *Men! They have absolutely no modesty.*

Afterward, he shoved her aside with his hip and washed his hands in the sink, then used the washcloth to wipe off his mouth, and the trail her peanut butter and honey journey had followed. The whole journey!

Meanwhile, she just stood there like a dunce watching him. Belatedly she realized that he'd freed himself from her scarves . . . easily, considering how soon he'd followed her

into the bathroom. The implications of that realization seeped
in slowly. Finally she said, in a choked voice, "You let me do
all those things to you when you could have gotten untied at
any point along the way. Didn't you?"

He shrugged.

"Why?"

"Do you need to ask, sweetling?"

"Now I'm really embarrassed."

"Me, too." He was wiping his hands on a dry towel. "Ready
to try for three?" he inquired lazily.

Which would probably mean four for me. Holy cow!

Back to leaning against the door jamb, he clearly intended
to block her exit in case she tried to bolt, which she was considering.

"Actually, Max, it's oh-three-hundred. I'm thinking you'd
better head on back to the base before you get into trouble."
*Not that I want you to. Nope, I've got visions of sugar in my
mind, and I don't mean plums.*

"I don't have to leave for at least an hour," he contended.
"There's a lot to be done before then."

Okay, time to call the Macho Man's bluff. "Like what,
hot stuff?"

"Like showing you the famous Viking S-Spot."

"Don't you mean G-Spot?"

"Nay. The S-Spot is a Viking invention, far better than
the G-Spot." He made a face of mock lasciviousness at her.
Or maybe not so mock.

"Is it on the man or the woman?" She pretended indifference. *Like I'm fooling anyone!*

"It is *in* the woman, but only a Viking man can find it.
With his tongue." He smiled lazily at her.

"You're teasing me."

"Dost think so? Is that a dare, milady?"

"No, no, no! I wouldn't dream of any more dares tonight. I've had enough dares for one day. In fact—"

But it was already too late. Max picked her up in his arms and carried her back to the bedroom, whispering wicked, wicked things in her ear the whole time.

Exactly one half hour later, Alison discovered that the Viking S-Spot was indeed better than any mere G-Spot. And she "embarrassed" herself for the fourth time that night.

But then, Max hit three and a half—*who knew there could be half an orgasm?*—which he'd declared was *not* a record for him. Six had been his top performance, or so he claimed, but he'd been eighteen at the time and trying to outdo his brother. A dare, you could say.

God bless dares.

Not a bad performance for a thousand-year-old man! . . .

Ragnor sat at the kitchen table, fully dressed, eating the rest of the chocolate cake, washed down by a can of mead. After a night of strenuous sex play, there was naught better than a hearty meal.

While he ate and drank, he studied an odd parchment document he'd found hanging from Alison's cold box. The sheets were attached to each other with the individual pages divided into numerous blocks with numbers that had a significance he could not comprehend. Although he was getting better at understanding the Saxon English spoken here, much of the written word still puzzled him.

Alison was fast asleep in her bedchamber, thanks to his fine work. And it had been his finest work, he thought with a grin. She had an S-Spot for sure, and he'd had the pleasure of helping her discover it, over and over. The gods knew what they were doing when they blessed men with the occasional uninhibited woman. He grinned some more.

He heard a rustling in the bedchamber and the padding of feet to the bathing chamber. "Oh, my God!" he heard her exclaim. She'd probably looked in her mirror and seen what he'd seen . . . the face of a woman who had been good and truly tupped. Bed-mussed hair, whisker-rasped cheeks, and chin, bruised mouth. Every man's fantasy lover.

"What are you reading?" she asked, walking into the kitchen a short time later. Her short hair had been wetted down and combed off her face. She must have applied some tinted ointment to hide the redness of her skin, though there was no hiding the kiss-swollen lips. Barefoot, she wore a big, thigh-length tea-ing *shert* with the words "Navy Brat" on the front.

He glanced down at the document in front of him and said, "I do not know. What is this?"

She walked closer. "A calendar." Then she frowned at him. "Why wouldn't you know what a calendar is? Every country in the world has a calendar to record the days of the month."

He frowned now, too. "But ne'er have I seen one in parchment form. Oh, I suppose the monk scholars keep track of time in their manuscripts. And farmers certainly need to follow the seasons. But this . . ." His words trailed off.

He was still confused, but more than that, he sensed that something important was about to happen. And it related to this calendar. Mayhap he was about to discover exactly what country he was in and why he had been spared death to be sent here.

"What is that?" he asked, pointing at some letters at the top.

"The name of the month. This is August." She flipped through various pages and remarked, "September, October, November."

"And those words?"

"Days of the week. Sunday, Monday, Tuesday, and so on. Max, you are really starting to scare me. You seem to have this Swiss-cheese kind of memory, where commonplace things have slipped through. I'm beginning to think I need to report you as a medical risk."

He ignored her misgivings and continued his questioning. "And what is this number at the top?"

"The year."

It was almost as if he rose outside his body then. He could see his own eyes widen with shock. He saw his mouth drop open on a gasp. He saw his body go rigid, braced for some death blow. But then he came to himself and said, "That is impossible. It is the year one thousand and ten."

"No, it is not, and stop fooling around. It's not funny."

"Do I look as if I'm laughing? If what you say is true, then I am more than a thousand years old. Or—oh, holy Thor! Could it be I have traveled a thousand years forward in time? That must be it. I cannot believe it. I do not believe it. But it answers so many questions."

"Max, there is no such thing as time-travel."

"I would think not under normal circumstances, but I am increasingly convinced that time-travel must be the answer. Inside," he said, patting his hand over his heart, "I sense that I have finally been given an answer."

"I repeat, there is no such thing as time-travel."

"I repeat, give me another explanation. I was born in the year nine hundred eighty-three. I live on the family estate at Norstead. I am a trained warrior, and a good one. I own a fleet of twenty longships. I am a far-traveled adventurer. My sister Madrene runs the family farmstead nearby. I was twenty-seven in the year one thousand and ten. I went to battle with Svein Forkbeard, king of the Danes. During the battle, he fled, but all his other ships and four of mine as well were lost to the bloody Saxons. I drowned. I swear I did. Or leastways, I thought I did. When I awakened, your brother the chieftain was holding my head underwater."

He kept shaking his head, as if to shake free of this most outlandish notion. *Time-travel? Me? Impossible!* But it was the first thing that made sense to him in the past sennight of senseless happenings.

"I'll give you another explanation," she said, sitting down in the chair next to him and patting his forearm with compassion. "You had a severe head wound. Scientists still don't know everything about the effects of head wounds. Sometimes they defy logic. For example, there was that American woman who had been in a coma for a long time, and when she awakened she had no memory *and* she spoke with a British accent."

"Is that supposed to reassure me?"

"No, I'm just saying there is a logical explanation for what is happening to you, but we don't know what it is yet."

"I never had a head wound and have no scars to prove it," he insisted.

"Maybe you're a quick healer."

"Pfff!" was his opinion of her theory. "If this is the year and the century you say it is, then I have time-traveled. I am not barmy. Confused, yea. Shocked, yea. But I am not yet demented."

Just then the tell-a-fone rang, jarring them both. Who would be calling her at this late hour?

"Hello," she said, picking up the black box on the cabinet

top. "Yes. Yes. Okay, he'll be right down." She replaced the black box on its holding tray, then looked at him. "That was your friend Cage. He's downstairs in a taxi, waiting to take you back to the base. He says it's important that you guys return right away."

"How can I go back now when I have just discovered that I am a time-traveler?" *Besides, with a little convincing, I might be able to manage another peaking.*

"You are not a time-traveler. Max, you have to go back. Otherwise, you are going to land in a hospital or the brig. Either way, you will be out of SEALs."

He waved a hand dismissively. "What do I care about SEALs when I have this more important issue to resolve?"

"There is nothing you can do tonight. Go back. Don't act hastily. I'll talk to you sometime tomorrow."

"Perchance that is best, as you say. My father always said that unplanned actions always lead to disaster, though I do not see what could possibly be more disastrous than this."

Within moments, though, he was walking out of the apartment with Alison and down the stairs. They must have awakened Sam, who was barking loudly behind Lillian's closed door. Ragnor opened the front door and waved to Cage that he would be right out.

Then, in the open doorway, he kissed Alison farewell, lifting her up onto her toes. "There will be other nights," he said against her mouth.

"Maybe," she replied dreamily, leaning up for another kiss. *No maybes about it!*

The driver of the yellow car beeped his horn.

Ragnor ignored the interruption and told her again, "There will be other nights." Setting her away from himself, he told her, "Go inside and lock the doors after you, both of them. I will watch till you are safe inside."

She did as he asked, and he took great pleasure in watching the sway of her arse up the steps, an arse he'd had the good fortune to become intimately familiar with tonight. Despite everything that had happened to him . . . or seemed to have happened . . . he could not be unhappy about tonight and his connection with this woman.

With a grin, he walked to the car and got inside to see an equally grinning Cage.

"Got lucky, did you, buddy?"

"More than you know."

CHAPTER TWELVE

❦

Sweeping the enemy with . . . brooms? . . .

By the time Ian arrived at his office Monday morning, the pile of paperwork on his desk had reached monumental proportions. A Master Chief's bane!

He'd been in D.C. over the weekend visiting his father and as usual suffering the constant exhortation that he go to officers' candidate school. Being the highest-ranking enlisted man never had been good enough for Admiral MacLean. His father raised guilt tripping to new heights. In the end, Ian had told dear ol' Dad that he'd think about it seriously, but dammit, he was happy where he was now. His personal life was the pits, but professionally, he was okay.

Two days away from the base should have resulted in rest and relaxation, but he'd returned with the mother of all headaches. Which was about to get worse.

Right off, he noticed that among the stack of memos was an urgent request from that goofball Magnusson that he see him as soon as possible. Six times he'd come in! And it was only ten A.M.

First, he had to take care of some more important matters. Like, how the hell would he know why thirty-seven broom handles had disappeared from the various SEAL trainee buildings? Maybe someone had developed a cleaning fetish. Jeesh!

Just then, his aide, Seaman Rogers, rushed in. "Excuse me, Master Chief, sir. Welcome back. Sorry to barge in, but, holy frickin' hell, you gotta come out to the Grinder and see what Magnusson is doin'." The expression on the young man's face was a mixture of amazement and bust-a-gut amusement.

Ensign Flaherty, one of the SEAL instructors, poked his head in and added, "At least we now know what happened to all the broom handles." Flaherty was laughing so hard he could barely speak.

"Broom handles, huh? And Magnusson? What have we got here?" Ian inquired, not so amused, as he rose from his chair and proceeded to follow what ended up being a stream of chuckling men leaving the SEAL offices and heading for the exercise arena. "A Viking Mary Poppins?" He couldn't help chuckling at his own joke.

He stopped dead in his tracks a short time later, no longer chuckling.

"Good God!" someone said behind him.

"Don't blame God," Ian countered, without turning around. He still stared bug-eyed at the spectacle before him. "God invented intelligence; man invented stupidity; Magnusson took stupidity to a new level."

Magnusson was standing alone at one end of the field while forty feet away his teammates were lobbing broom handles at him, like spears. But instead of the spears hitting him, Magnusson was deftly catching them in a hand, one at a time, twirling them about in the fingertips of the same hand, and sending the spears back to his "attackers," all within seconds.

Seaman Rogers informed Ian, "He says it's a trick he learned in the Norselands from his grandfather, a jarl named Eric Trygvasson, and Eric's brother Olaf."

"Not that it matters, but what in God's name is a jarl?"

Rogers shrugged. "Hell if I know. Something like an earl, I think. Anyhow, Magnusson says this trick comes in handy when attacked by a troop of spear men."

"Now this trick I learned from my great-uncle King Olaf," Magnusson yelled to his teammates.

A king now? As if anyone here gives a rat's ass if he's related to a king or the Pope or Genghis Khan.

Now he was throwing two spears at once and aiming them directly at the chests of Cage and Pretty Boy, who presumably were supposed to twist them agilely in their fingertips and fling them back at the dingbat. Instead, the two SEAL trainees ducked. *Smart men!* But even before the double spears had sailed over their heads, Magnusson threw another set. A regular spear-throwing machine he was. His teammates were laughing and ducking like crazy.

Men all around him were laughing like crazy, too, and some were actually impressed. Meanwhile, jackhammers were doing the rumba in MacLean's head.

Enough of this nonsense! "Magnusson! Get your hairy butt over here! I swear you are going to be in Gig Squad till graduation . . . if you last that long."

"Dost speak to me?" he asked, genuinely puzzled.

Ian wanted to cross his eyes in frustration. If ever he was inclined to shake a trainee silly, this was the time. "Of course I'm speaking to you. Who else would think nothing of stealing thirty-seven broom handles, making a spectacle of himself, and taking time away from real training exercises?"

"I do not have hairy buttocks . . . leastways, that I am aware of. That is why I wondered if you addressed me, or some other person with hairy hindquarters."

Ian did cross his eyes then.

"And it is not a waste of time to demonstrate a skill which could be handy during battle," the numbskull argued.

"Seen a lot of broom handles in battle lately?" MacLean asked several SEAL instructors who stood next to him, lips twitching with suppressed laughter.

"Not a one," Ensign Brown answered.

"You missay me, chieftain," Magnusson had the nerve to reply. "Not broom handles. Spears."

"Seen a lot of spears in battle lately?" Ian asked the SEAL instructors.

"Nope," they answered as one, still fighting laughter.

"Come with me," he ordered Magnusson. "Not that I would mind chewing your ass out in public, but you have pushed some boundaries today that are going to take at least an hour for me to detail for you, and I don't plan on doing it standing in this hot sun."

After a brief discussion with the instructors about the morning program, Ian set off for his office with Magnusson trailing behind him. Well, not behind him. The idiot caught up with him and walked alongside him, as if they were equals.

"Actually, there are some things I need to discuss with you, too, Chieftain," Magnusson said.

"I know. You came into my office six times this morning."

"Where were you?"

"Out of town. Not that it's any of your business."

"Well, truth to tell, it is my business when your sister is involved."

Ian stopped stock-still and turned slowly to glare at the

ensign. "Am I going to have to hit you for mentioning my sister's name?"

Magnusson frowned. "I do not know. I mean, I would not let you hit me. But, yea, you might want to hit me. I did compromise your sister, but my intentions are honorable."

Ian growled. He was pretty sure he knew what compromise Magnusson referred to, and he was equally sure he did not want to know for sure. What could his sister be thinking, to involve herself with this joker? Never one to avoid trouble, Ian took a deep breath and demanded, "Explain yourself, and make it quick."

"Could we not do this in private?" Magnusson asked.

Ian realized that they were drawing curious stares from passersby. He continued to walk.

"I am worried about Alison."

"Alison?" Ian said so softly it sounded like a shout to Ragnor's ears. "You dare to use her given name? She's your freakin' superior officer." The compromise was becoming clearer and clearer to Ian, and the ramifications could be ominous for both his sister and the SEAL trainee.

Magnusson waved a hand airily.

"Why are you worried about my sister?" They entered MacLean's office, and he slammed the door loudly behind them. He sank down into the chair behind his desk, mainly to put some distance between them. He couldn't recall a time when he'd been so tempted to wring a man's neck, except maybe for the slimeball that had screwed his fiancée when he'd been OUTCONUS on a field op.

Magnusson, ignoring protocol, sat down in the chair in front of Ian's desk and sighed wearily. Apparently, broom-handle tossing was hard work. "When I was at her keep last night, there was a man loitering in the side courtyard. That on top of the stalking telephone calls, and her quarters hav-

ing been entered on another occasion. Even though she called
the policing man for help, I believe she needs guarding. And
not just from that puny dog of her landlady's, either."

Ian pressed the fingertips of both hands to his eyeballs in
a futile effort to calm his pounding brain. Besides, if his
hands remained idle, he just might leap over the desk and
throttle him-who-had-no-brain.

Taking Ian's silence for permission to proceed, the dimwit did just that. "I understand that our SEAL teams will be
going to jump school soon in far off George-hah, though I
find it hard to believe that jump school is what Cage tells me
it is. Surely you would not make your soldiers jump out of
the sky and float to the earth like bloody birds. I for one refuse to kill myself by splattering my body in a thousand
pieces; a sword to the heart would be preferable, if you ask
me. Besides . . ." His words trailed off as he noticed Ian's
red face and bulging eyes. He concluded quickly, "That is why
I needed to speak with you. Together we must needs come
up with a plan to smoke out Alison's enemy, and to keep her
safe whilst doing so."

"Do they ever shut up on your planet, Magnusson?"

"Huh?"

"There is a rule about holes."

"Is this another of your bloody motivating sayings?"

Ian glared at him, though he had to smile inside, knowing how the trainees felt about his irritating motivational
quotes. "As I was saying, the thing about holes is, if you are
in one, stop your damn digging."

"Huh?" the dingo said again.

Ian counted to ten silently, then said icily, "Let me see if I
understand you. One, you were in the home of a superior officer of the opposite sex last night for reasons I do not want to
know. Definitely a high-level infraction of Navy rules. Two,

I was aware of the Breather phone calls Alison received in the past, but you are saying they continue and that her apartment was broken into, police were called, and that last night you personally saw a man in her yard. But no one thought to let me know, least of all my sister. Three, there is a guard dog at Alison's house that I was unaware of. Four, you are telling me that you do not *choose* to go to jump school. Is that the whole friggin' story, Mister Good News?"

"Well, there is one little other thing."

"I am afraid to ask."

"It appears I am a time-traveler."

Ian grinned. *What a fruitcake!*

"And methinks your sister is my destiny."

Ian started to laugh then, and once started, could not stop. What else could he do?

Clean sweep it was not . . .

By mid-afternoon, Ragnor had run from one end of the Coronado beach to the other at least a hundred times, had completed endless numbers of pushing-ups and jump-in-jacks, had survived the O-Course three times including the Slide for Life, climbed a rope wall as tall as a small mountain five times, having fallen off only twice, and had sand in every wrinkle and orifice of his battered body. In between, he'd been in the lean-and-rest position for long periods of time, which involved the body being parallel to the ground with no sag and his weight being held up by his extended arms and tips of his boots. And he'd been told to "hydrate"— which meant drink water from a vessel attached to his belt—so many times that his bladder was about to explode. Still, the chieftain was not satisfied that he'd been punished enough.

And, to give the chieftain and other instructors their due, they were in prime condition, working just as hard as the poor trainees.

The chieftain grumbled now at being forced to give him a reprieve in order for Magnusson to keep his appointment with Doctor Fine-gold. Holy Thor, did he have a lot to tell the head healer!

Nobody had been willing to listen to his claims of time-travel. Mostly they'd just laughed at him or shaken their heads sadly at his assertions. Bloody hell, he couldn't blame them. He could hardly believe it himself.

Actually, his teammates had been more interested in knowing what had happened betwixt him and Dr. MacLean for those missing six hours afore he'd returned to the sleeping hall. Of course, he'd told them nothing. That had not stopped them from speculating in a most crude and rude fashion.

"One hour, Magnusson," the chieftain bellowed at him now. The man had perfected the art of fine bellowing. If he was not careful, the chieftain would burst that vein in his forehead one of these days. By thunder, but he would make a good mate for Madrene. They could nag each other to death. Of course, now that Ragnor believed he had time-traveled, there was the little problem of how to send the chieftain back to Madrene, especially since he hadn't a clue how to get back himself. Besides, he wasn't so sure he wanted to return, now that he'd met Alison. Mayhap he could lure Madrene here by some trickery; she would ne'er leave her beloved farmstead willingly, not even at the prospect of a half-bald, ill-tempered SEAL chieftain for a bed mate. Problems, problems!

"And you'd better be back here ready for advanced surf rescue. We all want to see if you can set any more records for swimming. Ha, ha, ha! And remember, if something is hard, it must be worth doing."

Nag, nag, nag! I swear, if I hear one more miserable in-spirational dirge out of your mouth, Chieftain, I might just see how much sand can be stuffed down that hole. He tried to swagger away from the exercise arena, just to annoy the chieftain, but his legs felt like butter and every muscle in his body burned and his bones actually creaked. So all he managed was a careful walk. Pride was great in him, but by the time he arrived at the medical building, he felt like collapsing.

Then he saw something that made him perk up immediately. Rather, some*one*.

Alison.

Her lips were still kiss-swollen from their love-making of the night before, and he liked to think that her pinkened cheeks showed a blush as she recalled all that they had done. Bloody hell, even he might consider blushing over all they had done. On the other hand, perchance she was having sec-ond thoughts about having been intimate with a thousand-year-old man. And whilst on that subject, he gave himself a mental pat on the back for being so virile at such an old age. *Ha, ha, ha! This is just wonderful. Making jests in my head, and then laughing at my own jests.*

In one hand, Alison carried a parchment sack imprinted with "Noble Barn," or "Barn and Noble," whatever the hell that meant. What a peculiar country, to give nobility to a barn!

But that was neither here nor there. The important thing was Alison, who was headed toward him with steely determi-nation in her green eyes. He did so appreciate a determined woman!

He smiled.

She did not smile back.

Uh-oh!

There is the Triple Crown, and then there is the Triple-S . . .

Alison had awakened that morning with a smile on her face.

No second thoughts. No recriminations over casual sex. Who was she kidding? There had been nothing casual about her encounter with the Viking SEAL trainee. Even during her routine five-mile run before breakfast, she'd kept on smiling. Then she had smiled during a quick stop at a bookstore before heading to work.

No way did she buy Max's time-travel nonsense, but clearly something had happened to his memory as a result of the concussion. She should report his condition to authorities, but that would mean an automatic dismissal from SEAL training. Instead, she'd bought him a bunch of *English as a Second Language* books and audio books on CDs to be played on her old Walkmen which he could use even when sleeping at night. Later, he could get an MP3 player or an Ipod and download books himself. In addition, she'd tossed in some rudimentary math and history books and tapes. If these didn't jog his memory, or if he didn't heal more on his own, she would be forced to take action.

But that was before. This was now. So much for her good mood! Her smile had frozen on her face only seconds into a meeting a few moments ago with her brother. Max, the man she had built so many foolish dreams on, had gone blabbing to her brother. The jerk! Max, not her brother. Well, actually, her brother, too. Why didn't either of them realize that she was a strong woman? She could take care of herself. And if she couldn't, she would be the one to arrange additional security, not either of those Neanderthals.

"You are in such trouble, buster," she said, seething, as she came up to the grinning moron and poked a finger in his

chest. He must have come to his appointment with Dr. Feingold right from the morning exercise evolution because he
wore a grungy T-shirt, equally grungy shorts, and heavy,
scuffed-up boots. His face, neck, and arms were marked by
equal parts perspiration and sand.

Max looked wonderful. And she remembered just how
wonderful he looked under all that grunge. *Aaarrgh!*

"Me? Why am I in trouble, sweetling?" he asked in a silky
purr, coming way too close to her for a public corridor. He put
up a hand and rubbed a strand of her hair between thumb and
forefinger, as if fascinated.

Before he had a chance to lean down and sniff her hair,
which he seemed inclined to do, she shoved him away and
said, "Because you betrayed me, you jerk."

"Me?" He frowned. "How so?"

"By talking about me to my brother. Behind my back."

"Oh, that," he said as if it were nothing.

"Yes, that. Here." She shoved the shopping bag into his
hand. "These are some books and CDs I bought for you . . .
before I realized what a snake you are."

"You bought me a gift?" The expression on his face was
priceless. You would have thought she'd given him a Rolex.

"Don't distract me, you louse. Take the stuff and enjoy it,
because I don't plan on seeing you again."

"Of course we will be seeing each other again," he said,
peering into the bag, then setting it down on the floor.

Before she had a chance to realize what he was about, he
lifted her by the waist, opened a large broom closet behind
her, and walked them both inside. It was as black as coal inside till he pulled the string on the ceiling bulb. He must be
familiar with the broom closet for some reason, she thought.
But that was beside the point. Way beside the point!

"What do you think you're doing?" she squealed as he

backed her up against a rolling utility table, then lifted her up so she sat with her feet dangling off the floor. He shoved her skirt up and stepped between her spread thighs.

"Thanking you," he murmured as he sniffed her hair and murmured something about strawberries, which was the scent of her shampoo.

"For what?" she gasped out. Little tingles of sensation were ricocheting throughout her body just from his breath near her ear.

"Your gift today. Last night. What is about to happen. Take your pick." Now he was outright blowing in her ear, and it felt damn good . . . dammit.

"A simple 'thank you' outside would have sufficed. And get one thing straight—nothing is going to happen now." She tried to turn her face away from the kiss she sensed was coming, but he plowed his big fingers into her hair, holding her face in place.

Then he kissed her.

And she surrendered. Just like that. She couldn't help herself. Like a wanderer in the desert who had been thirsty for too long, she welcomed him. There was no explanation for her behavior. He was just a man, like any other she'd known before. Her heart and her traitorous body didn't see him that way, though. Every time she saw him, even from that day on the grinder when he'd returned without medical permission to BUD/S, it was as if some inner being recognized him, saying, *There you are, sweetheart. I have been waiting for you forever.* And it was the same every time she saw him again. Strange!

"I missed you," he murmured after kissing her into a panting blob of hormones.

"How could you miss me when you've been working out so hard today?" she argued. "I can see that Ian gave you a grueling workout today—as punishment for something or other, I suspect."

"Brooms," he said, of all things, and smiled against her mouth. "Dost think I cannot run and think at the same time? I am a many-talented man."

Boy, do I know how many talents you have! She smiled back against his mouth. "I'm mad at you," she said and nipped his lower lip.

"I'm mad *about* you," he replied. "What are these things anyhow?"

She glanced down and saw that he was running his palms over her stockings from knee to upper thigh and back again. No wonder she'd been tingling in that region! "Stockings. Pantyhose, to be precise. And you've probably put a dozen snags in them with those calluses on your hands."

"How far up do they go?"

There he went again with that stupidity about everyday things. "To the waist."

He groaned. "Another form of chastity belt." She was about to correct him, but he'd raised her skirt and proceeded to pull down her stockings, all the way off, including her high-heeled pumps.

"Max, this is not a good idea. If we get caught in here, we're both going to be busted."

"I am not precisely sure what 'busted' means, but whatever it is, we will be happily busted." With those ominous words, he pulled her butt to the edge of the table, then released a very impressive erection from his shorts and entered her all in one fluid motion.

Her heart practically stopped with the intense pleasure that one stroke generated.

But then he pulled back out. All the way. With horror. And said, "Oops!"

"What do you mean, 'Oops'? Come back here." She tried to grab for him, but he stepped away and held out his arms to keep his distance.

"I didn't use a cone-dome, and I have none with me. Do you perchance have any cone-domes with you?"

"No, I don't have any condoms with me," she replied with visible consternation. "Jeesh, do you think I have sex at work every day?" *Any day?*

"I hope not," he said, then grinned at her. She loved the way he grinned . . . kind of lopsided and sexy. "Not to fear, dearling, I will just have to show you the Viking S-Spot." With those words, he threw her legs over his shoulders, causing her to topple backward onto the table.

"Eeeekkkk! You already showed me the Viking S-Spot," she pointed out with a little gurgle of embarrassment at her vulnerable position.

"Ah, but this will be different. 'Tis the Triple-S, known by only a few Norsemen and used only on very special women . . . those who are strong enough to withstand the torture and worthy enough to be given the gift of supreme ecstasy. Legend says that women are unable to speak afterwards, so intense is the pleasure. Legend also says that the woman is ruined for any other man afterwards, her standards for peaking having been raised so high."

He was right.

Blind man's bluff . . .

Ian was stomping down the hallway of the medical center searching for the blight on his life when a utility-closet door swung open. To his shock, out stepped his sister and the idiot-from-hell. They were pretty freakin' shocked to see him, too.

His sister's hair was mussed and her uniform was wrinkled. In fact, he could see sprinkles of sand in various places, and there were a half-dozen runs in her stockings. The dodo bird was no better. He had a bite mark on his bottom lip, and the look of a man who'd just had his ashes hauled.

"Sonofabitch!" Ian exclaimed.

"Now, Ian . . ." his sister started to say. She, at least, had the good sense to be blushing.

"Chieftain, it is not what you—" dodo bird started to say.

Ian raised both hands to halt the two of them. If he reported this incident, and he should, his sister would lose as much as the dodo bird . . . everything she'd worked so hard for as a woman in the military. He couldn't do that to her. Not without giving her a second chance. "Don't say anything. Either of you. I did not see this. I am a blind man as of five minutes ago."

"Thank you, Ian," she said in a shaky voice.

He nodded his acknowledgment of her thanks. They both knew how difficult it was for him to bend military rules, no matter what was at stake.

"Thank you, Chieftain," the dodo bird added.

"Shut up!" The dodo bird probably didn't have a clue how much personal integrity he was sacrificing to remain quiet.

To both of them, he warned, "Next time, I won't be so blind."

Meanwhile, back at the commune . . . bikers' commune, that is . . .

"How's your head today, Tor?" asked Serenity Morgan, a middle-aged woman with blond hair accented by black roots, which hung down to her leather-clad butt. She had eight rings in each ear, two gold studs in her nose, and tattoos up one arm and down the other. Not surprisingly, she was a tattoo artist.

Her husband, George Morgan, also known as Spike, a former Microsoft engineer who now sold classic Harley parts on the Internet, was equally longhaired, pierced, and tattooed. While Serenity did body art in her spare time, George did body piercings. They lived in a remote commune of thirty-some bikers somewhere in northern California. Actually, it was a cozy trailer park called Hog Heaven. Sort of a commune for bikers.

Torolf shrugged. "My head doesn't hurt anymore, but my memory is still a blank. I sense that I'm running away from something, and that I'm angry, but I have no clue what that might be."

The only way he knew that his name was Torolf Magnusson was because of his driver's license. When they'd found him and his Harley Road King along the side of a rural road two weeks ago, the bikers had decided that his shaved head bespoke a background in the military or prison. They doubted whether it was Hare Krishna or some such cult, because that didn't jibe with the expensive vehicle he'd been driving. In addition, he'd sustained some kind of head wound, which had been stitched and treated, and there was an odd bruising about his neck. Could it be from a prison garroting, or from a neck chain being yanked from his neck by a burglar, or an accident while engaged in some clandestine military op?

The only other items in his wallet were three hundred dollars in cash, a credit card, and a photo showing an older blond-haired version of himself, an older black-haired woman, and a pigload of kids of various ages. Was this his family? If so, he didn't recognize a one of them.

Respecting his privacy, no one in the motorcycle community had tried to contact anyone at the Sonoma address on his license, nor did George use his Internet expertise to do a search on him or that address; these were people who felt a person's past was his or her own business. Thus far, Torolf hadn't felt inclined to call Information for a telephone number attached to the address, either, fearing what he would find out about himself. The memory loss itself and what physical ailment it might signify scared him, too. Also, he'd been having strange, strange dreams the last few nights. In some, he was a Viking in some Dark Age wooden castle, almost instantly morphing into some guy tending a modern-day vineyard, then switching to a sailor in a military-type rubber boat bobbing out at sea, or was it a longship? Every time Torolf tried to reason it out, his head wound started to throb.

For now, he did mechanical work on motorcycles for various residents around Hog Heaven to earn his keep, especially for the Morgans, who'd opened the second bedroom of their RV to him. He didn't know where he'd learned the skill, but somehow he could break down and put back together a Harley with ease. Maybe he'd learned how on his own, as a Harley owner, or maybe he'd been a mechanic.

"You are not to worry about anything," Serenity said, patting him on the shoulder. He was in the process of repairing the trim on one of the RV windows. "Take your time, and everything will eventually fall into place. God has a plan for all of us."

Or the gods, he thought. *Now, where did that idea come from?*

"It's sad that no one has come looking for you, though," Serenity added. "And that's all I'll say on the subject."

Torolf thought it was sad, too. "Perhaps I'm all alone in this world, and no one cares about me."

"We care," Serenity said, tears brimming in her eyes.

He smiled, and it was his turn to pat her on the back. Serenity and Spike had been married for thirty years and had never had any children. He suspected his dropping into their lives fulfilled some need of theirs . . . and his, too.

"What say we go have a beer?" she suggested, swiping at her wet eyes.

"A horn of mead cures many an ill," he replied with forced cheerfulness. *A horn of mead? I really am losing my mind.*

Son of a gun! . . .

"Has that son of mine lost his mind?" Magnus Ericsson raged at his wife Angela for the hundredth time in the past two weeks. "Torolf may be twenty and seven years old, but I swear he is as insensitive as a boyling."

"Now, Magnus, I'm sure he is all right. He'll call when he is able."

"I think I should call him."

"Don't you dare. Torolf specifically said he is not able to take calls. He will contact us when he gets a chance."

"But it is unlike him to go more than two weeks without—"

"No!" she said emphatically. It was one of the things that had attracted him to her from the beginning—her take-no-nonsense attitude.

They were in the Blue Dragon vineyard, checking the status of their latest crop of grapes as they talked. It would be one month till harvest, but every day some new catastrophe might swoop down on them . . . a sudden frost, too much heat, wind, worms, fungus, just about anything.

But the catastrophe he feared most at the moment involved his son Torolf. He had the oddest premonition that all was not as it should be.

"'Twas a demented idea to begin with, his wanting to become a Navy SEAL. Did he not learn from his Uncle Jorund how hard the fighting life can be? Why could he not be content to be a farmer, as I was most of my life, or a vintner as I am now? 'Tis a good life. Bloody hell, even his brief stint as a smoke jumper putting out forest fires was less nerve-wracking than this."

"He has to find his own way, honey," Angela said, reaching up to kiss him fondly on the cheek. Ten years they had been wed now, and he loved her as much or more than when he'd first seen her. In truth, that was what he wished for all his children—love.

She looped her arms around his neck and smiled, as if having read his mind. "You always said that your grandmother believed every man had a woman he was destined to love. Maybe Torolf has finally found his destiny, and he has been too busy to think of us."

"Dost think so?" Magnus asked, hope ringing in his voice. "Yea, that is what it is. Torolf's destiny has finally caught up with him."

CHAPTER THIRTEEN

※

When brothers become a bother . . .
     By the time the security specialists, the police, the
FBI, a private detective, telephone reps, and Lillian had left
her apartment late that afternoon, Alison was ready to pull
out her hair . . . or what little her brother had left.

"This was not necessary, Ian," she insisted, fixing herself a cup of herbal tea—the soothing-the-nerves kind.
Security lighting that would make Lillian's residence resemble a Wal-Mart parking lot, a new unlisted telephone
number and caller I.D., triple-bolt locks, a movement-detection
system . . . holy moly, she feared entering her own apartment. She wouldn't be surprised if Ian had called in Henry
Lee to double check for fingerprints.

Meanwhile, Ian was chowing down on a plateful of
Lillian's white chocolate macadamia nut cookies. "Yes, it
was necessary. And before you protest that you can take care
of yourself, I'm aware of that. But I'm still your brother. And
by the way, thanks for the wallet, even if my birthday's not
till tomorrow."

She made a face at him.

He grinned at her.

"Listen, Allie, it's always better to be safe than sorry. I
can take care of myself, too, but the title for my home in San

Diego is listed under an alias, I use a secure cell phone only when in my home, and I have protective devices throughout the structure. Doesn't mean I'm a scaredy-cat. It means I'm smart."

She exhaled with disgust. "You did all that stuff when you were an active SEAL working on covert antiterrorist ops. Hiding your identity and location was essential then to keep the tangos from infiltrating intel in this country."

"It still is essential. When are you gonna learn? You are a Navy officer with security clearance to a military base. You are the daughter of an admiral and sister to a SEAL, a pilot, and a midshipman living on important Naval Academy grounds. Hell, those Middle East terrorists whose plot was thwarted by David's team five years ago may still be looking for revenge, and what better way to get it than through his fiancée? Or me."

He blinked several times to stem the tears that welled in his eyes. Sometimes Alison forgot that Ian had been on that Lebanese op, as well . . . the only SEAL survivor. Once he got his emotions under control, he continued, "You are a potential target, whether you like it or not, whether you ever become a SEAL yourself."

He was probably right, but she'd heard the lecture many times before. "Go home, Ian. I need to take a nap for fifteen hours or so . . . until tomorrow at least . . . to recover from you."

He still grinned. Then his face went sober. "Are we going to talk about you and Magnusson?"

"No, we are not. Definitely not."

"You are treading dangerous waters, sis."

"Professionally or personally?"

"Both."

"Let me just say one thing on the subject, then drop it. It's been five years since David died. I haven't been involved with anyone in all that time. Not one single man. I just haven't been interested. If I've finally found a man who catches my eye . . . well, would you deny me that?"

"Does it have to be a subordinate? Does it have to be the goofball of SEAL Class 500? Does it have to be the number-one splinter in my behind?"

She shrugged. "I certainly didn't choose him."

"Can't you unchoose him?"

"Unchoose?" She laughed and grabbed for one of the sinfully delicious cookies. She sighed and closed her eyes with delight.

"Yeah, unchoose him."

"Don't make too much of this thing with Max. Just because a girl, or woman, surrenders occasionally to the temptation of a cookie, it doesn't mean she is dumb enough to suddenly maintain a steady diet of sweets."

"That's a helluva analogy, sis. Some women have been known to let themselves go because they get addicted to sugar."

She laughed. "You're right. It was a bad comparison. Not to worry, though. I can control my appetites."

"Oh, God, I wish you hadn't said that. You're starting to scare me. Surely it hasn't gone so far that you can't end it here. Call it a blip on your hormone screen and move on to someone more suitable. A different cookie, so to speak."

Her eyes went hard. No longer in sugar heaven or amused by the analogy game, she said, "Lay off, big brother. I'm a big girl. It's my life. Whether I make the right choices or mistakes, they're mine to make."

"Oh, shit! It's too late, isn't it? You now have a sugar craving."

Alison feared that was true. But then she smiled to herself. She couldn't wait to indulge again.

If wishes were fishes, they'd all be whales . . .

Ragnor had been on San Clemente Island for one sennight, engaged in war games. Thor's teeth! War was too serious a business to call it a game, but that was what these lackwitted military men did here.

He now knew how to shoot a rifle at both a stable or moving target with some precision. That was fun.

He now knew how to plant an explosive device that blew away everything within five hides, including buildings, trees, birds, and human eardrums. That was fun.

He now knew how to employ escape-and-evade and search-and-rescue tactics at night, with a team of instructors and other sadists hot on his heels. That was fun.

He also now knew how it felt to be captured by the enemy, subjected to endless grilling questions, forced to live with one's own less-than-aromatic unwashed body, squeezed into a small bamboo-cage prison too small for a grown man to stand upright, and nigh starved to death, except for eating roots and loathsome grubs, which did not taste like chicken no matter what anyone said. That was not fun.

The only thing that could be worse, in Ragnor's opinion, would be jumping out of sky machines called arrow-planes and floating to the ground under canvas tents, which was to be an upcoming "evolution" for the SEAL trainees. Demented, that's what it was. He chose not to think about it, lest he shiver in his boots . . . an ignoble thing for a Viking to do.

They were seated in a small building waiting for a large

motoring boat to take them, and a large number of other teams, back to Coronado. He'd tried to call Alison on her tell-a-fone before they left the base, but he kept getting a message that her number had been disconnected. Her brother Ian, who'd been along on the trip-from-Niflheim, had told him to stop worrying about her, that she was in safe hands now. Hah! As if that would reassure him! The chieftain had also told him to bug off where his sister was concerned. He'd had the poor sense to tell the chieftain where he could put that bug, which had earned him several dozen more running punishments. By the time this time-travel nonsense was over, Ragnor was going to have limbs of steel . . . and a very nice arse, too.

"You're muttering to yourself again. And smiling," Cage pointed out. Cage sat next to him on a long bench. On his other side were Cody and Sly. Across the aisle from them were JAM, Flash, Pretty Boy, and F.U.

"I wish I was back in Loo-zee-anna, swimming in the bayou, catching a few crawfish, scarfing down a bit of my grandma's gumbo. A little *joie de vivre*, Cajun style. Nothing fancy, just the slow, easy, uncomplicated life. Of course, if you wanna throw in a Southern belle with hot pants as well, I wouldn't object." That was Cage speaking, of course.

"I wish I was walking down Forty-second Street in Manhattan, breathin' in all the smells and sounds of the Big Apple." Sly lived in a place that was alternately referred to as a man's hat or an apple. What a country!

"Me, I wish I was in Nashville, at a Toby Keith concert," Flash called over to them. "Man, I love that guy's singin'. He's a man with an attitude. Doesn't hurt that he likes us guys in the military. 'How do ya like me now?'" That last was sung as Toby Keith presumably did.

"Nah!" Cody said. He and Flash were always squabbling over their preferences in music. Bloody hell, till he'd landed in this mad country, Ragnor hadn't known there *were* different kinds of music to pick from. Even now, he could not care. It was all just loud, in his opinion. "Better I be back in Asbury Park, cruisin' the beaches for chicks," Cody continued, "maybe lucking out with an impromptu Springsteen concert at the Stone Pony. Yeah, a little brew and The Boss, that's the ticket."

F.U., who was known as an extreme sports enthusiast, said, "I'd love to be in Wyoming, skiing down Mount Moran's Skillet Glacier."

Vikings skied, too, but only when the snow was so high there was no other way to get from here to there, like from the great hall to the privy on a cold winter day. Not Ragnor's idea of a grand fantasy.

"Or mountain climbing—I wouldn't mind that either," F.U. added. "The north face of the Grand Tetons . . . man oh man, that is heaven on earth."

Hah! Ragnor had climbed more than a few mountains, usually when attempting to chase some bothersome, land-grabbing band of Danes who'd dared invade his land. 'Twas not an activity he would willingly seek out.

Pretty Boy's wish was pretty straightforward. Being a former race-car driver, he said, "Just one more time I'd like to compete in the Daytona Five Hundred."

JAM had a totally different view of what he'd like to be doing. "I'm thinking about getting engaged."

"Oh, jeez! JAM's got a bad case of the hornies, but he's too guilt-ridden by all that Catholic teaching to do anything about it outside of marriage," Sly said. "You're not a Jesuit anymore, son."

JAM smiled, not at all offended. "I never was an actual

Jesuit. I attended seminary, but never took holy orders. Besides, it's not my religious background that makes me think about getting engaged. I've known Laura forever. She's an elementary school librarian in Los Angeles. I love her." He shrugged as if that said it all.

"Well, don't tell the brass about getting engaged," Pretty Boy advised.

JAM frowned with confusion. "There's no rule against being engaged or married in SEALs."

"No rules, per se, but if the Navy wanted you to have a wife, they would have assigned you one. What they don't know at this point, before you graduate and are deployed to a team, is your business," Pretty Boy said. "My opinion only."

Several of the others nodded, apparently sharing his opinion.

"How 'bout you, *cher*?" Cage asked him. "What's yer wish?"

Without thinking, Ragnor said, "I wish I was back in the Norselands, in my own time."

For some reason, they all turned on him with shock.

"Not that I believe all that time-travel crap, but why would you want to live in such primitive conditions?" Cody asked.

"Some modern inventions I would miss. Like cone-domes. And some of your foods, like cheeseburgers and pizza. But what need has a man for motoring vehicles when a good horse or a fast longship will do in most circumstances? Yea, your bathing rooms are cleaner, with all that flushing and running water, but a privy is a privy, when you get down to it. Besides, I have house servants aplenty to scrub out the garderobes; thus mine are less stinksome than many. You have nice keeps here in Ah-mare-ee-ca, as far as I have seen, but the timber castle I have at Norstead is magnificent, even by your standards. As for battle tactics and weapons, yours are far superior, but when the fields are level, as in sword against sword, I have no need of a repeating rifle." He could see that everyone was gaping at him as if he'd lost his mind. He must have, to be blathering so. And he hadn't even mentioned the one thing he would miss if he returned to the past. Alison.

"*Mon Dieu*, you are scarin' me," Cage said, patting him on the arm. "I thought you were gettin' better with all those CDs you've been listenin' to at night."

"I am getting better at adjusting to your country, but it does not change the fact that I was born in 983, a very different time from yours."

"Shit, that would make you about a thousand years old," Pretty Boy hooted. "You do age well, buddy."

"I want to know how he manages to get his pecker up after all these years," F.U. chimed in. "And without Viagra even."

"So horniness doesn't go away with time, eh?" JAM asked, an appropriate question since they'd just teased him about being horny in love.

"You ever meet Attila the Hun?" Cody teased, bent over with laughter.

"I believe Attila the Hun was a bit before my time."

"How 'bout Genghis Khan?"

"Who?"

"Never mind."

"I didn't think anyone was before your time, except perhaps Jesus," Flash offered.

"I have met Leif Ericsson, though. The Viking who supposedly discovered your country. A more arrogant Norseman there never was. He probably claimed to have invented sex, as well."

"You are a piece of work, Max," Flash said with a grin. "And you say it all with a straight face."

"You can all make jest at my expense. Go ahead. Enjoy yourselves. But know this: I ne'er believed in time-travel afore either . . . until it happened to me. Remember that move-he *Starman* that you told me about, Cage, where a man from another plan-hat arrived here?"

"He's talking about that old Jeff Bridges movie where an alien lands in Colorado and impregnates a modern woman," Cage explained. "Oh, *Dieu*, you didn't knock up Lieutenant MacLean already, did you?" Cage asked in horror.

Whaaat? Where did that idea come from? Ragnor shivered with horror at even the hint of his impregnating a woman in the midst of all his other turmoil. Shades of his father! "Would you all stop interrupting?" Ragnor said with exaggerated disgust. "What I was trying to say is, if an alien is possible, why not time-travel?"

"Max, Max, Max!" Sly shook his head sadly at him. "That movie was fiction . . . make-believe . . . not real life."

"And you, JAM," Ragnor persisted. "With all your religious studies, surely you believe in miracles, don't you?"

JAM's face flushed, which was remarkable for a dark-skinned person such as he. "Yeah, I believe in miracles."

"So . . . what? You're a friggin' miracle?" Cage wanted to know.

It was Ragnor's face that heated up with embarrassment now. "That's exactly what I think I am. A friggin' miracle of a time-traveler." He burst out laughing.

Until the chieftain walked into the building and came up to loom over all of them.

"Dum-dee-dum-dum," F.U. sang in an undertone.

"Magnusson!" the chieftain bellowed. Did the man ever

talk in a normal tone of voice? He made an abrupt signal with his thumb, indicating he wanted Ragnor to follow him to the back of the room.

"Uh-oh! What did I do now? Are you going to make me run up and down the length of this room? Or have you changed your mind about meeting my sister Madrene?"

The chieftain looked as if he'd like to hit him.

"Have I mentioned that Madrene resembles a cross between two famous women whose pictures I have seen on various SEAL lockers. A bit of Faith Hill and Pamela Anderson," he lied.

The chieftain's jaw dropped open before he had a chance to catch himself. He was interested, despite himself, Ragnor could tell.

"Shut your trap," the chieftain said bluntly.

"She is tall and blond and beautiful like Faith Hill, but she has two of Pamela's attributes, if you get my meaning." Madrene would kill him if she ever heard him describe her thus. He was not about to mention Madrene's shrewish disposition or the fact that she would as easily wallop a man as kiss him.

His SEAL trainee friends laughed uproariously as they blatantly eavesdropped on his and the chieftain's conversation.

"Shut . . . the . . . fuck . . . up!" Ian said. He was not laughing.

When they got to the back of the room, the chieftain told the two instructors there to go to the front, giving them some privacy. Then he sliced Ragnor with a glare intended to intimidate, which intimidated him not in the least. "Sit," Ian ordered.

They both sat down, and Ragnor started to ask him about Alison, whether he had heard from her, whether there were any more stalking calls, but the chieftain put up a hand. "I have a few things to say to you. I don't want to be interrupted."

"I have a few—"

"Did I give you permission to speak?"

"Nay, but—"

"Are you in love with my sister?"

"Huh? I hardly know your sister."

"That's what I thought. Just a notch on your sword, right?"

Ragnor drew himself up straight. "Do not dare to speak for me. Chieftain or not, you have no right to misspeak me. You asked about love . . . an emotion I have ne'er experienced afore, so I cannot say for sure how it feels. I do know that your sister is my destiny."

"Destiny? What kind of bullshit is that?"

He shrugged. "I cannot explain it. I just sense that Alison and I were meant to be together."

"And the sex just happened to take place along the road to your destiny."

"That is correct. I am pleased that you understand."

"You kumquat! I don't understand anything. How my sister could be interested in a goofus like you. How you managed to make her acquaintance, let alone an acquaintance with her bed sheets. How you even remotely think there's a chance of a future between a SEAL trainee and an admiral's daughter."

"I would have you know my grandfather was a high noble in the Norselands. My great-uncle was king. I am a jarl. My lineage is as high as your family's any day, in any country, in any time."

"That's another thing. This time-travel nonsense you keep spouting. I'm ordering a complete mental and physical reassessment of you when we get back to the base."

"Whatever you choose," Ragnor said. "I know what I know, and it has naught to do with some head injury."

"Why don't you just ring out, Magnusson, and save us all a heap of trouble?"

"Because you want me to."

"What? What the hell does that mean?"

"It means that you push and push me, hoping I will quit. That just makes me more determined to finish. We Magnussons are a stubborn bunch."

"And stop trying to fix me up with your sister."

Ragnor grinned.

"And stop grinning."

"So grinning is against the rules now, too?"

"Shut up!"

"By the by, wouldst thou give me Alison's new tell-a-fone number?"

"No. Have you heard a word I've said to you? Stay away from my sister. I don't want you contacting her. She doesn't want you contacting her."

"Did she say that?" His heart constricted painfully.

"She said you were just a passing fancy. In fact, her exact word was 'cookie.' You were a cookie that happened to be available at a time when she had a sudden sugar craving. She's probably on a diet now, though. Most women are, most of the time."

"Alison referred to me as a passing fancy . . . a mere cookie?" Ragnor felt the oddest lump lodge in his throat.

"Yep. You're not the only one who dodged the love bug."

"She is my destiny," Ragnor insisted.

"Ships that pass in the night," the chieftain insisted back. "A little sugar to satisfy her sweet tooth. That's all." The chieftain just smirked then, as if finally he'd scored some points in the battle betwixt them.

Ragnor asked for permission to be excused, which was given. As he walked back to his seat, he remained silent, but what he thought was, *Beware, m'lady, you will find out just how this cookie crumbles.*

CHAPTER FOURTEEN

If you want sweet, I'll give you sweet . . .

It was past midnight when Ragnor made his way to a coin tell-a-fone in the corridor of the sleeping hall.

Using a code of numbers that Cage had given him, he got the sequence for Alison's landlady from a woman whose name was, oddly, Information. He knew that because when she answered his call, she said, "This is Information." He dialed the number she gave him.

"Hello," a female voice answered groggily.

"Greetings. Is this M'lady Lillian?"

"M'lady? Max? Is that you? What time is it?"

"Sorry I am if I awakened you, but 'twas the first opportunity I had to call. How is Sam?"

"Just fine. He's stopped barking at every moth and mosquito that goes by, but now he has this chewing fetish going on. He's especially partial to chair legs . . . thinks they're bones, I guess."

He laughed.

"How can I help you, dear?"

"Can you give me Alison's new number?"

She hesitated. "I'm not sure I should be giving out a private number."

"Alison would want you to give it to me," he said, not at all sure of that fact.

"Well, if you say so." She gave him a series of seven numbers. After hanging up, putting more coins in the black box, and dialing again, another sleep-ridden voice came on the line.

"Hello."

"Alison?"

"Max?" Her sleepy voice sounded immediately alert. "What's wrong? Are you hurt? Where are you?"

Aaah, she must care about me if my safety is of concern to her. "Nay, I am not hurt. I am in a corridor outside the sleeping hall. We got back today from San Clemente Island, but the chieftain and his cohorts have been watching me like a hawk to prevent my going to you. They even followed me into the privy." One time he had ducked into a stall, crawled over the top, come out stealthily, and ended up behind the chieftain. An ill-humored man, the chieftain was; he had not been amused. Not even when he'd told him he'd been practicing escape-and-evade tactics. "This is the first chance I've had to escape their scrutiny."

"You'll be in trouble if you get caught making an unauthorized call."

"Pffff! I am always in trouble. And if I hadn't gotten through to you on the tell-a-fone, I would have come to your keep. That would have been a UA, an unauthorized absence."

"I know what a UA is, Max. I'm in the Navy, too."

"I forgot." *When I see you in my mind, sweet witch, I see you naked with me atop you, panting with lust. I do not see you in uniform, sword in hand, ready to do battle.* "In any case, a UA would mean even bigger trouble for me, so you are not to worry over a mere tell-a-fone call."

He imagined she was lying in her bed while they talked. Preferably naked. *I certainly have naked on my mind tonight. Well, every night, where you are concerned, Alison.* More likely, she was wearing one of those big tea-ing *sherts*. But she would be naked underneath. *Thank you, Odin, for the gift of male fantasy*, he thought with a grin.

"How are you?" she asked. Her voice was soft and caring as she spoke.

Oh, yea, naked for sure! "Fine, now that I am talking to you."

"Have the CDs and books helped at all?"

"Yea, they have. Thank you very much. Though they raise more questions than answers about this new time I have landed in."

She sighed. "You're still persisting with the time-travel stuff?"

"Of course. By the by, I do not relish the idea of being likened to a sweetmeat."

"A what?"

"Sweetmeat. Your brother told me I am naught more than a cookie to you. That a nibble satisfied your appetite, and you are no longer hungry. For me." *Give me a chance, and I will show you just how much of a sweet craving you have. My fellow trainees wolf down candy bars to get a "sugar high." I will show you a sugar high, all right . . . more like a Ragnor high.*

"I'll kill him."

"That is a good idea." *Or match him up with Madrene.* He thought a moment. *Why do I keep thinking about the chieftain and Madrene? 'Tis odd.*

"I was trying to explain to Ian how I could have behaved in such an uncharacteristic way. I don't engage in sex indiscriminately, you know."

"I would think not, if you waited five years for me."

She chuckled, and was probably shaking her head at his hopelessness. "Just out of curiosity, what prompted Ian to say such a thing? I mean, he couldn't have said something like that out of the clear blue sky."

"He was asking me if I loved you."

Her silence rang out like thunder.

Finally he inhaled for courage and said, "I do." Ragnor was no dummy. He had realized, the minute he'd told the chieftain that he barely knew Alison, it had been the wrong answer. Betimes he needed to remind himself to be charming.

She laughed. "You liar!"

So much for charm! "Well, I told the chieftain that I did not love you, but now that I've had a chance to think on it, I have decided that I do."

"Liar!" she repeated.

"I *think* I love you. I *probably* do. I *should*."

He could hear her laughter through the tell-a-fone. He was not sure if he should be offended or not. "And you, milady? Dost love me?"

"I like you, Max, and that is saying a lot. There hasn't been a man that I've cared enough to get to know, let alone love, in a long, long time."

"That is something. Isn't it?"

"Yes, it is something." Her voice was so low, steeped with emotion, that he barely heard her words. He was making inroads. He could tell. Vikings had a way with female inroads. "But I've been thinking—"

"Nay, nay, nay! Do not start thinking. A woman's thinking is a man's doom." *There go my inroads!*

"I've been thinking," she continued, despite his protest, "that it was good you had to go away this week. We needed some time apart. Everything happened way too quickly with us. Fast and furious is a sure path to disaster."

"Fast and furious is not necessarily a bad thing." *In truth, I can think of several scenarios where fast and furious would be a decided advantage.*

"We did things in reverse. Most people get to know each other first, decide whether there is an attraction, then they may or may not make love. We skipped all those steps and jumped to the finish line."

And what, pray tell, is wrong with that?

"Now, the only recourse we have is to start all over, or end things."

Panic overtook him of a sudden. "Do not dare to suggest that we end things. You are my destiny."

"I wish you would stop saying that. It's no more believable than your being in love with me."

"Stop being so unbiddable. If I were with you now, I would convince you otherwise." He closed his eyes for a brief second, picturing what he might do. It was a very nice picture.

"Making love isn't the answer to everything."

Is she reading my mind now? Over a tell-a-fone? "Nay, but it makes women amenable to a man's reasoning."

"And a man's reasoning would be that hopping in the sack solves everything."

Time to change the subject. Get her off guard. She is too sharp by far. "I dreamed of you last night, sweetling. I swear, I could smell your skin. You were making that soft purring sound when you arch your back."

"Are we about to have phone sex?" she asked shakily.

He liked the shaky part. And the sex part, too. "Fone sex? Hmmm. That sounds intriguing. In fact, have you ever . . . ? Oh, bloody hell!" Just then, Ragnor saw the night patrol man approaching. He put the phone back in its cradle and stepped back into the shadows.

Give me a buzz, baby . . . and I mean a real buzz . . .

The line went dead.

Alison stared at the phone, then put it back in its cradle. She had to admit to being intrigued by the train of Max's last words. *Do I purr? Really? Well, so does he. Sometimes. Just thinking about purring is making me feel like . . . purring. God, I am pathetic. But, God, I love it!* She lay back on the pillow and smiled, thinking. Just as she was drifting off to sleep, a smile still lingering on her lips, the phone rang again.

"Max, what happened?"

"The night patrol came by, probably with special instructions to check on me. I had to hurry back to my pallet and pretend to be sleeping. I snored a bit just to be convincing."

His childlike demeanor softened her. "You shouldn't have called back."

"I wanted to. Don't you want to talk with me?"

"Yes. No. I don't know. This is such a mistake. You and me." *But it feels so right. Really, how can something so obviously doomed to fail feel so right?*

"Can we have fone sex now?"

Talk about a one-track mind. To her surprise, she liked that about him, whereas she would have been repulsed by it in any other man. "No, we cannot."

"Talk to me, then. I feel so lost here, except for you. You have become my anchor."

I do not want to be your anchor. My life is weighted down with enough baggage as it is.

"Because you are my destiny, of course."

And I do not want to be your destiny either. That calls for responsibility and commitment and way too many other important things that I cannot give at this time. Still, it is a compliment. Isn't it? "Do you tell that to many women?"

"How could more than one woman be my destiny?" He seemed genuinely perplexed by her question.

"Max, Max, Max. What am I going to do with you?"

"I have a few suggestions. But for now, just talk to me, dearling."

"About what?"

"Yourself. Why you are a doctor. Why you are in the military. Why you want to be a SEAL."

She nodded, as if he could see her. "I grew up in a family of men. My father, Rear Admiral Thomas MacLean, is a member of the U.S. Government's Task Force on Terrorism. You already know my older brother, Ian. My younger brother Ross is a Navy pilot, and my still younger brother, Clay, is a midshipman at Annapolis. My mother died of cancer when I was eight. Because Dad was a Navy lifer, we traveled all over the country. There aren't many military bases where I haven't lived at one time or another. By the time I was sixteen, we had lived in twenty different cities in four countries. Luckily, I was really smart. Not a prodigy or anything, like you might be, but smart enough to graduate from high school at sixteen and med school by twenty-two. Because we had no mother and because we moved so much, my family became very close-knit. Navy Brats 'r Us. We were our own best friends. It's partly why Ian is so overly protective of me."

She grew quiet, pensive with memories.

"Go on," Max prodded.

"I'm probably boring you."

"Nay, I enjoy learning about you. I like hearing your voice. Why did you choose the healing arts?"

"Well, my brothers and I are very competitive. Doesn't matter if it's sports or school or whatever. My dad was a SEAL. One of the early webfoot warriors. From a young age, it's all I wanted to be. Ian, too. Ross and Clay will probably become SEALs someday, too. We've grown up knowing firsthand what a threat terrorism is to our country, and the SEALs are some of the best fighters of terrorism."

"But they won't let you in because you're a female."

"Right. So my second choice of career was medicine, Navy medicine, and, really, it's not a bad choice. I love medicine. If I'm barred from SEALs much longer—I'm already approaching the age limit, you know—I hope to be assigned to some teams as auxiliary staff. Often they need medical personnel to go out on field ops."

"That could be dangerous, couldn't it?"

"Of course."

"I do not like the idea of my woman placing herself in danger."

She sat up straight in bed, miffed at his wording.

Before she had a chance to voice her outrage, he said, "Oh, do not get your back all stiff over my calling you my woman. 'Tis how I think of you, no matter what you say. By the by, what do you think of tattoos?"

"Huh?" His change of subject startled her.

"I am thinking about getting a tattoo. What would you think of that?"

"First, it's none of my business what you do to your body."

"I beg to differ. My body is your body . . . so to speak."

"Second, it would depend on what kind of tattoo."

"Well, many of the SEALs and trainees have frogs on their arses or other body parts. 'Frogmen' was the name for SEALs in prior generations of the Navy," he told her, as if giving her a history lesson. It was adorable of him, really. "But I do not favor frogs all that much. Too many warts and slime."

"Hey, I've kissed a few frogs in my time."

"Huh?"

"Never mind. How about a Viking in a horned helmet?"

He made a sound of disgust. "We Vikings do not wear horned helmets. But a sword or battle axe would not be amiss. I like the chain tattoo on Cage's upper arm, and Flash has a heart on his shoulder that is rather attractive. Do you have any tattoos?"

Once again, he'd disarmed her with his quick change of subject. "No."

"We could go get tattoos together."

"No way! Ear piercing is the extent of my body mutilations."

"When can I see you?"

Another change of subject. "I don't know. I said from the beginning that we need this time apart, to reevaluate our relationship."

"I was ne'er much for rethinking. I want to make love with you again."

She said nothing. What could she say?

"Are you angry with me again?"

"No."

"But you do not want to make love with me."

"I didn't say that."

"Ahhhh." She could hear the smile in his voice.

"We need to slow this train down, honey." She could have bitten her tongue for her inadvertent endearment.

"Honey? I like that. We have a half day off on Saturday. Will you do something with me?"

"No."

"Not *that*. Well, leastways, not totally that. I want you to go to a lie-berry with me."

"Why?"

"JAM told me about lie-berries. Methinks there are answers to some of my time-travel questions in a lie-berry."

"All right," Alison said. What harm could there be in going to a library with him?

"And then mayhap we could go to a furrier."

"A furrier? Whatever for?"

"I have a strong desire to lie with you in a soft, silky bed fur."

He hung up before Alison could say anything more. No matter. She was speechless.

I like you, you like me, knick-knack paddy-whack . . .

Alison picked Max up on a street corner outside the naval base on Saturday afternoon.

With a wave and a smile, he opened the passenger door of her Mazda and slid inside. His six-foot-four frame filled every inch of free space in her compact vehicle, and then some.

She leaned down to help him adjust the seat. On the way back up he put a hand to her nape and tugged her closer, planting a sweet kiss of welcome on her lips.

"I missed you," he said huskily.

"I missed you, too," she admitted. Probably not a wise thing to say, but damn, it was the truth.

"What kind of garment is that?" His eyes swept the bare skin of her shoulders and arms and her legs from the knees down to her sandals. There was a mixture of appreciation and disapproval in his scrutiny.

"A halter sundress. You don't like it?"

"I like it way too much, but I am not sure I will like other men looking at all that exposed skin."

She should be offended by his proprietary air. Instead, she savored the idea of his being jealous.

"Your hair is wet," he observed, still holding on to her nape and kneading softly.

"Goop," she said, stifling a groan at her hairtrigger reaction to his mere touch. Well, his kiss, too.

"Poop? You put poop in your hair? Doesn't smell like poop. Smells like apples to me."

"Not poop," she said with a laugh.

He made an exaggerated sound of relief. He must have been teasing her.

For a brief second, Alison relished the simple joy of being teased by a good-looking man. She couldn't recall such a light-hearted moment in a long, long time. "It's Goop to hold my hair down. Without it, my hair gets all curly."

"I like your curly hair."

"Do you?" she said, inordinately pleased with his compliment. She'd always hated her red, curly, Little Orphan Annie hair, but maybe it wasn't so bad.

"*All* of your curly hair," he added.

She made a tsk-ing sound at his crudity. "You're a dangerous man, Mr. Magnusson. Softening me up with teasing and flattery."

He gave her nape a final squeeze and sat back in his seat. "Dangerous, huh? Give me half a chance and I can show you real danger." He winked at her.

"I like you, Max," she blurted out, then smiled at him.

"I like you, too." He smiled back at her.

"So, where to? I'm your servant for the day."

"Oh, sweetling, you should not make such offers to me. A love slave for the day? Odin must be smiling on me."

Love slave? Holy moly! "Enough fooling around! Which library do you want to go to?"

He shrugged. "An adult one. JAM's betrothed-to-be is a lie-berry-anne in a school for young children. That would not do for me. Is there another kind?"

"Yep. San Diego Public Library should do for a start. If that doesn't have what you want, we can try one of the college libraries."

"First, I would also like to stop somewhere to buy more of those books and CDs you got me before . . . especially the CDs. It is easier for me to understand the spoken word."

She nodded.

"Can we hurry, though?"

"Why? You don't have to be back till oh-twenty-hundred, do you?"

"Yea, but once we are done at the lie-berry, I have other plans for us."

She didn't ask what he meant.

She knew.

His life was an open book, or so he hoped . . .

They'd been at the library for two hours and Alison was getting increasingly more concerned and confused.

Max had difficulty reading text, but his mind was sharp as a whip. He could remember the call number of all twenty reference books they'd skimmed through so far, as well as repeat back verbatim the material she read to him about ancient Vikings. Either he held a doctorate degree in late tenth- and early eleventh-century history with an emphasis on Vikings, or he was a freakin' time-traveler, which was of course impossible. Still, he knew even the minutest details about the culture, the geography, famous and lesser known figures of the time, clothing, even the sagas.

He gazed about the shelves of books with wonderment, as he had been doing incessantly since they'd arrived. "So many books! Dost know how rare they are in my time? Why, only kings and men of vast wealth have any books at all, and then only one or a few. Except for the monasteries, of course, where the scribes prepare the illuminated manuscripts, taking as much as a year to complete only one."

What could Alison say to that? He was correct about the method of writing or copying books then. Printing presses didn't exist in the tenth and eleventh centuries. Heck, there wasn't even any paper, per se, just thick parchment.

"Tell me how to find Olaf Trygvasson," he said.

She pulled the name up on the computer catalog and saw at least three dozen books listed. Glancing over her shoulder, she saw that the amazing man was instantly memorizing all the call numbers as they flicked by.

When they went to the stacks and found the books with the information he wanted, Max was further engrossed.

"This is the guy you claim is your great-uncle or something, right?"

He nodded. "My grandfather's brother, the all-king of Hordaland, which is known as Norway today. I was hoping that in some discourse on King Olaf, my uncle, there might be mention of my family and what happened to them."

Suddenly Alison realized why they were there. Max, in his conviction that he had time-traveled, was attempting not only to prove his theory to her and himself, but to find the key to his future. If he found some historical reference to his immediate family, including himself, he would know whether he would stay here in the future or return to the past. For example, if the book listed his name or that of his children, it would mean that he would return to his own time.

Aaarrgh! I sound as if I actually believe this nonsense. Which I don't. Not even remotely. Poor Max!

"Listen, sweetie, let's take some of these books home with us," she suggested.

"Will they allow us to do that? Do I have enough money with me to purchase them?" Max had been paid today, and he had no concept of dollar values, as evidenced in the bookstore earlier where he had handed the clerk three hundred-dollar bills for fifty dollars' worth of CDs.

"Yes, and there is no cost. They'll lend them to us, on condition we return them in three weeks."

"Amazing!" he said, caressing one of the covers as if it were a precious object.

"These books, on top of the CDs we already bought, should do you for a couple weeks. Besides, I'm hungry and I know an ideal spot where we can have a picnic lunch."

"I know what a pick-nack is. Cage often talks about pick-nacks back in Cage-hun land, usually by the water. Our pick-nack better not have sand within shouting distance. I am sick up to my eyeballs of sand."

"No sand," she said, chucking him under the chin. "How would you feel about a picnic in bed?"

He just smiled.

CHAPTER FIFTEEN

⚛

Whining over wine . . .
They stopped at an upscale wine and cheese shop
to gather items for their picnic lunch.

Alison put into her basket warm French bread, brie and
Stilton cheeses, various fresh fruits, olives, and hard salami,
while Max wandered the wine aisles. She found him standing rather dumbfounded in front of a display of Blue Dragon
wines.

"Max? What's wrong?"

"I don't know," he said softly, putting both hands over his
heart as if he were having trouble breathing. "Blue Dragon,"
he murmured as if rolling the words on his tongue, seeking
answers.

"Blue Dragon? That's a California vineyard, but I don't
think I've ever tried their wines. Have you?"

He shook his head slowly from side to side, reached forward to touch one of the bottles, then drew back sharply as if
he'd gotten an electric shock.

"Come to think of it, your family are vintners, aren't they?
Is this theirs?" she asked.

"My family is dead, and my father was a farmer. He ne'er
grew grapes that I can recall. And Frisian wines were the
only ones I ever saw at his table."

She could have sworn she'd read something different in his file, but perhaps she was mistaken. "Then what's the problem?"

"I don't know. It's just . . . I don't know . . . odd, I guess. I feel drawn to this section of the merchant's stall. There is some connection . . . I sense it . . . something important . . . but I cannot place it." He threw her a sheepish look. "You must think I am totally barmy now. First time-travel, and now bonding with a bottle."

"No, I don't think you're barmy," she said, throwing an arm over his shoulder and giving him a squeeze. "You're rather adorable, actually."

"Adorable? *Adorable?*" he protested a short time later as they left the shop and headed back to the car. "Vikings are not adorable. Unless . . ." He deliberately let his words trail off and gave her a lazy, half-lidded look.

"Unless what?" she said, laughing.

"Unless you plan on doing something particularly wanton to show your adoration."

"For sure, baby. For sure."

Baby, you move me . . . or is it your vibrating recliner? . . .

Ragnor tried to hide his distress from Alison as they returned to her keep. She had gone off to prepare their picknack feast, and he wandered aimlessly around her front solar, touching things, glancing out the window, thinking, thinking, thinking.

He was lost in time; there was no other conclusion he could come to. For a Viking whose uncomplicated life usually amounted to eat, sleep, make love, fight, or go a-Viking, it was particularly alarming not to know what he should do next.

After declining an invitation from Mistress Lillian and Doctor Fine-gold to partake in a backyard feast of beef-steaks cooked over hot coals, they'd come up to Alison's apartment. *People today have all these modern conveniences, like electrical stoves, my-crow-waves, and toast-hers, and what do they do? Cook outdoors over a fire, like people of my time do. Demented, that's what they are.*

On entering her apartment, Alison checked her answering machine, which had been thankfully silent of Breather calls ever since she'd changed her number. The conclusion she had come to regarding that silence was that her Breather must have been making random calls . . . in other words, she was not necessarily the target. Ragnor was not so sure about that.

But he worried more about other things.

He had crammed so much information into his brain of late that he felt as if his head might explode. *American history, world history, math, English, science, daily news, football, baseball, hockey, shooting a gun, using a fone, driving a car, birth control, natural childbirth . . . was there any other kind? Like unnatural childbirth? Ha, ha, ha! On and on and on. Why did modern people need to know so much?* He was nigh killing himself to succeed in a program he was not even sure he liked. *A man should really, really want to be a SEAL to suffer so. Shouldn't he?* Or as the chieftain often said, "Ask not what the Navy can do for you, ask what you can do for the Navy."

If he had indeed time-traveled, whether due to some scientific marvel or a whim of the gods, he had to wonder why. What was the purpose for his being here? He had thought he was sent to save someone—Alison, in particular—but she had folks aplenty to help her here. Mayhap she was not his destiny, after all. *If not, for the love of Odin, who or what is?*

More important, would he be slung back in time one day as quickly as he'd been slung here? Without prior notice? And did he want to return? *Bloody hell, I hope I do not have to drown again.*

He just did not know. Anything.

Suddenly tired, he sank down into the velvety chair and leaned it into a reclining position. To his surprise, when he inadvertently pressed a button on the side, the chair began to vibrate softly under his buttocks and back.

He grinned to himself and thought, *I have an idea.*

But then he drifted off to sleep. The idea imbedded itself into his dreams, though. *Holy Frigg!*

He was so excited by her, he fell asleep . . .

Alison lit a dozen candles, laid an old checkered tablecloth over her bed, and prepared for a sumptuous indoor picnic. Wine rested in an ice-filled bucket. All the tempting foods were laid out, along with silverware and plates. She was ready.

But when she went to get Max, she found him fast asleep in the Lazy-Boy. And it was set on "low vibration." *Whoo-ee!*

She smiled gently as she stared down at him. Poor guy! He had to be exhausted. SEAL training was physical and psychological torture under the best of circumstances for even the fittest men, but Max was suffering the additional mental stress associated with whatever memory problems assailed him due to his concussion. His arms were crossed over his white T-shirt, his ankles crossed on the footrest. He breathed evenly through slightly parted lips.

What was it about him that appealed to her so? He was handsome, of course. And funny, in his own way. Sexy . . .

oh, yeah! But it was more than that, and she just couldn't pinpoint what.

Leaving Max to sleep for a while, she got herself a glass of white wine—one of the Blue Dragon vintages they'd purchased. Carrying the wineglass with her, she went over to the sofa and began to peruse the library reference books on the coffee table. Ancient-history books tended to give little information about individuals or families unless they were big shots for that time. Yes, there was stuff about Olaf Trygvasson, his wives and children, but nothing about his siblings and their families. But wait, in the acknowledgments at the back of one book, she saw mention of a thesis written the previous year by a UCLA student astonishingly named Magnusson . . . Kirsten Magnusson. It was titled: "A Study of an Old Norse Family in Eleventh-Century Vestfold."

Hmmm. Usually theses weren't widely published, and she wasn't about to travel to Los Angeles to go looking through the library stacks for a copy, but maybe . . . just maybe . . . she might find some information on the Internet. Moving on automatic, she grabbed her laptop, set it up on the coffee table, and soon booted up. A quick search of Kirsten Magnusson on Google brought up two links. One, a website about her thesis. The other, weirdly enough, was connected to Blue Dragon Vineyard.

She clicked on the first entry. There wasn't much there, just the author's name and e-mail address, a short bio describing her as a twenty-five-year-old teaching assistant at UCLA who'd written her master's thesis on this small segment of Viking history. Alison decided to write a short e-mail to this Kirsten Magnusson, identifying herself as a physician at the Naval Amphibious Base at Coronado, asking if there was any chance she might download a copy of the thesis. As she hit "send," she looked up and noticed that Max was still in the same position on the recliner, but his eyes were open and staring at her.

"I fell asleep. Sorry, sweetling." He yawned widely as he spoke.

"That's okay. You needed the rest."

"I have so little time with you. 'Tis a waste to spend any of it sleeping."

"Well, I got some work done. Do you want to hear what I found out?"

"Not now," he said, opening his arms to her in a beckoning way. "I have a better idea for making the best use of our time together."

"I'll bet you do." She shut down her computer and walked over, letting him lift her by the waist so she ended up straddling his lap. "You're throbbing, honey," she pointed out with a little laugh.

"It's the chair."

"I don't think so," she disagreed, swaying her hips from side to side to show him just where she sensed his throb.

"By the by," he said, chuckling, "I have been wondering all day what you are wearing under that siren dress."

"It's a sundress, not a siren dress. And not much."

"Hmmm. That bears some investigating." With deft fingers he undid the tie at her neck, which caused the dress to fall to her waist, exposing her breasts. Then he ran his rough palms up her thighs till they touched the edges of her bikini underpants. "You are wrong, dearling. You are wearing way too much." With those words, he soon had her out of the panties and dress, straddling him totally naked.

"You're still dressed," she complained as he arranged her the way he wanted her, straddling his lap again, her butt on his thighs.

"Just for a second. I want to look at you." His voice was husky with arousal, which in turn aroused her.

"I'm a little embarrassed."

"Do not be. The future seems so unclear to me, especially today. If anything should happen to me to send me away from here . . ."

Panic swept over her at the prospect of his going away. *Oh, God, when did he become so important to me?*

". . . I want to remember you . . . all of you." He winked wickedly at her. "I am making a mind picture of you."

"I can give you a real picture . . . a photograph."

He shook his head to indicate he didn't mean that kind of picture. "Your red curls," he explained and gently brushed the back of his fingertips over the hair on either side of her face and then between her legs.

With that sweet gesture, his throb became her throb, too. Like an electrical circuit pulsing between them where their private parts met.

"Your skin, like fresh cream it is, all over your body. I saw a piece of priceless porcelain once in the market town of Birka. It came from the Eastlands, but 'twas not as fine as your skin."

"What a nice thing to say!"

"'Tis the truth. And these," he said, a twinkle in his blue eyes; "like berries they are, floating in cream." He touched the tips of her breasts with his fingers.

She bowed her back reflexively, like a cat yearning for more.

"Your pleasure in sex gives me back equal pleasure. Like now. I can see in the haze of your green eyes, in the parting of your lips, that you want me."

"Are you trying to say I'm wild?" The tone she tried for was saucy, but she was unaccustomed to playing games.

"In a good way, yea." He pulled her down so that she half lay on him. When she extended her legs so that her feet rested atop his, she did in fact cover him. He kissed the side of her head softly and said, "There was a time, before this whole time-travel business, when I had lost my enthusiasm for the bedsport."

"Oh, no, not the enthusiasm talk again."

He pretended she hadn't interrupted. "I was bored with women, no matter how beautiful, no matter how talented. Even with King Svein's daughter Inga."

"Oh, please. I have to compete with a princess now?"

"No more interruptions, milady," he said, chucking her under the chin. "Now one look at you, and my enthusiasm is back with a vengeance."

"I can tell." She rubbed herself against his erection for emphasis. Saucy was coming easier to her now.

He swatted her behind. "Behave, wench. You must needs maintain a proper respect for a good enthusiasm."

"Oh, I do. I do." She raised her head and looked at him, serious now. "I would miss you if you went away. Don't go."

"I do not know if my going or staying is within my control, but know this, heartling, I would miss you, too. And while many things seem out of my control, one thing I can promise: I can make the here and now we share memorable."

"Got a little humility problem, do you?"

"I am a Viking. Humility is not in our makeup."

She lowered her lips to his, kissing him softly but thoroughly. When she raised her head, he tried to pull her back down. "You taste good. What have you been eating? Grapes?"

"Not eating, drinking. I had some wine."

"The Blue Dragon wine?"

She nodded. "Are you going to get an electrical shock just from tasting it on my tongue?" she teased.

"I do not know. We'd better try again and see." This time it was Max who kissed her, softly but thoroughly. When the kiss ended, he said, "No electrical shock, just a sexual one."

"Did you bring any condoms with you, cowboy?" she asked, helping him pull his T-shirt over his head without her getting off of him—a real feat!

"Only a dozen," he answered as he toed his shoes off.

And he was serious.

By the time they got his jeans off—which was not easy, with his refusal to get off the vibrating recliner and his not wanting her off his body—they were both more than ready for sex. After he helped cover his awe-inspiring "enthusiasm" with a condom, she eased herself down onto him. She could have wept for the sheer ecstasy that slow slide provided her.

"I want to touch you," he murmured.

But she slapped his hands away. "Not now. Too many sensations hitting me at once. I want to concentrate on one thing at a time."

He arched his eyebrows in surprise at her orders. He complied, though, by folding his arms behind his head.

Max filled her, and her inner folds adjusted to accommodate him. When she felt in control enough that she wouldn't go off like a rocket at the merest touch, she leaned forward, bracing her arms on his shoulders. She spread her legs wider, so that a certain spot between her legs would hit his pubic bone. Only then did she begin to move on him, slowly, rocking.

He muttered something in a foreign tongue that probably translated to "holy friggin' hell!" which was pretty much how she felt. His eyes went wide and he blinked.

She blinked, too.

"Are you done concentrating now?" he gasped out.

"Why?"

"Because . . ." he said, and showed her. Putting his hands under her buttocks, he lifted her high on him so that she took him even farther inside herself.

She could swear he grew even thicker and longer in that blink of a second.

"I did not know I could do that," he said, wonderment in his voice. "That is what you do to me . . . for me," he declared joyfully.

"I didn't know I could, either," she said and began to undulate her body with the rhythm of some sexy music video. *Beyonce, eat your heart out!*

Max made a low growling sound of masculine agony deep in his throat.

She was wet, she was throbbing, and she was about to come.

So what did her Viking do? In one fluid movement, he rolled them over so that she was on the bottom and he was on top, still embedded in her.

"Oh, boy!" she said.

"Nay. 'Oh, man!' is what you should say."

But she was speechless, with the velvety chair vibrating under her tush and Max torturing her with long, way-too-slow plunges into her body . . . plunges that hit her *right there* every time he came home, and left her throbbing when he left.

She began to beg. "Please. Harder. Faster. Now!" She spread her legs wider. She wrapped them around his waist. She dug her nails into his back.

He laughed. The brute. But he did as she'd ordered. Perhaps not such a brute.

She shattered then into about a million sex-charged pieces as he pounded into her one last time. The only saving grace for her was that he was the picture of male-pushed-to-the-limit as he threw back his head and roared out his own awesome climax. She liked to think she had a little to do with that. Okay, a lot.

"You're smiling," he observed once they both panted themselves back to normal. He bit her chin as punishment.

"So are you." She bit his shoulder as punishment.

"Some pick-nack you throw, m'lady," he said.

"Oh, my goodness! I bet the candles all burned out." She started to jump up, but Max winced and held her down till he eased himself out of her.

As they strolled back to the bedroom, Max remarked with a bit of consternation, "*My* candle is not at all burned out, that I assure you."

Burning the candle at both ends, and then some . . .

It was not the first time Ragnor had sex and food at the same time, but it was the most fun.

Whilst naked, they ate hard and soft cheeses slathered on slices of Frankish bread, washed down with delicious cool wine. The chunks of spiced meat were palatable to him, but the bitter olives were not. They saved the fruit and the remainder of the wine for dessert, which consisted of what Alison aptly called "wild monkey sex."

They had cleared the bed, taken a shower together, and were now lying on the bed and talking softly as lovers are wont to do. He had to return to the military base within the hour.

She told him of her work as a healer, particularly the patients she'd dealt with this past week. He laughed when she described Flash having bruised his thigh during underwater demolition practice and wanting her to sign a weekend liberty for him to go home to recuperate. "The reason I knew that Flash had an ulterior motive," Alison explained, "is that there was to be a NASCAR race taking place this weekend, and he was one of four SEAL trainees who had the same brilliant idea."

"You can't blame them for trying," Ragnor said, grinning. "But I can think of better things to do when given free time than watching cars chase each other around big circles."

"Like?" she asked, slanting her eyes at him seductively.

"As if you don't know, you insatiable wanton," he answered.

Ragnor told her of the grueling week he'd had in SEALs training. "Do not take offense, milady, but your brother has a cruel streak on occasion."

"His bark is worse than his bite."

"Hah!" *I have known black bears less vicious than he is.*

"Really."

"When I tried to voice my concerns over this jumping-out-of-the-sky nonsense, he told me, 'It's a case of mind over matter, boy. We don't mind. And you don't matter.'"

She laughed. "That's an old military saying. Don't take it personally. And you have to understand that Ian's been through a lot lately." She told him how Ian had been betrayed by his betrothed, how the only thing the traitorous woman had left behind was a fat old cat.

"A cat? A *cat*?" he hooted. "I knew it! The chieftain is destined to be with my sister Madrene. She has a cat, too."

"I'd like to see you convince him to travel back in time, with a cat yet, to be with *your* sister." She smiled impishly at him. He knew she didn't accept that he'd time-traveled, but he blessed her for accepting that he believed it.

He loved this impish, playful side of Alison. And he realized that the one thing he had missed about sex for years and years was laughter. The best love-play had smiles in there somewhere. "If I ever do get sent back to my own time, methinks I will become a monk," he declared. "You have ruined me for other women."

She laughed softly against his chest, then kissed one of his nipples, causing a jolt in his manpart, which amazed him. After all the sex they'd engaged in, his enthusiasm should be all worn down . . . for today, at least.

"If you're going to be a monk, then I guess I'd better become a nun," she said.

"You will be the first hard-bodied nun in history, I warrant." *Hmmm. I have ne'er had sex with a nun afore. I wonder if Alison would . . .*

"And you'll be the sexiest priest. All the ladies will want to confess their sins to you."

I could wear a monk's tunic. I already have the shaved tonsure. You would wear a religious habit. And . . . "Dost have any sins you would like to confess to me, m'lady?" He waggled his eyebrows at her with mock lasciviousness.

"I've been having wanton fantasies of late."

Uh-oh, is she reading my mind? But I like the sound of "wanton." "Hmmm. Tell me more, my child."

"Well, there is this certain Viking—"

"Ah, Vikings! They are a temptation." *Especially Viking monks.*

"That they are," she agreed.

"Methinks I should levy an appropriate penance." *By the gods, methinks I would make a grand priest.*

"Something involving sex? Tsk-tsk-tsk! That would compound the sin."

They smiled at each other.

He kissed her lips softly, then grew serious. Time was creeping up on him. "I do not know when I will see you again. We will be leaving for George-ha in a few days for jump school. I shudder to think of all that will entail. Bloody hell, I shudder to think of getting into an airplane to go to George-ha to begin with. But that is neither here nor there. You must take extra precautions for your safety whilst I am gone. I really wish you would move into the bachelor officers' quarters on the base. Or go to visit your father."

She shook her head. It was an argument they'd had before, and he hadn't won yet.

"Then be extra careful. Try to come home afore dark. Carry that pistol with you. Take no chances."

"Max! You're as bad as Ian and my father. I'll be all right. You're the one who must take care of yourself. Stop worrying about me." She kissed him gently to reassure him. A futile gesture.

"When I get back, we will talk," he told her. "There are many things I have to decide, and all of them involve you."

Like, *You are the most important thing in my life.*

Like, *You really are my destiny.*

Like, *Just looking at you takes my breath away.*

Like, *I do love you.*

Like, *I want to spend the rest of my life with you.*

That was what he thought, but he was unable to say the words . . . and mean them. Yet.

CHAPTER SIXTEEN

❧

Flying through the air with the greatest of unease . . .

Ragnor sat in the window seat of the airplane as it soared through the skies. His fists clutched the armrests with a death grip, his stomach roiled with nausea, and he kept his eyes squeezed shut from the minute they went "wheels up" back in Coronado and their officer yelled out to them, "Good to go!"

Not him. He was definitely not "good to go."

There were about seventy-five SEAL trainees on the plane, along with a few instructors. Chieftain MacLean had stayed behind at Coronado. They would join up with another two hundred or more soldiers from various military "boot camps." He had no idea what a boot camp was and didn't care to ask.

Once they disembarked from the metal death trap at the Fort Benning military base in George-ha, he sank to his knees on the ground and gave thanks to Odin for his safe journey. The worst part of getting off that airplane was knowing he would have to get on again in three sennights. Even worse, he would soon be jumping out of it, or something similar, whilst the plane flew in the skies.

Insanity, that's what it was.

"I thought you were a smoke jumper at one time." Cage frowned as he patted him on the shoulder. Ragnor stood and bent over at the waist, trying to breathe.

"What's a smoke jumper?" Ragnor asked.

"Never mind," Cage said, shaking his head at him.

"You gotta earn your wings, man," F.U. told him.

He told F.U. what the Navy could do with his wings.

"You'll love it," Pretty Boy said. "You get such a rush the first time you fall. Just like the first time I took the checkered flag at Darlington. Wow! Better than sex."

"Mayhap better than your sex play," Ragnor countered, "but not better than my sex play."

"Seriously, Max, you better get your act together or you'll be FUBAR before you make your cherry jump," Flash advised in a kindly fashion.

"Foe-bar? Do you refer to my sword Foe Fighter?"

All his fellow trainees said, "Huh?"

"It's foo-bar, buddy. FUBAR means Fucked Up Beyond All Recognition," Flash explained.

"Oh, well, I am already that," Ragnor said. "We Vikings have a similar word we use betimes. UFWABL."

"Oooof-wobble? You pullin' our leg, Max?" Cage asked with a laugh.

"'Tis the truth. Up a Fjord Without a Bloody Longship. Same thing."

Just then a man with a commanding presence yelled out, "At-ten-hut!"

Everyone within hearing range jerked to attention, including Ragnor.

The man, who resembled a bull, stood right in front of Ragnor's group and seemed to be addressing him personally, though he was surely talking to them all. "I am Sergeant

Major Williamson of the United States *Army* Airborne, and we are not about to put up with any crap from a bunch of hairy-assed leg swabbies."

Ragnor learned later that all combat troops called sailors "swabbies," implying that all they did was stay safely on ships and swab decks. The term "leg" was used to define anyone who hadn't yet been jump qualified.

"Is that clear, mister?" the bull bellowed, and, yea, he *was* looking directly at him.

"Who? Me?" Ragnor said, which was really lack-witted, of course. *When will I learn to be quiet?*

"No, I'm talking to that tree over there. What's your name, boy?"

"Ensign Magnusson, sir," he said, staring straight ahead. *I think I am going to throw up the contents of my heaving stomach.*

"I'm gonna remember your name, Magnusson."

That is just wonderful. It appeared the sergeant major was demonstrating to them all that they were Navy men at an Army base. Unfortunately, he intended to use Ragnor as his whipping boy.

"Dost think it is fair to pick on me? In my opinion—" he started to say before the sergeant major put up a halting hand.

His comrades groaned with dismay, and some of the Army troops grinned. *Mayhap I should not have spoken.*

"And your crybaby, whiney-assed opinion would be what, Ensign Mag-nuss-on?"

"Nothing, Sergeant Major, sir," he replied, suddenly gaining the wisdom to shut his teeth. "What was that word you used before?" he asked Flash in an undertone once the Army man turned away.

"FUBAR," Flash murmured back.

"For a certainty!" Ragnor concluded.

"I have another one for you," Cody said. "This is a classic SNAFU." Ragnor didn't even bother to ask. Cody explained all on his own. "Situation Normal, All Fucked Up."

"That is us," Ragnor agreed with a sigh.

"Not us," JAM said. "You."

Meanwhile, back at the . . . base . . .

All hell broke loose after Max left town.

Alison and Ian had both been ordered to move into bachelor officers' quarters at the base, thanks to a sudden escalation of her breather/stalker situation. Armed military police followed both of them wherever they went, even to the bathroom. Lillian and Sam moved in temporarily with Dr. Feingold, to everyone's surprise except Alison's.

The Breather calls had started up again, despite Alison's private number. There were messages now, in the same or a similar foreign-accented voice—definitely Middle Eastern, according to the Intel—and they were threatening.

A tracing device had been found in the wallet Alison had given Ian for his birthday. Apparently, the device had been planted there by the person who had entered her apartment weeks ago, as a way to find out where Ian was living.

As a result of the tracing device, Ian's home had been entered and his phone lines wired. He was also being threatened by the foreign-accented culprit.

Someone was up to no good, and it involved both Alison and her brother. Her father, alerted to the danger, had arrived from D.C., accompanied by an armed guard worthy of a visiting king.

No one knew why they were being stalked, but some of

the best military and private Intel in the country was at work on the case. Terrorism in any form was taken seriously these days.

But that wasn't the worst of Alison's problems. She was pregnant. *Pregnant!* No one knew but her, and she was less than one month along, but that didn't change anything. *Pregnant!*

Who would have thunk it?

A physician. A superintelligent woman. A Navy SEAL aspiree. A woman who had her whole future mapped out. A control freak personified. Pregnant. Was that dumb, or what?

She and Max had used condoms every time they'd made love . . . lots of condoms. *Except* for that one bleepin' nano-second in the broom closet. God must have a sense of humor to have thrown this roadblock her way. Or maybe He had some plan for her. Was it destiny, as Max kept saying?

She had to laugh or else she would cry.

Well, Max would be coming home at the end of next week.

Would that make things better, or worse?

Are we having fun yet? . . .

The first two weeks weren't too bad.

The grueling physical exercise required of SEALs was cut in half, and there was no Gig Squad, no long swims, or nighttime evolutions.

Same old constant running as in SEALs training, though. No one ever walked here, either. The men and women were ordered to run everywhere. "Move it, move it, move!" But here the running was called the Airborne Shuffle, running in step with the left foot slamming down. Some half-brain sitting in an off-his somewhere probably thought it had a musical lilt to it.

Really, the military in this time and this country was a bit barmy, placing so much emphasis on running. They ought to put more time on swordplay, catapulting, laying siege, boiling oil, forcing battering rams through heavy doors.

The Army people here appeared not to like the Navy people much, for no apparent reason, possibly because they'd given their barracks a special name, the Frog Pond, setting them apart from the others.

Sergeant Major Williamson had singled Ragnor out for particular dislike, also for no apparent reason. But the Viking could handle that kind of torment easily. Real torment would have been serving under someone like Svein Forkbeard, who had a free hand with his broadaxe. Cage summed up Ragnor's situation succinctly: "Sometimes you're the dog. Sometimes you're the hydrant." Ragnor didn't know precisely what a hydrant was, but he got the gist.

He and the other SEAL trainees had survived these two weeks. That was the most important thing.

This fifth phase of SEAL training in George-ha was designed to teach the men how to fall in progressively more dangerous situations. The PLFs (parachute landing falls) started with a thirty-four-foot tower simulating an airplane exit. *And wasn't that great fun!* Then they moved on to 250-foot captive jumps. *Even greater fun, that!* During the upcoming final Jump Week they would all be required to make five qualifying jumps, one in full combat gear and another a mass jump with all their comrades. Out of an airplane. Up in the sky. *I can't wait. Ha, ha, ha!*

The work was tedious at times. Over and over they practiced the proper way to fall into the sawdust pits, to avoid breaking a leg or other body part. They must needs fall on

the flat of their feet with the legs acting as springs to absorb
the shock, upper body twisting to the side. Not as easy as it
at first appeared. Sometimes he missed his brother Torolf,
who would have enjoyed hearing him tell of lessons in falling, of all things. The two of them had done way too much
of just that as youthling boys bent on mischief.

Today was Saturday, and they'd been given the only liberty day to be dispensed whilst in George-ha. Ragnor had
been calling Alison's tell-a-fone number every half hour, to
no avail. All he got was her answering machine—a torture
device, to be sure.

"Where could she be?" he complained when he returned
to the table in the drinking hall where his friends were
sloshing down beer and eating pizza, an Ah-mare-ee-can
delicacy that looked like manchet bread with cheese and a
bloodlike substance on top. Actually, it was delicious.

"She's still not there, huh?" Cage asked, patting him on
the shoulder as he sat down.

Ragnor shook his head and decided he just might have to
drown his sorrows in his mead. He'd been unable to make
any fone calls the first two weeks they'd been here. Now, at
his first free time, she was unavailable. Why he would think
she should have made herself available, without prior notice,
he had no idea, but he was chagrined nonetheless.

Just then a female Army person sat down in the empty
chair on his other side and said, "Hiiiii, baby."

He looked to his left and then behind him to see whom
she addressed. "Are you talking to me?"

"Oh, yeah! My name's Tamara Blue. I'm from Savannah.
Y'all can call me Tammie, y'heah?" She talked with the same
lazy drawl as Cage.

"Just call me Max," he replied, a mite baffled. Usually
women latched onto Pretty Boy first, attracted by his supe-

rior good looks, as he so often reminded them. Or JAM if they were more tempted by dark, mysterious men. Ragnor was not a humble man. He knew his assets, and they were plenty, but still he asked, "Why me?"

"Honey, I reckon you got a butt to die for. I noticed when you went to make a phone call."

He grinned. *Bloody hell, I wish Torolf were here. He would be hooting with laughter that a woman is attracted by my arse.*

"Y'all gonna buy me a beer?"

"Oh. Yea. Of course." He felt as clumsy as an untried youthling. Cage laughed and raised a hand in the air to signal the serving wench. Ragnor's other comrades smirked at his awkwardness.

He recognized the woman now. She was in their jumping class. Whilst some of the men shivered in their boots afore leaping from the high towers, she had launched herself out with a wild yell of "Yahoo!"

"Sooooo, Max, is it true what they say about SEALs?" she inquired lazily after taking a long swig of beer straight from the bottle. Holding his eyes, she did the most outrageous thing. She took the long neck of the bottle into her mouth, all the way, then slowly drew it out, licking the sides the whole time.

Son of a dragon! I wonder if Alison can do that?

He heard Cage mutter at his other side, "Sonofagun!" The other men muttered things more explicit than that.

"Well?" she asked.

"Well, what?" He gulped as he spoke. Tammie was short, petite, and blond, with a tattoo on her arm that read "Born to be Wild." She was not his type at all; still, a part of his body appreciated her assets very much . . . and the bottle trick, he had to admit. He shifted in his seat to accommodate that growing appreciation.

Tammie noticed and grinned at him. "I asked if it was true what they say about SEALs?"

That they are demented? That they talk too much about women? That they are braggarts? "What do they say?"

"That y'all have great staying power. All that long-distance swimming and stuff tends to build muscle." She put particular emphasis on the word "muscle," which let him know which muscle she was referring to. As if he and said muscle didn't know exactly what she meant.

"I do not know about SEALs, but we Vikings are known far and wide for that particular talent," he told her truthfully.

"Oh, my Gawd! You're a Viking, too. I luuuuve football."

Flash burst out laughing, and beer shot out of his mouth. "Good thing he's not a Ram. Think of that picture."

"Do you think the Minnesota Vikings wear horned helmets?" Cody was laughing so hard he kept hitting the table with his fist as if to catch his breath.

"Or that the Rams know how to *ram*?" Sly added with a chuckle.

In truth, they were all making mirth at his expense and that of the young woman.

"I mean that I am from the Norselands," he explained to Tammie.

"Jerks!" she said to the entire table, including him. Then she stood, about to stomp away.

Ragnor couldn't insult a woman, even a stranger, especially when tears welled in her eyes. He put a hand on her forearm and drew her back down. "My apologies, m'lady, I meant no offense. I really am a Viking by birth. And my friends"—he cast a warning glower around the table— "well, they are nigh *drukkinn* and will surely suffer the ale-head in the morning, if that is any recompense."

She nodded her acceptance of his apology. Some of her

friends came to join them at the table, which shut the crude mouths of his comrades. In the shuffle of gathering extra chairs and ordering drinks, Tammie asked, "Wanna dance?"

Well, actually, he didn't "wanna," but he couldn't offend her further. So he stood with a sigh of resignation and walked out onto the dance floor. There were no musicians, but music blared from a lighted box.

Tammie came only to his chin, so she wrapped her arms around his waist and rested her face on his chest. Not knowing what to do with his hands, he placed them on her shoulders. Then they swayed from side to side.

I am getting quite good at this dancing. In fact, I like it.

Then she moved her hands down to cup his buttocks.

On the other hand, it would not be wise to like it too much. He knew he had to say something. "I am complimented by your interest in me, but I am committed to another."

She drew her head back. "Married? I didn't see a ring."

"Nay, not married."

"Engaged?"

"Not precisely."

"Are you jerking me off?"

Ragnor had a pretty good idea what that meant. "Nay. 'Tis true. I have a lady love back in Coronado waiting for me." *I hope.* "Whether we wed or not is in the hands of the Norns right now, but mayhap it will happen someday." *If I'm still here.* "All I know is that I would feel disloyal to her if I rutted with another woman." *Though I am sorely tempted.*

"Rutted?" She laughed. "Maybe you oughta be a ram instead of a Viking, like your buddies said."

They continued to sway back and forth, quiet now. Another song came on the box, and still they swayed.

"Is there no man in your life back in Save-anna?"

"There was," she said, "but we had a big fight before I re-upped this time. He's in the Army, too, but he wanted to get married and for me to stay home and take care of his kids."

He frowned in confusion.

"He's divorced but has custody of his two kids, three- and four-year-old boys."

"Well, I know how that is. My father had custody of thirteen children at one point. None of the women wanted to stay and take care of them."

"Thirteen?"

"Yea. I suspect that not all of them were his, but my father had a kind heart and could not turn any child away. In any case, he was a very handsome man. Women loved him, obviously, but none of them would stay because of the children. A more bothersome lot there ne'er was, myself included." *Why do you not take up blathering as an occupation, Ragnor? You are getting quite adept at it.*

"Oh, Jake's kids aren't a bother at all. They're adorable. And their mother is a bitch. Wants nothing to do with them. Poor munchkins! And Jake, he's a great father. I can't help loving him, kids and all."

"Let me understand this. You love the man. You love his children. But you left him?" *Now I am giving love advice. Aaarrgh!*

"I'm only twenty-four years old. I want a military career. For a while anyway. And despite loving his kids, I want my own. I don't know. I'm so confused."

Let me tell you a thing or twelve about confusion, milady. "Betimes it is difficult for me to understand people of your ti . . . country. You make everything so complicated."

"How so?"

"A man protects those under his shield. That is the way it has been from the beginning of time. Oh, do not get your hackles up. I am not saying that women cannot have their own lives and interests. But I understand this Jake fellow. 'Tis in the nature of man to want his woman and children home where he is better able to care for them."

"That is a load of male chauvinist crap."

He shrugged. "I do not have easy answers. But let me say this. You live in dangerous times here in Ah-mare-ee-ca. Terrorists. Deranged despots. And military people are in even greater danger than average folks. How would you feel if you heard tomorrow that your Jake had been killed?"

"Devastated."

"And would you have any regrets?"

"Probably."

"On the other hand, if you were killed tomorrow, how would your Jake feel?"

"Devastated," she answered without question.

"Would he have regrets?"

She shrugged. "Probably. What's your point?"

"My grandmother believed that for every man there is one woman. She would say, find a way to make it work. Life is too short to live it unhappily." *Does this apply to me, too?*

"Why is it always the woman who must compromise?"

"I ne'er said that." *Did I think it?*

"Well, I suppose that my parents and Jake's parents could help with the kids when either of us was on active duty. We'd be able to save some money for a house if both of us were working. And it's not like it would be forever. I don't know. It's not the best solution, but . . ."

". . . a compromise?" *Why am I thinking that this applies to me, too?*

She smiled and hugged him warmly. "Thank you."

"For what?"

"Listening."

Several hours later, when Ragnor and his friends were leaving the drinking hall, after five more unsuccessful calls to Alison, he noticed Tammie leaning against the wall speaking on the tell-a-fone. "I love you, too, Jake. And, darlin', we are gonna make it work. If we love each other, nothing can stop us. Y'hear?"

Ragnor smiled and tipped his cap at her as he passed. In his heart, though, he wondered if love really could overcome all odds. Especially when the man was a thousand years old.

CHAPTER SEVENTEEN

❦

*D*addy Dearest . . .

Alison was as spit-shined as any Navy girl could be when she went to the opulent, one-hundred-plus-year-old Hotel del Coronado to meet her father and Ian for dinner.

The Del was a magnificent architectural extravaganza, which had been visited by numerous celebrities and politicians over the past century. The movie *Some Like It Hot* had been filmed here with Marilyn Monroe, Jack Lemmon, and Tony Curtis in 1958. Wallis Simpson and Edward, then Prince of Wales, were said to have met here. It even had its own resident ghost.

But that was neither here nor there. Alison barely paid attention to the surroundings as she made her way toward the Palm Court, followed by the ensign who'd been assigned to guard her this past week, even when on base. She was about to be grilled by her father, and she felt like a little girl on the carpet again.

"Hey, Pooh Bear," her father said as he stood and gave her a quick kiss and warm hug. *Pooh Bear? Jeesh! I'm twenty-seven freakin' years old and he still calls me Pooh Bear!*

"Daddy," she said, hugging him back. *Wait till he finds out that Pooh Bear is gonna have a mini-Pooh.*

Over his shoulder, Ian grinned at her . . . probably delighted to have some of the attention diverted away from himself. Their father had been in town for three days now, and Alison had managed to avoid him, after their initial meeting, having pleaded a heavy caseload with her patients.

Once they sat down, she noticed her father had his usual martini sitting in front of him. The Palm Court was known for its award-winning martini menu, but that wouldn't have mattered. Her father had had a ritual of drinking two martinis, graced with one olive each, every night as long as she could remember. No less, no more. The Del wouldn't have dared give this austere, highly decorated Navy big shot anything but the best, whether it be lodgings, food, or drinks.

His admiral's uniform with all its medals and insignia was impeccable. The brass gleamed. As always, not a hair on his short-cut gray head was out of place. Thirty years of "high and tight." He sat erect, even when at ease. The man commanded respect without uttering a word.

Ian was drinking Scotch, straight up. A bad sign.

"What'll you have, Pooh?" her father asked.

"Just water with a twist of lemon," she said.

"No wine? You usually have white wine."

She shook her head. "Not tonight." Or for another eight or so months. *Oh, God! How am I ever going to tell these two? Well, not tonight, that's for sure.*

While her father updated them on the investigation, Ian sipped at his drink and she picked at the appetizers. She hadn't realized she was so hungry, and the calamari in filo dough was delicious, followed by crisp house salad with raspberry vinaigrette dressing. She ate all of hers, as well as part of Ian's and her father's, too. Her appetite had become voracious, probably due to the baby. *How soon will I show? Ha,*

ha, ha! I'm a doctor. I already know that. Three months.
Maybe four.

"It can't be those Lebanese terrorists from five years ago
that are stalking me and Allie today," Ian said. "They all
died in the bombing, along with a bunch of civilians and our
entire SEAL team, except for me. A bunch of friggin' nut-
cakes!" He glanced at Alison and winced at his own bad
language.

Really, Ian and her father both treated her like a little
girl, as if she'd faint at bad language. *Not so little now . . .
and about to be bigger.*

"We don't know for sure yet, but we think one of these terrorists lost civilian family members in the blast, and they're
out for revenge," her father explained.

"Revenge?" Alison exclaimed. "They were the ones who
set off the bomb."

"Terrorist logic, I guess," her father said. "An eye for an
eye, we're thinking. Your family destroyed in return for the
tango's family."

"What about Clay and Ross? Are they in danger, too?
And how about you, Daddy?" she asked, suddenly worried.

"They wouldn't be able to get to me. I'm too insulated in
the capital. But, yes, Clay and Ross could be targets, and the
necessary precautions have been taken."

Their entrees came: stuffed flounder with wild rice for
Alison and rare filet mignons with big baked potatoes for Ian
and her father. As they ate, her father continued to discuss
the investigation. At one point he stared at her oddly, and she
realized that she'd put sour cream and chives on her rice
and was eating it with relish. "Right now we are in a holding pattern. Everyone's safe. But at some point we may have
to send some pigeons out there to catch a hawk or two."

"Pigeons? I hope you don't mean a decoy for me," Ian protested. "I'll go back to my house and act as bait. I don't need anyone to take my place."

"Me either," Alison said, equally irritated.

"Opinions noted, and they will be passed on. Those decisions are out of our hands, though. Changing the subject, I have some good news for you, Pooh Bear."

I'm not pregnant? It was just a dream ... or a nightmare?

"We've just gotten the president's and the Congressional Armed Services Committee's confidential approval to go ahead with a new set of military teams ... the Liberty Teams. It's all hush-hush so far. They'll be made up of representatives of special forces from all the armed services ... Green Berets, SEALs, Delta teams, all the Special Forces, computer experts, pilots, medical personnel. To start, there will be twelve teams of fifteen hand-picked operatives each."

Her father looked her directly in the eye and winked.

The hair rose on the back of her neck. "Me? You think I might have a chance?"

Her father patted her hand. "No promises, and I know it's not the SEALs, as you've always wanted, but I do have a little bit of pull."

Can my life get any better ... or worse ... than this? I'm pregnant. There is no way in the world they will accept a pregnant woman. And it's doubtful they'd take a new mother, either. Lack of focus. Oh, my God! Oh, my God! What should I do? Tears welled in her eyes.

"Now, sweetie, don't go bawling on me. You always hoped for something like this."

I feel like bawling. Could the timing be any worse?

"How about me?" Ian asked, giving her a bit of breathing time.

"Aren't you happy in SEALs?" the admiral inquired. They both ate as they talked. Alison did, too, like an automaton.

"Yeah. But this new program sounds exciting. It would be good to be back in the field again."

His father nodded, considering. "Maybe you should go to officers' candidate school first."

Ian crossed his eyes at her when their father turned to signal the waiter for a second martini. She knew about this standing argument between Ian and their father over his becoming an officer.

"So, who is this person Max who keeps calling you?" the admiral asked out of the blue.

Alison choked on her fish and had to take a drink of water to wash it down.

"The FBI guys listening to your answering machine say this guy Max called you twelve times yesterday."

Ian just smirked.

"He's a friend," she said. *Who happens to have time-traveled here. Ha, ha, ha.*

"Only a friend?" her father asked. The old bird saw way too much.

"For now," she said, feeling her face heat with a telling blush. *And, by the way, he's the father of your grandchild.*

"You know I'm going to want to know more," her father said with mock sternness.

That's what I'm afraid of.

"Leave her alone, Dad." Ian, bless him, came to her rescue. "I've already pushed her far enough on her personal life. There are some things she's gotta do herself."

Sometimes Ian could be a pain in the tush, but sometimes she just loved him to pieces.

The admiral raised his eyebrows at Ian's standing up to

him, but fortunately, he didn't insist that she tell him more about Max. Not yet. But he would eventually, that she knew.

Heck, what could she say? There's this guy I may or may not be in love with. He thinks he's an eleventh-century Norseman come to visit here for a short time; then he'll be off on his longship to go a-Viking or something. And if or when he goes, he'll have left something precious behind.

Me.

And a baby.

"Anyone want dessert?" she asked. "I'm dying for some double fudge mousse cheesecake."

Falling in love with falling . . .

Ragnor knew with his cherry jump that this was a sport he could love.

He was fifth on the stick out the door. Everyone was visibly scared, even those who'd done this before. But the minute the jump master called his number and Ragnor stepped to the exit, all fear left him in a rush of exhilaration. He had one hand on each side of the doorway, legs slightly bent, one foot slightly behind the other. When he jumped up and out, he executed a perfect jump, arms hard at his sides as he'd been taught, hands gripping the reserve chute, chin tucked into his chest. As his main chute billowed out above him, Ragnor grinned and let out a fierce Viking battle cry of victory.

Pretty Boy had been wrong. It wasn't better than sex, but it was a close second.

Ragnor would have done all five of his required jumps that day if they'd allowed him to. He suspected his fellow SEAL trainees felt the same way. There was a bit of the ad-venturer in them all.

After the Jump School graduation ceremony at the end of the week at which they received their silver wing brooches, Sergeant Major Williamson surprised Ragnor by coming up to him and shaking his hand. "Good job, sailor," he said.

Ragnor was too stunned to speak, despite being inordinately pleased.

But the thing that pleased him most was that he was on his way back to Coronado.

And Alison.

She's got mail . . .

Ian was back in his own home as part of a combined FBI and Navy Intel plan to draw out the perps, but Alison was not so lucky.

Ian's and Alison's homes had been wired for sound and video. Snipers were now located surreptitiously around the two neighborhoods, but it was hoped no blood would be shed on either side; the military always said that in the most successful op no shots were fired. Ian himself wore body armor under his regular clothing, just in case, but only after he completed his regular duties at the SEAL Command Center at Coronado and returned to his home in San Diego.

Admiral MacLean had gone back to D.C., reluctantly. His presence could cause suspicion and extra caution on the part of those stalking the family. The last thing they wanted at this point was a cautious tango. Cautious tangos hid out in their hidey-holes, impossible to detect.

Meanwhile, Alison bristled at being out of the loop. Forced to continue living on base, she raged at anyone who would listen. The only promise she'd obtained was that she'd be bait, along with Ian, if they didn't capture anyone this week.

Even while Alison stormed and railed, she had mixed feelings about the whole mess:

1) Here was an opportunity for her to finally engage in an active op involving possible terrorists. At the same time, she thought, placing a hand over her flat stomach, she had another life to consider now.

2) She wasn't even sure if she wanted this baby. Well, actually, she was sure. There'd never really been any question about that.

3) Worried sick over the fanatics who had targeted her and her family, she floundered between rage and fear. She'd like to be the one to engage the cowardly weasels, to put a bullet between their beady eyes. But then, she was deathly afraid that she or Ian or her father would suffer the same fate as David. She knew too well that good didn't always win out in the end.

4) She was mad at Max for getting her pregnant. Oh, the logical part of her brain argued that she was equally to blame. After all, she'd allowed him to lift her skirt. But who said pregnant women are logical?

5) The thing that confused her most was herself, and her constantly shifting emotions. Did she love Max . . . almost a perfect stranger? Did he love her? Did it matter in the scheme of things? She was a take-charge woman. She wanted to control her own destiny. But how?

Destiny? Now, why did that word come to mind? Max always said that she was his destiny. Was it possible?

So many confusing thoughts! And so few answers!

Alison solved her dilemma the way pregnant women have since the beginning of time. First, she bawled for five minutes. Then she went to pee for the hundredth time that day. Then she ate everything in sight.

A tiny voice in the back of her mind whispered, *Why do you worry about things beyond your control? What will be will be.*

Was it Max sending her a telepathic message?

Yeah, right!

Or God?

Hmmmm.

Either way, Alison felt oddly better. Besides, Max would be back tomorrow. Time enough then to resolve things . . . or get even more stirred up.

It was still early, too soon to go to bed, so she decided to get caught up on some paperwork related to her patients. When she was done, she went online to check her e-mail. To her surprise, the queue showed something from a <kmagnusson>. Oh, my goodness, it was the woman she'd e-mailed several weeks ago about her graduate thesis.

Quickly opening the e-mail, she read:

Dear Doctor MacLean (or should I call you Lieutenant MacLean?):

Sorry it has taken me so long to reply. I've been home at Blue Dragon on a term break. With all my brothers and sisters, chaos reigns there, so I haven't had a chance to log on to a computer till now.

Yes, I can send you a copy of my thesis as an attached file, as long as you understand that even theses are copyrighted material. Frankly, I consider it a compliment that anyone would be interested. It is such a specialized area of interest.

You mentioned knowing someone with the name Magnusson. Could that possibly be my brother Torolf you refer to? I ask only because your signature line indicates U.S. Navy, and he is a Navy SEAL trainee. By the way, if it is Torolf, tell him our father is upset that he hasn't called in ages. (Just like a man, right?)

But it's probably not Torolf, because he would know my name, of course, and be aware of the research I've been doing for years.

In any case, let me know what you think of my material. And, if there are any other questions, feel free to ask.

    Kirsten Magnusson
    Doctoral candidate in medieval studies, UCLA

At first, Alison was stunned.

She reread the letter. What stood out was the fact that Max had brothers and sisters, despite his having said they were all dead, except for someone named Madrene back in Norway. The third time through, she homed in on the Blue Dragon connection. She hadn't mentioned Kirsten Magnusson to Max the day she'd sent the e-mail, so Kirsten's comment about that didn't apply. Still, why would he have gone to the trouble of doing research at the library if he already knew all this stuff?

Very troubling!

Another quick read and she noticed something else. Kirsten had an AOL address, just as she did. On the remote possibility that Kirsten might be online right now, Alison sent an Instant Message:

Hey, Kirsten! Thanks for the attached file. Haven't had a chance to read it yet. Yes, I know someone named Magnusson—Max. He's off at jump school right now in Georgia. I have so many questions. Any chance we could get together sometime?

Dr. Alison MacLean, Lt. (jg) U.S. Navy

Within minutes, she got a response:

Questions? I don't know. What would Torolf . . . I mean Max . . . say about that? I wouldn't want to do anything behind his back.
    Kirsten Magnusson

To which she replied:

Not to worry. I would do nothing to hurt Max. In fact, I believe meeting with you might help him. He's had some problems since the accident. It's up to you, though.
    Dr. Alison MacLean, Lt. (jg) U.S. Navy

She had barely hit "Send" before there was a response:

What accident? Oh, my God! What happened?
    Kirsten Magnusson.

Alison couldn't believe that Max hadn't told his family about the accident and his concussion. On second thought, maybe he wouldn't. *Some of these Navy SEALs are so macho, they would consider a concussion a sign of weakness. It really isn't that surprising that Max wouldn't have told his family, now that I think about it. Besides, I don't know what his relationship was to his family before the accident.*
She put her fingers on the keyboard again and typed:

Listen. We really do need to meet. I don't feel comfortable discussing Max in this way. And as a physician, there are some things I can't disclose anyway. So, what do you say to our meeting Friday, the 20th, at 3 p.m.? I can come to your office if that's okay.

Dr. Alison MacLean, Lt. (jg) U.S. Navy

Kirsten agreed, although Alison could tell that she would have liked to ask more questions. They both said good-bye, then signed off.

Could my life get any more stressful than this? Do I really need to be involved with a man who has so many issues?

On the other hand, how can I not do everything to help him? Maybe meeting Kirsten will unravel some of the mystery surrounding Max.

So it was a hopeful Alison who crawled into bed that night . . . hopeful because Max was coming back tomorrow, hopeful that she would be meeting a person next week who might shed some light on the mysteries surrounding him, hopeful that the dark cloud that had been hanging over her head would suddenly burst forth with sunshine.

What a dreamer!

CHAPTER EIGHTEEN

❦

Her boyfriend's back and they're gonna be sorry...

The chieftain waved peremptorily to Ragnor the minute he stepped onto the airplane steps. Ragnor was pretty sure Ian wasn't there to welcome him home with open arms.

"Wow!" Flash muttered. "Max gets his very own Welcome Wagon."

To which Cody added, "Do you think he'll give him a big ol' kiss?"

"Just so it doesn't involve tongue," was Cage's contribution.

"Sarcasm ill suits you knaves," Ragnor observed with a laugh, adding his own conclusion: "He probably wants to give me another silver brooch, like my wings, for being such a good SEAL whilst away from the base . . . or just for being away."

"The only time the master chief would relish giving you any kind of decoration is if he could pin it on your ass," Pretty Boy said. "Or another objectionable body part."

"There is naught objectionable about *that* part of my body." Still, he pretended to shiver and cross his legs at the prospect of any sharp object going there.

They all had a good laugh then at his expense, which they

stopped abruptly when they got to the bottom of the airplane steps.

"Stay away from my sister, birdbrain," the chieftain said to him right off, pulling him over to the side of the tarmac.

"You say birdbrain as if 'tis an endearment." Ragnor smiled cheerily at the chieftain.

"Do I have to assign you to Gig Squad the minute you get back?"

So the chieftain is singing the same old song. Blather, blather, blather. "Where is Alison?"

"She is none of your concern."

Wouldst like to take a wager on that? "She is very much my concern. Either you tell me where she is and why she does not answer her tell-a-fone, or I will get the answers myself."

"Is that a threat, shit-for-brains?"

Ragnor inhaled and exhaled sharply for patience. Word insults need not pierce him. Finally he said, "Believe you me, a Viking with a purpose is a formidable foe. I do not make idle threats. And I do not want you for my enemy. In truth, you and I are on the same side of the shield when it comes to protecting Alison and having her best interests at heart."

The chieftain's eyes went wide at his words. "Un-be-freakin'-liev-able!" he muttered.

I think he's starting to like me. "Besides, once you meet my sister Madrene, you will be sticking to me like burrs on a bull's arse."

"I am not interested in you. I am not interested in your sister. I am not interested in anything that comes out of your stupid mouth."

"Not even if Madrene is a combination Julia Roberts and Charlize Theron?"

"You said she was a combination Faith Hill and Pamela Anderson. Make up your mind."

Ragnor just grinned. Obviously, the chieftain had been paying more attention than he'd pretended.

Then, taking Ragnor's forearm and following his teammates toward a nearby building, the chieftain disclosed, "A lot has been happening with the tango who's been stalking Alison . . . and me, too. She's moved into the bachelor officers' quarters on base. An armed guard follows her everywhere. Me, too. She's so stressed out, she's eating chocolate by the bucketfuls. Now, will you leave her alone till all this is resolved?"

Alarm rippled over Ragnor. "Is she safe? Was she hurt in any way?"

The chieftain shook his head. "The attacks have been just verbal. So far. But this is no everyday weirdo making idle threats. This is bigtime serious. Do you understand?"

He nodded.

"So you'll stay away?"

"Why would I stay away? I am no threat to her. I want to help."

The chieftain groaned with frustration and probably would have pulled at his hair if he had some of any length. "You've got to give the FBI and Navy Intel room to work. Don't distract them with your presence. And, frankly, if I were you, I wouldn't want to call attention to myself in any way . . . if you get my drift."

Ragnor got the chieftain's drift. That didn't mean he would follow those ridiculous orders. Nothing would keep him away from Alison now that he was back in town.

Apparently the chieftain suspected his intentions, because he immediately ordered Ragnor and his classmates to the sleeping barracks, where they were to stow their gear and report to the Grinder within the hour. To make sure that Ragnor didn't stray, he told the other seven members of his team, "If Magnusson leaves your sight for even one minute before reporting back for duty, *all* of you are going to be doing push-ups for the next twenty-four hours. Is that clear?"

They all, Ragnor included, stood at attention, then saluted the chieftain as he stomped away.

"Asshole!" Sly said, to which the rest of them concurred with simultaneous grunts.

Once they returned to duty, the instructors immediately launched into a discourse on what would be the final phase of their training for the next three weeks: SCUBA, which meant diving . . . all kinds of underwater diving. The whole purpose was to teach them ways to get from one point to another underwater without being detected. It meant they had to learn to exhale in one steady stream for a minute and a half, which turned out to be harder than anyone had anticipated. It meant they had to learn to swim with underwater breathing devices. It meant they had to understand the medical aspects of this type of dangerous work, which Ragnor hoped would be taught by Alison. It meant they had to know which fish were friendlies and which were not; sharks and barracudas being in the latter category, both of which he had encountered in his previous life. It meant they had to become true frogmen, as comfortable in the ocean depths as they were in a jungle environment. Webfoot warriors!

All of them were so exhausted by the time they got back to their sleeping barracks that night that they wished they were back in Georgia jumping out of airplanes.

The men took quick hot showers and fell onto their pallets, asleep practically before they hit the mattresses.

Ragnor had other plans, but they would have to wait till

the morrow. Even if he had had the energy, a guard standing at the doorway ensured he wouldn't be using that energy for anything but sleep.

But he dreamed. Sweet, sweet dreams.

Running with the wolves . . . rather, SEALs . . . uh, same thing . . .

Alison finished her morning rounds and decided to go run with the SEALs.

She was a little upset that Max hadn't come to see her yesterday, even though she knew it wasn't his fault. Ian, her father, the FBI, and Navy security had practically built a glass wall around her to keep the tangos from getting to her. If she wanted to see Max, or talk with him, she would have to take the initiative . . . and even then, it would take a little creative planning. That would be risky—calling attention to herself and Max and a possible relationship between them, which was a U.S. Navy no-no. So maybe that wasn't such a good idea.

But running would be okay, she told herself. Lots of people liked to run with the SEALs, and not just military personnel at the base. Visiting celebrities, politicians, even presidents loved to run with them, looking upon the exercise as both an ego boost and a promo opportunity.

Butterflies fluttered in her stomach as she warmed up on the Grinder, knowing she would be seeing Max soon. Then she jogged slowly to the beach, where she planned to catch up with the various SEAL classes running together this morning, like any other morning. To her surprise, they were stopped up ahead, standing around, while Ian, Lieutenant George Igo, the XO of the SEALs command center, and several instructors stood arguing with Max and his team-mates. Max's swim partner, Cage, was sitting on the beach rubbing his ankle. A whole lot of yelling was going on.

She began to run faster when she realized Cage was hurt.

"I'm not volunteering out," Cage shouted, getting clum-sily to his feet with the help of Max. The tears in his eyes were a testament to the pain he was trying to hide. Either that, or a testament to his fear that he would be expelled from the training program.

"You ring out or I ring you out," the XO said stonily. "You've injured your ankle, Seaman LeBlanc, and are unable to com-plete the rest of SEAL training. That's that!"

"The hell it is . . . Lieutenant Igo, sir!" Cage insisted. Turn-ing to Ian, he pleaded, "Master Chief, sir . . . you allowed Max to continue after his concussion. Give me a chance, too."

"Let me look at it," Alison said, pushing to the forefront. She barely made eye contact with Max, who looked so good her mouth watered, before getting down on her knees in the sand and taking Cage's foot in her hands. The ankle was al-ready starting to swell, and the skin was turning a reddish blue. She probed, she pressed, she massaged, and she asked Cage questions the whole time. He denied being in pain, but she knew better.

"His ankle is sprained, not broken," she pronounced to the XO and Ian as she stood up. "Probably a torn or stretched ligament. At worst, a sprain. At the least, a bad strain."

"What does that mean?" Lieutenant Igo growled.

"He's in a lot of pain."

"No kidding!" Cage said.

Ian scowled at him in a silent message to be quiet.

"He should ice the ankle down, wrap it tight, and keep his weight off the foot for at least a week. And get an X-ray as a precaution."

"No way!" Cage knew full well that one week out of training and he'd be dropped from this class, maybe from SEALs training forever. All the other SEAL trainees standing around grumbled their support.

"You know the rules," Ian told Cage, his voice soft with compassion. "If you can't do the work along with your teammates, you have got to ring out."

"He is not dropping out," Max said, stepping in front of Cage and going down halfway on his haunches, his back to him. "Put your arms around my neck and wrap your legs around my hips," he told Cage. "We've got a run to complete, buddy."

Cage grinned and shook his head at Max. "Nice try, Max, but you can't carry me and run at the same time."

"I am a Viking. We can do anything we set our minds to do." He gave a quick glance at Alison to emphasize the double meaning in his words.

Her heart did a little flip-flop. She knew then that he was just as aware of her as she was of him, even in the midst of this disaster.

"Do it! Do it! Do it!" the other SEAL trainees started chanting.

Max said something in an undertone to Cage about him and the other guys having carried him for weeks and now it was his turn. Although Max had several inches in height on Cage, and the Cajun was much leaner in build, it would still be a formidable task.

"*Mon Dieu*, they will never believe this down on the bayou." Cage embraced Max from behind, piggyback style, and Max stood up clumsily. Once he got his bearings, he began to jog along the beach. The other SEAL trainees smiled widely and joined in with Flash who began calling out a jubilant jody call:

"I don't know but I've been told,
I don't know but I've been told,
Navy SEALs have hearts of gold,
Navy SEALs have hearts of gold,
Never leave a man behind,
Never leave a man behind,
The extra trouble we don't mind.
The extra trouble we don't mind.
He's my brother . . .
He's my brother . . .
He's no bother.
He's no bother.
Sound off, one, two . . .
Sound off, one, two . . .
Three, four.
Three, four."

Alison wasn't the only one with tears in her eyes as she watched the very slow jogging of the troop moving up the beach. No one insisted that they run at their usual pace.

She looked at her brother and he looked at her.

"I'm beginning to understand what you see in the dodo bird," was all he said.

They caught up with the troop and jogged along silently. At one point, Sly, who was about the same height as Max, came up beside him and they arranged Cage between them and resumed stride. Now Cage's weight was equally distributed between two men, his arms looped over each of their shoulders, his feet off the ground. When two other men took over for them after fifteen minutes or so, Max jogged in place till Alison caught up with him. The XO and several instructors gave him a dirty look as they passed by, but not Ian. He just shook his head hopelessly at the two of them.

At first, Max just jogged along beside her, staring straight ahead. But when she glanced over, she saw that he was smiling.

He's the only man I know whose smile is like a kiss. "What's so funny?"

"Not funny."

"You're smiling."

He looked at her then, giving her the full benefit of his smile. His smile said it all. He was glad to see her.

Yep, kiss-smiles, for sure. She wanted to be mad at him for getting her pregnant. She wanted to keep her distance from him emotionally till she understood her feelings. She wanted to tell him he was an idiot for calling attention to himself like he'd just done back there. But his smile melted her. And she couldn't help herself. She smiled back.

"I earned my wings," he told her.

The delight on his face is precious. "I know. How was it?"

"Exciting. I want to do it again."

Oh, Max, you are becoming a SEAL, whether you want to or not. That is pure SEAL mentality. She laughed. It was the reaction of lots of guys . . . women, too. Bone-deep fear at first, then a huge adrenaline rush afterward. "You'll have lots of opportunities if you become a SEAL."

"Mayhap we can do it together sometime."

Not while I'm pregnant, sweetie. "Mayhap," she said back, teasing.

The teasing was lost on him. "I missed you. When can I see you?"

"I don't know. Things are dicey right now."

He nodded. "Your brother told me."

My brother doesn't know the half of it.

"Meet me tonight," he said.

"I can't. I have a guard assigned to me all the time." She

glanced pointedly at the ensign who jogged right behind them.

Max, instead of being more cautious now that he knew they were being watched, reached over and patted her bottom. To the scowling guard, he remarked, "Just brushing off a sand fly."

The guard was not amused. In fact, she could have sworn he gave Max the finger.

Max couldn't have cared less. "I will come to you, then."

"Don't do that," she said quickly. "Jeesh, you'll get yourself kicked out of SEALs for sure. It's one thing to defy Ian and the other instructors. Another thing all together to butt heads with the FBI and Navy Intel."

"Huh?"

"Never mind."

"They fed us good in George-ha," he said, as if that were relevant to anything.

"Uh, well, great!"

"But do you know what I asked for with every meal?"

She couldn't even guess, and she probably looked ridiculous gaping at him in question.

"Peanut butter and honey sand-witches." He grinned and waggled his eyebrows at her.

You are such a child. She couldn't help but grin back at his playfulness.

"I heard your father was here. I would have liked to meet him. By the by, what is your bride price?"

Another quick change of subject and, whooee, it was a zinger. Was he deliberately trying to throw her off balance? *Well, I've got news for you, buster, I've been off balance ever since I met you.* "Why?"

He cast her a tsk-tsk look, as if she'd asked an odd question. "You know why."

*No, I don't. At least, I don't think I do. Oh, no! He
wouldn't!* No way was she going to go down that path. Time
for her to do the quick-change thing and throw him off balance.

"Does the name Kirsten Magnusson mean anything to
you?"

Max's head jerked to the side to look at her. "I had a sister
named Kirsten at one time."

"Had?"

"She died when she was fourteen years old, along with
the rest of my family. Why do you ask?"

Alison was spared from answering by the roar of *"Magnusson!"* from her brother, who was jogging back to them.
"What the hell are you doing back here all this time?"

"Just talking."

"Talking? *Talking?* Is that what we friggin' pay you to do
in BUD/S? Get your ass in gear to the front of the squad.
And since you're in the mood for talking, how 'bout you call
out a jody so we can all benefit from your wisdom."

Ragnor winked at Alison and loped up to the front, where
two of his classmates were transferring Cage onto another
set of shoulders. When they finished running, Alison planned
to check Cage over more thoroughly and bind him up so that
no further harm would be done.

"Is your brain melting, to be associating with a trainee in
public?" Ian inquired, watching her watch Max as he jogged
to the front.

Probably. "I wasn't associating. I was just running with
the teams, and he happened to be running beside me."

Ian snorted with disgust.

Just then, Ian was given more reason for disgust, though
she noticed his lips twitching with mirth, as Max called out
his own version of a jody call:

"I don't know but I've been told,
I don't know but I've been told,
Navy SEALs are like men of old.
Navy SEALs are like men of old.
Elite warriors, did you say?
Elite warriors, did you say?
Sounds like Vikings in Norway.
Sounds like Vikings in Norway.
Look good . . .
Look good . . .
Love good . . .
Love good . . .
Best fighters in the neighborhood.
Best fighters in the neighborhood.
Women love them, yea, they do.
Women love them, yea, they do.
Vikings, SEALs . . . same crew.
Vikings, SEALs . . . same crew.
Heroes through and through.
Heroes through and through.
Time-less!
Time-less!"

That last, rhymeless word was added for her benefit, she was pretty sure. In fact, when Max glanced back at her and winked, she knew for certain.

She put a hand over her belly and said to herself, *Oooh, baby, we are in big trouble.*

CHAPTER NINETEEN

When love comes knock, knock, knocking . . .

Alison was in the shower that night when she heard a soft knock on the glass door of the shower stall.

At first, she was alarmed. How had someone entered her unit on the second floor of the officers' quarters? Could it be the tango? She grabbed for a loofah back scrubber and crouched down into a defensive position.

When the tango entered, she raised her "weapon" and was about to whack him on the head, but the culprit grabbed the handle in mid whack and threw it to the floor. The tango was Max.

"Are you crazy? You almost gave me a heart attack. And I could have really hurt you."

"With that?" He glanced disdainfully at her "weapon."

"Why are you here?" she asked, wiping water out of her eyes from the continuing hot spray. Barefoot and bare-chested, wearing only nylon running shorts, Max was already wet . . . not that he appeared to mind.

"Because I am dirty?" He smiled at her, giving special meaning to "dirty."

"How did you get here?"

"I rappeled down from the roof and came through your

living-room window. Sorry I am, but I had to break the lock. Well, not too sorry, since I am here."

"The roof? You rappeled down from the roof?" she asked incredulously.

He nodded. "Finally some of the training on the O-Course is beginning to have some merit . . . though my brother and I used to rappel on occasion when we wanted to enter a Saxon castle for a bit of raping and pillaging." He waggled his wet eyebrows at her to show he was teasing. "Flash is up on the roof still, holding the rope and keeping watch for me."

"I've heard of nut-case antics on the part of SEALs and SEAL trainees before, but this takes the cake."

"You have cake?"

His interest in a sweet at a time like this was equally adorable and asinine. But perhaps he'd just been teasing again, because he was already backing her up against the wall and leaning down to kiss her.

Against his sexy, sexy mouth she groaned and said, "Max, this is insanity. We have to talk."

"If this is insanity, it feels bloody hell damn good. If this is insanity, then no wonder half-wits walk about with silly grins on their drooling faces." He laid his lips over hers and kissed her deeply. In fact, he kissed her so deeply and so thoroughly that her knees started to buckle. Luckily, or not so luckily, he lifted her by the waist and held her up with his hips pressed against hers.

She said nothing, but she did make a whooshy exhaling sound, like a woman in labor, or, better yet, a woman in heat. *Yikes!*

"I have five minutes, ten at most, afore Flash and I have to be back at the barracks. My teammates can cover for us only so long," he said quickly, letting her know he had heard her plea for talk. "So, talk or tup?"

"What a choice, you smooth-talker, you!"

He shrugged. "There is a time for smoothness and a time for crudeness. Art thou offended, m'lady?" Meanwhile, he insinuated himself more intimately between her legs *right there*, and she bit her tongue to stifle a groan. "Hmmm?"

Alison had grown up in a household of men, she worked primarily with men. If she were going to be put off by a little blunt talk, it would have happened long ago, and it hadn't. "Hardly," she replied with a laugh.

"So, talk or tup, sweetling?" He let her body lower to the floor, sloooowly.

His question had been a rhetorical one, really, because he'd already dropped his shorts and was naked underneath. Surprise, surprise! "Do cone-domes work in water?" he asked, slipping one on.

She started to tell him a condom was no longer necessary, but surely there would be a better time than this. Without any preliminaries or waiting for her to answer his question, he lifted her again, spread her legs with his knees, and in one sweet thrust was in her to the hilt. All of her inner folds were practically doing the hula, they were so happy to have him back. And she wasn't the only one who was pathetically enthusiastic about it; she could swear Max's penis was throbbing inside her.

She stood on tiptoes to fit better. Correction. He lifted her even higher by the buttocks and levered her legs around his hips. The hot water spraying over them turned tepid, but neither of them cared. Who was she kidding? It could be freezing and they'd still be hot.

As Max began to undulate himself in and out of her, he held her gaze. She couldn't have looked away if she'd wanted. His eyelashes were black spikes surrounding clear blue eyes. His lips were parted.

She put a hand to his cheek. He turned slightly and kissed the palm. Then immediately returned to watching her.

"I want to see you peak," he said.

"I want to see you peak first," she said.

He appeared about to balk—even as he continued to stroke in and out of her while he spoke, talented fellow that he was—but then he said something surprising. "Make me."

Now, how would I do that? Especially with you watching me like that. But then she became bold. She put her hands behind her neck and bowed her back so that her breasts jutted outward.

His rhythm faltered into a jerk before he resumed his slow thrusting pattern.

"How was that, sweetie?"

He laughed. "Not bad."

"Not bad? I'll give you 'not bad.'" She ran her hands over his shoulders, down his back, and under his buttocks. He grinned. But she wanted more of a response than that. Coming back to her own body, she took her small, very sensitive breasts in hand and thrummed the nipples to hard points with both thumbs.

"Holy Frigg!" he exclaimed through gritted teeth and slammed into her one last time.

To say that they had a simultaneous orgasm would be the understatement of all time. *Think fireworks and earth moving. Think fast and furious with finesse. Think love.*

But Alison didn't want to think anything just then.

Max let her slide to a standing position and was disengaging quickly after checking his wristwatch and muttering, "Two minutes to go! I hate to tup and run, sweetling, but I am going to be in big trouble if I don't get back."

She reached over and turned off the faucets. He pulled his shorts up, and she wrapped a towel around herself. They both emerged from the shower into the bathroom, laughing, only to see a Middle-Eastern-looking guy in a Navy uniform pointing a pistol at them. The uniform, which was much too big for him, and the pistol probably belonged to the guard who had been stationed outside her door, who she prayed was still alive.

Max shoved her behind him, but not before the tango gave her a sweeping glance of disgust and snarled in broken English, "Bitch! Infidel! Whore! You die today." He held the pistol in two hands and crouched a bit into the firing position. Clearly, he was more interested in her than Max, though he probably wouldn't mind—in fact, wouldn't hesitate—to take them both out.

"Nobody is dying here today," Max said calmly, motioning with his hands behind his back that she should move into the shower stall.

"No move!" the perp shrieked. "Go to side." He motioned with his gun.

This guy was a loose cannon. No telling what he would do. Alison moved back to Max's side. The room was a fair size, and the guy—Lebanese, she would guess—stood in the open doorway of the bathroom, putting about ten feet between them. She could see that the bedroom door out to the corridor was closed. No help from that quarter.

"Just relax. Just relax," Max said, holding his palms out in front of him. His voice and demeanor were cool, but Alison saw the fire of anger in his blue eyes. "Let's talk about this," he told the tango.

"No talk. Today, Allah be praised, my family be avenged. Today the Jew-loving U.S. of A., the Nav-hee SEALs, the MacLean family . . . today they pay price for their support of Israel. Murderers, all of you!"

"Murderers? Not us," Alison argued.

"Shhh," Max cautioned her.

"Don't tell me to be quiet. I have no idea who this jerk is, but he doesn't scare me." *Actually, he does scare me, but I can't let him know that.*

"This lady has nothing to do with you," Max said, slowly backing up and pulling her with him, an inch at a time.

"She has everything to do . . . she and her cursed family. I lost my father, two brothers, and a sister in that bombing. Her betrothed rots in hell for his crime; no business he had coming to my country. No business! Her brother will suffer the same fate, too . . . soon as he enters his home tonight."

"Oh, God! He must have planted a bomb in Ian's house," she murmured to Max.

He nodded that he'd heard her.

"How did you get on this base? In this building?" she asked, though she wasn't entirely surprised. After all, Max had managed to get in, too.

"Carefully. I plan for five long years. You think your military the only one knows covert tactics?"

"Killing me is not going to solve anything," Alison said.

His dark face went rigid with fury. "Do not speak to me, American harlot. Soon you burn in the fires of your Christian hell."

"You'll never escape alive."

"I die glady for just cause. A family jihad—"

In the middle of his sentence, Max shoved her hard so that she fell backward onto the tile floor while he launched himself forward. The gun went off as Alison watched in horror while the two men struggled on the floor. The gun went off a second time.

Alison heard someone screaming and realized it was herself. As she crawled up on her knees, then stood, making her way over to the two still bodies, she sobbed. *Oh, please . . .*

oh, please, God, let him be alive. Already a pool of blood was forming on the white tiles in an ever-expanding circle.

As several military men, weapons raised, broke through the outside door—apparently the tango had locked it from inside—and Flash came crawling through the window, alerted by the gunshots, Max moved slightly and raised himself up to a sitting position, gazing about groggily. The tango was dead, a bullet wound showing between his eyes. And Max had been shot in the shoulder. Alison dropped to her knees beside him.

"Somebody hurry! Find Ian! A bomb has been planted at his house," she yelled to one of the Navy guards. "And please, call the medics right away. Max is bleeding." Already she was examining the shoulder wound and stanching the flow with her towel, leaving herself naked. That didn't matter. He was probably just stunned, but still she cried, "Wake up, Max. Don't you dare die on me."

Just then, Ian rushed in. Apparently, he hadn't gone home yet. Drawing Alison to her feet, he wrapped a blanket around her and drew her shaking body into his embrace. "What the hell is going on here?" he yelled. Medics followed close behind him and were soon working on a now awake and pro-testing Max, trying to talk him into getting onto a stretcher. She explained shakily what had happened. Before long, the tango's body was removed and a bomb squad was sent to Ian's home.

In the end, Max had no choice. They forced him onto the stretcher. Just before they took him out, he glanced over at Alison, probably to say something teasing. But instead, his eyes latched onto her hands, which were held protectively over her stomach. It was a reflexive action that mothers throughout time had been taking. His eyes shot up to hers in surprise, then shock, then accusation. He said nothing. *Nothing!*

Luckily, he was the only one who'd noticed. Once the room was emptied, except for her and her brother, who would be joining the bomb squad shortly, Ian hugged her tightly.

It was over.

I've got a secret . . .

By the time Alison got to the medical facility two hours later, Max had already been stitched and bandaged up and was preparing to return to his barracks. Obviously, if a concussion couldn't hold him down, a mere bullet wound wouldn't either.

Ian had called her a half hour ago to tell her that the bomb in his home had been disabled. Without her warning, not only would his house have gone up in flames, but possibly the entire block.

Lieutenant Igo spoke with her in the corridor. "This boy Magnusson has got a lot of questions to answer. You do, too. First thing tomorrow morning. What was he doing in your room tonight? And what the hell was Petty Officer Gordon doing up on the roof? Major breaches in Navy regulations and security. *Major!*"

"Yes, sir," she said with a sinking heart, then added, "Ensign Magnusson saved my life, sir, and that of my brother. Possibly others. I hope that will be taken into consideration."

Her superior officer glowered at her for a moment. "Duly noted." He walked stiffly away.

Once the doctor on duty came out of the examining room, shaking his head over his irascible patient's complaints, he told her, "He's all yours, and good riddance."

Max was in the bathroom attached to the examining room.

When he came out, looking wobbly and very, very tired, she started to go to him, arms open for an embrace. "Oh, Max!"

He put up a halting hand and stepped back, eying her coolly. It was as if they were strangers.

"You are such a fool." A tiny sob escaped her. "You could have been killed, throwing yourself at that tango like that." Now that the danger was over, a war of emotions was playing out inside her. She found herself angry with Max, but so very happy that he was alive.

His jaw clenched and unclenched visibly. "I am a Viking. We protect those under our shields. And you, wench, are under my shield, whether you like it or not."

"I am not . . ." she started to say, then stopped herself at the fury she saw boiling just below the surface.

"You are breeding." It was not a question.

She nodded, placing a hand over her tummy, as if protecting her baby from its father's anger.

He blinked, profound hurt clouding his eyes. "Were you going to tell me?"

"Of course."

"When?"

"Soon. Well, probably not till after graduation. Or—"

"Or mayhap you were waiting to see if I would be around. Or if you even wanted me around." Another idea seemed to occur to him, and his nostrils flared with fury. "Were you going to kill our child? I have heard how easy it is to do that in your enlightened modern time. And a child would not fit in with your plans for a military life, now that I think on it."

"No!" Now it was her turn to be hurt. "If I were going to abort this child, I would have done so as soon as I found out I was pregnant."

"I should be honored that *you* decided to have my child."

"There was no opportunity for us to make a joint decision."

"Do not tell me you couldn't have found a way to make contact with me these past three weeks in George-ha."

Her face heated at his accusation, which was well founded. And he was right about something else as well. She had considered this her decision to make, not theirs.

He exhaled with disgust. "So much for all your modern marvels! I thought those cone-domes were supposed to prevent conception."

"They do."

He arched an eyebrow at her.

Her face heated with embarrassment. "That one time in the broom closet when you weren't covered."

"*What?* That was only for a second."

"It only takes a second."

His lips twitched and he almost smiled, but then he quickly suppressed it. "Bloody hell, I am as bad as my father. My seed is way too virile."

She was the one who almost smiled then.

"When will we wed?"

"What? Oh, no! We are not getting married just because I'm pregnant."

"I beg to differ. This child will have my name. Do not doubt that fact."

"We are not getting married.

"We are, do not doubt that for one instant."

"Be reasonable, Max."

"Reason has naught to do with paternity."

"Do you still think you are a time-traveler?"

"Yea. What has that to do with this?"

"It has everything to do with this. If I believe you are a blooming Viking from the eleventh century, why would I want to marry you?" She regretted her words the moment they left her mouth.

"Indeed," he said sadly, his blue eyes piercing the distance between them.

A hot tear rolled down her cheek.

He was unmoved.

"What I meant by that was, if we got married tomorrow, how would I know that you would be there the next day?"

"There are no guarantees in this life, even without time-travel. Consider what almost happened to us. Consider your fiancé David."

"That was a low blow."

"That is real life. Bad things happen. But people don't stop living to avoid dying."

"Max, this is not the time to—"

"You are right, as usual," he interrupted her stonily. Sarcasm coated his voice. "When will be the right time?"

"I don't know," she said with a dull ache of foreboding.

"So be it." He turned and proudly walked away from her and out of the medical facility.

Intuitively, Alison understood that something momentous had just happened. She feared what it might be.

Running as fast as he can . . .

Ragnor did not see Alison at all during the following week. By choice. He was afraid of what he would say or do in his present mood.

Ragnor was relieved, of course, that Alison was no longer in any danger. That did not mean he could forgive everything in his relief.

He had been called on the carpet by the XO, the CO, and

the BC for being in Alison's keep that night. Being "called
on the carpet" was the modern way of saying "screamed at"
so shrilly they could have peeled rust off armor in a moldy
Saxon castle. XO and CO were military terms for execu-
tive officer and commanding officer, while BC was Ragnor's own affectionate term for bloody chieftain. In the
end, he'd been given permanent Gig Squad, which Cage
had assured him was a mild punishment for boinking his
superior officer . . . "boinking" being a crude term for swiving. Apparently, his saving Alison's, the chieftain's, and a
large number of other lives had weighed in his favor.

Alison had sent him several notes asking him to meet
with her to talk, but eventually she stopped asking when he
ignored her pleas. He was in no frame of mind to talk at the
present time. He was too angry. Too hurt. Too confused. Too
tired. Besides, when women wanted to talk, it usually meant
they wanted to tell the man what he should think and do.
Well, that was not going to happen. He would be the one doing the telling when he finally met with her. The problem
was, he didn't know what he wanted to tell her at this point.

Everything was happening too fast.

As the BUD/S training wound down to its last phase,
which would culminate next week with a rock portage exercise, the instructors were working the team extra hard, trying
to get every bit of education in. There was so much to do
and so little time.

Luckily, Ragnor's wound had been minor and he had not
missed any training. Cage was healing fast, too.

They were all excited about the upcoming graduation,
which was scheduled a week from tomorrow, to be followed
by two glorious weeks of liberty. Amazingly, only fifty men
remained of the 145 who had started in the program four
months earlier. That was before Ragnor ever got to Coronado,

though no one would believe him when he said so. The ending of BUD/S did not mean they would become SEALs or that they would be given the coveted trident pin. Nay, that would come six months later after serving successfully on an assigned team.

He was unable to sleep more than a few hours each night, and his heart raced all the time. He was edgy and had to keep moving, as if his body was readying itself for some big event. He listened to CDs and even read books as fast as he could get them. His mind felt like a sponge soaking up knowledge about anything and everything related to this modern world where he had landed.

And, yea, some of the books had been on childbirth. He kept coming back to those pages that showed pictures of an unborn child at one month, two months, all the way to delivery. His fingertips traced the images, over and over. Who knew *it* had fingers and toes, even eyelashes, at such a young age? Would it be a boy or a girl? Would it look like him or her or a combination of them both?

To Ragnor's mind, it was a sign of weakness that he'd become so confused. He brushed his teeth twice a day and blew into his palm to make sure he was minty enough. Yesterday he'd caught himself sniffing his own armpits to see if his dear-odor-ant still worked, when good manly sweat had sufficed in the past. He said "Yes, sir!" and "No, sir!" to men he did not necessarily respect. He thought about learning to drive a car. Food had become too important to him, especially sweets. He'd developed a particular fondness for peanut butter and honey grain bars. Soon he would be soft . . . oh, not soft in body . . . he had more muscles now than any man had a right to, except for some berserkers he knew . . . but soft inside. Womanish. He thought about Alison all the time, and when he did, his heart ached.

He was losing himself, that was his fear. Real men did not sit about questioning their life paths. They just lived. For that reason, he sought out Doctor Fine-gold repeatedly. His instructors gave him permission to see the head healer once each day because they were concerned about his continuing claim of being a time-traveler. This was his fourth visit since the shooting. Doctor Fine-gold was the only one he'd told about Alison's pregnancy, and then only on condition that the doctor keep the secret.

"I think we should talk about the baby," Abe said, for about the tenth time in the past four days. Abe was his other name. Doctor Abe Fine-gold.

And here they went again with the "we" business, when what Abe really meant was that Ragnor should talk about the baby.

"Do *you* want this child?" Abe asked bluntly.

Ragnor sighed. "That is the question I wrestle with in my head in the dead of night when I cannot sleep. I was always repulsed by my father's breeding excesses; I told you afore that he had thirteen children in all."

"Some men measure their manliness by their reproductivity, which is foolish, of course. It doesn't take a real man to make a child, but it takes a real man to raise one."

Ragnor waved a hand dismissively. "You missay me, Abe. My father fulfilled his duties admirably. Everyone said so, even when they laughed at him. Seemed like all he had to do was look at a female and his seed flew out of his body and into her womb. But then, he cared for them. That is neither here nor there. What I was saying was that I always thought I hated large families and everything they represent . . . babies, whining children with runny noses and smelly bottoms, noise, chaos, overwhelming responsibility."

"And now?"

"Now I am wondering about my low spirits of the past year and my lack of enthusiasm for the bedsport."

"Max, Max, Max. It is a known fact that depression can cause impotency."

"Aaarrgh! I had no trouble raising my staff. I just did not want to."

"Ah, yes, I see," Abe said, unconvinced.

No doubt the doctor liked to think that Ragnor's cock wouldn't . . . well, cock . . . because that would provide a neat answer to all his problems. Cage had explained to Ragnor last night that shrinks—*that's what they called mind healers, and didn't that conjure up unpalatable images . . . mind shrinking?*—liked to boil all problems down to one thing: sex. Too much, not enough, perverted, lacking perversion, whatever.

"I am wondering if perhaps you protest too much," the doctor said.

Aaarrgh! The man does not listen. The wick in my candle is just fine, thank you very much. "Now all I want to do is tup," he went on. "With Alison, that is. Tup, tup, tup. I would wear my staff down to a nub if I could. But am I getting any tupping now? Nay! Dost want to know why? I will tell you. Because I am a bullheaded lackwit who does not know what in bloody hell he wants."

Abe's jaw was hanging open.

Mayhap I am blathering again. Hah! Forget mayhap. For a certainty, blathering comes second nature to me now. They ought to call me Ragnor the Blatherer.

Once Abe shut his jaw, the mind healer said, "Can we get back on the subject? I asked if you wanted the baby."

"Of course I want the baby. What a question! But I was trying to explain why I feel that way . . . why I am surprised that I feel that way." *Thor's teeth! Am I really talking about feelings? Next I will be weeping or taking up the needle arts.* "Truth to tell, I miss my large family, even the chaos. The things I thought I hated about my father's household have become precious memories to me."

"That is entirely normal, Max. In fact, I suspect that seventy-five percent of all adults go through a period when they hate their homes, their hometowns, their families, everything they associate with childhood."

"Did you?"

Abe smiled. "Absolutely. Now I am thinking of retiring someday to Long Island and maybe even returning to synagogue."

Ragnor had no idea what a sin-a-grog was, but it sounded interesting. He wondered idly how Lillian, Abe's companion of late, would feel about his going to a sin-a-grog place.

"So, you say that you want this baby. What are your plans?"

"Huh?"

"Come, Ragnor, there are lots of decisions you must make."

"Like?"

"Well, you will be assigned to teams after graduation next week. Perhaps you might want to consider requesting assignment to a team here in California so you can be nearby when the baby comes."

"They would assign me to a team outside Coronado?"

"Certainly. The men in your class will be going to assignments all over the world, some of them even on ships."

"I will not go."

Abe laughed. "You'll go wherever they send you, or end up in the brig or out of SEALs or both."

"Well, this certainly complicates things. I must go to the chieftain right away and make my preference known. But, nay, I cannot do that without Alison's permission to disclose her pregnancy."

"You've got to talk to her," Abe said.

Ragnor let out an exhale of surrender, though he had hoped to hold out longer. "I suppose I must."

"Why are you avoiding her? That's what I don't understand."

He gave Abe a grimace of disgust. "I told her we would wed, and she refused me."

Abe smiled. "You *told* her?"

"Yea, and, unbiddable wench that she is, she said her pregnancy is not a good enough reason for marriage. Hah! I would like to know what is."

"Alison has a lot on her mind these days. It has to be horrendously disappointing to her that after all these years waiting to join the SEALs, she's finally being given an opportunity to be part of those new Liberty Teams, but—"

"—she's pregnant," Ragnor finished for Abe, even though he had no idea what a "Liberty Team" was. Sounded like something similar to SEALs. Another secret that Alison was keeping from him. When had she been going to tell him of this fine opportunity she'd been offered, and how his planting his seed in her belly was causing her to lose her dreams?

"Don't look so unhappy, Max. Things will work out. They always do. Love prevails, and all that."

"She never said she loves me." *By the heavens! I sound like a whiney lackbrain.* "Do you think she does?"

"Why not ask her?"

"'Tis not the kind of thing a man asks." He stood. "I must needs get back to the pool arena. The chieftain wants to teach me to stay underwater for longer times by nigh drowning me."

Abe smiled, then stirred the papers on his desk as if suddenly recalling something of importance. "I forgot to give this to you. Alison dropped it off earlier today. She said you might find it of some interest."

Ragnor frowned and was about to ask why she couldn't have given it to him herself, but then stifled himself because he knew the reason. He'd refused to see her.

He took the folder in his hands and opened the top. Inside was a pile of parchment sheets. The top one said, "A Study of an Old Norse Family in Eleventh Century Vestfold," by Kirsten Magnusson. Ragnor's brow furrowed with confusion. Hmmm. Alison had asked him if he knew anyone by that name, he recalled now. Then he shrugged. There had to be many Kirsten Magnussons in this huge world today. He wondered if this was yet another secret Alison had hidden from him.

He waved to Abe as he left, but he noticed something about his other arm. He was getting the same ripple of shock running over his body, emanating from the folder, as he had from that bottle of Blue Dragon wine.

How odd!

CHAPTER TWENTY

❧

Looking for clues . . .
All week Max had refused to meet with her. By Friday, Alison was fed up. She'd gotten along without him before she met him, she'd get along without him now, or so that old song went.

What was it about men and their blasted pride? Yeah, she'd done something that might have offended him, but mainly it had been a sin of omission. And easily explainable if he'd only give her a chance. Heck, her brother Ian was the same way. He probably would have been able to work things out with his fiancée if his pride hadn't got in the way.

She'd done enough groveling with Max. The next step would have to be his.

In the meantime, she had that appointment to meet with Kirsten Magnusson in her UCLA office. Alison got up early, did her usual five-mile jog, then ate a huge breakfast in line with her increased I'm-bound-and-determined-to-get-fat appetite. After that, she made the more than two-hour drive to Los Angeles.

Kirsten Magnusson was gorgeous, even with glasses perched on the end of her nose. She was tall, about five foot nine, with glorious blond hair hanging halfway down her back. Her features were Nordic, with a slight resemblance to

Max. Wearing faded Gap jeans and an Aerosmith T-shirt, she greeted Alison in her sixth-floor office—little more than a closet really.

Alison liked her almost immediately. She was warm and intelligent, with a self-deprecating sense of humor, especially about her office, which she referred to as Trump's Other Tower.

"What did you think of my thesis?"

"I enjoyed it very much, although it ended rather abruptly."

Kirsten studied her closely. "With the ship being lost in the fog, you mean?"

"Yes. Max always talks about his family having gone down in a shipwreck or something. Even so, it seems as if there should be more to the story."

"Maybe someday, if you get close enough to Torolf . . . sorry, I can't get used to his being called Max . . . he'll tell you more."

Alison frowned. How much closer could she and Max get? Was he hiding something from her? Hah! He had a nerve accusing her of secrets when he had a few of his own.

Flipping through the thesis pages, Alison pointed to the bibliography. "I notice that you cite lots of source material on the time period and events that occurred in Norway, but most of the personal information about the Magnusson family came from the journal of a fourteen-year-old girl, Kirsten Magnusson, who lived there then. Same name as yours."

Kirsten's face flushed . . . with embarrassment, Alison supposed. "Yes, you could say that she was my ancestor many, many times removed. I was lucky enough to . . . um . . . discover her long-lost journal."

"How interesting! I didn't know girls did much writing

then. In fact, I didn't know anyone did much writing in the tenth or even eleventh centuries."

"They didn't, but Kirsten was a very unusual girl."

"Apparently." Alison studied the still blushing Kirsten for a long moment. There was something about her and the whole story that struck an odd note, but she couldn't quite put her finger on it.

"You mentioned Max having had an accident. When I told our father, he almost went through the roof. We had to practically sit on him to prevent him from driving right down to Coronado."

"I don't think that would have been a good idea." Briefly, she gave Kirsten the details of the accident and Max's concussion.

"How like him! To jump right back into SEALs training after a blow to the head. I always knew his head was thick, but that's ridiculous."

"The problem is that he's suffered some memory loss." At the expression of shock on Kirsten's face, she immediately added, "I'm sure it's temporary. But that's why we were looking for information on his family history. We wanted clues that might help him remember."

"Does Torolf know you're here today?"

She shook her head. "Oh, don't worry about betraying any confidences. It's just that he's been away at jump school and winding down to graduation. There hasn't been time to discuss much of anything." *Talk about telling whoppers!*

"You know, he hasn't invited any of the family down for his graduation," Kirsten told her, hurt ringing in her voice. "Do you think we should call him up and ask for an invitation, or just show up?"

"I don't know. My first inclination is to say, wait till he

gets his head together. I'm not sure if the shock would jar him into remembering, or cause other damage. Besides, he's not graduating into SEALs yet, just out of BUD/S training."

Kirsten nodded. "This has always been a dream of Torolf's."

"Really? Most of the time, he acts as if he's just biding his time."

It was Kirsten's turn to say, "Really?" Then, "If Torolf doesn't remember his family right now, who does he think he is?"

Alison smiled. "An eleventh-century Viking from the Norselands who has time-traveled here."

"Oh, my God!" Kirsten said, but she wasn't shocked. More like dismayed. "What should we do?"

"I was thinking . . . once he graduates, he'll have a two-week liberty. What would you think about my driving him up to Blue Dragon Vineyards? Just to see if it jogs his memory?"

"That would be great! I have an idea. Harvest Festival will be held on September eighth. Would that fit in that time frame?"

"Yes. Yes, it would." Alison wasn't sure she'd be able to talk Max into going anywhere with her, but she would try. They exchanged various addresses and telephone numbers.

Just before she left, Kirsten asked, "What exactly is your relationship with my brother?"

Alison paused. "I wish I knew."

The Story of Me . . .

Max called Alison's office number on Friday morning between the morning run and breaking fast and was told that she wasn't coming in today. *Why not?*

Between breaking fast and his first almost-drowning of the day, he called her home. Nothing but the ring-ring-ring, then the bloody answer machine. No one was home. *Why not?*

Between three almost-drownings and some IBL maneuverings among rocks designed to kill the trainees or compel them to ring out, he called Lillian. "She went to Los Angeles this morning, dear. She should be back by mid-afternoon." He thanked her for her help and hung up, but wondered, *Why?*

They were being given a half-day liberty today because the instructors were involved in some hush-hush (that was Cage's word) meeting with some bigger chieftains from the nation's seat. Probably something related to terrorism, which was all everyone talked about. Dangerous times they were here, even worse than his own harsh time. At least back then, a person didn't have to worry about being blown into a thousand pieces just walking down the road of a busy market town.

Since his classmates had gone into San Diego and Alison was not yet home, he decided to look over the folder she'd left for him. He still had trouble reading the Saxon language, but if he sounded out the more difficult words, he should be able to manage.

First he sounded out the title, "A Study of an Old Norse Family in Eleventh-Century Vestfold." That sounded interesting, especially since it was written by a person who had the same name as his sister.

It took him a long time to read the document, but when he finished, he was more puzzled than before he'd started. It was the story of his very own family. Every one of them, himself included. It ended with his father's longship being lost in a haze of fog.

First, how did this person know so many details about his family? All of the family's names and ages, even his father's wives and mistresses, were set down. There were descriptions of his father's farmstead, right down to the runic carvings about the great-hall lintel. Episodes that only a person who had been there could have related, like the time his father's hirdsmen had tried to find a non-fertile woman for him by presenting him with everything from a hugely pregnant cow-maid to a half-bald wench who was older than Magnus himself. There were sagas he'd forgotten, but which this person had written down. Descriptions of all his family members, himself included, were accurate, though he did not think that he and his brother Torolf had been as vain or mischievous as they were portrayed. This person had even included Madrene's shrewishness.

Second, why would someone here in modern times be so interested in such a small segment of ancient history, and why his particular family?

Third, where had Alison gotten this document, and why had he only found out about it now? Another of Alison's secrets!

An idea came to him unbidden then. What if this Kirsten was one of his own descendants? Or what if someone on that longship had survived in some far-off land, like Greenland, and this was his or her descendant?

One thing was certain: He would have to meet this Kirsten person. But first, he had about fifty questions to ask Alison. He tried her number, but again no answer. He decided to go there himself and wait for her.

Suddenly, excitement rippled through him at the prospect of seeing her again. And it wasn't just because he had questions.

Hog Heaven was turning into Hog Hell . . .

Torolf was going to have to leave this madhouse soon or else become one of the inmates.

He had more repair work than he could handle. In fact, he could probably make a good living as a Harley mechanic if he wanted . . . which he didn't.

The Morgans continued to be great hosts and friends to him, but they were driving him nuts with their not-so-subtle attempts to make him stay. The latest tactic was to throw one biker babe after another at him in hopes that he would fall in love and not want to leave.

Like Lizzy, who had come last week to watch him adjust the carburetors on a Harley Heritage Springer. Lizzy was a thirty-something teacher who spent her summer vacations here at Hog Heaven. She had stood there leaning against the concrete wall of the garage while he squatted down on his haunches. Then she'd blurted out, "I've got balls."

"Whaaat?" He'd shot up, almost hitting his head on the handlebars.

"Ben Wa balls."

"Whaaat?" he'd said again.

"You know, those heavy metal Oriental balls you can buy in sex shops. Man, they sure do vibrate when I ride my hog."

But she had been no worse than Linda, a part-time stripper who claimed to be eighteen but was more likely jail bait. He'd been working on Granny Olsen's valves when Linda had asked him, "Wanna see my nipple rings?"

"No!" he'd shouted.

Too late. Linda had lifted her T-shirt to display two very nice breasts ornamented with shiny gold rings.

Ouch!

Speaking of breasts, a part-Cherokee trucker named Tissee-woo-na-tis, or She Who Bathes With Her Knees, wanted to show him her breasts, too, but for a different reason. Tissie had told him, while he'd been detailing a classic Harley Electra Glide, that the only parts of her body that had been tattooed were her two breasts, which had been made to look like ice cream cones.

He must have frowned his confusion. Big mistake! Tissie took that as her cue to reveal all. And, yep, her breasts were tattooed to resemble two waffle cones, filled with vanilla ice cream and topped with cherries.

Holy dairy products!

Serenity and Spike had set him up, hoping to keep him here as sort of an adopted son. The worst thing was that he noticed them eyeing him lately like a fresh palette for their tattoo and piercing arts. That hunch proved true when he awakened one morning to find Serenity drawing a picture of an eagle with a marker around his navel. He was pretty sure that it had been a preliminary sketch for one of her tattoos. On him! And George had been looking at that region, too. Probably the eagle would have had a ring in its mouth, also known as his belly button.

I ... don't ... think ... so!

Torolf's memory was coming back in bits and pieces. In fact, he kept a small tablet in his back pocket listing all the things he remembered. A Navy uniform, which was pretty clear evidence to him that he'd been in the military, not prison. But why would he have gone UA? A vineyard. A Viking longship. A shipwreck, or a ship lost in the fog. An accident in which he was struck by a truck. A brother, or someone, who looked a lot like himself.

His progress was much too slow. So finally he decided to research the address listed on his driver's license. He used George's computer to call up the address so he could get a telephone number. Two names were listed at the same Sonoma Valley address, which was incidentally home to Blue Dragon Vineyards, Angela Abruzzi and Magnus Ericsson. A prickling sensation passed over his body at that second name.

Not giving himself a chance for second thoughts, he dialed the number.

A male with a deep voice answered. "Hello. Magnus Ericsson here. Who is this?"

"I don't know. But I think I might be your son."

Working my way back to you, babe . . .

When Alison got home from Los Angeles that afternoon, Max was sitting on the top step of her porch, talking with Lillian as she dug among her rosebeds. An empty glass and dish were sitting next to him, which she assumed had held milk and the lemon meringue pie she'd smelled baking this morning.

He looked so good sitting there. Just an average guy, wearing a Harley T-shirt, jeans, and white athletic shoes, but of course there was nothing average about him.

Lillian waved. Max just stared at her. And she did what pregnant women throughout time have done; she started to bawl.

Max glanced at Lillian, and Lillian glanced at Max. They both shrugged in confusion, then walked over to meet her.

"What's the matter, dear?" Lillian asked, patting her on the shoulder.

"Did I do something?" Max opened his arms to embrace her.

But she stepped back, hugging her briefcase in front of her chest with both hands and continuing to sob. "No-o-o," she blubbered.

"Do you want me to go?"

Panic shook her. "Don't go."

Lillian and Max seemed to communicate something

between them, and Lillian walked away. He put an arm over Alison's shoulders and led her toward the house.

"What in bloody hell is going on?" he asked. They were walking up the steps to her apartment now.

"I was happy to see you." *Finally.*

"You were crying with happiness?" He cast her a skeptical glance.

She nodded. "And relief." *And became I'm pregnant, you fool.*

Once they were in her apartment, she set her briefcase down and went into the kitchen to put the teakettle on to boil. He followed her and leaned against the counter, arms crossed over his chest. "Where were you today?"

"I went to see Kirsten Magnusson."

She could see that surprised him. "The person who wrote that document you sent me?"

"Yes."

"Why?"

"Why did I go see her?"

"Yea. Why did you go see her? Why did you not tell me you were going? Why didn't you invite me to go along?"

The teakettle whistled. "Do you want a cup of tea?"

"Nay. Do you have any mead?"

She smiled tentatively. "Would a Bud Light do?"

He nodded.

They both sat down at the table, she drinking sweet tea and he sipping beer. "I went to see Kirsten because I was intrigued by her research. If you had talked with me this week, I probably would have asked you to go along." *Or maybe not.*

"What did you learn?"

"Not much that wasn't in her thesis. She's your sister, Max. Oh, I know you don't believe that, because you insist on saying you came from another century. But I think, and she thinks, that you're her brother."

"That's impossible."

"She is very hurt that you didn't invite her and the rest of your family to your graduation next week."

"How could I invite people I do not know?"

"Will you make love to me?" *Oh, God, my brain is melting.*

"*What?*"

Her request had obviously surprised him. Heck, it had surprised her, too.

"You are in the middle of drinking tea. You just got done leaking tears all over yourself. You're pregnant. And that makes you want to jump in the bed furs?"

"Did you think pregnant women never got horny?" *He doesn't want me anymore. Some men get turned off by pregnant women. Oh, jeez, can I be any more humiliated?*

He smiled for the first time that day. "I never had an opinion on that subject . . . until now."

"Well, for the record, I'm not horny at the moment." *If you believe that one, I have a bridge to sell you, honey.* "Just lonely." *And guess whose fault that is?* "And you're acting so remote and everything." *Like a horse's ass.* She shrugged.

"Are you going to start weeping again?"

"No. Maybe." *Better yet, how about if I hit you?*

"Sex isn't the answer to everything, and I cannot believe I actually said that. See what you have done to me?"

It was her turn to smile . . . sort of. *He does want me. Yep, he does. I can tell.*

"I'm not remote. Just bloody hell confused. By the by, when were you going to tell me about the Liberty Teams and how I have ruined your life and destroyed all your dreams?"

So, Abe must have blabbed to him. "You've got a whole lot of mistruths tossed in there with a few facts."

He just arched a brow in question.

"Yes, there are going to be Liberty Teams." She explained briefly what the Liberty Teams would be and why there was a need for secrecy. "I learned about them when my father was here. And, yes, I probably would have had a good chance of making one of the teams. And, yes, at one time, I would have been delighted."

"So where's the mistruth?"

"It's a mistruth to say that you ruined my life or destroyed my dreams. Let's get one thing perfectly clear. It's my body, and it was I who made the decision to carry this baby. There was never a question of that. Should I have discussed that decision with you? Maybe. Okay, yes. But in the end I would have had the ultimate say-so."

"I just don't understand you."

"That makes two of us."

"How could you change directions so quickly? You said over and over that your life path was set on becoming a SEAL. Now you have a similar opportunity, and you don't care?"

"Of course I care. But there is a famous saying that when one door closes, another door opens. There's also a saying that if you're handed a lemon, make lemonade." *Holy moly, now I'm turning into my brother with all these motivational quotes.*

"Are you calling my babe a lemon?"

She laughed. "So to speak. Listen, I'll find some other dream . . . something I can get equally excited about. All I know is that this child"—she put a hand over her still-flat tummy—"is surprisingly important to me. I never realized how much I want to have a child. I can't give you details on what I'll do yet. Maybe I'll go off to some desert island with this little mini-me or mini-you or mini-us and play doctor to the natives."

"Where do I fit into that picture?"

"Where do you want to fit?" *With us?*

"I already suggested that we wed, and you rejected me."

"No, you did not suggest. You ordered."

"So if I asked nicely, you would agree?"

"I don't know. Probably not. I would have to know lots more before I would agree to marry you. I definitely wouldn't do it for the sake of a child."

He rolled his eyes in frustration.

"I'm starving. Would you eat if I made some lunch?"

He nodded. "Or we could call Dome-nose for some pizza. I've become partial to that pepper-only meat as a topping."

She made the call, then leaned against the wall, chomping on an apple. "Actually I'm always starving. Betcha I turn into a blimp, with all the food I've been shoveling in. The SEALs could use me as an IBL."

"One of my father's wives looked like a walking longboat by the time she was about to give birth."

"That's a nice image."

He grinned. "I'm sure you will look lovely."

"You charmer, you."

"Has the baby moved yet?"

"Max! I'm only about one month pregnant. The baby won't move for months yet." She loved the fact that he was interested, as he should be.

"You know that I will convince you to wed with me, don't you?"

"You could try." *Please try.*

"A challenge? Milady, you dare much if you think you could withstand a Viking assault of the magnitude I will wage."

"Talk, talk, talk! I've already experienced all your secret Viking spots."

"You think so? Didst not imagine I would show you all my tricks at once, did you? Tsk, tsk, tsk! Seduction is my second greatest talent."

A sense of relief washed over her at the lightness of the moment. No more anger and recriminations. "Changing the subject for just one second . . . Max, will you go with me to the Harvest Festival at the Blue Dragon Vineyards after graduation? It's at least an eight-hour drive. We could leave on Friday, stay overnight somewhere midway, maybe San Luis Obispo, and arrive Saturday afternoon."

"Huh?" She could tell that her quick change of subject had disconcerted him.

"I promised Kirsten Magnusson I would bring you."

"This Kirsten person has a connection with that wine we drank . . . the one that felt so odd in my hands?"

She nodded.

At first he balked, but then he nodded.

She smiled and walked over to sit on his lap. "About that seduction business . . ." she said, nuzzling his neck.

CHAPTER TWENTY-ONE

*O*ne is the loneliest number . . .

Forty-eight members of the original 150 in Class 500 of BUD/S graduated into teams the following Friday. Ragnor Magnusson, in full dress uniform, was one of them.

And he'd never felt so lonely in his life.

He hadn't been prepared for all the ritual and pomp given to their ceremony . . . or to its importance. Parents, sisters, brothers, and friends had traveled from all over the world to be with these forty-eight men on this special day. Except for Ragnor himself, who had no one, unless he counted Alison, who'd waved to him when he'd entered the arena and taken his seat.

Her father, Rear Admiral Thomas MacLean—a dignified man with short gray hair, who displayed more brooches on his chest than Ragnor had ever seen—was one of the speakers, along with an older man who had been in one of the original SEAL classes. There was also a senator from California . . . a senator being sort of like an ealdorman on the king's Witan in the Saxon lands, he surmised. JAM, as honor man for his class, also gave a talk. Mostly the subjects were honor, stamina, and courage . . . subjects dear to the hearts of all Norsemen.

Ragnor's mind wandered as it hit home just how alone he

was in this land and time. And how the moment had come to make some decisions about what he would do here, since returning to the eleventh century didn't appear to be an option.

Cage elbowed him from the right side and said, "Stand up, you idiot. They just called your name."

After the ceremony, a small feast was held under tents near the beach. Alison came up to him immediately and hugged him warmly. "Congratulations, sweetie. You look so hot."

He laughed and hugged her back. "Hey, I thought I was supposed to be the one doing the seducing. Hot *is* a compliment, is it not?"

"The ultimate, babe. The ultimate."

"Max," the chieftain said then, reaching out to shake his hand. "Congratulations." Interesting that Ian would call him Max; usually he called him something derogatory, like "jerkoff" or "goofball." And his congratulations seemed sincere enough. Perhaps he wouldn't say anything to irritate the chieftain today, like, "My sister Madrene could teach you about the famous Viking S-Spot."

"Did you say Max?" Admiral MacLean said then, stepping around the chieftain. He raised his eyebrows at Alison in some meaningful way.

She blushed and took her father's hand, at the same time lacing the fingers of her other hand with his own. "Daddy, I'd like you to meet Ensign Magnusson. He's a good friend of mine. Max, this is my father."

Good friend, eh? More like good lover. They shook hands, but her father eyed him in the way fathers have since time began, asking the silent question, *What have you been doing with my daughter?*

Tupping. More tupping. And then . . . tupping.

After some awkward conversation about the ceremony

and the team Max had been assigned to at Coronado, the admiral asked Alison, "Are you sure you can't come back to Washington with me for a few days of R & R?"

She shook her head. Her fingers, still intertwined with his, clenched even tighter. "No. Max and I are driving up to Sonoma Valley, leaving later today. We want to visit Blue Dragon Vineyards tomorrow."

"Really?" the admiral and the chieftain said at the same time.

Ragnor could tell that Alison was unsure what to say. So he blundered ahead on his own. "Alison and I are looking for a nice site to hold a wedding."

Alison's face turned blood red and she made a sort of gurgling sound in her throat. Slowly she looked at him, alternating between daggers and disbelief. Her only response was, "Oh, my God!"

Her father and brother settled for mere daggers.

But Ragnor . . . he was bloody well pleased with himself. Sometimes a Viking just had to take a stand.

Home sweet home . . .

Torolf was tooling his way home on his Harley by early Saturday morning. And, yes, he now recognized that Blue Dragon Vineyards was his home, and had been since he was sixteen years old. His memory was coming back in leaps and bounds.

There had been lots of weeping and promises to keep in touch as he left Hog Heaven, and truly he was thankful for all the help Serenity and George had given him. But now, he was ready to resume his old life, whatever that might be.

It was a balmy early September day, with the smell of

grapes in the air. He turned onto the long private drive lined with a low stone wall and stately oak trees. Every ten feet or so big, dragon-shaped pottery urns spilled forth lush red flowers.

He revved the motor on his Harley and came to a screeching stop in the wide circle in front of the rambling Victorian house with its wraparound porch. He was not surprised to see most of his family already rushing down the wide steps to meet him: his father, whose long blond hair had more than a few gray strands, some of them put there by him; his step-mother Angela, his step-grandmother Rose, the housekeeper Juanita, and about eight of his half-brothers and sisters.

Once the chaos of reunion subsided, his father—the same six foot four as himself though much more burly in build—released him from an embrace and held him away from himself. "Where have you been, boy?"

"Hog Heaven." He grinned.

"I sense a story coming," Angela said, winking at him.

He told them about his accident, his medical leave from SEALs training, his loss of memory, and his sojourn at the biker commune.

"But Kirsten said . . ." His father's forehead furrowed with confusion.

"Kirsten? Where is she?"

"She'll be here later this afternoon. She's driving up from Los Angeles after her early-morning class," his father informed him, still frowning. "Your uncles Rolf and Jorund are here with their families for the Harvest Festival. They're out back."

"Great!" Rolf, once known as Rolf the Shipbuilder, and his wife Meredith operated a replica of a Norse village up in Maine, where his uncle built authentic longships. Jorund, a famous warrior at one time, not surprisingly called Jorund the Warrior, ran some kind of exercise facility for mentally and emotionally challenged people in Texas.

"Back to Kirsten and what she said." His father was frowning again with confusion. "I still don't understand why—"

"Shhh," Angela said, looping her arms in each of theirs to propel them up the steps. "We can discuss everything later. We had an especially good harvest this year, Torolf, and an early one, too. You're just in time for the Harvest Festival."

"Oh, boy!" he said, but he had a strange feeling that something else was about to happen, too.

In the war of the sexes, females have an advantage . . .

On Saturday morning, Alison and Max did a little sightseeing after a late Southwestern-style breakfast in San Luis Obispo before resuming their car trip to Blue Dragon Vineyards. Good thing she'd gotten that extra walking in, since she'd gone back to the buffet table twice, much to Max's teasing delight.

They drove Ian's red Mustang convertible, which he'd surprisingly loaned to them for the trip once he'd gotten over the shock of Max's announcement that they were planning a wedding. She, on the other hand, still wasn't over the shock, even though she'd immediately told her father and brother that he'd been kidding. When her father and Ian had looked to Max for confirmation of her denials, he'd just grinned. She could have wrung his neck.

Despite all that, she was enjoying herself immensely, even though Max had not made love to her since before her pregnancy. Last night, he'd slept in the other double bed in their small mission-style hotel. He'd claimed exhaustion, but

Alison suspected it was all part of some macho-dumb plot to seduce her into marriage. Surrender by way of lust overload, or some such thing.

He might just succeed.

She wouldn't let that ruin her trip.

And Max was enjoying himself, too. She could tell. Right now he was leaning back against the headrest, basking in the sunlight and breeze as they cruised up I-5. His right arm rested on the open window, his left arm was draped over the back of the driver's seat.

At Max's urging, she wore her halter sundress, the same one she'd worn the day they went to the library—white background with red flowers—and skimpy white sandals. She'd painted her finger- and toenails flame red and wore bright lipstick, also at Max's urging. It was a strange little game of sexual teasing they were playing.

She liked it.

He wore khaki shorts and a white U.S. Navy T-shirt with flip-flops. The odd note was the ancient arm rings he wore today. He'd gotten the confiscated items back from her brother once training ended. His hair was still very short, but he was so handsome it did not matter. He looked suntanned and healthy.

He glanced over and caught her watching him. He winked.

Whoo-boy, she felt that wink all the way to her toes and some places in between. "You seem extremely relaxed now that graduation is over and we're away from the base," she remarked.

"I suppose I am. I may not know why I was sent here or what my destiny truly is, but it feels as if I am heading in the right direction."

"I thought I was your destiny," she teased.

He tugged on one of the curls at her neck as punishment and said, "From the time I saw that white light when I was drowning . . . oh, do not frown at me so . . . near-drowning, then . . . you seemed to be in danger, and I thought that meant you were my destiny. That the gods had sent me here to save you."

"But you did save my life, Max."

"If that is so, then what is my destiny now?"

She wanted to say *Why not me still?* But the words would not come out. Placing a hand protectively over her stomach, she wondered why he didn't view their baby as his destiny, as well.

He noticed her gesture and said, "There is no question in my mind that you and I will wed, and that I will be a father to this child. Do not doubt that, Alison."

"Not that I'm agreeing with you, but if that's the case, what's the problem?"

He put a hand to his forehead as if to press out the creases of worry. "I am uncertain. 'Tis a sense I have, not unlike what happens afore a big battle. Something is in store for me . . . something big . . . bigger than what has occurred so far."

"A premonition?"

"Possibly. It is as if there is an answer just beyond my grasp."

"An answer to what?"

"I know not. Just that 'twill be the kind of thing that, once discovered, makes one feel like hitting oneself aside the head for not realizing it sooner. Does that make sense?"

"Very much so. Tell me, what are you hoping to get out of our visit to Blue Dragon today?"

"You are the one who made these arrangements, not me," he pointed out. "But there are several possibilities. One, it could be just a coincidence that there is a person with the same name as my dead sister, who is connected to a vineyard that I have ne'er visited but feel oddly connected to. Two, and this is alarming, perhaps this Kirsten is one of my descendants, which would mean that I will travel back to my own time. Three, it could be one of Madrene's descendants. Four, perhaps there was a survivor of that long-ago ship lost in the fog, and that person lived in a far-off land, like Greenland, and now this is a descendant of one of my brothers or sisters who I thought had died."

"Wow! You've got a whole lot of theories going there." The one that bothered her most was the idea that Max might be going back to his own time, which was ridiculous, since she didn't believe he'd ever come from that time.

"I see your disbelief. What do you think, then?"

She shrugged her opinion. "I think you got hit on the head during BUD/S, have a loss of memory, and hopefully will regain some or all of it when you are reunited with your family at the vineyard where you grew up."

He laughed and tugged again on the curl at her neck. "You think I'm demented, do you?"

She smiled at him. "Only temporarily."

"And you love me still?" She could tell that he immediately regretted those words, even though he'd only been teasing.

Not wanting him to go all serious on her, she teased back, "What's not to love about a bald Viking SEAL wannabee with an ego the size of the Pentagon?"

"Was that a yes?"

Oh, yeah! "I am not going to answer that question, especially when you are playing these sex-deprivation games with me."

"Sex what?"

"You know exactly what I mean. And listen up, buddy, I

am on to you. You can deprive all you want, but I can hold out as long as you can."

"Oh, really? Is that a challenge?"

"If it walks like a duck and quacks like a duck, it must be a duck."

"You will not win in any war with me, dearling. Best you surrender now, agree to a wedding date, and we can pull over to the side of the road for a quick swive."

Sounds good to me. "You are unbelievable," she said, laughing.

"'Tis one of the best things about me."

You male chauvinist Viking, you! "Do you ever have trouble finding hats that fit?"

"Nay. Why?"

"Because you have such a big head." *And other biggies, too.*

"Oh. You mean I have much conceit. Well, there are other things big about me, too."

"Puh-leeze!" *He must be reading my mind.*

"I like.it when you beg."

"Puh-leeze!" She took the next exit and said, "We'll be there in less than an hour. While you're basking in the glow of your own wonderfulness, and congratulating yourself on how you can seduce me into doing whatever you want, keep one thing in mind, darling."

After a speaking pause, he asked, "And what would that be?"

"I'm not wearing any undergarments under this dress."

He glanced sharply at her and looked as if he'd swallowed his tongue. Once he recovered, he grinned. "Congratulations. You have won the battle."

"I know," she gloated.

"But the war is far from over."

If children are a gift from the gods, the Ericssons were overblessed . . .

Magnus sat with his son Torolf on a wooden swing behind the house, watching the preparations for the day's festivities. In all the chaos of his return, they hadn't had much of a chance to talk yet.

A farmer at heart, Magnus still relished the smells of earth and growing things. Sweet breezes. The warm sun. He led a good life with few regrets.

His wife Angela, along with her elderly grandmother Rose and equally aged housekeeper Juanita, were laying a veritable feast of foods out on the tables that had been arranged nearby for the annual harvest celebration. He would go to help her soon. Despite being wed for more than ten years, he still liked to stay close to her.

There would be plenty of Italian dishes, some Mexican, and even a few Norse ones, though Magnus had forbidden his wife to provide the hated lute-fisk. His two sisters-by-marriage, Meredith and Maggie, had taken charge of the beverage arena, which would soon offer a tun of mead—a Viking requirement; wine—a Blue Dragon requirement; and Kool-Aid—a children's requirement.

His brothers Rolf and Jorund were playing croquet on the side lawn with the youthlings, whilst the teenagers and older children listened to loud music down by the pond. It was hard for him to credit that he had bred babes who now passed twenty winters, but then, he was nigh a graybeard himself, approaching the age of fifty way too fast. A band had already set up its instruments and would begin to play once their guests arrived later today.

But this was a quiet time for him and his oldest son Torolf.

Well, nay, Ragnor was one sennight older, but he was back in the Norselands.

"Dost ever think of Ragnor?" Torolf asked him of a sudden.

Magnus's head shot up. "Do you read my mind now, son?"

"It's funny," Torolf began tentatively, "but ever since my accident, Ragnor has been on my mind constantly. I even dream of him."

Magnus nodded. "I do, too. What do you think it means? Is he in some trouble? And what could we do from here?"

"I do not know."

"Was I wrong to leave Ragnor and Madrene behind?" He blinked back the tears that misted his eyes.

Torolf squeezed his arm. "Nay. You did what you thought best, and we intended to go back. Besides, it has turned out well for all of us, hasn't it?"

Yea, it had. Torolf had gone to college and entered the military. Kirsten was a teacher at a college, where she studied the old Norse ways. Storvald, at twenty-four, worked with his uncle Rolf at Rosestead, a replica of an old Viking village, where he made fine wood carvings to decorate homes and ships. Dagny, only twenty-three, was an artist whose oil paintings sold in local galleries. Njal, ever the mischievous son, was still a mischievous man at twenty; though he was still a student in college, young women called here all the time for him. And seventeen-year-old Jogeir, bless his heart, intended to try out for the Olympic running team this year . . . and this the boy who had been born lame. Hamr had finally gotten his bow and arrow, but at sixteen was more interested in football and wenches. Kolbein, the shy one, was still quiet and studious at fourteen; Angela thought he might have a religious vocation one day, but Magnus could hardly imagine any child of his being a priest. Lida was still the joy of his life at twelve and spoiled beyond belief, but no more so than ten-year-old Marie, the child he and Angela had created together.

And things had worked out well for his brothers, too. Rolf and Meredith had two children who brought them great joy, thirteen-year-old Foster and eleven-year-old Rose, even though Meredith had thought she was barren. Ah, well, the Ericsson men ever were known to be virile. Meredith had quit her college teaching job last year and worked alongside her husband at Rosestead now.

Jorund was the one who'd surprised them all. He'd wed a head doctor, who'd already had two children, twins Suzy and Beth, now twenty and studying to become doctors themselves. Jorund and Maggie had three children of their own, ten-year-old Eric and the eight-year-old twins, Mack and Mike. Jorund, a famous warrior, now taught exercising to demented people.

Life is strange.

"Yes, it is," Torolf said.

Magnus must have spoken aloud. "But tell me, Torolf, what have you been doing? I must admit to being hurt that you did not invite us to your graduation."

"Huh? What graduation?"

"From SEALs training. Yesterday."

"Father! I was forced to drop out of training when I got the head wound almost two months ago. I'll be resuming training with the next class. Probably I'll be given another Navy assignment for the interim, now that I'm feeling better."

"Then where in bloody hell have you been all this time?"

"Hog Heaven, I told you before. I lost my memory for a while, but now it is back."

"Methinks it is not as back as you say. Kirsten said you

were about to graduate and that you would not know us if we arrived for the ceremony; in fact, we might do you harm."

"And Kirsten knew all this . . . how?"

"By talking to your woman friend, Alison."

"Aaarrgh! I have no woman friend named Alison."

"She is a physician, I believe, and she went to Kirsten on your behalf to study the story of our family."

Torolf frowned some more. "Alison? A physician? Bloody hell! She couldn't be referring to Lieutenant Alison MacLean, could she?"

"That is the one."

Torolf laughed uproariously. "Father, Alison MacLean wouldn't give me the time of day. She told me to drop dead one time. Does that sound like a woman friend?"

"Nay. Mayhap Kirsten will have some reasonable explanation when she arrives."

"'Tis more likely that you misheard her, being in your dotage and all."

Magnus gave his son a playful punch in the arm at his teasing, then rose to his feet. "Let us go help the womenfolk. They must needs have a man to direct them, though they would never admit such."

Torolf wrapped an arm around his father's shoulders and squeezed. "You are so out of touch."

When past and present collide, hold on, baby . . .

They had just turned off the highway onto a road with a sign that read "Blue Dragon Vineyards." The narrow lane they traveled on now was a scenic corridor with tall trees, a low stone wall, and bright flowers in picturesque urns adorning both sides. Wildflowers covered the extensive lawns. To one side there was a pond with willow trees. Up ahead a considerable distance was a great white house with black shutters. Behind it were many, many hides of land covered with orderly rows of grapevines.

None of it was familiar to him, and yet Ragnor felt every fine hair on his body stand to attention. His heart raced madly, and he could swear he heard his blood roar in his head. He was more fearful than he'd ever been afore a battle, more fearful even than when confronted with Madrene in a nagging rage.

"Pull over," he ordered Alison.

"No way!" she said with a laugh. "That's the tenth time you've asked me to pull over since I told you I'm naked under this dress. We are not going to have roadside sex."

He shook his head, wanting to tell her seduction wasn't his goal right now, though the image of what lay under that little wisp of a garment tantalized him mightily and he would not mind some roadside rutting, regardless of his odd mental state. But his tongue seemed glued to the roof of his mouth.

The stubborn wench did not stop until they reached the clearing afore the front of the house where other vehicles were parked, even a motoring-cycle. In the side yard, Ragnor could see several dozen people—adults and children—playing games and lounging about. Music provided a raucous backdrop.

"Are you okay, Max?"

He shook his head.

"Was this a mistake? Should we leave?"

He could tell he was scaring her. Holy Thor, he was scaring himself. But, nay, he had to find out what was here. It must be important.

He undid his seat belt and got out of the car. Walking

slowly toward the side yard, he saw several people stop and stare at him. One young woman put her hands to her mouth and cried out, "Oh, my God!" A little girl started to rush forward, but a youthling boy held her back.

Stoically, Ragnor plowed forward, leaving Alison behind.

Coming around the back side of the house were two men . . . one older and one about his age. Both were blond, though one had long hair rippled with gray, while the other's was cut short, military style.

Ragnor stopped in his tracks.

They did the same.

He cocked his head to the side in puzzlement.

They did the same.

The older man's eyes went wide with sudden understanding. Then he started to weep as he stepped forward, arms outspread in welcome.

"Father?" Ragnor inquired tentatively. How could this be? It was impossible. Wasn't it?

The older man nodded and grabbed him into a mighty hug, nigh cracking his ribs with the vigor of his embrace. "Praise the gods! My son Ragnor, my son Ragnor! I have missed you so."

The younger man stepped up then, a mirror image of Ragnor except that his hair was blond and his eyes brown, while Ragnor's hair was black and his eyes blue. "Torolf," he said joyfully. "I ne'er thought we would ever be reunited."

"You are a sight for sore eyes." Torolf kept hugging him and pulling back to look him over, then hugging him again. In the end, he held him at arm's length, then observed, "You wear a Navy shirt, and your head is practically bald. Why is that?"

"Because I have just completed Navy SEALs training. I

am beginning to wonder . . . hmmm . . . perchance were you in that program? And didst you leave of a sudden?"

Torolf nodded slowly.

"By the gods, I underwent all this torture in your place. Now it finally makes sense."

Torolf slapped him on the back, laughing. "Oh, this is rich. I get to go to the SEALs teams without all the hard work. That is better than any prank we played as young men back in the Norselands."

There was no time to puzzle it out then as Ragnor was overrun with all his brothers, sisters, stepmother, cousins, uncles, and aunts . . . some of whom he had not seen for eleven years, some of whom he'd never met. It was over-whelming.

But not so overwhelming as it must be for Alison, who stood at the edge of the parking area, watching the reunion unfold. How could he have forgotten about her? He walked over and took her hand, leading her to the group.

"Father, I would have you meet my betrothed, Alison MacLean."

Alison was making that cute little gurgling sound of hers again at the word "betrothed." Come to think on it, Vikings were especially good at making women gurgle.

His father's jaw dropped. "In such a short time, you have met a woman you want to wed?"

"Not just that, but we are going to have a baby," Ragnor blathered on.

Gurgle, gurgle, gurgle!

"I can't believe it. Already you are outdoing me," Torolf complained, a grin on his lips. "Betcha her brother Ian is livid, especially if he thought you were me." He grinned at that statement, too.

"A grandfather? Me? I am too young," his father pro-

claimed, but the smile on his face showed his great pride.
He hugged Alison warmly, and Torolf gave her a little wave
of greeting.

Everyone else was offering congratulations afore Ragnor
thought to glance Alison's way.

She glared at him.

Uh-oh!

Leastways she no longer gurgled. He just smiled back at
her and hugged her to his side. *I know the best way to make
her smile again. It involves siren dresses and bare skin . . .
and, well, what we Vikings do best to make a maid smile. I
wonder if they have any broom closets here.*

She bared her teeth and growled at him.

On the other hand . . .

CHAPTER TWENTY-TWO

⌘

T *alk about older men, younger women! . . .*
Alison didn't know if she was more angry or confused.

Well, the anger was only a small part of her roiling emotions of the moment. What else could she expect from the arrogant louse she had come to love? After all, he'd made the same outrageous announcement to her father and Ian. And, yes, she did love the arrogant louse. She'd known that for weeks now.

But confusion? Lordy, Lordy! Everyone talked at once. They appeared to be family . . . all two dozen of them. Father, stepmother, brothers, sisters, uncles, aunts, cousins. They were a veritable Norse version of the Beverly Hillbillies. One of them was almost a twin to Ragnor . . . that was what they called Max . . . except for the difference in their hair and eye colors. And it sounded as if Torolf had explained that he'd been injured, which she was well aware of, but that he'd left Coronado and suffered a memory loss while off at a hog farm or something. Meanwhile, Ragnor had just bopped in and completed BUD/S for him. Simple as that. Ha, ha, ha! Amazing! Impossible! But still, amazing!

The most alarming, confusing thing of all was that, if she accepted that all these people were who they claimed to be, then Ragnor Magnusson truly was a time-traveler. She had made love with a freakin' thousand-year-old, albeit remarkably well-preserved man. *Eeew!*

Ragnor had gone off with his father and uncles and Torolf to chat some more and probably chug down beer. Alison was helping the stepmother Angela, the two aunts Meredith and Maggie, and the newly arrived Kirsten to set the tables for the upcoming feast. She'd already spoken at length with Maggie's twin daughters, who were in pre-med at Berkeley. They had lots of questions about her own practice, especially since it involved Navy SEALs, always an appealing subject for twenty-year-old females.

"I don't understand any of this," she said in an aside to Kirsten, once all the tables had the appropriate china plates, silverware, and cloth napkins.

"The feast? Our fancy way of eating outdoors? Or the time-travel?"

"What do you think?" Like she would care whether they used Royal Doulton or supermarket paper plates.

"Let's sit down," Kirsten suggested. The other women came over, too, probably knowing all too well how Alison was feeling. They sat down on blankets that had been arranged on the grass, and Angela brought them glasses of the new wine.

Alison declined hers, and Kirsten asked her, "You really are pregnant?"

"Yep. I know some people think wine is okay in moderation, but I don't want to take any chances."

"Good thing the world isn't pregnant or we'd be out of business," Angela remarked drolly.

"When's the wedding?" Meredith asked.

"There is no wedding. Max . . . I mean, Ragnor . . . is jumping the gun a bit."

"Oh?" the three of them said at once.

"Now, there's a surprise," Meredith said. "A Viking taking things for granted."

They all laughed.

"He did ask you to marry him, didn't he?" Kirsten wanted to know, as if every man who got a woman pregnant did the "right thing."

"He *told* me we would marry."

"Men! They are so clueless," Meredith said.

"Yep," they all agreed.

"I never considered abortion once I knew I was pregnant, but, man, this little one"—she put a hand over her belly affectionately—"interferes with everything I'd always planned for my life."

"You will marry eventually, though, won't you?" Angela stared at her with motherly concern.

"Maybe. Probably. I don't know. This happened rather fast. I still haven't reconciled myself to who he is . . . or appears to be. Today's the first time I came even close to thinking it was possible. Even then . . ."

"Ah. The time-travel business," Meredith said. "What finally convinced me was all the knowledge Rolf had about that time period. Little details, like the name of a sword or a longship. I was a medieval-studies professor and I didn't know half of what he did. The man even built me a longboat." She grinned sheepishly at them and took a sip of her wine.

"For me the final straw was when my daughters and I went with Jorund to Rosestead, the Viking village that his brother founded in Maine," Maggie said. "Of course, we didn't know it had any connection to Rolf at the time. To see him in that element, it was impossible to deny that this was what he had come from."

Alison was having trouble fathoming how a college pro-

fessor and a psychologist . . . seemingly intelligent women . . .
could accept such a preposterous notion as time-travel.

"Well, I know that time-travel exists, because I experienced it firsthand." Kirsten set aside her empty glass and
looked directly at Alison. "In the year 1000 A.D., my father,
myself, and eight of my brothers and sisters were on a longship somewhere beyond Greenland. A strange fog enveloped
the vessel, causing us all to fall asleep. When we awoke the
next morning, we were on a Hollywood movie set. I was
only fourteen at the time, but I remember every detail. Of
course, I couldn't put any of this in my thesis. Either my aca-
demic superiors would have thought I was nuts, or if they
did believe it, they'd have sent the whole lot of us to some
research lab for testing. Viking guinea pigs, that's what
we'd be."

Alison burst out laughing at the image of a bunch of Vikings being stranded in Hollywood and at the preposterous
notion of time-travel. "Honestly, how can you explain time-
travel?"

"Oh, there is no explanation. It's a miracle, that's all,"
Maggie said, throwing her hands up in the air. "Sometimes
you just have to trust that God—or the gods, if you listen to
my husband—have a different plan for us."

She must have still looked skeptical.

"Honey, do you believe in God, or some higher being?"
Angela asked, putting a hand on her forearm and caressing
it in a motherly way.

"Of course."

"Why? You can't see Him. There is no science to prove He
exists. Sometimes you just have to trust." Angela shrugged as
if that said it all.

"You're still not buying it, are you?" Kirsten narrowed
her eyes at her with exaggerated dismay.

"No."

"You will."

After that, Alison relaxed and enjoyed herself. She loved watching Ragnor—she still stumbled over that name—bask here in his own element. Everyone, including Ragnor, kept coming over to where she sat in a cushioned lounge chair on the back patio to make sure she was okay. If she didn't fit in, it wasn't because she was ignored.

But Alison felt the need to get away by herself, to assimilate all the astounding news she'd been hit with today, to sort out the implications of what this would mean to her and Ragnor. Torolf would probably resume his position on the SEAL team to which he—rather, Ragnor—had been assigned. Becoming a SEAL had always been Torolf's dream. But what would Ragnor do, assuming he was here to stay? Become a vintner? A SEAL under his own name? He was an extremely intelligent man. With some major tutoring, he could choose any career he wanted.

Where do I fit in the picture? And our baby?

It was all more than Alison could handle at the moment.

So in the early evening, while it was still daylight, Alison pulled Ragnor aside. He grinned, thinking she wanted to make out a little and pulled her into a somewhat secluded grape arbor, more decorative than utilitarian.

While he nuzzled her neck and tried to ruche up her dress, letting out a hoot of joyous laughter when he discovered that she was indeed naked underneath, she kept swatting his hands aside. "Listen to me, you lech, I have to tell you something."

"Does it have aught to do with marrying me?"

"No."

"Then it cannot be all that important."

"Yes, it is. Oh, my goodness! Stop that. Someone might come in here." He had backed her up against one supporting post and had her dress up to her waist. His big hands were palming her bare buttocks.

"You are right, as always, milady, but I am a Viking. We Norsemen know what to do in such situations." With that, he plopped down onto the bench behind him, taking her astride him. He billowed the skirt of her dress out and over his lap and knees. "Anyone walking in unannounced will think you are just sitting on my lap," he proclaimed proudly.

"Yeah, if they are stupid and unaware of the Viking one-track mindset when it comes to sex."

He smiled, then reached under and touched her, thus getting the last word in, so to speak.

She almost screamed, so intense was the pleasure.

Quickly he pulled down his shorts and arranged his erection to press against her folds. "Your woman dew welcomes me," he informed her in a silky voice. "Like warm honey it is."

"Warm honey on a hot rock?" she teased.

"For a certainty." He nuzzled her neck and kissed his way up to her mouth. "Thank you, *sweet*ling," he whispered against her parted lips.

"For what, *sweet*heart?" She rubbed her mouth back and forth across his. It had been so long since she'd been with him. More than a month. But it seemed like a year.

"For finding Kirsten. For coming here with me. For giving me back my family. For everything."

"It was my pleasure."

"Nay, *this* is your pleasure," he said, thrusting himself inside her.

That is for sure, sure, sure, sure, sure, sure . . . she stuttered mentally.

When it was all over, she still sat on his lap with his wilted penis inside her, her head resting on his shoulder, both of them panting. "I love you, *heart*ling," he said then.

She went stiff. This was not the right time. He was speaking out of gratitude and the joy of his homecoming. Even so, she whispered back, "I love you, too, my *heart*."

He smiled at her repeating back his endearment in her own way. "What was so important that you lured me here?"

"Hey, buster, I was the luree, not the lurer." But then she grew more serious. "I called the hospital a little while ago to check on a patient. One of the covering physicians was called away on an emergency, and I have to go back tonight." It was a lie, of course, but for a good cause.

"Oh, nay! Can we not wait till the morrow to return?"

"No, no, no! You stay here for a few days, or longer. I'll drive back myself."

"I am not going to remain here without you."

"Now, don't go getting excited—"

"I thought you liked it when I got excited."

She chucked him playfully under the chin. "You need this time with your family. I need to be back at Coronado. Relax and enjoy the gift you've been given here. I'll call you tomorrow night, or you can call me. Please."

She could tell he was divided—wanting to stay, but feeling obligated to go with her.

"Really, I'll be all right."

"Well, only if you will give me a proper goodbye." He wiggled his hips from side to side to show what he meant, as if the moving, hardening object inside her didn't already proclaim the message loud and clear.

She laughed. "You know how you're always braying about this or that famous Viking S-Spot?"

"Vikings do not bray." Then, "You do not like the Viking S-Spots?"

"I love the Viking S-Spots."

"Well?"

"What you do not know is there is a famous Navy SEAL S-Spot as well."

"How would you know? You are not a Navy SEAL."

"Ah, but I was engaged to one."

"Hmmm."

"Is that a *hmmm* you are interested, or a *hmmm* you are not open to new and creative ideas?"

"Definitely interested. Where is this SEAL spot on your body?" He pretended to lean down and peek under her dress.

"Not there, silly. The difference between the Viking S-Spot and the SEAL S-Spot is that this one is on *your* body. It will be my gift to you."

His blue eyes lit up with interest.

A short time later, as Alison stood and whisked her hands together dramatically, Ragnor lay back on the bench and pretended to have died. "You give good gift, milady."

Alison only hoped that this wouldn't be her last gift to him.

Beer wisdom . . .

He should have gone with her, Ragnor realized almost immediately.

"You should have gone with her," Torolf said, as if reading his mind as he'd always been wont to do. Some things never changed.

It was past midnight, the party long over, and they were

seated on rocking chairs on the back porch, swilling down more mead on top of all they'd already imbibed. He wondered idly if he'd be able to walk to his bed in the spare bedchamber when he got up, or if he should just sleep in this chair tonight. More likely, he would end up face down on the wooden floor.

"She said she would call me when she arrived at her hotel tonight, but she has not called."

"Don't worry. She's all right. She probably didn't want to disturb you. Women are stubborn that way."

"But she said she would call."

"Women lie."

"Men lie, too. Remember the time you told Olga Cross Eyes that she looked very pretty in the hay byre with her dress up over her head."

"That is beside the point. I cannot picture you with children."

"Not *children*, for the love of Frigg. One child."

Torolf laughed. "Both of us grew up in that madhouse of screaming, whining children. We made a pact when we were twelve never to have children of our own."

"I believe we were changing Kolbein's shit-laden nappy at the time," Ragnor pointed out. "That alters a man's thinking somewhat."

"So now you want children?"

Ragnor had to ponder for a moment. "If you had asked me that three months ago, I would have said nay. But the instant I learned of this babe growing in Alison's belly, I knew . . . I just knew it would be precious to me."

"It's Alison who makes the difference, then?"

"Methinks so. Plus, I have been thinking of late that the big family we grew up in was not all that bad. Not that I

would want to have a *large* number of babes with Alison.
One will do. Or two, if I am coerced."

"Don't try to tell me she coerced you into bed. That I will
never believe." Torolf grinned at him. "She would have
nothing to do with me. Even when I only tried to be friendly,
she gave me the cold shoulder."

"Ah, but I was always the more handsome of us two."

"Your conceit hasn't changed at all."

"Are we *drukkinn*?"

"Absolutely."

The two brothers grinned at each other.

"Why did you say I should have gone with her?" Ragnor
tried to lick his lips, but they seemed to have disappeared.

"Because women say one thing when they mean another.
They want us to guess what they really think," Torolf explained.

"So, when Alison said she didn't want me to go with her,
she probably meant the opposite?"

"Exactly."

"And this philosophy of yours was taught to you by what
fool?"

"Our father."

The two of them grinned at each other some more.

"He seems happy here . . . you all do."

"We are. I'm not sure why we were all sent here, or how,
but every member of our family seems to have found a
niche."

"A niche, huh? What do you suppose my niche is?"

"Well, with a baby on the way, I would say your niche is
with Alison, wherever that might be."

"But what work would I do here? I ran the family estates
in the Norselands. I fought in wars when so inclined. It was
a different world, calling for different skills."

"Pfff to that! You can do whatever you want here. You could help Father run Blue Dragon."

"I know naught about grapes."

"You could work with Uncle Rolf at Rosestead, prancing around like a Viking warrior."

Ragnor reached over to punch his brother's arm and almost fell out of his chair.

"You could teach mentally ill people to exercise at Uncle Jorund's clinic."

"Oh, that sounds like fun."

"Hey, maybe you could go to medical school and be a doctor. You and Alison could be a team."

"Somehow I do not see myself sitting in a classroom for years. And I have ne'er been drawn to the healing arts."

"Father has a friend who will get you some forged documents stating that you were born here. Don't want them putting you on display in a museum somewhere to show what a thousand-year-old cock looks like."

"*It* is fine."

"Well, I guess so if you got the good doctor pregnant already."

"How about you, Torolf? What will you do now?"

"Return to SEALs," he replied without hesitation. "It's always been my dream. In some ways, your coming here helped keep my dream alive, brother. With my injury, they never would have let me continue." Torolf gave him a quick shoulder squeeze to show his thanks.

Ragnor frowned with concern. "Since I went through the last few weeks of training in your place, won't you find it difficult to just pick up where I left off?"

"Nah! I already have a pilot's license, and I jumped more times than I can count when I worked fighting forest fires. Besides, I'm not saying it will be easy, but training isn't over,

just because you . . . rather, I . . . graduated from BUD/S.
It's just the first phase, buddy. And if that's not enough,
I'll confide in Cage. He's a good guy. He'll help me catch
up."

Ragnor nodded. If he could survive after being dumped
in the middle of SEALs training hell, his brother could
surely survive the continuation. They were Vikings, after
all.

"Back to you and Alison, they do have condoms here,
you know."

"I know, and I used them all the time. It was just a momentary slip."

"A momentary slip. Do not dare stop there."

"In a broom closet."

Torolf's mouth gaped open with disbelief; then he let out
a burst of laughter. "Oh, Ragnor, I have missed you sorely."

You never know what you've got till you lose it . . .

After stopping midway back to Coronado for a late dinner,
Alison decided to drive through instead of staying in a hotel
for the night alone. She should have called Ragnor, but it
was midnight, and she didn't want to awaken anyone at Blue
Dragon. She would call in the morning.

She was not unhappy as she made the trip home. Those
eight hours gave her lots of time to think and plan. If Ragnor
were here, he would say, "Nay, nay, no thinking!" Alison
smiled at his words in her head. But she was a logical person,
and she thought with her head now, not some other body
part, like her heart.

One, she refused to marry Ragnor for the sake of the
baby. Not even for the love they both professed. That love

had not stood the test of time yet. That did not mean that they wouldn't marry at some point. They needed to spend time together, maybe even live together for a while. He wouldn't like that, but that was her decision on the matter . . . for now. He would try to change her mind. She couldn't wait.

Two, if they didn't marry, Ragnor would share custody of the baby. No way would she deny her child a father. And, man oh man, what an extended family this little one would have!

Three, she would have to inform her father and her brothers of her pregnancy, ASAP. And her superior officers at the base, even though her work shouldn't be affected.

Four, related to that, she would decline the unspoken offer to join the new Liberty Teams. Oddly, she did not feel all that bad about it. She was beginning to wonder if perhaps the dream of becoming a SEAL hadn't begun to fade a long time ago.

Five, she would tell Lillian about the baby, and perhaps the widow would be willing to help her with some childcare.

With all these decisions made, Alison smiled and patted her stomach. "You and me, baby . . . and maybe your daddy, too."

She arrived back at her house about four a.m. and went immediately to bed, where she slept soundly till daylight crept through the windows. But it wasn't daylight that had awakened her. It was cramps . . . no, more like mild contractions in her belly. And she felt wetness beneath her on the sheets.

Oh, my God! Oh, my God! She stumbled to the bathroom, where she discovered what amounted to a heavy menstrual flow. As a physician, she knew that she was losing the baby. Quickly she started to dress in hopes of making her way to the clinic. Perhaps the doctors there could do something to stop this.

But there was no time. Every five minutes or so, she was passing clots along with the flow. In the end, she just sat on the bathroom floor, propped against the tub, and cried. *Oh, baby! Sweet baby! I am so sorry. Please, God, take this little child into your arms. If there is a heaven, please welcome my baby there.*

Later, she would go see her gynecologist/obstetrician, but, barring complications, she hadn't been far enough advanced in her pregnancy to require a D & C or any other procedure. She knew what the doctor would say. Some pregnancies were doomed from the beginning. It wasn't her fault. There would be other children. The whole routine.

Alison washed herself, now that the worst was over, put on a heavy pad and a long flannel nightgown—her comfort attire—and crawled into bed. Maybe when she woke up this time, she'd find this had all been a dream. No, she wouldn't delude herself.

Before she went to sleep, she realized there was one thing she had to do first.

I have to call Ragnor and tell him our baby is gone.

Goodbye, baby . . .

"There's a phone call for you."

Ragnor sat up so abruptly in the bed that his head swam and his eyes blurred. But then, that was probably due to the excessive amount of mead he'd imbibed the night before.

He turned toward the doorway where his new stepmother, Angela, stood staring at him with amusement. There was a mean streak in some females that gave them enjoyment on seeing men suffer from the alehead.

"It's Alison," she said, handing a cordless tell-a-fone to him.

"Oh." He took the tell-a-fone from her, meanwhile glancing at the clock on the bedside table. Noon! Holy Thor, he had never slept this late.

Angela gave him a little wave and closed the door after her.

"Alison, where are you? I should have gone with you. I realized that as soon as you left. Are you back in Coronado?" He was blathering, and he was not sure why. Perhaps he sensed something bad about to happen, but that was a ridiculous notion.

"I'm home. And, no, you shouldn't have come with me, and I don't want you blaming yourself, do you hear me?"

Ragnor's skin prickled all over and not from the effects of his foolish overdrinking. Alison's voice was soft, as if she'd been weeping. Something must have happened. *Blame? For what?* "What is it, dearling?"

"I lost the baby."

"What baby?" His fuzzy brain appeared to have shut down.

"Our baby."

"Where did you lose it?" He still wasn't comprehending what she said.

"Oh, Ragnor, I had a miscarriage this morning."

A low groan of agony emerged from his throat afore he had a chance to catch it. "I am so sorry." And he was. Truly, until that moment, he had not realized how much he wanted the babe. And, dammit, it *was* his fault. He should have gone with her. He might have been able to prevent this from happening.

"Me, too." She was definitely weeping now.

"Are you all right? Are you in a hospitium?"

"No. I'm home. And I'm all right physically. Mentally . . . emotionally . . . it will take me a few days to accustom myself to not being pregnant anymore."

"I'll come back right away."

"*No!*" she said in a panic. "Don't come back . . . not right away. Spend this time with your family. I'm thinking about going to visit my father for a few days."

She was lying, Ragnor sensed. Her father had not known of the pregnancy. She wouldn't want him to know now.

"I'm coming home," he insisted.

She said nothing, probably because she was holding in her sobs.

"Wait for me, heartling. Please."

CHAPTER TWENTY-THREE

The Vikings are coming . . . and coming . . . and coming . . .

Alison was awakened late that afternoon by a loud knocking on her door. She'd taken a sleeping pill after talking with Ragnor and probably hadn't heard the initial knocks.

Groggily she made her way to the door, peeked out through the peephole, then groaned. "Ragnor! I told you not to come," she said, even as she opened the door and he stormed in, taking her immediately into his arms.

She'd told him that she didn't need him here, that she was all right, but she realized now as he held her tight against him, making soothing noises against her hair, that she did in fact need him. She broke down, sobbing against his neck, wetting his T-shirt.

"I am sorry, dearling. I should have been here with you. But I will make it better now."

"Ragnor, you can't bring this baby back."

"I know I cannot bring the babe back, but we will make it through this ordeal together. And we will make other babes, that I promise you."

"You don't want children," she blubbered out between sobs.

"Yea, I do. With you, leastways. But mayhap you will not want children with me now that you have a chance to join those Liberty Teams."

"I can't think about any of that now."

"I know, I know." He sat down in the rocking chair and arranged her on his lap, rocking gently. "Like a small, wounded animal you are. My heart nigh breaks for you . . . for us, actually."

"Where do you want this stuff?" It was his brother Torolf speaking from the open doorway. He'd carried up two pieces of luggage and a white ice-cooler chest. To Alison, he winked and said, "Nice negligee, sweetheart."

"Huh?" She wore a floral-printed flannel nightgown that covered her from neck to wrists to ankles. "Drop dead," she told Torolf, seeming to recall that it wasn't the first time she'd said that to him.

"I think she likes me," Torolf told Ragnor. "Best you watch your back, brother. She might be making a move on me."

"When aliens land in Coronado."

"One of them already did." Torolf looked pointedly at Ragnor.

Oh, yeah, Ragnor is a regular Mork. What does that make me? Mindy? Yikes, I must be going into shock. "Were you two always like this together?" Alison asked.

"Always," they both said, grinning at each other.

Meanwhile, Torolf made himself at home, carrying the ice chest into the kitchen, where she heard the refrigerator door open.

"They insisted on coming with me on the airplane," Ragnor told her in an apologetic tone.

"*They?*" she practically squealed.

His face turned red with embarrassment. "Really,

twenty-seven years old and my family can still reduce me to a bumbling youthling, unable to say them nay."

"Don't feel bad. My father and brothers do the same to me. So, who exactly came with you?"

"My father, Angela, Torolf, and Kirsten. My uncles Rolf and Jorund and their families stayed behind to tend the younger children. Otherwise they would have come, too."

"Good Lord!"

"My sentiments exactly."

"What's in the ice chest?"

"Angela contends that pasta is the comfort food you need to recover. She brought all the ingredients with her, along with a few leftovers from the feast. A few? Hah! We could feed an army."

"And your father? And Kirsten?"

"Kirsten drove to her office in Lost-Angel-Less, but she will come here tonight. My father is down in the front yard giving Lillian advice on soil and plantings. Last I heard, they were discussing the merits of cow shit over goat shit."

"You do have a way with words. Where are they all staying?"

He ducked his head sheepishly.

"Here?" She tried not to sound too alarmed.

"Angela said a woman needs family around her at a time like this."

She smiled at him, wiping her wet cheeks with the sleeve of her nightgown, which was god-awful ugly, as Torolf had implied. "I told you not to come, you big lout."

"I did not heed you, lout that I am."

"Thank you."

"For what?"

"Coming."

He laughed. "What a contrary wench you are!"

Just then, another visitor arrived. "Who the hell are all these people?"

"'Tis your brother," he informed her, as if she didn't already know. "No one else bellows like he does."

Of course, Alison started wailing again, and soon she was in Ian's arms, telling him about the lost baby. She could tell that Ian was conflicted over whether to be angry over the pregnancy or sympathetic over the loss. The latter won out. He kept patting her back as he held her, saying things like, "Shhhh, Allie. There will be other babies. Shhh."

After that, Ian kept glancing from Ragnor to Torolf with confusion. *Uh-oh! This could mean bigtime trouble with the U.S. Navy. We need to come up with a game plan before we divulge the deception that took place right under his nose.* Luckily, the two brothers had had the foresight to shave their heads before leaving Blue Dragon. Since Torolf's hair had been growing out during his absence, it would have been clear that he was blond. "Which of you is which?" Ian's eyes narrowed with suspicion.

"I'm Torolf," they both said at the same time.

Which caused Ian's eyes to narrow even more.

Then Torolf said, with a straight face yet, "I'm the one who graduated into teams. This is my brother Ragnor. He's thinking about joining the next SEAL class."

"I am?" Ragnor said.

"Good thing I won't be there," Ian said. "I'm not sure I could take another Magnusson goofball."

Alison felt as if she were in the middle of an old Laurel and Hardy skit. But at least the brothers' antics kept her mind off her loss.

But that wasn't the end of the farce that had become her life. Alison had forgotten to tell Ian not to tell anyone about the miscarriage, so, once returning to his home, he called their father.

By nightfall, her father arrived, too, with Ian in tow. *Laurel and Hardy meet Abbott and Costello. Unbelievable!* Looking as if he were in shock, her father, in full uniform, came immediately into her bedroom where she was resting, and sat down on the side of the bed. "Ahhh, Pooh Bear!" was all he said. And she, of course, started wailing some more. This strong military man, who had probably fought dozens of battles with a stony face, wept unabashedly with his only daughter.

Later, everyone—his family, her family, Lillian and Dr. Feingold—sat outside eating platefuls of pasta with marinara sauce, which Ragnor described to her as "white-wormlike food covered with a red-bloodlike sauce," warm Italian bread, and salads which Ragnor described as platefuls of weeds with raspberry vinaigrette dressing, sipping at the fine wines his father had brought along.

To her surprise, Ragnor's family mixed exceedingly well with her father and Ian, despite their vast differences. Who knew that her father had an interest in ancient methods of warfare? Ragnor, who supposedly had been a famous warrior at one time, talked at length on the subject, which kept her father enthralled. Ian still studied Ragnor and Torolf suspiciously.

The evening progressed, and now Ragnor was in Alison's bedroom, where she had been ordered to rest by one of the Navy's top physicians, whom the admiral had insisted come to the house for a second evaluation. She'd eaten a small amount of food and was leaning back on the pillows. Ragnor half reclined next to her on his own set of pillows.

"Do all these people bother you?" he asked, twining his fingers with hers. "If so, I will order them to leave."

"No, it was sweet of them to come. And, actually, it was the best thing for me today. I needed to get my mind off the . . . baby." Her voice cracked on that last word.

He squeezed her hand.

"Everyone keeps saying that bad things happen for a reason, even though we don't understand it at the time. I can't see any reason for this," she said.

"Well, you never would have wished for it to happen, but it does give you more options for the future. Like the Liberty Teams."

She nodded. "You, too. I know that you felt compelled to ask for an assignment close to Coronado because of the baby. Now you can go wherever you want. Even back to your own time."

"So, you believe in time-travel now?" He chuckled.

"No, I can't say that I do. I try not to think about it at all. I choose to think you and your family are all just a little bit eccentric."

He laughed. "Time-traveler. Eccentric. Same thing. But tell me this, sweetling, would you not miss me if I returned to my time?"

She pulled her fingers from his grasp and rolled over on her side to face him. Caressing his face with her fingertips, as if to memorize him, she said, "I would miss you desperately."

"Good," he said, "because I am going nowhere."

"For now," she emphasized.

"For now," he agreed.

It was not the answer they both needed, but it would give them time to unravel the tangles of their separate lives. She hoped.

Taking a break . . .

Ragnor had been at Blue Dragon for the past three weeks. Alone. Well, as alone as any man could be when surrounded by the most bothersome, meddlesome family in the world.

"Why don't you just go back to her if you're so miserable," Torolf asked him.

"Because Alison and I agreed to spend one month apart so that any decisions we make about the future will be based on logic and not emotion."

"And whose half-brain idea was that?"

Ragnor blushed. "Hers. But I agreed. I fear that Alison will limit her career choices because she feels obligated to me. In essence, I am giving her a choice."

"You are pathetic!"

That pretty much summed up his own thinking, as well.

At times, Ragnor was miserable, but mostly he was excited about embarking on a new life here in Ah-mare-ee-ca. His father had arranged for his false birthing papers. Ragnor had taken driving lessons and now possessed a paper that said he was entitled to drive a moving vehicle. It turned out his arm rings were worth a fortune, so he sold one and used only a small portion of the funds to purchase himself a new Jeep Cherokee. Torolf had tried to talk him into a Corvette, which he called a single guy's badass toy, but Ragnor had told him he didn't feel single.

To which Torolf had repeated, "You are pathetic."

His father had hired him a tutor, and between the tutor and the computer he was still mastering, Ragnor was learning so much, he could hardly keep up with his spinning mind. In fact, Ragnor had become enthralled with computers—not just what they could do, but how they worked, and their potential for the future. The two computers he'd bought—a PC and a laptop—along with scanners, printers, and various related devices, had cost him as much as a longship in the old days. He wasn't certain yet, but he felt drawn toward a career that would combine his military background, all that he had learned in BUD/S, and computers.

On the other hand, if it would help him in his pursuit and holding of Alison, mayhap the combination could be computers and medicine.

Then, too, he had to decide whether he wanted to be a SEAL, like Torolf. If so, he would have to do the whole torturous program all over again, starting in about five months, assuming he was accepted.

Last week, Torolf and Cage had gone off with their new team to Louisiana, where a special military training camp to counter terrorism had been set up in the swamplands. Ragnor and his father planned to fly down there tomorrow on a two-day trip to observe the goings-on. Perchance Ragnor would be closer to a decision by the time he returned, when his one month would be up.

In this mish-mash that had become his life, there was only one certainty, and that was Alison. She was his lodestone.

But that lodestone shattered for him two days later when Torolf told him something alarming. The entrance requirements for the new Liberty Teams had just been announced. One of them was that members must be unmarried and willing to sign a promise not to wed for at least two years.

After much agonizing over this new information, Ragnor knew what he must do. He must give up Alison. He would sacrifice his dream of a lifetime with her, in order for her to fulfill her own dreams. It would be his gift to her. But she must never know.

It was the only way.

Breaking up is hard to do . . .

Alison fidgeted nervously, waiting for Ragnor to arrive.

It had been one month since they'd seen each other . . . one month too long. She had been the one to suggest a separation, but she'd also been the one to regret it the moment he was gone.

He'd called last night to say he was driving to Coronado today and would be here by late afternoon. His voice had sounded rather cool on the phone, but then he was probably still uncomfortable with modern telephones.

She'd changed her clothes three times and finally settled on a short jeans skirt, tank top, and sandals. She added a spritz of Dream cologne, some mousse to fluff out her hair, and a light covering of makeup. Just then, looking out her window, she saw a Jeep pull into the driveway. Forgetting pride, she ran out the door, down the steps, and into his arms.

At first, Ragnor seemed startled by her effusive welcome, but then he hugged her back, hard.

She kissed his face and neck and ears and mouth so enthusiastically that Ragnor finally pulled away, laughing. "What is this all about?"

"You stayed away too long."

"You ordered me to stay away this long."

"Did you have to listen to me?"

He laughed some more and began to walk her toward the house, his arm over her shoulder. A tiny prickling of apprehension swept over her. Ragnor wasn't being cold, but he wasn't being hot either, and that was unlike him.

She knew for sure that something was wrong when he didn't immediately take her into the bedroom to make love. That was what she'd expected. It was what she wanted.

"What's up, Ragnor?" She stiffened her body with pride

and put some distance between them in her living room. "I thought we'd be going at it like Energizer bunnies by now."

"We need to talk." His eyes shifted, looking everywhere except at her.

The fact that he hadn't said, "We need to talk *first* was a glaring omission to her. "So talk," she said icily.

"Have you been offered a place on the Liberty Teams?"

Huh? That was not the question she had expected from him. *Do you love me? Will you marry me? Can we make another baby?* Those had been her expectations, foolish girl that she was.

"Yes."

"Have you accepted?"

"I haven't given them an official answer yet."

His shoulders sagged, and he let out an exhale of . . . what? Disappointment?

"I think you should accept," he told her then.

She cocked her head to the side, trying to figure out what was going on. "Why?"

"It's what you've always dreamed of. It's the opportunity of a lifetime. To be on the first of the Liberty Teams . . . well, you will be making history."

"And that's what you think I dream of?"

"It's what you've always said."

"Am I being dumped, here?"

"No! Absolutely not." He licked his lips and gulped several times. "I am walking away so that you can be free."

He's walking away. Oh, my God, he's walking away. Tears burned her eyes.

"Please don't cry. I cannot bear it when you cry." He started to come to her, but she put up a halting hand.

"You big ignoramus. You don't have the right to declare me free or not. That is totally my decision." She patted a hand over her heart in emphasis. "Just for the record, what are you going to be doing, now that you are flying fancy free?"

"Mayhap I will go to Norway to see if I can locate the place where my family holdings once were."

"I could go with you." *Oh, jeez, I'm not going to beg, am I?*

"Why would you want to?"

"To help you." *Yep, begging.*

"You can help me by becoming the first female Liberty Team member."

"You said you loved me." *I can't believe I've become that kind of woman. I don't recognize myself.*

"I do."

"What kind of love gives up at the first hint of trouble?" *Okay, that's my last grovel.*

"'Tis the kind of love that wants what's best for you."

"And you get to decide that? In what macho world are you living?" *Definitely the last. Pull yourself together, girl. Get some dignity.*

"It is over, Alison. I wanted to do this amicably. I did not want to hurt you. In truth, I want only the very best for you."

"I think you'd better go."

"Perchance we can talk again once you are less emotional."

"Perchance you can go to hell."

"Mayhap I am already there."

On that odd note, he looked at her for a long time, then silently made his exit.

Alison stood stock-still, unable to move or breathe or scream, which was what she really wanted to do. Ragnor had left. He said he loved her, but still he left. Something was wrong with this picture.

I should go after him and karate-chop him to the ground. Or I should go jump his bones.

Am I really going to let him go so easily, without a fight? Hell, no! No way can I let Ragnor go this way. No way!

She went to the door, opened it and was about to run down and catch him before he left, but what she saw stopped her cold.

Ragnor was at the bottom of the steps with his forehead pressed against the front door. His shoulders shook slightly.

Alison inhaled sharply with sudden understanding.

Her Viking was weeping.

Vikings take clueless to a whole new level . . .

Ragnor sensed, rather than heard, Alison behind him.

Oh, this is too much! Now I leak like a sniveling youthling. How pathetic! And how do I explain it to her? He turned reluctantly and saw her standing at the bottom of the steps, arms folded over her chest, eyes glaring. She would have looked fierce if not for the ridiculous black marks running down her cheeks from the kohl she must have put about her eyes.

"Uh, I got a cinder in my eye." *Holy Thor, is that the best I can do?*

She walked up and punched him in the stomach as hard as she could. It didn't hurt all that much, but he flinched anyway.

"Why did you hit me?"

"For scaring me like that. For making me think you didn't care."

"I ne'er said I did not care."

She drew back to punch him again, but he grabbed her wrist.

Meanwhile, Sam was barking like a mad dog behind

Lillian's closed doors. Lillian must be out, otherwise she would come to investigate.

With a sigh of surrender, he lifted her in his arms and began to carry her up the stairs. Alison kept slapping him about the ears and shoulders. Once he set her down in the middle of her solar, she demanded, "What was that all about?"

"Sacrifice." It didn't sound as good now as it had when he'd rehearsed it on the way here.

"Whose? Mine? You were sacrificing *me* for what?"

"Not you. Me. I was being noble." He could feel his face heat up on those last words. How noble was it when a man told people he was being noble? Didn't that take the nobility away?

She eyed him as if he'd lost half his brain.

Maybe he had.

"I know you have some affection for me—" he started to say.

"Affection, you lunkhead? Love. L-O-V-E."

She was not making this easy for him. "Knowing that you care and probably feel some obligation toward me . . ."

Rolling her eyes, she walked over to the sofa and sat down. "You'd better sit, too, baby, if it's going to take you this long to spit it out."

"Sarcasm ill suits you, m'lady."

"Blustering ill suits you, m'lord," she mimicked back at him. "Get to the freakin' point."

He sat down next to her. "I heard about the rules for the Liberty Teams. Only unwed men and women, and those promising not to marry for at least two years. I did not want you to give up your dreams because you were bound to me."

"So you were giving me a choice?"

"Yea, I was." He brightened at her finally understanding his motives.

"Are all Vikings as dumb as you?"

"Huh?"

"Ragnor, when you walked out of here today, you weren't giving me a choice. You were telling me how things would be, based on your choice. You gave me no choice as to whether you should stay or go."

He put his face in his hands, then looked sideways at her. "If I were not here . . . if we'd never met . . . would you join the Liberty Teams?"

She shrugged. "Maybe. Probably. But I'm not joining them now."

"You're not? But you said—"

"I said that I haven't *officially* given them my answer, but I've already said no informally."

"Because of me?" he asked with a huge sigh.

"Because of you," she said softly. "Oh, Ragnor, I love you. I want to be with you. I'm a physician. I can work anywhere you go . . . whether it be Norway or America or Timbuktu."

"Tim who?"

"Never mind," she said, laughing.

He stood then and smiled for the first time that day. Picking her up by the waist, he twirled her around, hugging her tightly to him. "I love you, too, heartling."

"Does that mean you are going to continue to seduce me till I agree to marry you?"

"Nay."

"Nay?"

"I figure I am all nobled out. 'Tis your turn to do the seducing." He kissed her then, a warm, hungry press of lips upon lips, a silent promise that everything would work out now.

When the kiss ended, she stared at him adoringly—Vikings had a way of bringing such an expression to a woman's face.

"I love you," she said.

"I love you," he said. "For all time."

"So, Viking . . ." She slanted him a half-lidded sultry look, which put him immediately on guard. *Beware of sultry-eyed wenches.* "I don't suppose you have any more of those Spots up your sleeve?"

He threw his head back and laughed. "Actually . . ."

EPILOGUE

⊗

Ragnor Magnusson married Alison MacLean in a mid-October wedding held outdoors at Blue Dragon Vineyards.

They had originally planned to move in together and wait till the following spring, but then Alison had balked, claiming she wasn't giving her Viking another chance to go noble on her . . . or go off a-Viking. He'd pretended to hesitate, but he wasn't giving her a second chance to escape, either . . . or go off a-Navy SEALing.

The members of Ragnor's—rather Torolf's—BUD/S team, along with the bride's brother Ian, came in dress whites and formed a beautiful arch of swords for the bride and groom to pass through. Ragnor's family formed an arch of swords as well, except theirs were ancient pattern-welded swords a thousand years old.

Torolf acted as best man and Kirsten as maid of honor. Rear Admiral Thomas MacLean gave his daughter away and seemed to have taken quite a fancy to Angela's brazen cousin Carmen, a rabid feminist who was said to have told the admiral, "Making war to get peace is like screwing for virginity." At which the admiral had howled with laughter and countered, "Screwing a feminist is like digging for gold in a mine field."

Ragnor wasn't sure what career to pursue, but he was taking myriad computer courses and boning up on his school studies. To his and Alison's surprise, the plans for the new Liberty Teams were cancelled. Instead, there was talk of a female SEAL program called WEALS. By the time that happened, Alison figured she would no longer be interested because she wanted a family. Ragnor said one child, Alison said three, but they had plenty of time to make that decision.

In the meantime, the happy couple planned to honeymoon in Norway. No one was sure what Ragnor hoped to accomplish by going there, but the entire family wanted to go along. Wisely, the couple declined the offer.

One strange thing happened during the wedding reception. Ragnor took Ian into the house to show him a painting hanging above the library mantel. It had been painted from memory by Ragnor's talented artist sister Dagny. A lovely blond woman, unsmiling and haughty in her demeanor, stared down at them. Dressed in regal Viking attire, complete with fine gold embroidery on the gown and amber jewelry, the woman was magnificent. It was Madrene, of course.

Long after Ragnor returned to the reception outdoors, Ian stood gazing up at her. Entranced, some said later.

When the reception was winding down, Ragnor took his bride aside and said, "I think I know why I always thought you were my destiny."

"Oh?" she said, linking her arms around his neck. She'd told him earlier that she wore nothing under her wedding gown. He couldn't wait to discover the truth of that statement.

"I assumed that destiny meant I was called here because you needed me."

"And now you think that's not true." She cocked her head to the side in surprise. "Here I was getting used to being your destiny."

"Oh, you are still my destiny. 'Tis just that I am the one who needed you, not the other way around."

"Oh, Ragnor, what a sweet thing to say."

"That is the best thing about us Vikings. Our sweetness." He waggled his eyebrows at her.

"But, honey, you told me something else was the best thing about Vikings."

"That, too." He laughed. "Shall I demonstrate?"

"I thought you'd never ask."

READER LETTER

❧

Dear Reader:

I hope you liked this first of my Viking Navy SEAL books. When I first wrote this book back in 1994, it was a venture into new territory. Not just Navy SEALs, but Viking Navy SEALs.

Personally, I think it was a great idea. What do you think?

At first, the idea sounded outlandish. In fact, there's a great tongue-in-cheek comic strip on the Internet about my books called 'I love you Sandra Hill.' http://www.questionable content.net.php.comic=1281

But really, Viking to SEALs was a natural progression. The similarities between these men, whether they be modern SEALs or tenth-century Vikings, are striking. Fierce, fighting men. Love ships and the water. Handsome and well-built. Brave and loyal. Appreciate humor, especially when laughing at themselves. Great lovers, even greater family men. I could be describing Vikings or SEALs.

It's important to me that I get the Navy SEAL details correct, but at the same time, please be gentle with me readers. This is a fantasy novel. In some cases, I took deliberate liberties, such as *yellow* inflatable rafts, and the way in which Ragnor and Alison bent the military rules barring a relationship between an officer and a subordinate. And, yes,

I know there's lots more to SEAL training than I portrayed here and that it would be nearly impossible for a man to step into the middle of training, undetected, even if he were a twin.

I admire the Navy SEALs tremendously and hope you all agree that they provide a great service to our country. They are indeed our silent warriors in the fight against terrorism. The same admiration applies to all who serve in the military to keep us safe and free.

Please keep in mind that while *Wet & Wild* is the first of the Viking Navy SEAL books, it is the fourth book in the story of the time-traveling Ericsson/Magnusson family, starting with *The Last Viking, Truly, Madly Viking,* and *The Very Virile Viking.* And it will be followed soon by *Hot & Heavy* (Madrene and Ian's story).

I invite you to visit my website where you can enter the occasional contest, sign up for my mailing list, watch book videos, download free novellas, check out genealogy charts, and just plain have fun.

Thank you, thank you, thank you for your incredible support and loyalty over the years. Some of you have been with me from the beginning, and believe me, I know who you are. Each and every one of you is appreciated.

As always, I wish you smiles in your reading.

Sandra Hill
shill733@aol.com
www.sandrahill.net

GLOSSARY

A-Viking—a Norse practice of sailing away to other countries for the purpose of looting, settlement, or mere adventure; could be for a period of several months or for years at a time.

Berserker—an ancient Norse warrior who fought in a frenzied rage during battle.

Birka—a trading town not far from present-day Stockholm, Sweden.

Braies—slim pants worn by men.

Brig—Navy jail.

BUD/S—Basic Underwater Demolition SEALs.

Danegeld—tax raised to pay tribute to Viking raiders to save the land from being ravaged.

Drukkinn (various spellings)—drunk, in Old Norse.

Ealdorman—chief magistrate, or king's deputy, in Anglo-Saxon England; later referred to as earls, appointed by the king; mostly noblemen.

Fjord—a narrow arm of the sea, often between high cliffs.

Frey—god of peace and plenty, also fertility.

Frigg—goddess of beauty, love, and marriage.

Garderobe—latrine or privy.

Gig Squad—a punishment inflicted during BUD/S whereby

a SEAL trainee is forced after a long day of training to do many vigorous exercises outside the officers' quarters.

Grody jodies—Jody calls, or jodies, the cadences called out by soldiers as they march or run. Grody jodies are vulgar ones.

Gunna—long-sleeved, ankle-length gown for women, often worn under a tunic or surcoat, or under a long, open-sided apron.

Hectare—type of land measure equal to 2.471 acres.

Hide—primitive measure of land that originally equaled the normal holding that would support a peasant and his family, roughly 120 arable acres, but could be as little as 40.

Hird—a permanent troop that a chieftain or nobleman might have.

Hnefatafl—a Viking board game.

Hordaland—ancient Norway.

Hospitium—ancient form of hospital.

Houri—beautiful woman, often associated with a harem.

Jarl—high-ranking Norseman similar to an English earl or wealthy landowner; could also be a chieftain or minor king.

Jihad—religious duty, or holy war.

Joie de vivre—joy of life.

Jorvik—Viking-age York, known by the Saxons as Eoforwic.

Jutland—Denmark.

Keep—house, usually the manor house or main building for housing the owners of the estate.

Loki—blood brother of Odin, often called the trickster or jester god because of his mischief.

Longship—narrow, open water-going vessels with oars and

square sails, perfected by Viking shipbuilders, noted for their speed and ability to ride in both shallow waters and deep oceans.

Lutefisk—dried cod.

Manchet—flat loaves of unleavened bread, usually baked in circles with a hole in the center so they could be stored on an upright pole, like a broom handle.

Mead—fermented honey and water.

Motte and bailey—form of building construction placed on a flat-topped hill or motte.

Muspell—in Norse mythology, the realm of fire.

Niflheim—a gloomy place of ice, snow and eternal darkness ruled by Hel, the gruesome Queen of the Dead.

Norns of Fate—gods or goddesses who spin the threads of fate for all people.

Odin—king of all the Viking gods.

O-Course—grueling obstacle course on the training compound, also known as the Oh-my-God! Course.

OUTCONUS—outside the continental United States.

Privy—outhouse.

Runic—ancient alphabet used by the Vikings and other early Germanic tribes.

Sagas—oral history of the Norse people, passed on from ancient history.

Sennight—seven days, one week.

Shert—medieval term for a shirt.

Skald—poet or story teller.

Straw death—the most ignoble death for a Viking, to die in his bed (straw-stuffed mattress).

Thor—god of war.

Thrall—slave.

UA—unauthorized absence (replaces AWOL).

Valhalla—hall of the slain, Odin's magnificent hall in Asgard.

Valkyries—female warriors in the Afterlife who did Odin's will.

Vestfold—section of eastern Norway, southwest of present-day Oslo.

Witan (or Witenagemot)—a king's advisory council made up of nobles and ecclesiastics.

Can't get enough of *USA Today* and
New York Times bestselling
author Sandra Hill?
Turn the page for glimpses of her amazing
books. From cowboys to Vikings, Navy
SEALs to Southern bad boys, every one
of Sandra's books has her unique blend of
passion, creativity, and unparalleled wit.

Welcome to the World of Sandra Hill!

The Viking Takes a Knight

⊗

*F*or John of Hawks' Lair, *the unexpected appearance*
of a beautiful woman at his door is always
welcome. Yet the arrival of this alluring Viking
woman, Ingrith Sigrundottir—with her enchant-
ing smile and inviting curves—is different . . .
for she comes accompanied by a herd of unruly
orphans. And Ingrith needs more than the leg-
endary knight's hospitality; she needs protection.
For among her charges is a small boy with a claim
to the throne—a dangerous distinction when
murderous King Edgar is out hunting for Viking
blood.

A man of passion, John will keep them safe—
but in exchange, he wants something very dear
indeed: Ingrith's heart, to be taken with the very
first meeting of their lips . . .

Viking in Love

*C*aedmon of Larkspur was the most loathsome lout
Breanne had ever encountered. When she
arrived at his castle with her sisters, they were
greeted by an estate gone wild, while Caedmon
laid abed after a night of ale. But Breanne must
endure, as they are desperately in need of protection . . . and he is quite handsome.

After nine long months in the king's service, all
Caedmon wanted was peace, not five Viking prin-
cesses running about his keep. And the fiery red-
head who burst into his chamber was the worst of
them all. He should kick her out, but he has a far
better plan for Breanne of Stoneheim—one that
will leave her a Viking in lust.

The Reluctant Viking

*T*he self-motivation tape was supposed to help Ruby Jordan solve her problems, not create new ones. Instead, she was lulled into an era of hard-bodied warriors and fair maidens. But the world ten centuries in the past didn't prove to be all mead and mirth. Even as Ruby tried to update medieval times, she had to deal with a Norseman whose view of women was stuck in the Dark Ages. And what was worse, brawny Thork had her husband's face, habits, and desire to avoid Ruby. Determined not to lose the same man twice, Ruby planned a bold seduction that would conquer the reluctant Viking—and make him an eager captive of her love.

The Outlaw Viking

As tall and striking as the Valkyries of legend, Dr. Rain Jordan was proud of her Norse ancestors despite their warlike ways. But she can't believe it when she finds herself on a nightmarish battlefield, forced to save the barbarian of her dreams.

He was a wild-eyed warrior whose deadly sword could slay a dozen Saxons with a single swing, yet Selik couldn't control the saucy wench from the future. If Selik wasn't careful, the stunning siren was sure to capture his heart and make a warrior of love out of **The Outlaw Viking**.

The Tarnished Lady

*B*anished *from polite society, Lady Eadyth of Hawks'* Lair spent her days hidden under a voluminous veil, tending her bees. But when her lands are threatened, Lady Eadyth sought a husband to offer her the protection of his name.

Notorious for loving—and leaving—the most beautiful damsels in the land, Eirik of Ravenshire was England's most virile bachelor. Yet when the mysterious lady offered him a vow of chaste matrimony in exchange for revenge against his most hated enemy, Eirik couldn't refuse. But the lusty knight's plans went awry when he succumbed to the sweet sting of the tarnished lady's love.

The Bewitched Viking

⚭

Even fierce Norse warriors have bad days. 'Twas enough to drive a sane Viking mad, the things Tykir Thorksson was forced to do—capturing a red-headed virago, putting up with the flock of sheep that follows her everywhere, chasing off her bumbling brothers. But what could a man expect from the sorceress who had put a kink in the King of Norway's most precious body part? If that wasn't bad enough, Tykir was beginning to realize he wasn't at all immune to the enchantment of brash red hair and freckles. Perhaps he could reverse the spell and hold her captive, not with his mighty sword, but with a Viking man's greatest magic: a wink and smile.

The Blue Viking

⊗

*F*or Rurik the Viking, life has not been worth living since he left Maire of the Moors. Oh, it's not that he misses her fiery red tresses or kissable lips. Nay, it's the embarrassing blue zigzag tattoo she put on his face after their one wild night of loving. For a fierce warrior who prides himself on his immense height, his expertise in bedsport, and his well-toned muscles, this blue streak is the last straw. In the end, he'll bring the witch to heel, or die trying. Mayhap he'll even beg her to wed . . . so long as she can promise he'll no longer be . . . **The Blue Viking**.

The Viking's Captive

(originally titled MY FAIR VIKING)

⊗

yra, Warrior Princess. She is too tall, too loud, too fierce to be a good catch. But her ailing father has decreed that her four younger sisters—delicate, mild-mannered, and beautiful—cannot be wed 'til Tyra consents to take a husband. And then a journey to save her father's life brings Tyra face to face with Adam the Healer. A god in human form, he's tall, muscled, perfectly proportioned. Too bad Adam refuses to fall in with her plans—so what's a lady to do but truss him up, toss him over her shoulder, and sail off into the sunset to live happily ever after.

A Tale of Two Vikings

⚘

*T*oste and Vagn Ivarsson are identical Viking twins, about to face Valhalla together, following a tragic battle, or maybe something even more tragic: being separated for the first time in their thirty and one years. Alas, even the bravest Viking must eventually leave his best buddy behind and do battle with that most fearsome of all opponents—the love of his life. And what if that love was Helga the Homely, or Lady Esme, the world's oldest novice nun?

A Tale of Two Vikings will give you twice the tears, twice the sizzle, and twice the laughter . . . and make you wish for your very own Viking.

The Last Viking

*H*e was six feet, four inches of pure, unadulterated male. He wore nothing but a leather tunic, and he was standing in Professor Meredith Foster's living room. The medieval historian told herself he was part of a practical joke, but with his wide gold belt, ancient language, and callused hands, the brawny stranger seemed so . . . authentic. And as he helped her fulfill her grandfather's dream of re-creating a Viking ship, he awakened her to dreams of her own. Until she wondered if the hand of fate had thrust her into the loving arms of . . . **The Last Viking**.

Truly, Madly Viking

*A Viking named Joe? Jorund Ericsson is a tenth-
century Viking* warrior who lands in a
modern mental hospital. Maggie McBride is the
lucky psychologist who gets to "treat" the gorgeous Norseman, whom she mistakenly calls Joe.

You've heard of *One Flew Over the Cuckoo's Nest*.
But how about *A Viking Flew Over the Cuckoo's Nest*?
The question is: Who's the cuckoo in this nest? And
why is everyone laughing?

The Very Virile Viking

☘

Magnus Ericsson is a simple man. He loves the smell of fresh-turned dirt after springtime plowing. He loves the feel of a soft woman under him in the bed furs. He loves the heft of a good sword in his fighting arm.

But, Holy Thor, what he does not relish is the bothersome brood of children he's been saddled with. Or the mysterious happenstance that strands him in a strange new land—the kingdom of *Holly Wood*. Here is a place where the folks think he is an *act-whore* (whatever that is), and the woman of his dreams—a winemaker of all things—fails to accept that he is her soul mate . . . a man of exceptional talents, not to mention . . . **A Very Virile Viking.**

Wet & Wild

W hat do you get when you cross a Viking with a Navy SEAL? A warrior with the fierce instincts of the past and the rigorous training of America's most elite fighting corps? A totally buff hero-in-the-making who hasn't had a woman in roughly a thousand years? A dyed-in-the-wool romantic with a hopeless crush? Whatever you get, women everywhere can't wait to meet him, and his story is guaranteed to be . . . **Wet & Wild**.

Hot & Heavy

In and out, that's the goal as Lt. Ian MacLean prepares for his special ops mission. He leads a team of highly trained Navy SEALs, the toughest, buffest fighting men in the world and he has nothing to lose. Madrene comes from a time a thousand years before he was born, and she has no idea she's landed in the future. After tying him up, the beautiful shrew gives him a tongue-lashing that makes a drill sergeant sound like a kindergarten teacher. Then she lets him know she has her own special way of dealing with over-confident males, and things get . . . **Hot & Heavy**.

Frankly, My Dear . . .

&

*L*ost in the Bayou . . . *Selene had three great passions: men, food, and Gone with the Wind.* But the glamorous model always found herself starving— for both nourishment and affection. Weary of the petty world of high fashion, she headed to New Orleans for one last job before she began a new life. Little did she know that her new life would include a brand-new time—about 150 years ago! Selene can't get her fill of the food—or an alarmingly handsome man. Dark and brooding, James Baptiste was the only lover she gave a damn about. And with God as her witness, she vowed never to go without the man she loved again.

Sweeter Savage Love

☙

The stroke of surprisingly gentle hands, the flash of fathomless blue eyes, the scorch of white-hot kisses . . . Once again, Dr. Harriet Ginoza was swept away into rapturous fantasy. The modern psychologist knew the object of her desire was all she should despise, yet time after time, she lost herself in visions of a dangerously hand-some rogue straight out of a historical romance. Harriet never believed that her dream lover would cause her any trouble, but then a twist of fate cast her back to the Old South and she met him in the flesh. To her disappointment, Etienne Baptiste refused to fulfill any of her secret wishes. If Harriet had any hope of making her amorous dreams become passionate reality, she'd have to seduce this charmer with a sweeter savage love than she'd imagined possible . . . and savor every minute of it.

The Love Potion

⊗

*F*ame *and fortune are surely only a swallow away* when Dr. Sylvie Fontaine discovers a chemical formula guaranteed to attract the opposite sex. Though her own love life is purely hypothetical, the shy chemist's professional future is assured . . . as soon as she can find a human guinea pig. But bad boy Lucien LeDeux—best known as the Swamp Lawyer—is more than she can handle even before he accidentally swallowed a love potion disguised in a jelly bean. When the dust settles, Luc and Sylvie have the answers to some burning questions—can a man die of testosterone overload? Can a straight-laced female lose every single one of her inhibitions?—and they learn that old-fashioned romance is still the best catalyst for love.

Love Me Tender

*O*nce upon a time, in a magic kingdom, there lived a handsome prince. Prince Charming, he was called by one and all. And to this land came a gentle princess. You could say she was Cinderella . . . Wall Street Cinderella. Okay, if you're going to be a stickler for accuracy, in this fairy tale the kingdom is Manhattan. But there's magic in the Big Apple, isn't there? And maybe he can be Prince Not-So-Charming at times, and "gentle" isn't the first word that comes to mind when thinking of this princess. But they're looking for happily ever after just the same—and they're going to get it.